**Praise for *New York Times* bestselling author
MICHELLE SAGARA
and The Chronicles of Elantra series**

"No one provides an emotional payoff like Michelle Sagara."
—Bestselling author Tanya Huff on The Chronicles of Elantra series

"Intense, fast-paced, intriguing, compelling
and hard to put down...unforgettable."
—*In the Library Reviews* on *Cast in Shadow*

"Readers will embrace this compelling, strong-willed heroine
with her often sarcastic voice."
—*Publishers Weekly* on *Cast in Courtlight*

"The impressively detailed setting and the book's spirited heroine
are sure to charm romance readers, as well as fantasy fans
who like some mystery with their magic."
—*Publishers Weekly* on *Cast in Secret*

"Along with the exquisitely detailed world building,
Sagara's character development is mesmerizing. She expertly breathes
life into a stubborn yet evolving heroine. A true master of her craft."
—*RT Book Reviews (4 ½ stars)* on *Cast in F...*

"Each visit to this am...
with its richness of place and cha...
—*RT Book Reviews (4 ½ stars)...*

"Another satisfying addition t...
and entertaining fantas...
—*Publishers Weekly* on *Cast in Chaos*

"If you are searching for a rich and rewarding fantasy read different
from the usual fantasy fare, then you can't go wrong with *Cast in Ruin*
and The Chronicles of Elantra series. Heartily recommended."
—*SciFiGuy.ca* on *Cast in Ruin*

"Sagara does an amazing job continuing to flesh out her large cast
of characters, but keeps the unsinkable Kaylin at the center."
—*RT Book Reviews* (4 ½ stars) on *Cast in Peril*

"Über-awesome Sagara picks up the intense action right where she
left off...while Kaylin is the heart of this amazing series, the terrific
characters keep the story moving. An autobuy for sure!"
—*RT Book Reviews* (4 ½ stars) on *Cast in Sorrow*

CAST IN FLAME

MICHELLE SAGARA

HARLEQUIN® MIRA®

Recycling programs
for this product may
not exist in your area.

ISBN-13: 978-0-7783-1708-1

CAST IN FLAME

Copyright © 2014 by Michelle Sagara

For questions and comments about the quality of this book, please contact us at CustomerService@Harlequin.com.

Printed in U.S.A.

First printing: August 2014
10 9 8 7 6 5 4 3 2 1

This year, Worldbuilders (www.worldbuilders.org), Patrick Rothfuss's charity drive for Heifer International (www.heifer.org), gave me an opportunity to contribute something to their series of auctions. I wanted to do this, in part because I like the charity, and in part because the money is used to make the world a better place.

But my contribution was…a manuscript for a book. This one. And in order for that contribution to have any value to the charity, someone was required to step up and bid on and win the auction. I was prepared to thank that person in the dedication to the book—or to thank anyone the bidder chose. I still want to thank Chad for his enormous generosity.

Chad, however, bid on and bought the book as a gift for someone else, and he has a few words he wants to say:

To that special someone in my life who shall remain anonymous.
Mainly because I would not likely be among the living
if her true name was mentioned.

There are so many things about you that I love,
like your stunning smile and laugh, which I never get tired of finding ways
of bringing out. The unconditional honesty you are willing to give
or how you sneeze when the sunlight kisses your face.
And the phrase "Oh Dear" will be forever special to me.

Life offers many challenges,
but I have never stopped loving you, always have, always will.

CHAPTER 1

On the second day after her return to Elantra, the city she policed as a groundhawk, Private Kaylin Neya fell out of bed, daggers in hands, knees bent. After one confused moment, she sheathed her daggers, took a brief look around the otherwise empty royal guest chambers that served as her temporary home, and let loose a volley of Leontine curses.

The small, translucent winged lizard that habitually slept above her head squawked in protest; she'd swept him out of the way without a second thought. He hovered in front of her face as she cursed; she didn't, at the moment, have anything left over for groveling apologies.

Leontine wasn't the usual language heard in the halls of the Imperial Palace. Nor was it generally heard in the function rooms, and when it was, it wasn't the particular phrasing she now indulged in. On the other hand, the thunderous sounds that had driven her from sleep pretty much guaranteed that no one who'd care could possibly hear her words. Kaylin could scream until she was blue in the face, with the same results. Anyone in the palace halls could, at the moment.

Dragons were having a discussion.

When she'd first heard Dragons converse in their native tongue, she'd thought of earthquakes or tidal waves. Distinguishing individual voices had been less important than covering both her ears in the vague hope she'd preserve some of her hearing. A couple of weeks in the palace with Bellusdeo for a companion had changed that. She could pick out three loud—painfully loud—voices in the crash of distant thunder: Diarmat's, Bellusdeo's and...the Emperor's. While she generally enjoyed the arguments between Bellusdeo and Diarmat, she had zero desire to ever interrupt—or witness—any argument which also contained the Emperor. Even mention of the Emperor was probably career-limiting.

It was dark, but the storm of sound in progress didn't seem like it would die down any time soon, and sleep was pretty much impossible—at least for Kaylin. The rest of the Dragon Court was probably in hiding, but Immortals didn't need anything as petty as sleep.

The minute—the *second*—she had the time to find a new place, she was *so* out of here.

The small dragon landed on her shoulders. She'd named him Hope, but felt self-conscious actually calling him that, and she hadn't had time to come up with a name that suited him better. He yawned, folded himself across her shoulders like a badly formed shawl, and closed his eyes. Clearly, Dragon shouting didn't bother him in the slightest.

Then again, he probably understood what they were saying.

The palace was never dark. Individual rooms had lighting that responded to the needs of the guests who occupied them, but the halls—the grand, wide, towering halls—were always fully lit. The Imperial Palace Guard also adorned those halls, standing like statues in a stiff, grim silence that suited their pretension.

They didn't stop Kaylin as she walked past them, heading to one of the only places that she was certain was somewhat soundproof. They knew her on sight, and if they'd had no issues treating her as one step up from a convicted felon in the past, she was now roommate to the Empire's only female Dragon. The Emperor didn't want anyone to piss Bellusdeo off.

Anyone, Kaylin thought glumly, but the Emperor himself. Dragons had never been famously good at sharing.

When she reached the tall and forbidding doors of the Imperial Library, she had second thoughts. It wasn't that the Imperial Library was home in all but name to the Arkon, the oldest member of the Dragon Court. It wasn't that the doors were closed; they were almost always closed. It wasn't even his extreme dislike of being interrupted.

It was the door ward that straddled them.

She'd woken to the sounds of angry Dragon, which pretty much defined Bad Day. Having to place her palm against this particular ward took Bad Day and made it worse. At the best of times, Kaylin's allergy to magic made door wards uncomfortable—but this ward could raise so much noise it might just interrupt the Dragons. One of whom was the Emperor.

There was no other way to open them. Kaylin briefly considered knocking. With her head. Before she could—and it was late enough, or early enough, that she might have—the doors surprised her by gliding open. No one stood between them.

At this hour, the library desk—the publicly accessible library desk—was unmanned. The display cases and the rows upon rows of standing files were shadowed. The robed clerks who kept the library spotless were conspicuous by their absence—but that was no surprise. No one sane visited the library at this hour.

As the doors rolled closed at her back, the sound of Dragon anger diminished.

The Arkon made his way toward her from the back of the large room, which surprised Kaylin; she'd expected to find him holed up in one of the many, many rooms that comprised his personal collection—none of which the public was invited to peruse.

"Thank you for opening the doors," she told him.

"I felt it best to avoid interrupting the ongoing discussion. No one involved in it is likely to be amused by the sudden need to attend to intruders."

"I live here, at the moment."

"Indeed. I imagine the only person present who might find a disaster of your making remotely convenient is Lord Diarmat."

"Who doesn't deserve it."

"You give him too little credit."

"Do I?"

The Arkon's smile was lined. It was also sharp. "Perhaps I will beg the Emperor's indulgence."

In theory, this sounded good. Given the way the day had started, it couldn't be. "How?"

"I might ask permission to teach you the rudiments of our language." His smile deepened as her eyes rounded and her brows rose.

"I'll go deaf!"

"Yes. Follow me, please. You interrupted me," he added.

"I don't know how you can work with that ruckus going on in the background."

"It is difficult. I do not have the concentration I once possessed in my youth."

"So, what are they arguing about exactly?"

"Bellusdeo's status at court, at the moment; the argument has touched on many subjects." The Arkon's eyes were a steady shade of orange, which wasn't a good sign, in a Dragon.

"What about her status? She's a Dragon, so she's technically a Lord of the Court."

"That is true only in mortal terms. She is not—as Diarmat has been at pains to point out—a Lord of *this* Court. She has not offered the Emperor an oath of fealty; nor has she agreed—in a binding fashion—to abide by the laws he hands down."

"She spends most of her free time with *me*," Kaylin replied. "I'm a groundhawk. She probably knows the law better than anyone who isn't."

"You misunderstand. Humans are not, of course, required to take such a binding oath—I believe they would not survive it. Bellusdeo has not been required to do so. Lord Diarmat correctly points out that she therefore poses a risk to the Court." He stopped at a smooth, flat wall. It was unadorned; Kaylin suspected it was actually a door.

The Arkon barked a sharp, harsh word and proved her suspicion correct; a part of the wall simply faded from sight. What lay on the other side of it was a disaster. It made Kaylin's desk at its worst look pristine and tidy. Hells, it made Marcus's desk look well-organized, which Kaylin would have bet was impossible.

The Arkon noted her hesitation. "Is there a difficulty?"

"Just how important is all the paper—that is paper, isn't it?"

"Parchment. Some paper. There is also stone and a few shards of smooth glass. I trust that you will disturb nothing while you are here."

"How?"

He raised a brow; his eyes didn't get any more orange, which was a small mercy.

"There's stuff all over the *floor.* There's stuff all over the chairs. I probably can't put a foot down without stepping on something."

"Then do not, as you put it, put a foot down." He gestured.

The hair on Kaylin's arms and the back of her neck rose in instant protest.

"Do not," he said, in a more severe tone of voice, "make me regret my foolish and sentimental decision to take pity on you and provide you some form of refuge."

Folding her arms across her chest, she walked into the room; her feet touched nothing. Neither did the Arkon's.

"Not to be suspicious or anything," she began.

"You do not think me capable of either sentiment or pity?"

"Not much, no. Not for me."

His smile deepened. "As you point out, Private, Bellusdeo did spend most of her free time in your presence. You have not, however, been in the city for the past month and a half. She has therefore had no anchor. No friends, if you prefer. In the last two weeks of your absence, she has spent a greater portion of her time in the fief of Tiamaris, speaking with the refugees there. When she chooses to enter the fief, she is met by one of the *Norannir.*"

"That would be Maggaron."

"The Emperor does not consider Maggaron to be a suitable guard in the fiefs; Lord Tiamaris, however, is. She has accepted—with poor grace—the Emperor's wishes in this regard."

"What happened?"

"She has taken to flying in the restricted air-space above the fief of Tiamaris."

"It's not Imperial land."

"No. She has pointed this out—at length. You might have recognized one or two of the words she used, if you were paying attention. She has, however, come close to the borders of the fief once too often for the Emperor's comfort."

"The *Norannir* live on the borders."

"Indeed. She has taken pains to point this out, as well."

"He's going to isolate her! The *Norannir* are the only other friends she has in this city!"

The Arkon's smile was softer, and infinitely more pained. "They are not her friends, Kaylin. They were once her subjects. She is not merely a Dragon to them; she is akin to a living god. Bellusdeo has her vanity. She has her pride. But she, like any Dragon, understands her role in their lives. She does not go to them for their sake, but her own. They remind her of who she once was.

"There is altogether too much in the Palace that reminds her of what she now is."

Kaylin's arms tightened. "And what, exactly, is that?"

"A displaced person. She is very much the equivalent of the *Norannir*. You think of her as a Lord of the Court, and you have some rudimentary understanding of the political power that title might give her. She lives in the Palace, and not in the mean streets of the fiefs that border *Ravellon*. She has food, should she desire it, and clothing; she has money. But the *Norannir* have more freedom than Bellusdeo now does."

"Why are you telling me this? Why not say this to the Emperor?"

"Do you think I have not?" His eyes shaded to a color that was more copper than orange. Kaylin couldn't remember what it meant, she'd seen it so rarely. In fact, she'd seen it only once: in Bellusdeo's eyes. "I have told the Emperor that Bellusdeo cannot live in a cage. He does not intend to cage her—but regardless, he does. She is too valuable to risk. We have already seen how close to disaster we came."

"Arkon—" Kaylin froze, and only in part because the muted draconic voices had risen in volume. "Please tell me this argument has nothing to do with my moving out."

"You are not, that I recall, fond of unnecessary dishonesty." He took a seat. It was the only seat in the room that seemed to have enough exposed surface to sit on. "If Bellusdeo can be said to have one friend in the Empire, it is you. She found your absence far more difficult than either she—or you—had imagined she would."

"She said this?"

"Of course not." He winced; it took Kaylin a couple of seconds to realize it wasn't because of anything she'd said. Unlike her, he could understand every word that was being said. Or shouted. "You have made it clear to Bellusdeo that life in the Imperial Palace does not suit you."

"Not in those exact words, no."

"Refrain from repeating the exact phrasing."

Because Kaylin loved her job on most days, she did.

"You intend to find another domicile?"

"Yes. As soon as I can." When he lifted a brow, she thought of the job she loved—none of which included pandering to annoyed Dragons. On the other hand, survival often did. "Look, there are people who would kill to live in the Palace. I'm certain of it. But they're the people the Hawklord goes out of his way to prevent me from meeting. Everything in my Palace rooms—everything—costs more than the clothing on my back. I feel like I should bathe *before* I step foot through the door.

"I can't leave or enter without an inquisition. I have to deal with Imperial Guards on a daily basis for no other reason than that I live here."

"They are there for the protection and security of our guests."

"Fine. But I don't want to *be* a guest in my own home. I want to be able to *live there*. Bellusdeo is a Dragon. When she dons Court dresses, they fit her *and* look good. She understands the powerful. She *has* power. I'm a groundhawk. I can barely make ends meet on my cruddy pay. I'm not in her class—and I know it.

"I came from the fiefs. I work on the streets. I don't belong here, and I can't be happy where I don't belong."

"You are a Lord of the High Court."

"The Barrani High Court, and you know damn well I don't have to live in the High Halls."

"You have visited them before."

"I visited them with *Teela*."

"And the difference?"

She grimaced. There was a difference. She wasn't certain what it was. "Teela's a Hawk."

"And Bellusdeo is not."

"Bellusdeo would never swear the oath the Halls of Law require."

"No. Lord Teela did?"

"Lord Teela doesn't give a damn about nonbinding oaths. They're just words, as far as the Barrani are concerned. There is no way Marcus would ever allow Bellusdeo to join the Hawks."

"Ah, yes. Your Sergeant's famous mistrust of my kind." His eyes, however, shaded toward gold. He clearly found Marcus amusing. "Your Teela understands the High Court, and she avoids it where possible. But if you enter that world, she enters it beside you—and she warns others, by presence alone, that there are consequences to any actions they might take against you. Bellusdeo cannot do that, here. And she is aware that she lacks that ability; the Palace is not her home. It is not an environment with which she is familiar, or over which she has ultimate control.

"Still, she tries. She targets Diarmat with the full brunt of her outraged disdain. Her outrage," he added, "is genuine. She feels your marks are not accorded the respect they are due. She does not fully consider the advantage in being underestimated—and I will say, now, that there is a distinct advantage to you, in my opinion. She feels a debt of gratitude to you."

"I didn't do anything for her gratitude. I did it because... because...."

"Oh, do continue. I'm certain it will be fascinating. You did it because that's what anyone would do?"

Kaylin shrugged. It was a fief shrug. Fief shrugs, on the other hand, were not a language with which the Arkon chose to be familiar.

"You grew up in the fiefs. You are aware that you are lying. Even if you aren't, there are very few—I can think of almost no one—who could do for Bellusdeo what you did. She would have died there." His gaze slid off hers. "I am not certain, at this moment, that fate would not be preferable in her mind. Yes, the discussion in progress—and to my mind it will be some hours before it is done—involves both your residence and hers." He closed his eyes. "She is in pain, Kaylin. She is grieving. For us, the grief is long past; it exists only in echoes, when we turn our thoughts to the past.

"For Bellusdeo it is new. It makes her reckless. More reckless," he added, as if this were necessary. "You see her as a Dragon, which is fair. You will age, you will die; she will live forever. She is favored by an Emperor we still consider it wise that you never meet; she is given leeway that would be granted no one else. All of this is true. It is not, however, the only truth.

"I understand that the loss of your home was due to her presence. Believe, Kaylin, that she understands this, as well. If you do not resent her for the loss—if you do not speak against her companionship—she will go where you go."

"You...want me to move out with her."

"No. I feel it prudent to advise you that her presence *will* make your life far more difficult than it might otherwise be. I want *her* to move out with *you*. I am of the opinion—at the moment—that the benefits that accrue will go in one direction; I am aware—as you are—of the risks that move entails. If Bellusdeo does accompany you, the Imperial Treasury will cover a large portion of your rental costs."

Kaylin's arms tightened, but she said nothing. She'd been able to afford her one-room apartment, even with Bellusdeo as a roommate. She wasn't so flush with money that money itself was irrelevant. But...she really didn't like the idea. At all. "She hasn't even asked me, you know."

"I know. She will not ask if she cannot argue the Emperor around; it would be too humiliating."

And having a screaming fight that an entire *palace* had no choice but to hear wasn't? "I don't want my home surrounded by bloody Imperial Guards."

The Arkon raised a white brow.

"I mean it. I don't want home to be a jail."

"Bellusdeo will have a security detail."

"*I* apparently have a security detail, if by that you mean Imperial spies. I can't stop them from watching my every move. I just want to *pretend* that they don't."

"Why?"

Dragons. Ugh.

"And your other demands?"

Kaylin had none. She felt guilty, because one of the things

she'd been so looking forward to was having a place of her own again. She'd had nothing when she'd come from the fiefs. But she'd had hope for the future—with the Hawks, within Elantra. What hope did Bellusdeo now have that was similar?

"Yes," she heard herself say.

"You will consider it?"

She nodded. The small dragon, silent as cloth for most of the interview, raised his head and batted the side of Kaylin's cheek with it.

"Good. I now have work to do."

"Midwives' guild?" Clint asked, as Kaylin trudged up the stairs of the Halls of Law.

"Dragons," was her curt reply. If the midwives had kept her awake through the small hours of the night, she'd've had something useful to show for the lack of sleep.

"If you don't want to see Dragons," Tanner told her, "I suggest you avoid the office for the next couple of hours."

"Why?"

"Bellusdeo is there."

She hadn't been in the apartments they shared at the palace when Kaylin had dragged her butt out of her rooms in the morning.

"Alone?"

"No. Lord Sanabalis is with her. So are six of the Imperial Guard. The color of Barrani eyes in the office is almost midnight blue."

Could this day get any worse? "Thanks for the heads-up." Kaylin considered turning tail and finding breakfast, but she didn't have much money on hand.

"You're going in?"

"Trouble'll find me when I leave the office if I don't; I might as well get paid for enduring it."

The Imperial Guard always set the office, as a whole, on edge. Caitlin didn't mind them, but they were so stiff, so officious, and so smugly superior, Caitlin was an island in the Halls. Bellusdeo was standing to one side of Marcus's desk as Kaylin entered the office. Kaylin glanced, once, at the duty roster, saw her name—beside Severn's—on the Elani beat, and allowed herself to relax. She wasn't late. Yet.

She didn't, however, see Severn.

Sanabalis was standing to one side of Bellusdeo; his eyes were a very clear orange, and if Dragons didn't physically require sleep, he looked like he could personally use a week of it. The Imperial Guard were like breathing statues.

"Private," Marcus growled. His sense of smell had probably alerted him to Kaylin's presence, as there were too many tall people between them for her to even see him, seated as he was at his desk, and behind the perpetual stacks of paper that girded it. She couldn't see the color of his eyes, but the tone of her rank pretty much gave it away. The Imperial Guard moved to allow her through.

She stood at attention in front of his desk and—as expected—his very orange eyes. She saw that he had reflexively gouged a few new runnels in the surface of that desk. Clearly, it hadn't been a pleasant interview, whatever its subject.

"Your services are apparently being seconded by the Dragon Court."

Standing at attention didn't allow for the usual facial tics or gestures that indicated dismay. It was the only good thing she could say about it.

"You are apparently not content living at the Palace."

It also didn't allow for nuanced commentary, which was

fine; surrounded by Imperial Guards, she didn't feel particularly nuanced.

"Well?"

"No, sir."

"And you intend to find other accommodations."

"Yes, sir."

"With a Lord of the Dragon Court."

She didn't hesitate; not with Marcus in his current mood. "Yes, sir."

"The Dragon Court feels that such a search should not be an after-hours affair. Cognizant of the difficulties Lord Bellusdeo encountered the last time she chose to live outside of the Palace, they've taken it upon themselves to assure that your search for a new domicile is secure. You are therefore relieved of your regular duties until that search is completed. To Imperial satisfaction."

"That is not," Bellusdeo said, speaking for the first time since Kaylin had entered an otherwise raptly silent office, "what was said." She stepped forward, until she was standing shoulder to shoulder with Kaylin, who, at attention, couldn't otherwise turn to look at her. "Private Neya's sense of responsibility to the Halls is quite strong; she understands the city far better than I, a recent refugee." She used the Elantran word for refugee. Kaylin almost cringed to hear it. "If, in Private Neya's considered opinion, such a search can be effectively conducted outside of her working hours, that is acceptable to *all* concerned." The swish sound her hair made clearly indicated that Bellusdeo was pinning someone—or several someones—with a glare.

Sanabalis cleared his throat. In the silence of the office, it sounded like a distant earthquake. "Bellusdeo wishes to accompany Private Neya on her rounds, as she did before the private was sent out of the city to the West March."

Great.

"Private," Marcus barked. "At ease."

As if. She did, however, relax her posture slightly. "Permission to speak freely, sir?"

Her Sergeant snorted. In general, there was nothing but free speech in the office.

"I'm not going on my rounds with a half dozen Imperial Guards as escort. Members of the Hawks *don't* require babysitters, and we don't want to imply they do; it'll hurt the force. If the guards come with Bellusdeo and can't be separated, I'll take the time to find a new apartment. If they can be detached, I can find us a place to live on my own time."

For some reason, this answer didn't appear to please Marcus, although he clearly agreed with it.

"Is Lord Bellusdeo a Hawk?" a familiar voice asked. Kaylin couldn't see the speaker, but cringed anyway. It was a Barrani voice. Mandoran's. She hadn't even *seen* him in the office, which answered her question about the day getting worse; clearly it could. A Barrani from the West March, frozen in time in the Barrani version of puberty, was now in the Halls of Law. She hoped Teela was standing on his feet.

"I am not," was the frosty, Draconian reply.

"I was under the impression," Mandoran continued, moving around the back side of Marcus's desk with care to avoid the now-bristling Leontine that occupied it, "that tourists were not allowed to accompany on-duty Hawks."

Marcus was either breathing heavily or trying to stifle a growl. Kaylin put money on the latter, and would have refused to bet on his chances of continued success.

"Lord Bellusdeo," Sanabalis said, "is a member of the Dragon Court—the governing body that advises the Eternal Emperor. It is well within her purview to ask for—and receive—permission to inspect the forces assembled within the Halls in light of those duties."

"Whereas I am merely a Barrani Lord visiting your fair city, and therefore have no responsibilities and no duties?"

Kaylin risked a glance at Sanabalis's eyes. He was annoyed, but not yet angry.

Mandoran, having navigated the desk, came to stand beside Kaylin. He was grinning, and his eyes were almost green. Certainly greener than Barrani eyes generally were in this office. He winked at her. This did not make the Leontine Sergeant any less bristly.

"I see Teela hasn't strangled you, yet," she said, in as quiet a voice as she could.

"Why would she want to do that? At the moment, she's not bored."

"She is," Teela said, "considering the concept of boredom with more deliberate care."

Mandoran's grin didn't falter.

"Where is Corporal Handred?" Kaylin asked, hoping to stem the tide of this particular conversation.

She'd've had better luck with a tidal wave. "He's closeted with the Wolflord," Teela replied. "The duty roster hasn't been updated, but apparently you and I are now covering Elani street." She turned and offered a correct bow to Sanabalis. Unfortunately, Kaylin now recognized it as a correct bow for the Barrani High Court. "I ask that you overlook any impertinence from my guest. He is in a situation very similar to Lord Bellusdeo's; the Empire—and the Eternal Emperor—did not exist when last he walked these lands."

Bellusdeo frowned. "I was not aware that the Barrani could voluntarily enter the long sleep."

"I'm certain there are many things that would surprise you about the Barrani," Mandoran replied. His voice, however, had taken on both edge and chill, and his eyes had darkened to blue.

This predictably caused unrest among the Imperial Guard, subtle though it was; it caused Sanabalis's eyes to shade toward a brighter orange, and it caused Teela's eyes—Teela, who had made her way to the other side of Mandoran—to narrow. They were, on the other hand, already as blue as they could safely get.

Bellusdeo, however, lifted a brow; her eyes were no longer slightly orange. They were gold. She was amused.

Mandoran wasn't.

Bellusdeo then turned to Teela. "If you have now had cause to reconsider your attitude toward boredom, I have not been so fortunate. Even for the Immortal, time can pass incredibly slowly. I believe I will find the patrol of great interest on this particular day." She turned to Mandoran and added, "as a visitor to the city that is my current home, I bid you welcome. I am certain you will do nothing to disgrace yourself or your Court should you be forced to accept the company of a Dragon for an afternoon, and I am certain the Sergeant will relax his rules enough that you may join us."

CHAPTER
2

Although Bellusdeo had the last word, there were several hundred other words—thankfully none of them in native Dragon—before it. Kaylin thought it unfair when Sanabalis asked for a private word with her before she could leave the office.

The lack of justice didn't notably ease when he marched her to the West Room in which her magic lessons were taught, and practically shut the door on her shoulder blades—without bothering to touch it. He did, on the other hand, activate the door ward with his own hand.

"What," he asked, in Elantran, "do you think you're doing?"

"I *thought* I was going on patrol in the Elani district."

His eyes darkened a shade. "If there is ever a time to play games with a Dragon, Private, it is not now. The Emperor is not pleased by the current state of events."

"Not even I could have missed that."

He grimaced, and his eyes lightened a shade. "He has granted Bellusdeo his very reluctant permission to leave the

Palace. He is placing the fate of the race in your hands." And clearly, while Sanabalis held Kaylin in some affection, he didn't consider her the appropriate receptacle for that responsibility.

She stared at him. She remembered to close her mouth after the first few seconds. "The same Emperor who initially thought I should be destroyed because I presented too great a risk?"

"We have not notably changed rulers in the interim." His eyes gained more gold as he studied her face. "Tell me about this new Barrani. He is a recruit?"

She started to say no, stopped, and shrugged. "I don't know. He's a friend of Teela's. An old friend."

"He is to my eye one of the Barrani young."

"She's known him practically all her life," she replied, trying to dodge the question he hadn't yet asked.

"And you trust him?"

Did she? "I don't know him well enough to trust him." That was true. "But I trust Teela."

"Teela is a Barrani High Lord. She owes her loyalty to—"

"She's a *Hawk,* Sanabalis."

Sanabalis was silent for a moment. "Kaylin, you have been the most difficult student I have ever accepted. The rewards are few; the frustration is legion. But you are not—as I'm certain Bellusdeo will tell you—boring. In my fashion, I have grown accustomed to your eccentricities. My opinion carries some weight at court. It will carry exactly *none* if Bellusdeo comes to harm." He lifted a hand as Kaylin opened her mouth. "Yes, I am aware that she is not a child. So, too, is the Emperor.

"But you have told anyone who will listen that you are no longer a child, either. The Emperor therefore wishes you to understand what is at risk for you. Bellusdeo has a home in the Palace. She will be as safe there as she would be—"

"In a grave."

Silence.

Kaylin watched the color of Dragon eyes closely; she'd folded her arms and widened her stance without conscious intent. But if Sanabalis felt insulted, it didn't anger him; the color remained a constant, pale orange.

"You do not understand the politics of the Dragon Court."

"Then I recommend better information be taught in racial-integration classes." She exhaled through clenched teeth and forced herself to relax. "Look, Sanabalis, I don't understand the problem. The Arkon had no objections. He doesn't think Bellusdeo *can* be happy in the Palace. Not right now."

"The Arkon is being astonishingly sentimental for one of our kind."

"No, he's just being perceptive. I don't know what went down at the end of all the wars. I don't know what choices the surviving Dragons were given—but I'm guessing that many of the Dragons didn't survive to make that choice. I don't know what choice Bellusdeo has been offered—but I'm guessing almost none. She's the only female Dragon. She's not being asked to choose between death and eternal servitude." He started to speak, and she held up one hand. "She understands what's at stake. She has a sense of responsibility. But she's not a piece of property. The Emperor already *has* a hoard."

"No choice has been demanded of Bellusdeo."

"That's not the way Diarmat sees it."

One pale brow rose into an equally pale hairline.

"...Lord Diarmat."

"Lord Diarmat is concerned for the rule of law. The Emperor's law. He is younger than the Arkon, and he is aware that female Dragons are not an entirely different species."

"They're not technically a different species at all."

"Exactly. Lord Diarmat is the only member of the Dragon

Court who will risk open hostility to make that point. Bellusdeo is a Dragon, but she is not accorded the responsibilities that exist, for Dragons, in the Empire."

"Meaning she's not forced to swear the same oath the rest of you swore."

"Yes." Sanabalis fell silent. He did not, however, give Kaylin permission to depart, and she was very much aware, given the turn of the day's events—or at least the evening's prior—that permission was required. "She is not happy," he surprised her by saying.

Kaylin waited.

"It may come as a surprise to you, but her happiness is of some concern to the Emperor; he balances it with a desire for her safety that is second only to his desire for the safety of his hoard. If you will not take the detachment of guards, I will have them dismissed. Go on your patrol. I will arrange a suitable escort for your...apartment hunting."

"Who would that be?"

He ran his hand over his eyes. "In all likelihood, Private Neya, me. I may attempt to saddle Lord Emmerian with that duty; he has not, to my knowledge, offended Bellusdeo in the last several weeks. Largely," he added, with a more toothy grin, "because he has avoided her entirely."

"Why," Teela said, in the clipped, cool voice that implied annoyance, "are you sulking?"

"I'm not sulking." Kaylin did not kick a stone, which took effort.

Mandoran grinned. "You don't look like you're sulking to me—but I'm not as conversant with mortal expressions. Why exactly do your eyes stay that fixed color?"

"Human."

"Doesn't it make the other mortals wonder if you're not just animals that talk?"

"Frequently." She reached out and caught Bellusdeo's elbow as the Dragon drew breath; it was the kind of slow, heavy breath which sometimes preceded fire. "Either that or it makes them suspicious, because clearly we're hiding something. Or we're insane."

"Well, I won't argue *that,*" he replied. He was looking at the buildings that lined the streets, the people that walked them, the stray cats and dogs, and the clouds that scudded overhead, as if everything was both new and fascinating. It probably was. He had spent the past many centuries trapped inside the green, which had a tenuous understanding of physical form. At best. His eyes were a shade of blue-green, and he kept to the side of Teela that happened to be farthest from the Dragon. Kaylin had inserted herself between Teela and Bellusdeo, which meant Mandoran and Bellusdeo were as far apart as they could be while still heading in the same general direction.

They both turned heads, though.

Mandoran wasn't encumbered by the regulation tabard that Teela wore, and Bellusdeo looked far more like a Lord of the Dragon Court—by dress, at least—than the average pedestrian. Most women who could afford to dress the way she did didn't walk anywhere—they took carriages, and usually stayed behind their guards and footmen.

Kaylin grimaced. She almost wished Bellusdeo were in one of those carriages, because Elani street was the home of wheedling, enterprising frauds, most of whom could happily accost anyone that appeared to have money.

They were usually better behaved when their victims had Hawks as escorts. Mandoran, on the other hand, didn't appear to understand that he *was* a victim. He responded to the offers—in this case, fortune-telling—with unfeigned curiosity and quick delight.

Teela raised a brow. Mandoran stiffened. Neither spoke out loud. They didn't have to, if they wanted their conversation to be private; they knew each other's true names. It had been centuries since either had had call to use them, if one ignored the past few weeks.

"Teela," Mandoran said, "doesn't want me to have fun here."

"She's working. You'll add to the paperwork if you do."

"Yes, that seems to be one of her fears. The other is attempting to throw me into...jail if I misbehave?"

"I imagine that would be a lot of fun," Kaylin replied.

"I've offered to visit the High Halls instead of the city streets," was his cheerful counter. "There, it won't matter if foolish or stupid people die; it's considered a form of suicide, and it isn't Teela's job to prevent that."

"Why did we think this was a good idea?" Kaylin asked her fellow Hawk.

"I never thought it was a good idea, if I recall. I merely pointed out that compared to your induction into the Hawks, Mandoran was far less likely to be in danger. Or to indirectly cause it. I was perhaps optimistic about the latter."

Mandoran snorted. So did Bellusdeo.

"I thought you were here to keep an eye on Annarion."

At that, Mandoran's smile dimmed. The color of his eyes shifted, but not into the midnight blue that generally meant upcoming injury or death. He glanced at Teela; Teela was studying the occupants of Elani street as if they were fascinating, dangerous, or both.

"You will have to tell me," Bellusdeo said to Kaylin, "exactly what did happen on your pilgrimage. It seems you've acquired companions."

"They're Teela's companions, not mine. And there are—at the moment—two of them in the city. You've met Mandoran. He's the outgoing, friendly one with the questionable sense of humor."

"It seems a fairly standard Barrani sense of humor, if less subtle than rumored."

"He's young for his age."

"Not so young," Mandoran cut in, "that he enjoys being talked about in the third person."

"And not so mature," the Dragon countered, "that he doesn't enjoy talking about other people present in the same way."

He grinned. His eyes were still a wary blue. "Fair enough." He spoke Elantran. Kaylin doubted a similar phrase existed in Barrani.

"Where is Annarion anyway?"

"Kitling."

Mandoran raised a black brow. "He's visiting his brother."

Nightshade.

"And no, before you ask, it's not going well."

"Why didn't you go with him?"

"I wasn't invited. Or rather, I was specifically *not* invited. Lord Calarnenne was willing to entertain Teela, but for some reason, Teela didn't choose to accept his invitation."

"I am uninterested in playing games of power with Nightshade."

"But Annarion—"

"Is not in danger. Whatever else Nightshade intends in future, the death of his youngest brother is no part of his plan. It is safe for Annarion to rage only in the absence of witnesses. Nightshade didn't invite me because he was concerned for Annarion's safety; he wished to confine Annarion's wrath. I," she added, with a slender, sharp smile, "did not." She glanced pointedly at the mark Nightshade had left on Kaylin's cheek. It was just so much skin to the younger Hawk, but it never failed to annoy Teela.

"Heads up. Margot on the prowl," Teela added.

Margot was possibly the person on Elani street Kaylin disliked the most, not that there was any shortage of rivals for that position. She was a tall, gorgeous redhead, and she made the color look natural. She was statuesque, her skin was fair, her eyes striking, and she could milk money out of stone by oozing wisdom and charm.

Neither of which Kaylin privately believed she had.

"She won't come here," Kaylin replied. "She's seen me."

If Kaylin played the least-favorite game, so did Margot. Kaylin was on the top of the Hawk's list, and possibly near the top three across the board. She still blamed Kaylin for the loss of one of her most lucrative clients, which cost Kaylin no sleep at night, ever.

"Pretty," Mandoran said, which didn't help. Margot was not an idiot, whatever else one could call her; she cast an equally appreciative look at Mandoran, but kept her distance. Barrani affairs were seldom safe for mortals, and attempting to bilk a Barrani out of money was a mug's game; it required stupidity and overbearing ego, and Margot only had one of the two. She pretty much failed to see Kaylin as Kaylin sauntered past.

"She is attractive," Teela said—which was obviously meant to irritate Kaylin, because there wasn't any other reason to say it out loud.

Bellusdeo shook her head. "By mortal standards, perhaps, but there's a brittle edge to the line of her mouth I find unappealing."

"Guys," Kaylin snapped. "A little less ogling and a little more patrolling."

"I'm not patrolling," Mandoran chuckled.

"Technically, you're not here."

He laughed. "You know," he said, "I think, when you have a place of your own, I'm going to be visiting a lot. You really are much less stodgy than Teela's become."

"Teela is *no one's* definition of 'stodgy.'"

"Kaylin will not be living on her own, and I don't do drop-ins," Bellusdeo pointed out. Her eyes remained golden. Mandoran's had edged toward green, but a stubborn streak of blue persisted. If he eventually chose to be comfortable around a Dragon, it wasn't going to be today.

He shrugged. "From the sound of it, you're not going to find much of a place of your own anyway."

"I can find a place," Kaylin said. "And Bellusdeo, despite appearances, doesn't require something palatial or even regal, given where we were living before."

"Oh, it's not your friend that's going to be the problem." He glanced at Teela's expressionless face, and added, "on the other hand, it could be worse for you. You could be living with Tain." His grimace looked nothing like a Barrani expression.

Teela cleared her throat. Loudly.

"You're living with Tain?"

"If you can call it living, yes. For some reason, he doesn't seem to want me to see much of your fair city. I want," he added, "to visit the Leontines I hear you have living here. I didn't even know they could function in cities. But your Sergeant seems fine wearing clothes."

Bellusdeo glanced at Kaylin. Kaylin turned a tight-lipped stare on Teela, who shrugged. "Surely you expected this?" the Barrani Hawk asked. "You know he hasn't lived in a mortal city before; he certainly hasn't lived in this one."

"The Leontines," Kaylin told Mandoran, in chilly Barrani, "are not animals. Nor are the humans. The Aerians are not birds. This is a *city,* not a zoo—and none of its inhabitants are here to be stared at through cage bars."

"Kitling."

Mandoran chuckled. "My apologies, Lord Kaylin. I seem to have touched a sensitive spot."

"You've reminded me of all the things I hate about Immortals. I don't know if you'd consider that a sensitive point or not." She didn't much care, either. The small dragon lifted a head and squawked. When Kaylin, still tight-lipped, ignored him, he nipped her ear.

"What?" She turned to glare at him, and he avoided her by leaping off her shoulders to hover in the air. When she still failed to understand whatever it was he was trying to tell her, he added sounds to the flap of wings, and when she failed to get *that,* he flew, head first, toward a window. A storefront window.

Kaylin ran after him, arms outstretched, while people in the street stopped to stare. She hadn't been patrolling on Elani for almost two months; the small dragon was still a novelty. Some of the gawkers were no doubt assigning a monetary value to him; she pitied anyone foolish enough to actually try to grab him and carry him off. Actually, scratch that. At the moment, she'd probably enjoy it.

It was only as she reached up for small and squawky that she recognized which window he'd threatened: it was Evanton's.

The door, habitually shut, now swung open; a wizened, bent old man was standing on the other side of the frame, his frown bracketed by a decade's worth of lines. "Don't stand there gawking," he said, matching tone of voice to expression. "Come in. I put tea on ten minutes ago."

Evanton didn't actually drink tea. He made it for guests. Given his current mood, those guests might as well have been tax collectors. Bellusdeo entered his store, her eyes rounding. If she'd been mortal, Kaylin would have assumed she was surprised at the clutter and the occasional moving cobweb. She wasn't. She turned to Evanton, in his apron, his jeweler's glass hanging on the edge of a tarnished silver chain, his white hair in wisps above the crown of his head.

And she bowed.

This seemed to mollify the old man. "You must be Bellusdeo," he said. "Rise, Lady. While I have a home here, you will always be a welcome, and valued, guest." His voice was deeper than usual, and to Kaylin's ear, stronger; it rumbled as if he were almost a Dragon. "I do not know who named you, or from whence they took the name, but it is yours in its entirety. I am honored."

Kaylin remembered, belatedly, to close her mouth. She stared at Bellusdeo. Bellusdeo's eyes were a luminous gold, and her lips were turned up in a gentle, almost reverent smile. "You have the advantage of me in many ways," she said.

"Ah, forgive me." He turned a far less reverent gaze on Kaylin. "Private, introduce us."

"Sorry. Bellusdeo, this is a friend of mine. He's called Evanton, around these parts; if he has a family name, he's never shared. The young man hiding in the kitchen is Grethan, his apprentice."

Bellusdeo frowned.

"Kaylin is, like the rest of the inhabitants of Elantra, very informal," Evanton said. He was, however, smiling in his slightly pained way.

"And you allow this?"

"Lady, she has twice saved my garden. In ignorance, she's borne the responsibility that has been the entirety of my adult life. She has never demanded reward greater than tea and snacks—and if I am to be honest, she doesn't so much demand as help herself if I am slow. I am willing to accept informality from her; formality would be so unnatural the awkwardness would likely kill one of us."

"Kaylin, do you understand who Evanton *is*?" Bellusdeo demanded.

"Yes. He's the Keeper."

"And do you understand what that means?"

"He—he stops the elements from destroying each other. And incidentally the rest of us, although I don't think they'd notice that as much." She hesitated and then said, "How did you know what he is if you didn't recognize who he is?"

Bellusdeo now turned to Teela. "Have you never explained?"

"Teela brought me here, the first time. When I wanted practical enchantments."

Evanton winced.

"Practical?"

"My daggers don't make a sound when I draw them."

The Dragon looked scandalized.

Evanton looked even more pained. "We all, as Kaylin likes to say, need to eat."

"I should have expected no better from an Empire that so denigrates the Chosen." Bellusdeo's eyes were now a deeper than comfortable orange.

"I am content, Lady," Evanton said, voice grave. "If the current Empire does not treat me with the regard or respect you now offer, it is a far less lonely place than it once was. Grethan," he added, his voice developing the gruffness and irritability of age. "You are being rude to a guest."

Grethan's stalks appeared from the left side of the door frame; they were followed, slowly, by the rest of his face. He didn't look comfortable. He was Tha'alani by birth, but although he had the characteristic racial stalks protruding from his forehead, they were decorative. He couldn't join the Tha'alaan. He couldn't speak to his own people the way they spoke among each other unless one of them touched him and entered his thoughts. The deafness had, in the parlance of the Tha'alani, resulted in insanity. In normal human terms, he'd been angry and isolated, and that anger and isolation had almost caused the death of a Tha'alani child.

A child whose life Grethan had, in the end, saved.

Evanton had taken him in; Kaylin often wondered if what had seemed an act of forgiveness and mercy wasn't just one long, extended punishment. But the only thing Grethan seemed to fear now was Evanton. He certainly wasn't afraid of Kaylin, Teela or Bellusdeo.

"Grethan," Kaylin said. "It's good to see you're still alive. Evanton seems to be in a bit of a mood today."

Bellusdeo's eyes almost popped out of her head. Kaylin made a mental note not to visit Evanton with Bellusdeo in tow.

The small dragon squawked and landed on Grethan's shoulder. Grethan looked at least as surprised as Kaylin felt. She recovered first. Grethan seemed entranced.

"So why is Evanton so cranky today?"

"Unfair, Private," Evanton replied. "Your tea is getting cold. And you've failed to introduce me to your other companion—although I suppose you could rightly attribute that lack of manners to Lord Teela."

"If she were unwise," Teela replied, her eyes an easy green. "Evanton, this is Mandoran. He has just returned to our lands after a long absence, and everything in them is new, except perhaps rudiments of our language. Mandoran, this is Evanton, the current Keeper."

"Mandoran?" Evanton frowned. It was a very peculiar frown; his eyes narrowed. In the dim light of the storefront, they seemed momentarily blue, although Evanton's didn't, as a general rule, change color. He extended a hand. Mandoran hesitated before extending one of his own. "Come, join us. Grethan, if you can detach yourself from Kaylin's companion, I would ask that you move refreshments to the Garden."

Grethan's eyes widened.

"The kitchen, while suitable for a private of the Hawks, is nowhere near suitable for Lady Bellusdeo." The official title was Lord, but Kaylin didn't bother to correct him. "We will therefore repair to the Garden."

"What is he up to?" Teela whispered. She was at the back of the line, because Evanton's rickety halls were at best one person wide. She had maneuvered into the position in front of Kaylin, who had pulled up the back, and had merely stopped walking until everyone else was far enough ahead.

Kaylin shook her head. "I don't know." She accepted Teela's suspicion because she felt some of it herself. "How did Bellusdeo recognize him as the Keeper? Did you, when you first met him?"

Teela exhaled. "Yes."

"How?"

"Mortals don't have true names, unless they've done something technically questionable."

"Meaning me."

"Meaning you, yes. No one is certain what having a name means for a mortal, and given you are—theoretically—mortal, you aren't considered enough of a threat that an answer must be found. The answer itself would take longer than the rest of your life to obtain."

"And that's relevant how?"

"Evanton doesn't have a name, per se. Not the way Immortals do. But if we meet his eyes for any length of time, we can see four words in their depths. They are names, they are linked to him, and they cannot be used to control him. It is the way the Keepers make themselves known to those who might otherwise intend them harm. If you look, you might be able to make out two of those names—but you might not. I'm not certain Evanton would stand still for long enough."

"He's not exactly fast on his feet."

"No, but in his fashion he knows how to intimidate. I've never noticed you engaging in staring contests with him."

"I'm not the one who does that, Teela."

Teela chuckled, but her eyes remained an alert blue. "I hate the Garden," she murmured, squaring her shoulders.

"It can't be any worse than paperwork."

Stepping through the narrow, rickety door at the end of an equally narrow, rickety hall was always a bit of a shock. Evanton's storefront couldn't, by any stretch of the truth, be called well lit, and the contrast between his work spaces and the Garden's brilliant, full-on sunlight made Kaylin's eyes water.

There was a roof, a domed high ceiling that would have fit right in in the Imperial Palace. There were no obvious glass ceilings or windows, and the roof, unlike the Hawklord's tower, didn't appear to open to the sky, so sunlight was in theory impossible. But nothing about this room conformed to what she knew of reality, and Kaylin had long since given up attempting to make sense of it.

She made her way across the flat-stone path laid into grass that would have made pretentious merchants weep with envy, pausing by the still, deep pool that sat, untouched by the breeze that moved almost everything else, in the Garden's center.

It was the heart of the elemental water, made small and peaceful. Beyond it, burning in a brazier that might have been used for incense, fire. Only in Evanton's Garden could the elements exist so close to each other in peace.

Beyond them was the small stone hut in which Evanton entertained the few guests he was willing to allow into this space.

"I don't think it's because of Bellusdeo that he moved tea," Kaylin said to Teela, as she made her way to the hut.

"No."

"I really hope Mandoran doesn't do anything stupid."

"He's not Terrano," Teela replied. "Terrano was the only one of us likely to throw his life away on a whim."

He was the only one of the twelve who had not chosen to come home. Somewhere in the spaces that mortals couldn't occupy, he was racing around the incomprehensible landscape discovering worlds and having fun. Kaylin fervently hoped he stayed there.

"Do you notice anything different about Mandoran? I mean, from before?"

Teela didn't answer.

When they reached the hut, the door swung open. Like any building of note in magical space, the interior didn't fit with the exterior; it was far larger than it had any right to be, for one. The floors were no longer rough stone; they were a gleaming marble, more suitable to a grand foyer than a parlor.

There were chairs of a style Kaylin had never seen in the Garden, and a low flat table that was the rough stone one expected to find outdoors. Tea, in Evanton's ancient, chipped tea set, was on the table, and steam rose from the spout of the pot. There were four cups, straight, tall cylinders absent handles. Kaylin didn't understand why cups made for hot liquid were ever without handles, but on the other hand, Bellusdeo was unlikely to burn *her* hand when picking them up.

The Dragon looked up as Kaylin entered the room; her eyes were golden. Clearly, the Keeper's abode suited her.

It suited her far more than the Palace.

"The Keeper was just regaling us with details of your first meeting," she said.

Mandoran, whose back was to the door, swiveled in his chair.

"It wasn't the first meeting," Evanton said, gently correcting her. "That was far less remarkable, although I remember thinking her unconscionably young to be keeping company with the Barrani Hawks."

"No talking about me as if I weren't in the room," Kaylin replied, taking the chair closest to Bellusdeo.

"You weren't in the room at the time."

"Here, now. Did small and squawky stay with Grethan?" The apprentice was nowhere in sight. Neither was Kaylin's most constant—and annoying—companion.

"No. He's in the fireplace." Bellusdeo nodded toward the fire in question. It was set into the wall, but reminded Kaylin—once again—of the Palace. Even the pokers looked like they were made of brass. And shiny.

"There's a fire in the fireplace," Kaylin quite reasonably pointed out.

"He doesn't take up a lot of room, and it's not like fire burns him. You can go and poke the fire if you want—he's there." Bellusdeo's expression made clear that if Dragons of any size didn't burn, mortals of any size did.

"I hope he puts himself out before he lands on my shoulders again." Kaylin turned back to her tea.

Squawk.

Mandoran grinned. "I have to say, I've never met a mortal a tenth as interesting as you are. I can almost understand why Teela is so attached to you."

"Teela," Teela said, "dislikes being spoken of in the third person even more than Private Neya. She is also far more effective at discouragement."

Mandoran laughed. "So she is. I don't know where you found the private, but I'd hold on to her, if I were you. Honestly, I wish everyone had descended on this strange, smelly, crowded place. Sedarias is beside herself with envy at where I am. In the Keeper's Garden!"

"It's not that exciting," Evanton said, his usual crankiness asserting itself.

"It is—she's the only one of us who'd met the Keeper. Not you," Mandoran added, as if that were necessary. "And Teela doesn't count. Can I talk to the elements?"

"Perhaps another day," Teela said, before Evanton could reply.

"But I hear the water," Mandoran said, his eyes green, his expression both familiar and strange. It took Kaylin a few minutes to understand why: it was very similar to the hesitant joy that the foundlings sometimes showed. She'd never seen anything remotely similar on a Barrani face before.

Evanton rose. "With your permission, Lord Teela, I believe the water wishes to converse with Mandoran. I will lead him there, and return."

Mandoran was out of his chair before Evanton had finished speaking.

CHAPTER 3

"I've never seen a Barrani so young at heart," Bellusdeo said softly, when they'd left.

"No. You wouldn't have," Teela replied. They were both speaking in Elantran. "We weren't considered of age to be meeting Dragons. I doubt very much that the rest of my friends would be considered so, now, were it not for the fact that they were born centuries ago."

"It can't be easy for them."

Teela's eyes paled; a ring of gold shifted the color of her irises. Bellusdeo had surprised her. Perhaps because she had, Teela answered honestly. "No. It won't be any easier for them than I imagine it is for you. We want home, in our youth. And when we've traveled far and suffered much, we want it more fiercely.

"But home is a myth. A tale. A children's fable. What will you do, Bellusdeo?"

Bellusdeo looked into her tea, as if she were scrying. "I don't know. What will your friends do?"

"At least one of them will take the Test of Name within the

next few weeks. If I can't talk him out of it, Mandoran will also take the test. I think he intends to accompany Annarion."

Kaylin found the tea too hot to drink, which was good, because she didn't choke on it. "He can't!"

"He can, kitling. There are no rules that govern the test—as you should well know. If you can enter the tower and read the word that will define you, you can traverse it. If you survive, you are Lord of the High Court. Annarion cannot be moved. His brother is furious. Mandoran might be more amenable to common sense."

"We're relying on his common sense?" Kaylin's eyebrows disappeared up her forehead.

"No. There is no 'we' in this equation. Mandoran is not—repeat *not*—your problem. Your problem at the moment is finding a place to live in the city. Focus on that, and keep your nose out of trouble while you do it. We'll take care of Mandoran." She broke off and looked to Bellusdeo, who was sitting completely still. "Kaylin knows most of the city reasonably well. She doesn't have our memory, but she doesn't need it."

"It's not her knowledge that worries me."

"No. But if you've listened to Evanton's horror story, you understand that she is capable of surviving much, much worse than a simple apartment hunt. Even with a Dragon or two in tow. She survived the loss of her home," Teela added, coming to the point in a way that she seldom did with anyone but Tain or Kaylin. "And between us, had she *not* been there, I don't think *you* would have survived." Eyes narrowing, Teela paused. "You don't think you would have survived, either." It wasn't a question.

"No. I had time to speak with the Imperial mages in your absence. I had time to assess their reports. But Teela, it's absolutely certain that the bomb would not have been thrown had I not been resident there."

Teela shrugged. "I didn't say Kaylin was *wise*. She's not. But in this case, accept her lack of wisdom as the gift it is. She means well—mostly—and sometimes you have to encourage that."

"Meaning well was not highly prized in the home of my childhood."

Teela chuckled. "It was actively discouraged, in mine. But mortal lives are so short; they believe, and they die before that belief is entirely lost. It makes them curiously compelling."

"Is that why you're a Hawk?"

"No." Teela hesitated, which was unusual. "And possibly yes. I didn't come to the Hawks looking for Kaylin Neya; I was surprised when I found her."

"Hello," Kaylin said, raising a hand. "I'm actually *sitting here*."

They both looked at her. Teela opened her mouth, no doubt to say something cutting, when the small dragon flew out of the fire, squawking at the top of his little lungs. Just in case volume wasn't attention-grabbing enough, he made a beeline for Kaylin's shoulders, landed with fully extended claws, and whacked her face with a wing.

"I don't know why you never had cats," Teela said, rising. "They couldn't possibly be any worse." Her eyes, however, had settled into Barrani danger blue.

Bellusdeo's were now orange.

"Can you understand him?" Kaylin asked, vacating her own chair before the small dragon bit a hole through her ear lobe.

"In this case, I don't think it's necessary." Teela rose and headed toward the door. It was awkward to have three grown women converge on said door at the same time, but Kaylin had the sinking feeling that awkward wasn't even on the list of their problems.

★ ★ ★

The door opened into torrential rain. The ceiling, such as it was—and the Garden was so elastic in shape and size, Kaylin didn't put much faith in Evanton's roof—was completely invisible; the skies were the gray-green of heavy cloud, and lightning illuminated the landscape in brief, bright flashes.

She couldn't see raging plumes of fire, and the ground just outside of the hut wasn't shaking in a way that implied it was about to break beneath their feet. But the wind was howling.

Literally.

Kaylin turned to the small dragon. "Where," she shouted, "is Evanton?"

He lifted a wing and plastered it against her upper face. He'd done this before, in the outlands, where vision was so subjective it was the only way to see what was actually in front of her. The Garden, in theory, didn't have that problem.

But when the wing covered her eyes, she could see past the driving rain; she could see past the flying leaves and the debris that might once have been offerings to each of the elemental shrines. She could see the clouds, and froze for a moment.

"Kitling!"

The clouds wore the shape and form of a woman. She was not familiar to Kaylin; she was too large—far too large—and too angry; her eyes were the size of the moons, even narrowed as they were. More disturbing were her wings. Kaylin had always loved Aerians because of their wings; she knew that those wings were weapons; that they could break a man's arm. But the wings of the storm—of the water—were like tidal waves; there was nothing beautiful about them, and the only freedom they implied was death.

"Can you see the Keeper?" Bellusdeo shouted. Her voice felt like rumbling earth.

"No—but the water is here, and it's enraged!"

"Only the water? Kaylin—can you see any of the other elementals?"

She started to say *air,* and stopped. The storm was entirely a thing of the water. "No."

The ground shook beneath Kaylin's feet. Leontine left her open mouth. But it wasn't the elemental earth joining the rumble; it was Bellusdeo. Bellusdeo, in her golden, draconian form. "Don't just stand their gawking—get on. That applies to you as well, Lord Teela."

"I am never," Teela said, complying immediately, "going to live this down."

Bellusdeo flew into the eye of the storm. Sadly, the eye was just above the jaws. The small dragon had wrapped his tail tightly around Kaylin's neck, and was digging new runnels into her right collar bone; he'd fallen silent, which was the only blessing. His wing was plastered against her face, above her nose and lips, which made breathing possible, although she was willing to bet more water than air was actually entering her mouth.

"Kitling—your arms!"

She'd noticed. The runic marks that covered over half of her skin were glowing brightly enough they could be seen through her sleeves; they were the color of Bellusdeo's eyes—and scales—as if only that part of her was now transparent. "Next time," she shouted, "we are leaving Mandoran at home!" She had no doubt that something Mandoran had done was responsible for the storm, and no certainty at all that she could stop it.

Which wasn't technically her job; it was Evanton's. Where in the hells was he?

Bellusdeo's flight was *not* smooth; it inspired no confidence at all. Since Dragons, unlike carriages, didn't come with built-in handholds, Kaylin's legs were rigid with an attempt to some-how hold on. She'd never gotten the hang of horses, either. But the Dragon was looking at something Kaylin couldn't see, and when she dove—through sheets of rain—for ground, Kaylin saw what: Grethan.

Bellusdeo caught him in her claws and lifted him. "Where," she demanded, "is out?"

"We don't *get out* without Evanton!" Kaylin shouted.

"Grethan can't stay here; he's half-drowned!"

"Can you land? Can he crawl up on your back?" She was already doing exactly that—but the ground here did not look promising; much of it was mud, and Dragons weighed enough she'd sink. Bellusdeo did, but she'd landed on her hind-legs and let them bear her weight while she set Grethan down.

Teela reached out and yanked Grethan out of the mud he'd barely had time to settle into. He was a bedraggled mess, but then again, so was Kaylin; Dragons and Barrani were exempt. Teela seated the apprentice in front of her.

"Grethan—where is Evanton? Can you reach him?"

Grethan swallowed air; his eyes were wide enough the whites seemed to have taken over half the space. "He's not answering!"

"Fine—but can you tell Bellusdeo *where he is?*" Teela had that calm-down-or-I'll-slap-you tone.

"He's—he's by the pond." Pause. "He's…in the pond."

"What pond?" Bellusdeo roared.

"Turn right!" Kaylin shouted. "Turn right and head toward the ground. Avoid the fire."

Right was a sheet of falling rain. Down was a sheet of falling rain. Kaylin was fairly certain there was no space in the Keeper's Garden that wasn't at the moment. "Teela—is Mandoran with Evanton? Teela?"

"Yes. And no."

"Which one is it?"

"…No."

Leontine and water didn't mix well. Kaylin tried anyway. She gave up and gave Bellusdeo directions, because she *could* see the pond. She could see it as the heart of the monstrous form water now wore: it was deep, dark, clear; it was no longer still.

The small dragon warbled; as his head was beside her ear, she heard him anyway. "Just one *normal* day. Is that too much to bloody ask? One day?"

Squawk.

The pond was the heart of the water. It didn't matter what shape it took, although Kaylin had very strong preferences at this point. It was anchored to one spot in the Garden. Storm aside, that anchor was still true. Kaylin had seen what happened when those moorings were broken, but by some miracle, they held.

Her arms were now aching, but she was used to that. When the marks began to glow, they often grew warm; warmth became uncomfortable heat.

"Grethan, can you be more specific?" Teela shouted.

But Kaylin said, "Never mind—I see him."

It was true. Evanton was standing *in* the water that rose like a pillar. His eyes were closed, his arms folded across his chest; for a moment, Kaylin stopped breathing. But his eyes snapped open before she could panic. Or, to be honest, panic *more*.

"Remind me," Teela shouted, "not to strangle Mandoran myself."

"Get Bellusdeo to remind you," Kaylin shouted back. "I'm thinking strangling sounds pretty damn good about now! I don't see Mandoran," she added. "Just Evanton."

"Worry about Evanton. Mandoran isn't dead. Yet."

★ ★ ★

Worrying about Evanton was easy. *Doing* anything about the worry, not so much. Bellusdeo had more or less found the pillar of water at the heart of the storm, but the storm was busy trying to swat her out of the air. As it was hard to maneuver around a constant stream of water, the flight was rocky. Kaylin tried to speak to the water, but the water wasn't listening.

And she knew that if she could call it by its name, she'd have its attention. Given what it was doing at the moment, that seemed like courting suicide. Given her very spotty record in Magical Studies, she wasn't certain of success. But... Evanton clearly had the water's name, and he was stuck in the middle of it, and the storm was still raging.

In spite of Teela's advice, Kaylin looked for Mandoran. Evanton was in the Keeper's Garden. Even if it looked like he was encased in water here, it wasn't likely to kill him—and if it did, they'd have far more pressing problems, none of which they were likely to survive.

"I swear," Teela said, "I'll kill him myself if he—" She broke off.

Bellusdeo had come to rest—if struggling to remain in flight and in position could be called rest—in front of Evanton. Evanton's eyes narrowed; he opened his mouth; no air escaped it. No words either. Frustrated, he spoke again. Slowly. Kaylin cursed as the movement of his lips resolved into three silent syllables.

"Teela—he wants us to find Mandoran!"

But Teela shook her head. "Speak to the water, Kaylin. Now!"

"Tried that. She's not *listening*."

"Idiot—*make* her listen!"

The name of fire always avoided Kaylin's grasp. She could stare at candles for three hours and fail to find the damned thing, although she'd used it before. The name of water was something she'd never consciously tried to call. The water spoke to her when it found her, and Kaylin responded in kind. She'd never come calling on her own.

Evanton knew the water's name. Evanton should have been able to calm the water down, if that was even possible. Offloading his responsibility onto the shoulders of a Hawk was low.

On the other hand it was just as possible that he was keeping the other three elementals in their peaceful, dozing state. The thought of dealing with angry earth, air *and* fire, on top of clearly pissed off water, killed all sense of grievance.

Bellusdeo, struggling in the storm, wasn't steady enough that Kaylin could reach out and touch the water's heart center. But Kaylin wasn't certain it mattered—water was everywhere, at the moment. Breathing was distinctly wet.

She tried, in her mind's eye, to see water's story, to find its elements, the way she could find fire's. Her arms ached with the heat of the marks that adorned her skin—and she wondered, briefly, if water's name was writ there, among all the other words she had no hope of reading.

While she could enumerate all of the things water personally meant to her, they didn't coalesce into a single name that defined those meanings. They were subjective words, not true ones—but mortals weren't gifted with true words; it was why it was so damned hard to remember true names: they *weren't* words.

They were the feelings and reactions you had to struggle to wedge into the words you did speak. They were subjective because they came from your life, not the life of the person you were trying to communicate with. You had to hope there was enough overlap in your lives that the words meant more or less what you thought they meant when you said them.

Only the Tha'alani seemed exempt from this constant stumble toward misunderstanding. The Tha'alani....

Kaylin closed her eyes. It changed almost nothing, but it allowed her to envision the water as she so often appeared: a young woman with an expression beyond her apparent years, who had clear, translucent hands. One of those perfect hands was extended toward Kaylin, as it so often was; Kaylin carefully reached out to grab it.

Her grip, as always, was that little bit too tight; she was grasping something she wanted—and had wanted—for her entire life. It wasn't, and couldn't be, hers. She was—at most—a welcome guest. But if the hand was water, it didn't slide through her fingers at the strength of that grip.

Even if she couldn't live here, she wanted to visit.

Kaylin.

She opened her eyes. The storm raged around the golden Dragon on which she sat so precariously; she felt, for a moment, that the whole of the water's attention was focused on her; water flowed down her flat hair; the stick that kept it off her neck had been lost. The small dragon was not impressed.

Tha'alaan, Kaylin said. She didn't need to shout, now; when she was connected with the water this way, she was certain to be heard.

"Whatever you're doing," Bellusdeo roared, "Keep doing it!"

She didn't need to be told. Even here, in the folds of storm, she felt the peculiar, particular warmth of the Tha'alaan. She heard the distant thrum of Tha'alani voices, and if she kept as silent as possible, it didn't matter; they didn't need words to hear or sense her.

The water became rain, and the rain ceased its fall.

Kaylin.

What happened?

I…was not aware of where I was. I heard a voice that I have heard in only one other place.

And you tried to destroy it?

It is not a voice that belongs in the Keeper's Garden, the water replied. *It is not a voice that belongs among your kind.*

It does, now.

No, Kaylin.

She thought of Mandoran. Of Barrani children, and Barrani childhood—artifacts, all, of ancient wars. *He's alive. He's here. He's—he's like Teela. He's Barrani. He—he wasn't, for a while.*

He is not, now. Silence again, and then a measured curiosity. Kaylin couldn't understand the question it contained—and that had never happened in the Tha'alaan before. *I understand how you see this…Mandoran. I understand that you see the name to which he wakened.*

But it is not, now, all that he is, and he brings danger with him. I sense his kin in the heart of the green; they are safest there. Send him back.

I'll talk to him.

Speak with care, Kaylin. You do not understand what he is.

Does he?

Silence. Then, *I…do not know. I think—I think he attempted to speak with me as he might once have spoken. I offer my apologies to the Keeper,* she added. *But it is best that Mandoran refrain from entering the Garden until either you understand what Mandoran has become, or until Mandoran does.*

Where is he?

Ah. He is with the Keeper.

Kaylin didn't ask where he'd been until now. Instead, she opened her eyes. The air was once again clear; she was on the back of a golden Dragon whose scales gleamed in the aftermath of an impromptu shower. Grethan was rigid in Teela's arms, and Teela was the color of alabaster, except for her eyes, which were the expected very dark blue.

The water itself was once again confined in the deep, still pond; the brazier in the fire looked no worse for the deluge. The breeze was warm, but gentle.

Evanton, however, was soggy. He resembled an elderly, bedraggled rat, but with less hair. "Do not give me that look, Private; I assure you I am drier than you are."

Bellusdeo, relieved of passengers, snorted smoke. "It occurs to me," she said, "that the Imperial Court is unlikely to be impressed."

"You didn't go dragon in the city streets," Kaylin pointed out.

"No. They'd be instantly aware of that transgression. I'm more concerned about the clothing."

"...Clothing."

"Don't make that face. I'm not about to parade naked through Elani street. I am, however, about to be reduced to wearing armor—a military look that I fear the Emperor doesn't favor." She cleared her throat, loudly.

"I think she's telling you to turn around," Teela said.

"Right."

Everyone was bedraggled except for the Dragon; Bellusdeo looked as if she were about to stride to war as an army of one. An impressive army, admittedly; she looked like the idealization of a warrior queen, more sculpture or painting than life. Teela was busy ringing water out of the perfect length of her hair, having done the same for her tabard. Mandoran was sitting on the ground, his knees folded into his chest, his chin resting on top of them. His eyes were ringed with shadow, but they weren't any darker than Teela's. Then again, black wouldn't have been much darker than Teela's at the moment.

Evanton placed a hand on Mandoran's shoulder; the Barrani youth looked up.

"It can't be helped," the Keeper said, in an incredibly gentle voice. Kaylin felt her jaw slide open; she'd expected fury and death threats, as well as forcible ejection. Evanton's frown reasserted itself as he looked at her. "I would, of course, be extremely angry if you did something this foolish in my garden." His tone implied that he expected Kaylin, at least, to know better.

Mandoran, however, slumped.

"Lord Teela," Evanton said.

"Keeper."

"Take Mandoran home. He will require both food and rest."

"What happened?" Kaylin asked. From Teela's expression, it was clear she already knew. "Evanton? Did you expect this?"

"Hardly."

"You don't look surprised."

"At my age, I seldom do. I can manage outrage, if you insist."

Since she had an idea of who that would be aimed at, she changed the subject. "I don't suppose you have a dress a Dragon could wear?"

"No."

"Access to one?"

"No."

"Are the Imperial spies still sitting across the damn street taking notes?"

"Yes. I imagine they were impressed that you brought Bellusdeo to visit."

Kaylin wanted to start the day over. The small dragon squawked.

"They'll be more impressed," Teela said, "when they see the results. You look like a warrior queen."

Bellusdeo was not immune to honest flattery, and smiled, inclining her chin. She clearly didn't have to deal with quartermasters.

"What did bring you here today?" Evanton asked Kaylin. She'd removed and wrung out her tabard, but that hadn't helped much. She was sloshing as she walked.

"You were waiting for us," Kaylin replied. "You don't know?"

"I am not an Oracle. You've been absent from your beat for almost two months." His eyes narrowed. "I had, of course, heard of Bellusdeo; I doubt there's a thinking being in the city who hasn't. I also heard—although in this the grapevine is less reliable—that you are now out of a home."

"An Arcane bomb," Kaylin replied. "It was intended for Bellusdeo; I was collateral damage."

"You both appear to be healthy, if a tad on the bedraggled side."

She nodded and glanced at the small dragon, who was flopped across her shoulders. He lifted his head—only his head—to stare at Evanton. He then squawked. Several times. "The Arcane bomb destroyed a quarter of the building I lived in. We were at ground zero—but he put up some kind of magical shield, which saved our lives."

"Yes, I noticed your companion." He bowed—to the small dragon. "My apologies for my lack of greeting. All Kaylin's companions this afternoon are worthy of note; I am too old to deal gracefully with a crowd."

The small dragon nodded.

"You are her familiar?"

Squawk.

"Ah. An interesting choice. I hope you don't expect a peaceful, tranquil life."

Snort.

"Evanton—can you understand him?"

Evanton's white brows lofted upward. "You can't?"

"I can figure out what he means—it's pretty obvious. But… none of his squawks sound like language, to me."

The Keeper's frown was a complicated network of lines. The small dragon squawked some more, and ended on a hiss that sounded very much like laughter. It didn't help when Evanton chuckled in response.

"Where did you find him?" Evanton asked.

"Long story."

"You are not notably shy about an excess of words on most days."

"I'm not usually in the company of a Dragon and a Barrani who can piss off the heart of the elemental water just by speaking to her." She grimaced. "I'm not usually a guest in the Imperial Palace, on a desperate hunt for a new home that won't have the Emperor turning me into a small heap of ash."

"Ah. I take it this means Bellusdeo intends to accompany you?"

"She's hoping to live with me, yes. We did okay before the bomb."

"I don't envy you."

"Evanton—you never envy me."

"Astute. I am, however, making the onerous attempt not to *pity* you."

"Thanks. I think." She glanced over her shoulder at the sound of a foot tapping. It was Teela's.

"Come back and have tea when you have more time to tell me about the past few months."

Teela didn't take Evanton's advice. She switched patrolling positions and let Kaylin—and the armored Dragon—take the lead. If Kaylin had privately envied the attention that Bellusdeo drew when they were together—and she pretty much drew it all—she repented; people were practically dropping their jaws at the sight of her now. On the other hand, very few of those people—some who were very familiar to the Hawks—dared to approach her, something the court dress hadn't seemed to discourage.

Bellusdeo looked like a Dragon now. Many mortals had no reason to ever cross a Dragon's path, and because they hadn't, it was easy to mistake them for human. From a distance, that's what they more or less resembled. Their eye color—and the inner eye membrane—were a giveaway only when you were close enough to examine the Dragon's face. Most people had no reason to get that close.

No one could mistake a Dragon in dragon form for a mortal—but when you were looking at giant scales, wings, claws and tail, that was understandable.

Dragon armor, even wrapped around a human-size body—albeit a tall one—was distinctive. And at least one of the gargantuan statues of the Eternal Emperor that littered the more respectable parts of Elantra sported it—with metallic leafing. The first time Kaylin had seen that statue, she'd thought the artist a pretentious nit. The first time she'd seen the armor in actual use—on Tiamaris—she'd silently apologized to that unknown artist, which she felt was fair, since it was the same way she'd dismissed him.

Bellusdeo therefore looked like a Dragon as she strode down Elani street by Kaylin's side. It made the day's work a lot easier, and as long as Kaylin ignored the probable consequences of the *need* for Dragon armor, she could be grateful.

CHAPTER 4

Mandoran was silent upon leaving Evanton's shop. He was silent throughout the rest of their patrol. Anything that had caught his attention when they'd first reached Elani street failed to grab it now; he was almost grim. No, Kaylin thought, Teela was grim. Mandoran looked as if he was walking to— or from—the funeral of a very close friend.

Kaylin wanted to speak with him, but given Teela's expression and the casual way in which she now hovered, it wasn't safe. But if it had been, what then? Words—especially words of comfort—weren't exactly Kaylin's strong suit. Sadly, inactivity wasn't, either. She wanted to do something to help, while being privately certain that any attempt would only make things worse.

"Kaylin?" Bellusdeo said.

"Sorry, just thinking."

"About?"

"If I had a suit of armor like yours, Elani street would be a lot easier to manage."

"Fear has that effect." The Dragon grinned. "The only thing your citizens seem to fear is the Emperor."

"Not true."

"No?"

"They fear starvation, disease, and homelessness. Among other things."

A golden brow rose in a distinct arch at Kaylin's snappish reply. "I touched a nerve."

She had. Kaylin's response was a fief shrug. "It's not easy being a mortal." Before Bellusdeo could speak, she added, "It's not easy being immortal, either. I'm coming to understand that. But our fears aren't your fears. I think there's overlap. Anyone, of any race, gets lonely. Anyone, of any race, can feel both grief and loss.

"But most of *our* lives aren't taken up with war and larger-than-life magical conspiracies. We die anyway, no matter what we do. And you won't. But the lives we live aren't insignificant to us; if we only have a handful of years, we *want* them more."

"I will not even argue that. Perhaps life is like friendship."

Kaylin glanced at her.

"If you have many, many friends, friendship is a given, a matter of fact. If you have—at most—one or two, it is rare, it is precious. The loss of a friend in that case is shattering because one cannot assume that there will necessarily be others. I did not mean to diminish either your fears or your experience."

"…No." Kaylin exhaled. "I used to think that people like you had it easy."

Bellusdeo didn't seem surprised by this.

"You're beautiful. You're charismatic. You never get old, or fat, you've never been plain—or ugly. You don't get diseases. The cold won't kill you. You don't need to sleep. You're never going to starve. If worse comes to worst, you can hunt.

I used to think—when I was a child—that if I were Barrani, I would never, ever have to be afraid."

"The Barrani are not without fear."

"No, I know that now. Neither are the Dragons—they just fear different things. All the things that terrified me as a child in the fiefs would never have been able to hurt me had I been you or Teela. It didn't really occur to me that other things *could*. My life was a desperate, mortal life. Until the marks appeared on half my body."

"And yet you do not seem to be comfortable with them."

Kaylin grimaced. Honestly, if she didn't stop doing that, her face would get stuck that way. "A dozen children were killed because these marks existed. Two of them were my family. I'd trade the marks, even now, if I could have them back.

"But I love my life. I mean, I hate parts of it—don't get me started on Sergeant Mallory or the idiots who demand nothing but paperwork—but I was helpless when I was that child. I couldn't have imagined living the life I have now; even escaping the fiefs was a daydream, something that other people did."

"What you love about your life now is that you can make a difference?"

Kaylin's nod was so instant and emphatic, she should have gotten whiplash.

"Even if that difference involves total strangers?"

"It's why I'm a Hawk."

"I will say that the *only* thing that makes me reconsider my opinion of the Emperor *is* the Halls of Law. It's the Hawks, in particular. There are many, many ways he could have approached ruling a city of this size. Or the Empire outside of it. To most of my kin, these laws of yours would be incomprehensible. They were made *for* mortals, designed for them, and are enforced *by* them."

Teela coughed. Loudly.

Bellusdeo chuckled. "Mostly enforced by them. In the Aeries of my youth, the suggestion would have been a joke—at best. Only the sentimental, the naive, or the foolish would have dared to suggest it."

"So...you think better of the Emperor because he's sentimental, naive or foolish?"

Teela coughed again. It was louder. "Do remember, kitling, that you're likely to be observed, hmm?"

"It's a *joke*."

"Yes. And Immortals are famous for their well-developed sense of humor."

Mandoran said, in all the wrong tone of voice, "I'm amazed that my kin have consented to be ruled by a Dragon."

"And I'm amazed," Bellusdeo replied, as Kaylin cringed, "that a Dragon has consented to rule Barrani, given the damage they've done to our people."

Kaylin turned to look over her shoulder; Teela had fixed her with a glare so pointed she should have spontaneously started to bleed. "Good job," she mouthed, in Elantran.

Arrogant, annoyed Mandoran was *probably* better than grieving, morose Mandoran. Probably. On the other hand, arrogant, resentful Bellusdeo?

By the time they returned to the office, Mandoran and Bellusdeo were figuratively bristling; had they been Leontine, it would have been literal. Color had returned to Mandoran's face, but it wasn't what Kaylin would consider particularly healthy. Color had mostly left Bellusdeo's lips, they were compressed so tightly. They had descended—ascended?—to raised voices half a dozen times; Bellusdeo apparently considered the loss of Kaylin's home and the possible loss of Kaylin's life almost unforgiveable. Kaylin's attempt to point out that Mandoran had not in any way been responsible for the Arcane bomb, given he wasn't even resident in the Empire, fell on selectively deaf ears.

It would have worked had Mandoran not called the bomb's lack of success regrettable. The fact that he apologized for the sentiment—to Kaylin—didn't appear to help much.

"I take it back." Teela's teeth were clenched so tightly it was a miracle she could wedge words between them. "You were definitely less of a concern than Mandoran, even when you were thirteen."

This wasn't much of a surprise to Kaylin. Mandoran was Barrani, after all. "Let's just never, ever take him drinking, okay?"

The guards—Clint and Tanner—that manned the outer doors of the Hall were on alert. Anyone would be, given that Bellusdeo's eyes were a shade of orange that could almost be mistaken for red, and Mandoran's eyes, a blue that could almost be mistaken for black. They didn't shift much in color as the small party made its way to the office, either.

Given that three of the four were still damp—which was a charitable description—silence descended on the office, rippling outward as people stared. It was broken by the usual whispers that implied gossip, but even that took longer than usual to start; no one wanted to piss off a Dragon or a Barrani. Well, except other Dragons or Barrani, apparently.

Marcus's facial fur—and ears—rose a good two inches as the Hawks made their way toward his desk. "Report," he demanded, growling on both *r*'s.

Kaylin glanced at Teela. Teela was staring at a spot about six inches above the Sergeant's eyes.

"We had a bit of a mishap at Evanton's," Kaylin said. She tried to keep her voice as quiet as possible.

"Wonderful. You're aware that Lord Emmerian is waiting for you in the West Room?"

She didn't cringe. It took effort.

"If this requires more paperwork on my part, I will take it out of your hide. Don't just stand their gaping—*go*."

Lord Emmerian was not wearing Dragon armor. The fact that Bellusdeo was couldn't be hidden, and his eyes—which appeared, from first glance, to be a cautious brass, shifted instantly into an orange that was in the same dark range as Bellusdeo's. Teela had all but grabbed Mandoran by the ears and dragged him as far away from Bellusdeo as office space permitted.

Since eye color was the first thing Kaylin noticed about Immortals, and his was bad, it took her a moment to look at the rest of him. She had briefly met Emmerian what felt like years ago; he had been silent, then. It was a better silence than the current one. She had seen him in the air above Elani street, with most of the rest of the Dragon Court—as a dragon. She thought his draconic form blue, although color did shift with mood.

At the moment, he was not in dragon form. He wore the usual expensive cloth of Court dress, but it was far less ostentatious than anything Bellusdeo wore. He had no beard, unlike Sanabalis or the Arkon. It made him look younger, not that the appearance of age meant much where Dragons were concerned. Aside from relative age, he looked nothing like the other Dragons Kaylin had met.

Oh, he had the eyes. But he was missing some of the arrogant bearing that she associated with Immortals. If it weren't for the telltale inner eye membranes, which were raised at the moment, she could have mistaken him for a regular person. A regular, rich person.

"Lord Emmerian," Bellusdeo said. To Kaylin's surprise, she bowed.

"Bellusdeo."

Bellusdeo smiled. Her eyes lost some of their murderous rage as she did. "I was informed by Lord Sanabalis that an escort would be provided for our apartment hunt—if that's the correct usage of the word hunt."

"It is," he replied. "I was pleased to be offered the opportunity—but I confess that I did not expect such a search to be… martial in nature. I am not perhaps suitably attired?"

She laughed. It was a lovely, low shock of sound—unexpected given the day. "It is, of course, I who am unsuitably attired; I'm tempted to retain the armor for the search. Any landlord who can overlook it is less likely to be troubled by having us as tenants."

Lord Emmerian said nothing, although he smiled.

The small dragon lifted his head; Kaylin could swear he opened only one eye as he surveyed the latest Dragon Lord. He then sighed in a whiffling sort of way and lowered both head and eyelid.

"If you will accompany us to the Palace, I will change there. With luck, the explanations likely to be demanded won't detain us until midnight."

Kaylin was willing to make bets on that. Sadly, most of them involved another sleepless night and a lot of Dragon shouting. "Let me talk to Caitlin before we leave? She had a few suggestions for places we might look."

Lord Emmerian froze.

"We have to find someplace I can afford," the private informed him, her voice a mix of defiance and apology.

Caitlin had a list, of course. She handed it to Kaylin, and Kaylin glanced briefly at the addresses while the office den-

mother dispensed advice. Since no one came to Caitlin's desk
expecting to avoid advice, Kaylin didn't bristle. "Don't mention the reason you're looking for a new place, dear. I realize
that might seem a tad unfair to the poor landlord—but I can't
think of many people who'd want to take that risk."

Kaylin could—but only one: the Emperor. "I don't think
the Barrani are likely to make another attempt; the only people who'll be more vigilant about possible attempts than the
Emperor are in the High Halls. They were embarrassed," she
added.

"I don't think that's true of all the Barrani."

"No," Kaylin replied, thinking of Mandoran. "But the Barrani Lords know the High Lord is angry; they'll walk carefully
for the next little while. Which, in Barrani terms, is a few
decades—possibly enough of them that I'll be dead of old
age and it won't be my problem. Or my landlord's. Thanks
for this."

Caitlin opened her mouth, shook her head, and closed it
again. As a send-off, it was ominous.

Bellusdeo did make it to the Palace, and to suitable clothing. She didn't make it out again without the need to tender
a report, but given the reportee was Sanabalis, it was quiet
and relatively brief. The small dragon was slumbering across
Kaylin's shoulders the entire time; clearly Sanabalis was not
worth the effort of waking up. On the other hand, Sanabalis
ignored the small dragon, as well.

Before they were cleared to leave, Sanabalis had insisted
they either take a carriage or a small platoon of Imperial Palace Guards. Kaylin had had enough of the Palace Guard. In
fact, she'd had enough of them the first time she'd met them
years ago. She made this as clear as only Kaylin Neya on a

tear could. Bellusdeo, however, didn't care for the officious, silent guard, either, and didn't demur.

During this discussion, Emmerian was present.

He remained silent. It wasn't a rigid silence; he wasn't—or didn't appear to be, given eye color—afraid of either Sanabalis or Bellusdeo. He simply had nothing to add to the argument on either side.

Given Kaylin's prior experience with Dragons and Dragon opinions—which were, of course, always smarter and wiser than hers, in the estimation of said Dragons—this was unusual. It wasn't that Emmerian looked friendly. He didn't. But he seemed content to be largely invisible, at least in comparison to the rest of the Dragons present.

This continued in the carriage as Kaylin sorted through addresses. Bellusdeo had, in the weeks Kaylin had been absent, studied Records-provided maps of Elantra; she probably knew the overall layout of the city as well as Kaylin did. The particulars were something she was willing to experience in person; she didn't expect crime statistics to tell her much about living in the various jurisdictions.

She did, however, seem to find the laws and their minutiae fascinating. Kaylin could understand this if she didn't think about it *too* hard; Kaylin sometimes found them fascinating. But Kaylin was pretty much paid to find them fascinating. Or to find reasonable ways to get around them in situations where the laws looked good on paper but were life-threatening in practice.

Bellusdeo now asked questions about the minutiae of said laws and their practical—or impractical—application. Kaylin, feeling self-conscious in the presence of a new Dragon Lord, answered as diplomatically as she could. Given that it was her job and the Halls of Law, this probably didn't say much.

Emmerian, however, listened politely; Kaylin noted that he

spent most of his time gazing out the windows at the passing street. There was just enough focus in the gaze that it implied attention rather than boredom, although his eyes did narrow as the Imperial carriage left the wider, grander avenues that surrounded the Palace, rolling past the streets that lead to the High Halls.

Bellusdeo was watching said streets at least as closely as Emmerian, but Kaylin wasn't worried; the small dragon who served as a primary alarm system was practically snoring in her ear.

When the streets narrowed, Emmerian said nothing. More loudly. Kaylin was glad that they weren't attempting to navigate by carriage during market day; carriage was probably the slowest way to get anywhere, although Imperial Crests reduced the waiting time by a fair margin. The streets were by no means dangerous by the time the carriage turned onto them, but Emmerian's silence had developed a hint of distaste.

Kaylin, who should have expected this, forced herself to remain quiet. Emmerian was used to a *palace*. He didn't have to live like a normal, working person. She exhaled. Bellusdeo didn't have to live like a normal, working person either—but she wanted to. Hells, given Bellusdeo, Kaylin didn't have to live like a normal working person. She was fairly certain most of the Hawks in the office would be appalled by her decision to move out.

But it was different, for Kaylin. Kaylin didn't fit in there. She didn't belong in rooms that made her feel dirty and clumsy and grungy just by existing. She didn't have the right clothing to walk the halls without attracting the disdainful glances of the *pages,* people who probably made less a week than even she did.

It was free accommodation, yes. But in every way except money, it was costly. She would have jumped for joy at the chance to stand in the Palace's *shadow,* as a child. She was a working, responsible adult, now.

Squawk.

Okay, a working, more-or-less responsible adult. Her job was the enforcement of the Emperor's Law; she didn't want home to essentially belong to that job. At the moment, it did.

"We're almost at the first place," Kaylin told the occupants of the carriage.

Bellusdeo had lived in Kaylin's old place, and didn't so much as raise a golden eyebrow. Emmerian hadn't, and raised a blue-black one as the carriage clopped to a smooth stop.

"You don't think the Emperor is going to like the place," Kaylin said, as a footman opened the carriage door and deposited a fancy stool before it.

Bellusdeo snorted as Kaylin stepped down. Emmerian followed Kaylin, and scanned the street before he nodded to a visibly impatient Bellusdeo. She disembarked last, by unspoken mutual consent.

"I am certain," the Dragon Lord finally said, "that he won't." He approached the doors to the four story building and frowned. "Is it possible that there's no door ward here?"

"It's not only possible," Bellusdeo replied, before Kaylin could. "But extremely likely. Our Kaylin doesn't care for door wards."

"'Our' is it?" Emmerian examined the door without touching it. He did not, however, use magic to do so—or at least not magic that made Kaylin's skin break out. "Private Neya, are the interior doors likewise without wards?"

"Which part of 'Kaylin doesn't care for door wards' was unclear?"

Emmerian stiffened. Bellusdeo had drawn herself up to her full height, and her eyes were now tinted orange. Emmerian's were likewise shading to bronze. The small dragon lifted his head and surveyed the situation—while yawning. His teeth were solid ivory, although the rest of his mouth suggested the same translucence as his body.

Both Dragons immediately turned toward him. He squawked. Given Bellusdeo's expression, Kaylin wasn't surprised she didn't squawk back. Contrary to Diarmat's constant criticism, Bellusdeo did have some sense of personal dignity; squawking at a winged lizard in the city streets was beneath it.

Emmerian was likewise silent, although he now looked mildly surprised. Kaylin, aware that she was the pedestal on which the interesting person was standing, nonetheless ducked between them and opened the door. The hall, at least on this floor, was lit; steep stairs the width of one person climbed up on the left of the door. The landlord's office—which was a fancy word, in Kaylin's opinion, for apartment—was down the hall to the right.

She was surprised at how nervous she felt. She couldn't remember feeling nervous when she'd gone apartment hunting with Caitlin the first time. Suspicious, yes. Bewildered. Not nervous. She mentally kicked herself.

What was the worst thing that could happen here? Besides Bellusdeo descending into full-bellow Dragon fury. The apartment could be terrible. The landlord might want too much for extras he hadn't bothered to mention to Caitlin. Bellusdeo might actually hate the place. None of these things was deadly; some might be minor humiliations, but Kaylin expected that from life.

She straightened both shoulders and knocked on the closed, residential door marked as an office. The floors on the other side of the door creaked. So did the floors on this side, but more ominously; Dragons were dense, and two of them were occupying pretty much the same square yard of flooring. The building was in decent repair, given Kaylin's admittedly slight experience; it was by no means new or modern.

The door opened on a man of middling age and similar height; he suited his building. "Can I help you?" he asked, in a tone of voice that implied he meant the answer to be no.

"Yes. I'm Private Kaylin Neya. I have an appointment to view 3B."

The man relaxed slightly; he glanced at Bellusdeo and Emmerian, his eyes narrowing. Neither of the two looked like they lived in this part of town. Ever. "Marten Anders. These your friends?" he asked, stepping into the hall with a very obvious ring of keys in his left hand.

"Yes. This is Bellusdeo. She'll be sharing the space with me for the time being." Kaylin failed to introduce Emmerian. Mr. Anders noticed, of course.

"She'll be marking the lease?"

"No."

The man shrugged. "We don't want trouble here," he told them both. "I run a respectable, quiet place."

"That's why we're here," Kaylin replied—quickly. Bellusdeo looked as if she was about to speak.

The small dragon squawked instead. The man's eyes rounded instantly as the transparent troublemaker sat up on Kaylin's shoulders.

"He's house-trained, and he doesn't bite. He doesn't make much noise." She resisted the urge to clamp a hand around his mouth, because she was fairly certain 'doesn't bite' would be instantly disproved.

"What *is* he?"

"A lizard."

The small dragon squawked.

"You know how there are albinos? He's like that, but with even less color."

Mr. Anders nodded slowly. Since Bellusdeo and Emmerian kept glacially stiff expressions plastered to their faces, he accepted the off-the-cuff lie and headed up the stairs.

There were actually two rooms, although the bedroom was about the size of the smallest of Bellusdeo's closets in the Palace. The floors were covered by a rug that had seen better decades, and the boards made a lot of noise. To Kaylin, this was familiar and almost comforting. There were windows; they were glassless, but shuttered—and barred.

"Are the bars necessary?" Bellusdeo asked.

"They're decorative, ma'am," the landlord replied.

"Good. You won't mind if we remove them, then. I don't particularly like the idea of living in a cage."

Emmerian turned to the landlord before he could reply. "Would it be permissible to make alterations to these rooms and the hallways themselves?"

This was not a question to ask a landlord who was looking less eager by the passing second. If Emmerian had been anything other than a Dragon, Kaylin would have stepped, hard, on his foot.

"What kind of alterations?" was the entirely reasonable response.

"They would be both physical and magical in nature. You clearly have rudimentary mirror grids within the building, but we would require something with a little more power. The windows would have to be changed; we would install glass—at our expense, of course. Are the rooms above this one currently occupied?"

"Yes."

"If we take this room, we would require it. For the sake of safety, we would also require the room directly below." Emmerian held up a hand before the man—whose mouth had compressed into a line that sort of matched his narrowed eyes—could interrupt. "We would, of course, be willing to double your current rents. Or possibly triple." It was the only thing the Dragon Lord had said that might possibly appeal to a landlord, but given the pinched expression on this one's face, it didn't appeal enough.

A thought struck Kaylin in the deepening gloom. "I'm not willing to pay triple the rent for *these* rooms—I can't afford it, given what I'm paid."

"No, of course not. We have agreed that we will not interfere materially with your living quarters."

"And *glass windows* that practically scream out to enterprising thieves aren't materially interfering?"

"No. They serve several functions, they increase security, and they add value to the building itself in the event that you choose to leave. The modifications will," he added, turning once again to the landlord, "remain your property when Private Neya chooses to vacate these premises."

When. Not if.

Kaylin could feel herself losing inches of height as Emmerian continued. This was possibly the most she'd heard him speak in one sitting, and she regretted the absence of his silence. The only thing worse was the shifting color of Bellusdeo's eyes. They weren't full-on red, but they were orange, and she'd dropped the inner membrane that muted their color.

And that, she thought, as she glanced at the pale man who was in theory a possible future landlord, was that. If he hadn't recognized Bellusdeo for a Dragon upon introduction, he recognized her as something non-mortal, now. Kaylin exhaled. It was the sound of total defeat. "Could you two wait outside?"

When neither Dragon moved, she added, *"Now?"*

The landlord did not insist on seeing them out. He did fold his notably burly arms across his chest when they were quit of the empty rooms.

"Look, I'm sorry. I'm sorry they were so insulting," Kaylin told him.

"Dragons, aren't they?"

"Yes."

"And you're a Hawk." He shrugged. "It's a job. They always like that?"

"Normally? No. Worse. They don't intend to be insulting—"

"But they think all mortals are money-grubbing merchants at heart."

She had the grace to look guilty. "In Bellusdeo's defense, she's spent a couple of weeks with us on patrol in the Elani district."

"So...fraudulent, money-grubbing merchants?" His lips twitched up at the corners. It was slight, but it was better than the frown that had taken up residence while Emmerian was talking.

"Caitlin wouldn't have recommended the apartment if you were—if you weren't... Can we just pretend I didn't start that sentence?"

His grin spread. "It's a bit of a pity," he said. "I think I could live with you. I think I could live with...new-fangled enhancements. They'd probably have to do something about the floors."

"But you can't throw people out of their homes, even for three times the money."

"No. Money's tempting, and I wouldn't get legal hassle for it—but, no."

"I like you better for it," Kaylin replied; it was true.

"Aye, well. If you're looking to make a home, it's a good

trait—for you—in a landlord. Tell you what—if you lose the roommate, and the apartment's still here, come back and we'll talk."

Emmerian and Bellusdeo were waiting in the carriage. The doors were closed. The windows, however, were slightly open, and Kaylin could hear Bellusdeo's voice the moment she opened the external door. She guessed that orange eyes were now deeply orange, and had Severn been with her, she'd've bet on it.

He wasn't, so she didn't make money. Then again, he might not have taken the bet, because he *had* ears in his head.

Since she wasn't feeling particularly charitable, she took her time walking to the carriage. She hoped Bellusdeo was figuratively chewing Emmerian's head off—but she didn't want the conversation to slide into native Dragon—not in the city streets. It would cause a panic, and she'd be at the center of it. Given the way things generally worked, Marcus would blame her.

If Marcus didn't, the Lord of Swords probably would—because when people panicked in any number, it increased the workload of the Swords. The footman jumped off the little shelf at the back of the carriage as she approached the doors. She let him open them, and climbed into a carriage that fell immediately silent.

The small dragon whiffled.

"He didn't mind a Dragon roommate," Kaylin said, first up. "It was the crap that came with the roommate that he found objectionable. What were you thinking?"

Emmerian looked momentarily disconcerted.

"You can't just demand that a landlord kick out two apartments full of people because you think you want rooms for your own purposes."

"I made no demands."

"They weren't exactly requests, Emmerian."

"They were. If the landlord did not wish to accommodate them, he was free to refuse to let the apartment."

"Which he did."

The Dragon implied a shrug without going through the down-market motion. "The modifications are not required should Bellusdeo choose to remain within the safety of the Imperial Palace. The measures are a compromise."

Kaylin turned to Bellusdeo. "You agreed to this compromise?"

"Hardly. I agreed to live with some surveillance. Given your current life, I expected that it would be subtle."

"My current life?"

"You are, as you well know, under Imperial Surveillance. I assumed that the security I would be offered would be of a similar variety." Her eyes were getting redder by the syllable.

"I think," Kaylin said quietly, "we're done for the evening. I'll mirror from the Palace and make my groveling apologies to the other two landlords."

CHAPTER 5

If Kaylin was done for the evening, Bellusdeo was not. Kaylin attempted to use the mirror in their Palace rooms—twice. She managed to more or less explain to Caitlin the outcome of the interview with Marten Anders, but the sound of Dragon fury meant Caitlin was reduced to lip-reading for half the call. Calling to grovel about missed appointments was out of the question. Caitlin offered to do it for her.

Apparently, sleep was out of the question, as well.

Staying in the Palace, however, had less than zero appeal; Kaylin didn't want to hide in the library with a sarcastic, cranky Arkon, although she did consider asking him if he had a spare bed in one of his maze of treasure rooms. She paced for a bit while the small dragon warbled in the breaks between Dragon "conversation." There weren't that many of them.

When she couldn't stand it anymore, she mirrored Teela. She almost cut the call when she saw the color of Teela's eyes: very, very blue.

"Unless Bellusdeo has burned down a city block or two, this is not a good time," the Barrani Hawk said.

"I think she's trying to burn down the Emperor, if that counts."

"It doesn't, unless she manages to succeed." Teela frowned as Kaylin lost sound. When it returned—or rather, when outrage receded between the long, long breaths Dragons could draw, Teela's brows had risen. "You're not half wrong," she said, in Elantran. "How long have they been going at it?"

"An hour. Maybe more. I have no idea how long they'll be at it either— Oh, I think that one's Diarmat."

Teela started to speak, rolled her eyes, and stopped. "Lord Diarmat. Honestly, kitling, when *in* the Palace, *try* to observe proper form."

"I'm heading out of the Palace because at this point, I can't. Try, I mean." She frowned. "Teela, where exactly are you right now?"

The Barrani Hawk grinned. It was a cat's grin. "You finally recognize the room?"

Kaylin was silent for a long moment. "Where's Severn?"

Teela glanced to the side of the mirror and held out her right hand, still grinning. "I win," she said.

Severn came into the mirror's view. He looked about as pleased to lose a bet as Kaylin would have, which wasn't her biggest concern. "Why is Teela at your place?"

"Teela," Teela replied before Severn could, "was bored."

"I mean it, Teela. I know what you do when you're bored."

"If you're not going to play with him, I don't see why you should be so proprietary; he's a big boy."

Severn raised a brow in Teela's direction. "I'm the substitute Tain for the evening."

"Why does she need a substitute?"

"The one she has is currently babysitting. I hear Mandoran caused a bit of excitement on Elani street."

"Where he wouldn't have been if you hadn't been in session

with the Wolves." Kaylin's frown deepened. She was certain Severn had heard maybe three words of the last sentence, but wasn't willing to bet on it; the Dragons weren't pausing for much. "What does she need Tain for?"

"She's not an idiot."

"Why, thank you," Teela drawled.

Severn didn't blink or otherwise indicate he'd heard her. "Tain's about the best backup she has."

"Why does she need backup? What's going down?" The small dragon sat up and leaned forward, adding his version of inner membranes to the mirror's surface.

Severn didn't reply. But he did glance—pointedly—at the Barrani Hawk. It was no answer, but it was answer enough for Kaylin. "Don't leave without me," she said abruptly.

Teela's eyes were already dark enough they didn't change color. "You are not—"

Kaylin cut the communication. The mirror was already doing a lightning jig as she grabbed her boots and daggers, putting them both on. It wasn't safe to ignore Teela when she was in this mood, but Kaylin was done, for the moment, with caution. Teela didn't *need* backup to go to a bar. She didn't need muscle. Nothing that could happen in a bar could threaten her life in any real way.

And there weren't a lot of places she could go that made Severn the ideal replacement backup. In fact, Kaylin thought, as she laced up her boots, there was really only one.

Nightshade.

Kaylin decided to accept the Imperial carriage offered as a matter of course to guests of any note living within the Palace. For perhaps the first time, she was grateful for the screaming fury of Dragon debate; it meant Bellusdeo wouldn't be able to follow her.

She wasn't expecting to be stopped by anything other than stiff, formal, condescending guards. These could be safely ignored. The person who met her in the halls as she all but raced toward the stable yards, not so much: no one ignored the Arkon if he didn't want to be ignored.

Teela wasn't going to wait forever. Severn could only stall her for so long. Damn it. She skidded to a halt; the only other option was running into the ancient Dragon.

"I can't talk," she told him, before he'd opened his mouth.

"Demonstrably untrue."

"I'm heading out for the evening."

"I had guessed you might, given the tenor of the unfortunate conversation."

"Is this something that can wait until I get back?"

He was looking, pointedly, at her daggers. "No. It might have escaped your notice, Private, but I am not currently *in* my library."

Kaylin bit back sarcasm with extreme difficulty. "Apologies, Arkon." A white brow rose as she slid into High Barrani.

"Accepted. There were apparently some difficulties this afternoon."

"Yes—we explained them to Sanabalis. Er... Lord Sanabalis."

"Indeed. I think the Emperor was not entirely sanguine about those difficulties; it is certain to come up in the conversation."

"It hasn't, yet?"

"No. Bellusdeo is extremely unamused."

"Diarmat—Lord Diarmat—doesn't sound all that happy either." It was the tiny silver lining on the gigantic storm cloud.

"He is not, but he is not a man who generally radiates either happiness or contentment. He is also not enough incentive for an old man to leave his library."

Kaylin took the hint and shut up, silently urging the Arkon to cough up his reasons as fast as humanly possible. Or dragonly.

"I am concerned about the difficulties, as well. The afternoon's," he added. "The current argument between the Dragon Court and Bellusdeo is nowhere near resolution and only an optimist or a fool would expect it to reach a satisfactory resolution in the near future."

"Please tell me the near future is within the next few decades."

He ignored this. "The Barrani, Mandoran. He was one of twelve Barrani children selected to undergo a significant rite of passage in the West March."

Gods. If he started asking about that, she'd be in these halls longer than Bellusdeo would be in the throne room. "Yes."

"Lord Teela was one of the same twelve."

"Yes."

"The only one of the twelve to return from the West March."

"Until very recently, yes."

"Your answers are evasive, Private Neya."

"They're direct answers to the questions you're asking when I have almost *no time,* sir." His brow rose, and she reddened. "Arkon."

"Very well. You will make the time to explain what occurred in as much detail as I require in future."

She'd age and die before she could live up to the level of detail he required. She kept the thought to herself. "I don't understand most of what happened, and I was there. But—"

"But Mandoran accompanied you home."

"Yes."

"He was not the only one of the twelve—Lord Teela aside—to travel to Elantra."

"...No. The other one didn't travel with us, though."

"Do your evening's plans include the other one, as you call him?"

"I don't know."

"But you suspect they do."

She hesitated before nodding.

"Very well. He is the reason I am here. Your Mandoran—"

"Teela's Mandoran, please."

"Lord Teela's Mandoran, if you prefer, caused difficulty in the Keeper's Garden. It was not a difficulty that the Keeper anticipated."

Obviously. She felt compelled to add, even given the agonizing passage of time, "Evanton recognized something in Mandoran, though. He didn't treat him the way he generally treats Teela. I think he wanted Mandoran to see the Garden."

"That did not work out as well as he'd hoped."

"No."

"Very well. Teela's other friend is, if our sources are correct, currently resident within the fiefs."

Kaylin suddenly felt very, very cold. "Yes."

"There are very few residences in which Barrani of any status might feel at home. I can think of only one—in each fief. I believe you are beginning to understand the possible difficulty."

She was. "The Castle."

"The Towers, yes. They are not, in architecture or constitution, like the buildings in which most of the citizens of the Empire live. They exist in a different space."

"...Like the Keeper's Garden."

"Very *unlike* the Keeper's Garden, but I see you have absorbed most of the point I wished to make. If your intent was to go to the fief in which Lord Teela's companion is situated, you have my apologies for wasting your time here. But

Kaylin—be careful. If Bellusdeo's brief account was accurate, Mandoran did not intend to cause the difficulties he did cause.

"It is likely that his friend might cause similar difficulties, with just as little intent."

"I don't understand *how*."

"No. You think of the lost as Barrani."

"They are."

"No, Kaylin. They *were*. They may even consider themselves to be Barrani now. Their interpretation of their own state is of little consequence. The Emperor does not yet feel threatened by their presence—or he did not, before the incident in the Keeper's abode. He will, however, be concerned."

Kaylin jumped out of the carriage before it had rolled to a full stop, which was well before the footman had time to jump down himself. Although it was now dark, the carriage attracted attention; she could see windows open as she headed straight for Severn's place, but ignored them. In this part of town, crossbows were unlikely to be trained on her exposed back.

Severn opened the door before she could knock. Teela was out in the street before she could talk.

"I'm against this," Teela told her. "For the record."

"That's fine, as long as you understand that I'm going anyway." She glanced at Severn as he locked his door. "We're going to Nightshade?"

He nodded and added, "I win," to Teela.

Teela was less graceful about losing a bet than Severn had been, probably because she had less practice. "I never said she was stupid."

That definition of never stretched the meaning of the word so far it was likely to snap. "I suppose it's too much to hope that we're not going to the Castle?"

"Far too much," Teela replied.

"Did Nightshade communicate with you directly?"

"With me? No. Before you ask, he didn't mirror Severn either."

"So we're heading there because Annarion was in contact with you directly."

"Something like that."

"Which means Nightshade isn't expecting visitors."

He is, now, the fieflord said, right on cue.

"There *is* a reason I didn't want you tagging along," Teela said. "In fact, there are several. Your mark is glowing." She strode at a fast pace past the idling carriage. No one took a carriage into the fiefs.

Kaylin lifted her hand to her cheek. Unlike the marks that had come to define much of her life, this one had arrived later, and she knew its source: Lord Nightshade, of the fief that bore his name.

"I take it this means he knows we're coming."

"...Sorry, Teela."

"Not good enough."

"You weren't exactly going to storm the damn Castle in secret."

"There's every chance we were going to do exactly that," Teela snapped.

Kaylin looked to Severn. "Was she drinking?"

"Alcohol doesn't affect me," Teela said, before Severn could answer. This wasn't strictly true, but close. Teela could, with effort, be affected by alcohol meant for mortal consumption—but almost anything could snap her out of it.

"Not an answer."

"As much of an answer as you deserve. Look—things at Castle Nightshade are in flux at the moment."

"Annarion is in the Castle."

"Yes."

"And he's the reason things are in flux?"

"That's our assumption." Teela picked up a pace that was already on the wrong side of punishing.

"Teela." The small dragon added accompaniment or the Barrani Hawk might have ignored Kaylin. She slowed, which, given her mood, was the equivalent of a dead stop.

"You can speak with Annarion. What's happened at the Castle?"

Teela exhaled. She didn't stop moving. "I can speak with Annarion," she said, in what should have been agreement. It wasn't. "At the moment, he can speak with me. But I can't understand at least half of what he's saying."

Kaylin almost missed the ground with her next step. "He's—he's speaking the way Nightshade and I do?"

"Yes."

"How can you not understand him?"

Severn caught Kaylin's arm. "She doesn't know. We're heading to Nightshade in part to find answers."

"And the other part?"

"To find Annarion."

"There's something else you're not saying."

She felt Nightshade's amusement and chagrin. *I believe what he wishes to conceal is the possible need to rescue...me.*

Kaylin did stumble, then. *Fine. You understand what's happening, right? You tell me.*

Annarion is having an argument, he replied, after a long pause.

With you?

It started that way, yes. Unfortunately it did not end that way, if it can be said to have ended at all. When he first arrived at my doors, I explained the nature of the Castle to him. The explanation was, of necessity, incomplete.

You couldn't explain the parts you don't understand.

No Barrani liked to own their ignorance; Nightshade was no exception. *Indeed.*

The argument that you were having was heated.

It was far less calm than most such discussions that occur within my domain.

How much less calm?

There was very little blood, but not none.

He tried to kill you?

I do not believe that was his intent. The Castle does not always judge intent correctly. There are rudimentary defenses under my control; there are subtle defenses which occur at the Castle's volition. The subtle defenses engaged when he attempted to strike me.

Kaylin uttered a loud Leontine curse, which caused Teela to raise a brow. And speed up again. *Where is he now?*

That would be the question. I have not managed to ascertain his precise location. He is alive; I believe him to be materially unharmed. He is not, however, within the confines of the Castle with which I am familiar.

You're familiar with all it! It's your castle!

So I would have said, although I would quibble with your use of the word familiar. *I have forced the Castle to conform to a shape and size—on the interior—that suits me. You are well aware that visitors who are unaccompanied frequently find that shape less fixed. Anna-rion is, at the moment, unaccompanied.*

So…your brother is arguing with your castle. A thought struck her as she jogged to catch up to Teela's back. *Is it still* your *castle?*

That would be the question.

The streets of the fief were empty. Kaylin could hear the occasional insect; that was it. The Ferals that hunted these streets were either absent or silent, which was almost a pity.

In Teela's current mood, Ferals on the hunt wouldn't last two minutes—and ridding the fief of Ferals was never a bad thing.

"Teela, can any of the others understand what Annarion's trying to say to you?"

Teela failed to hear the question. Since she had far better hearing than Kaylin, Kaylin assumed it was deliberate. She let it go.

Severn, however, answered. "Yes. Teela attempted to have them translate. It did not go well. Mandoran offered to enter the fiefs to find Annarion. She said no." He was walking in lockstep with Teela, but had taken the lead; it was work to keep it.

Kaylin had spent over half of her life in these streets—but almost never at night, if she'd had any choice at all. Night changed the texture of the map. Fear could change its shape. She glanced at Severn, took a deep breath, and reminded herself that she no longer lived here. The streets of the fief didn't own her. The fieflord didn't, either.

She was here with two Hawks. She was here because she'd chosen to cross the bridge; she could cross it again the moment she'd finished what she came to do. The fact that she didn't fully understand what she had to do here didn't matter. She was older, stronger, and she had backup.

If Nightshade's roving thugs attempted to stop her, she'd kill them. If they were Barrani thugs—and he had a few of those—she'd let Teela kill them. She'd help.

The only thing she should be worrying about—besides Annarion and Teela—was the damned entrance to the Castle: it was a portal. The only time portals didn't make her nauseated to the point of actually throwing up was when Nightshade literally carried her through the magical vortex.

Being sick all over his polished marble floor was probably the smarter choice.

"If you're worried about the portal," Teela said, as she finally slowed to a reasonable walk, "don't be."

"Easy for you to say. Portals don't bother you."

"That's probably not what she meant," Severn said, in exactly the wrong tone of voice.

Kaylin had been paying too much attention to the rest of the streets; she'd been listening for Ferals. The streets were not well lit, and in most cases, the light was moonlight. It was a clear night, but even if it hadn't been, Teela could practically see in the dark.

What Teela was looking at now didn't require Barrani vision to see; it was a black shape that rose into the sky. New buildings did not just appear in the fief of Nightshade. Even if the fieflord had a sudden change of heart, a building such as this one didn't appear over the course of a couple of months; it was constructed over a decade.

"Yes," Kaylin said, although Teela didn't ask. "It's new. And it appears to be standing on the only piece of prime real estate in the fief."

It looked very much like the silhouette of a Tower.

Within five fief blocks, they confirmed what they'd strongly suspected: the Tower occupied roughly the same amount of space as the Castle that had once stood there. The courtyard—small and decorative, if one counted the empty hanging cages as decoration—near the entrance to Castle Nightshade was also absent. So were the gates. The Barrani who usually oversaw those black gates—the armored guards more suited to Court than to fiefs—hadn't disappeared with them.

They no longer guarded gates, or a fake portcullis. They stood to either side of doors that seemed, even in moonlight, to be made of polished obsidian.

"This does not look promising," Teela murmured. "Kitling, are you still in communication with the fieflord?"

Since the mark on her cheek was warm enough it was probably glowing, the answer was obvious. Given Teela's mood, Kaylin answered anyway. "He's able to communicate with me."

"Ask him if this is what he expected the outside of his castle to look like."

The Tower was tall. It was taller than the Tower in Tiamaris, and looked infinitely less welcoming. The doors were its most striking feature, but the rest of the Tower wasn't exactly nondescript. It suggested cliff faces on stormy nights; it looked sharp, angular, an almost natural protrusion.

"He's remarkably silent."

Tell Lord Teela that I am not certain it is wise to enter the Castle at the present time.

No, thanks.

I make no attempt to mark territory, or to assume command. The Castle is dangerously unstable. Tell her.

Kaylin shook her head emphatically. *She's going in unless you forbid it. Given her mood, I'd be willing to bet she'd try anyway.*

A beat of silence followed. *Will you caution Lord Severn?*

Same problem, except for the mood. If I go, he's going, and if Teela's going, I'm going.

You will have to inform my men that I grant permission. At the moment, communications have been unreliable. Nightshade was at least partly amused. *They will accept your words as if they were, in this case, my own.*

The mark.

Yes. My brother dislikes it intensely; he wishes it removed. I have explained that its existence has saved lives, but he considers the practicalities incidental in this case.

Is he wrong?

You know he is not. When I consider the centuries in which I attempted to find solutions for his absence, I am reminded strongly of the mortal phrase: be careful what you wish for.

Can he take the Castle from you?

That is not my fear.

What are you afraid of?

He did not intend to do what I believe has begun. He is waking the Tower.

You mean he's talking to—to the equivalent of Tara?

Not deliberately. But something hears him, and I think it is struggling to respond.

Where is Andellen?

Within the Castle.

Getting permission to enter the doors was perfunctory. The guards took one look at Kaylin's face, and stood back from them. They weren't thrilled about Teela's presence, but said nothing; they were Barrani. These weren't negotiations. There was no partial obedience.

Severn unwound his weapon chain. The run through the streets hadn't merited full-on armaments. The unknown might.

In all, things worked about as smoothly as they ever did until it came time to enter the Castle. The doors didn't budge. Turning to the Barrani on the right, Kaylin said, "Are these doors a portal, like the portcullis used to be?"

"They do not function in the same fashion," the man replied, his eyes dark in the dim light. "Some can enter; some cannot."

"Has anyone who entered returned?"

"Their purpose is to reach the side of our Lord; they have no reason to return."

"That's a lot of syllables for *No*."

"Is there another entrance?" Teela asked.

It was Kaylin who answered. "Yes. But given the disaster of tea in the Keeper's Garden that's an absolute last resort. Safe arrival is dependent on a concentrated amount of elemental water, and I'm not taking chances on enraged water unless the alternative is something worse than enraged Dragon." She walked up to the closed doors and lifted a hand; her palm hovered an inch from its surface. Nothing made her skin ache.

"You were right," Teela said—in Leontine.

"About what?"

"They are far, far more trouble than you were when you wormed your way into the Hawks."

"It's not supposed to be a competition, Teela."

"At the moment it isn't—you're so far behind you couldn't catch up if you tried."

"Can Annarion open the door?"

"Annarion doesn't know the Castle," Teela replied, grinding her teeth. "He can't mesh the geography of what I see— and show him—with what he currently sees."

Which is pretty much what anyone sane expected from a Tower, although Kaylin had had hopes. She exhaled. "All right, small and scrappy. Can you open this?"

The small dragon squawked and launched himself off her shoulders. The Barrani guards didn't even blink as he hovered just above Kaylin's head.

I am not certain that is a wise idea, Nightshade said, with vastly diminished amusement.

It can't be any worse than whatever it is Annarion's doing.

You are devoid of an active imagination, which is disappointing considering the experience you have now amassed.

The small dragon chirped. He landed on Kaylin's shoulders in the alert position that involved more claw than usual, and extended his neck toward the door. Kaylin took the hint. She didn't touch the door itself, but approached it as if it were a portal—with a certain amount of dread.

"Corporal?" Teela said.

Severn nodded. He shifted his grip on the business ends of the unbound chain, passing a loop of links around Kaylin's waist. Teela grimaced but allowed him to do the same, while she murmured something about "foundlings" under her breath.

Only when Severn, attached to the chain by the blades, gave the sign did Kaylin suck in air and take a step forward.

"Charming," Teela said, voice dry.

Kaylin had always assumed that the passage through the portal was a misery—for her—because of the sensitivity to magic that had come to her with the runic marks that covered so much of her skin. No one else seemed to be hit as hard by the transition between the outside world and the interior of the Castle.

She revised this opinion now, because crossing through the obsidian doors didn't immediately slap her in the face with overwhelming nausea. To be fair to Nightshade, she'd never entered his castle with her small and squawky companion before. He was making quiet, snuffling noises. It sounded almost like he was snoring.

She glanced at him; he was alert and watchful, although his wings were folded. Whatever he saw, he expected her to see on her own. Severn was on Kaylin's right, and Teela, on the other side of him. Teela was pale.

"Can you hear Annarion any better?" Kaylin asked.

"Yes." The word was so sharp it forbid any further questions.

The portcullis had led, when used, to the grand, harshly lit foyer of Castle Nightshade.

The door did not.

It led, instead, to a room Kaylin had seen only once in the past: the statuary. She recognized it because some of the statues were still in the place she'd last seen them; the room was otherwise hollow. It felt strangely empty. The first time she had seen it, music had played, like the background discussion of a large crowd. The statues themselves had come to life, shaking off immobility with joy and excitement.

This room had been proof—if it were needed—that Nightshade was not mortal. He owned the statues, yes—but they hadn't started out as base stone. They had started out the way Severn or Kaylin had: messy biology. He therefore wasn't imbuing statues with life so much as allowing life to return to them.

There were humans here. A Leontine. They were beautiful in their frozen, stone encasement; they were far more beautiful when life returned to them. She could imagine that, had they continued to live in the world outside this Castle, they would have been loved or adored or followed.

She couldn't tell when they'd left the outside world, although she was certain historians would have had some guesses, given the style of the clothing they wore. Or, in the case of the Leontine, didn't.

But wherever they'd come from, they had ended up here, in a room that looked like a storybook throne room, with majestic pillars fronting the walls to either side. Between those pillars, a handful of statues remained. Kaylin didn't have Barrani memory; she couldn't recall whether or not they occupied the same positions they once had.

But she knew there were fewer of them, because she could see moving, half-dazed people wandering the interior of the room. It wasn't clear to Kaylin whether or not any of these people could see each other; they weren't talking if they could, but they weren't fighting either.

"Nightshade said that the Castle allowed him to transform his visitors," Kaylin told Teela. "...Was he lying?"

"Not necessarily," was the cool reply. "There are a handful of Barrani that might attempt—and succeed at—a similar transformation. Corporal?"

Severn let Teela out of the chain's loop. He didn't, however, release Kaylin. She didn't insist, either. She'd seen halls warp and elongate when she was standing on solid ground; she wasn't willing to bet that they were guaranteed to remain together.

The small dragon squawked. He caught Teela's attention, but the occupants of the room seemed unaware of his presence, or at least unconcerned by it. They seemed similarly unconcerned with Teela as she approached them. Her steps were sharp and heavy.

If it came to that, so was her sword; she'd unsheathed it. Barrani Hawks didn't—as a rule—carry swords. But the fiefs weren't home to the Hawks and the Halls of Law, and Teela hadn't chosen to carry sticks into the fiefs, on account of possible Ferals.

The small dragon hissed, tightening his claws. He also opened his wings, but they were high enough Kaylin assumed he was expressing his august displeasure, rather than giving her a different view of the world as he sometimes did with his wings.

Kaylin remembered her first reaction to this room. She remembered the stiff, tense, *hurt* outrage that Annarion had directed squarely at his older brother in the West March before he had departed.

"Can you tell Annarion that the statues *agreed* to this? It was a—a form of immortality. They were probably in love with his brother."

"Annarion is well aware of the effects Immortals have on the lesser races."

Lesser races. Kaylin rolled her eyes. She loved Teela like family, but there were whole days she had to work at it. "His words or your words?"

"He hasn't lived in this city. He hasn't experienced the changes that have come down with the passage of centuries. They're his words. But they could have been mine, once. They probably were. He sees mortals as essentially helpless."

"And you don't?"

Teela shrugged. "I see them as essentially mortal. If one confounds me, I put off thinking about them because they'll be dead soon, even if I do nothing."

Whole very long days.

"Annarion set them free?"

"That's the gist of it, I think. You could ask them. Some have rejected the transformation, but I don't think their decision will stand. Annarion is angry."

"Did he always have this kind of temper?"

"He was, of all of us, the most even-tempered." Teela slowly sheathed her sword; the Leontine standing in the center of the room looked almost docile, which was both striking and very disturbing. "And the most idealistic. Never anger the idealistic. They feel right is on their side—and right excuses much."

"I don't object in principle to his objections," Kaylin pointed out. "Just the condescension they're wrapped in."

"You can take that up with Annarion."

"If we can find him."

Teela nodded. "Can you find Nightshade?"

"I haven't tried. I forget just how much I hate this place

until I'm in it. Do you know if Annarion's found the vampires?"

"...Vampires."

Severn raised a brow, but said nothing.

"I don't know what you'd call them," Kaylin replied, trying—and failing—not to sound defensive. "They're Barrani. They're apparently ancient Barrani. They react to blood. I think they were already *in* the Castle when Nightshade took over. He said they chose the Barrani version of sleep here."

Condescension and arrogance drained from Teela's expression. Normally, this would have been a good thing. Today it was anything but.

CHAPTER 6

"Nightshade took the Castle," Teela said, her knuckles white as she gripped the hilt of the sheathed sword, "and he *left them here?*"

"I don't think he considered them dangerous." Kaylin hesitated, and then added, "They guard the Long Hall's doors. I'm not sure the doors open without their permission for anyone but Nightshade."

"Prior to this, I could say many things of Calarnenne—but one of them was not that he was a *fool.*"

"They've never hurt him," Kaylin pointed out.

"And how, exactly, do you know about them?"

Kaylin swallowed. This was not the direction she wanted the conversation to take. "I met them."

"And he told you they were…vampires?"

"Not exactly."

"I fear that exactly will have to wait. Although it occurs to me that any attempts to kill him have their best chance of success now."

She had her best chance of success in the West March, after the ceremony.

"They were sleeping," Kaylin said. "I mean, Barrani sleep. They weren't moving, and they appeared to notice nothing."

"Except you."

Kaylin failed to answer the question.

"And you were bleeding."

"Look—are they dangerous now?"

"I don't know. Do you think they can sleep through the changes that are now occurring in the Castle?"

"I don't see why they wouldn't."

Teela muttered something about mortals under her breath. "Annarion has not—yet—encountered the ancestors. He is now aware that they are present. And Kaylin, they were a danger, even in our time."

"By ours you mean yours and theirs."

"Yes. Unfortunately, this doesn't seem to have engendered a higher degree of caution in Annarion. It has, on the other hand, increased his disgust."

"What are the others doing?"

"They are speaking with Annarion. They are more effective, at the moment, than I can be."

"That's good." Kaylin was looking at her arms. Without another word, she rolled up her sleeve and pressed the gems on her bracer; the gems were already flashing.

"You wore the bracer when you knew we were coming to the Castle?" Teela asked, the words imbued with disbelief verging on outrage.

"I'm living *in* the Palace. You were the one who told me to observe correct form while there—and by Imperial dictate, I wear the bracer. Diarmat would probably reduce me to ash if he noticed it was missing; he'd be grateful for the excuse."

"Less talk about the Dragon Court while we're here," Teela replied, in a quieter voice. "Your arms are glowing."

"I'd noticed."

"Do they hurt?"

"No. Not yet. You know I was looking forward to a few weeks of boring report writing and whining about Margot, right? And finding a quiet place of my own again?"

"And that's working out well for you?"

"Very funny. On the bright side, it's not my fault this time."

"If you even suggest that this is *my* fault...."

"Yes?"

"You'll have a chance to personally compare my temper to Annarion's."

"I'll pass, if it's all the same to you."

"I thought you might. Roll up your sleeves," she added. As Kaylin was more or less already doing that, she considered this unnecessary nagging. She tossed the bracer over her shoulder, but Severn bent to pick it up. She didn't know why he bothered. The bracer was magical; no matter where she dropped it, it made its way back to Severn.

"You don't need to cart it around. It'll show up on your table, regardless," she reminded him.

"While you're living in the Palace, a certain amount of caution is probably wise. I'd be willing to bet a large sum of my personal money that it'll return. I'm not willing to bet your life."

The marks on her skin were a luminescent gold. They were warm, but not uncomfortably so. She wasn't terribly surprised when they started to swim in her vision. This didn't, on the other hand, mean there was anything wrong with her eyes.

The small dragon warbled and glanced at the marks. He flapped a bit, but not in an angry way. He was possibly the only non-mortal who wasn't nursing anger this evening.

"Don't eat them," Kaylin told him.

He snorted. She was surprised when he snapped at her arm and came away with a single word between his translucent jaws.

"Hey! I mean it!"

The small dragon flew to the Leontine who seemed to be standing in a quiet daze. Kaylin sucked in air and ran after him. A docile Leontine, while a bit surprising, wasn't going to be a difficulty. An awake, aware, and possibly angry Leontine was more than she could handle.

Teela joined Kaylin. Kaylin wanted free of Severn's chain, because it was bloody awkward to move at any speed while it was attached to his weapons.

"Do you **have** any idea what your small creature is doing?"

"About as much as I ever have. At least this time he's not insulting a water Dragon." Kaylin had never seen the small creature take an injury. She didn't want to start now, but he was well ahead of Teela, and as Teela approached the Leontine, she slowed. Barrani against Leontine wasn't a sure thing.

Without a lot of preparation, human against Leontine was, and not in the favor of the human.

"Can you stop him?" Teela asked.

"Probably not. Why?"

"I'm uncertain that this is likely to have a calming effect on Annarion."

"What would?"

"At this point? Very little. If Calarnenne was a more accomplished liar, we wouldn't be in this situation."

"Liar?"

"Annarion is disappointed in his brother. Disappointment— even betrayal—is something we all encounter as we gain experience; we learn that our hopes and our beliefs are not always based in fact. Usually, we're changing at the same time; we encounter ways in which our beliefs in ourselves are tested and found wanting. Annarion's and Mandoran's weren't tested, in their youth." She frowned. "Mandoran doesn't approve of his place in this discussion."

"Why?"

"He considers Annarion fecklessly idealistic; he feels a set down has been a long time coming, and is well deserved."

"Could he keep that to himself until we've worked out where Annarion—or his brother for that matter—is?"

"You've met Mandoran. What do you think?"

Kaylin's jaw ached, she was grinding her teeth so hard. "Why exactly did you miss these people?"

Teela laughed. "Probably because they're like this," she said, her eyes losing some of the saturation of blue. "I'm not ready to lose any of them again. Not yet."

The small dragon reached the Leontine, and alighted on his left shoulder. He'd never done that to Marcus, and Kaylin was pretty certain he wouldn't; Marcus had trigger reflexes, and things flying at his face—or his neck—were likely to set them off. Kaylin wasn't certain if the glow that illuminated the Leontine's face was the dragon's or the rune's, but his perfect fur reflected it; he was much richer in color than Marcus, and his ears didn't have the small scars that Marcus's did. The brunt of his entirely exposed fur was gold, but the light from the mark-lamp implied red highlights, like sunset or sunrise across a field of wheat.

His face was longer, his cheekbones more prominent; he apparently didn't have the bulk that caused Marcus to tower over his subordinates, even when he was seated. His eyes were Leontine eyes; at the moment, they were a peculiar shade of gray. Kaylin rifled through her very inadequate memory; she'd seen gray only a handful of times in her life, and never when things were going well.

She thought gray meant sorrow.

Speaking Leontine wasn't easy; if she had to do it for any length of time, it wrecked her voice. Only in Marcus's pridlea did she give up on rolling *r*'s and the growling tone that was half the conversation; she didn't care if his children thought she was a pathetic, mewling kitten.

Teela came to a full stop as the color of the Leontine's eyes became clear. Kaylin continued to walk, Severn attached by a slender chain at her waist. She held out both of her hands, palms up, fingers toward the ceiling to indicate sheathed claws. Not that she had claws.

He stared at her, his dull gray eyes at odds with the rich color of fur and the gleam of perfect, ivory fangs.

"I am Kaylin ni Kayala."

He blinked; his eyes narrowed. Kaylin noted that small and squawky still held the word in his jaws; he hadn't dropped it on the Leontine's forehead, and it hadn't disappeared. If he was using it just for the light it shed, she'd have words with him later.

"You cannot be kin," he finally said. "You are human."

Since human more or less meant hairless, mewling kitten, Kaylin nodded. "Kayala is our *myrryn*. Marcus is our leader. I have shared meat at their hearth-fire; I have protected the kittens. I have fought for my leader's survival. I wasn't born to the pridlea, but I am of it." She inserted all the appropriate sounds.

"Why are you here?" he asked. As he looked around the dimly lit room, his eyes turned down at the corners. "Where is Calarnenne?"

"He is at the heart of his castle," Kaylin replied, taking the same care to add all appropriate *r*'s and sibilants. "His pride-kin has returned after a long absence."

The Leontine's eyes widened, which Kaylin had not expected. "His brother?" he said, using the Barrani word.

She nodded, and added, "Annarion. He has not eaten at his pride-kin's hearth for hundreds of years. He finds the hearth fires hot."

"He is home," the Leontine replied. He closed his eyes. Opened them. They were now a shade of gold. "Calarnenne does not sing to his brother."

Kaylin blinked. "Does he sing to you?" Leontines were not notable for the quality of their lullabies.

"Yes, when he is restless. Have you heard him sing?"

"Once or twice. Mostly in the middle of battle."

"You have seen him fight? You have stood by his side?" The way the last question was asked implied that it was an undreamed of privilege. Kaylin revised her estimate of his age down. He looked, in stature, to be fully adult.

"Yes," she replied, because technically it was true.

"Do you travel to his side, now?"

"Yes." The fact that arriving there wasn't a certainty was unnecessary information.

"Will you take me with you?"

Kaylin faltered at the desperate hope in his eyes. And the fear, which was an edge of orange. When she failed to answer, he reached for her, grabbing both of her hands with greater than usual Leontine force.

"He woke me," the Leontine continued. "He must have intended to be with me." As if he were a child.

"Does he wake you often?" Kaylin asked, stalling. She could no more drag this Leontine into the wilds of Castle Nightshade than one of Marcus's own children.

"He wakes me when he can spend time with me," was the unadorned reply. "But he is not with me now. You are mortal."

She nodded.

"As am I. I will wither and die if I am left to live on my own. This," he continued, releasing her hands to trace an arc in the air that took in the whole of the chamber, "is my eternity, as promised."

"You spend most of it as a statue," she replied, before she could bite back the words.

He nodded, as if she'd just said water was wet. "How else can we live forever? We cannot live without aging. Age leads to death. If we wake only when he is with us, we are his forever."

This was *so* not one of Kaylin's life goals.

"He is busy. He is forever. If we live and breathe and walk as you do, we might never see him again. Do you understand? His life will lead him away from you. When he has time to return, you might be dead."

If only, Kaylin thought.

"This way, all our lives are spent in his company."

"And in no one else's," Kaylin pointed out. "Your family. Your pridlea. Your pack. They are gone."

"They were gone when he first came to me," was the quiet reply. "They were dead. I was carrion fodder. I remember."

"As if it were yesterday." Because, she thought, it might have been.

"I remember the vultures. I remember the war cries of the victors. I remember the color of blood on grass, and the wails of the survivors who would add to it. I remember my mother. My pack leader. I remember." He smiled at her, then. It was a smile tinged, of all things, with pity. "I remember Calarnenne. I remember his song. It stopped us all—enemy and family, both. I could not understand the words, but I heard them as if he was remaking language."

"Did you know he was Barrani?"

"I knew he was not kin," was the quiet reply. "I had never seen beauty in other races. Not until him. But he is not here."

Kaylin shook her head. "I don't think he wants you to leave this room, unless you want to. Stay here. I'm not—I'm not like you. I wasn't chosen for his—his eternity. Let me find him. Talk to your companions," she suggested.

"They are not my companions; they are his. We are his."

Kaylin nodded, mouth dry. "Keep them here. This hall is safe. Outside...there are predators."

"I think Annarion is both unhappy with this outcome, and simultaneously less angry. You, on the other hand, look green," Teela said, as she walked away from the Leontine.

Kaylin felt it, too. She was big on personal choices, and clearly, the Leontine had made his—but it left her feeling uncomfortable. "Have you found Annarion?"

"Have you found Nightshade?"

"No."

"Is half of what Nightshade says to you unintelligible babble?"

"No."

"Then don't ask."

Kaylin. Throughout the conversation with the Leontine, the fieflord had been silent. *An'Teela is correct. There is a danger here.*

For me, or for all us?

For all of you, he replied, with just the faintest hint of irritation. *Teela is not young for one of my kind, but she is not ancient. You have seen two of the ancestors; they are bound to the Castle and its service. The binding is older than either myself or Teela. I do not know its strength. It is my belief they were made outcaste for reasons far less political than mine. They would have been hunted, Kaylin. Had they been found, they would—with grave difficulty—have been destroyed. Ask her.*

Teela, understanding that the possible danger had passed, waited until the small dragon was once again anchored to Kaylin's shoulder, still carrying the rune. When he was she turned toward the most obvious set of doors available.

She allowed Severn to loop his chain around her before she opened the doors; they weren't warded, but she didn't bother to touch them. Kaylin was often surprised when Teela used magic as a tool. Hawks weren't supposed to be mages. They definitely weren't supposed to be Arcanists or former Arcanists. She didn't really care for this reminder of Teela's life before she'd been part of it, which wasn't reasonable or mature.

Some days, Kaylin fervently wished that she had already passed Adult 101 and could get on with being the person she wanted to be.

On the other hand, she had to survive if she was ever going to reach that near unattainable goal. She glanced at squawky. His eyes were wide, black opals; they reflected nothing. As he wasn't doing the small dragon equivalent of shouting in her ear, she assumed he didn't consider the door a danger.

"One day," she told him, "you're going to talk to me, and I'm going to understand you."

"And until then," Teela added, "she's going to talk to herself. A lot. Luckily the rest of us are used to this."

The doors swung fully open; nothing leaped through them to attack. Kaylin saw a lot of hall beyond the room itself; it wasn't brightly lit, but at least there was light. "Teela, tell me about these Barrani ancestors."

"Tell me," the Barrani Hawk countered, "why you call them vampires."

Kaylin shrugged. "They said something about my blood."

Teela closed her eyes for a couple of seconds, the Barrani equivalent of counting to ten. "They *spoke* to you." The words were so flat, they were hardly a question, so Kaylin didn't answer it. "What color were their eyes?"

"Teela, it was a long time ago."

"It was months ago. Not even mortal memory is that bad. Please do not tell me you don't remember."

But she didn't. "They were pale, even for Barrani. But perfect the way Barrani are. When we approached the door they guarded, Nightshade told them it had to be opened. Their eyes were closed until he spoke; they opened. But nothing else about them moved—not at first." She tried to remember her first—and only—walk through the Long Halls, as Nightshade called them. She could clearly see the Barrani standing to either side of the door like perfect statues. She couldn't, however, see the color of their open eyes. "They must have been blue," she finally said. "I'm sure I would have noticed if they were a different color. Green would have made them harmless. Relatively," she added.

"Were you bleeding at the time?"

"Maybe. I wasn't bleeding enough that it was significant." Kaylin hesitated. Severn held his weapons; she kept her hands on her daggers, but didn't draw them. "They asked Nightshade to give me to them as price for passage."

Teela's eyes were, of course, midnight blue, so it couldn't get any worse. "Passage through what?"

"Doors. They were door guards."

"They were not simple door guards. Do you know where these doors were?"

"Yes."

"Could you lead us there?"

"..."

"Could you make certain that you *don't* lead us there without some warning?"

"It's a Tower, Teela, in case you hadn't noticed."

Teela began to walk, and Kaylin fell in beside her. At Teela's frown, she fell back a bit; Teela didn't want Kaylin playing point. Kaylin didn't exactly want that position, either.

"I didn't notice the color of their eyes," she said, "because of their voices."

Teela stopped walking. "Their voices were different?"

"Not when they spoke to me or to Nightshade. But—I could hear them talking when we approached. Without, you know, seeing their lips move."

"I am beginning to understand why you feel boredom is not a fate worse than death," Teela replied, with a brief pause for a healthy, Leontine curse. "Did Nightshade hear their voices—their non-speaking voices?"

"I didn't ask him. It was the first time I'd been on the inside of the Castle, and it didn't seem safe or smart to ask questions. If *I* heard it, I assume he did."

That would be an unwise assumption. Amusement had been stripped from his voice; had he been standing beside them, his eyes would have been the same color as Teela's.

"Kitling, this is very important, and I will strangle you if you cannot answer me clearly. What were they *saying?*"

Kaylin was an old hand at exposing her throat, although she usually only did it when confronted with a raging Leontine Sergeant. Teela literally growled. "I couldn't understand them." Kaylin spoke quietly. "I could hear them, but they sounded entirely unlike any voices I'd heard before. I could identify it as speech—but I couldn't understand what was being said.

"I'd just come from an underground forest. I'd just touched

the leftover echoes of a message from the Ancients—or even an Avatar. I was very disoriented."

"Fine. Is there anything *else* you'd like me to know?"

"I'd like you to answer my question, now."

"It wasn't a question, that I recall." Teela exhaled. "The Barrani, like the Dragons, are ancient races. Mortals are relative newcomers. You've seen the Lake of Life. I don't know if you've seen the draconic birthing pits—I'm going to assume that you haven't."

"I haven't."

"I'd suggest you avoid it, although given it's you I shouldn't bother—you tend to do the opposite of anything resembling smart." She murmured something about having three wings, which was an Aerian expression that wasn't *always* used to imply innate stupidity. "You've probably heard the Barrani Hawks complain about boredom."

Anyone with functional ears had heard the Barrani Hawks make that complaint. Kaylin nodded.

"The Ancients liked to create. Much of what they created would make no sense to you—it barely makes sense to us. We were not—Barrani and Dragon—the first attempt at creating a self-replicating species."

"The Shadows—"

"We don't believe the Shadows were meant to be a distinct species. The Ancients' sense of either distinct or species, however, is poorly understood. You know that we require words to fully come to life."

"Names. True names."

"We require one," Teela continued. "And the one is drawn from the Lake, by the Lady. Without it, the vessel of our body never wakes. When our ancestors were created, there was no Lady. There were Ancients."

"Were you like the Dragons, then?"

"In what way? I am not aware that Dragons require two names."

"They don't *require* it. But I think they can contain more."

"*That* is a thought you will keep firmly to yourself. *Forever.*"

"The Dragons were supposed to be made of stone and imbued with life."

"Yes, well. It's probably true of the first Dragons. We are not entirely certain that it's true of the first Barrani. You think of stone as something that can be chiseled into the desired shape; it is why the word *stone* is used in these tales. The Ancients were not so limited in their building materials. Flesh could be—and was—shaped and changed."

The Leontines.

"Flesh could be merged and combined, while both living creatures somehow remained alive for the process. But flesh was perhaps a later concept, for the Ancients. You think of them as large, powerful *people*. Perhaps that is how they appeared to us, when they still walked the world—or the worlds. But it was only a facet of what they were in total, and they couldn't show us most of their faces. We couldn't perceive them; couldn't interact with them.

"It's my belief—and I am not a sage—that they could speak to us and we could not hear them unless they chose a form with which we could interact. We could not see them, unless they chose to confine themselves or diminish themselves in a similar fashion; we were too slender, too fixed, and too *small*."

"I'm guessing that's not the popular view among the Barrani."

"It is accepted as probable history. Popularity has very little to do with it. The earliest of our kin were not concerned with keeping records for their possible descendants."

"Did they *have* descendants in the traditional sense? Like, children, grandchildren, that kind of thing?"

"Not most of them, no."

"Then why are they even called Barrani?"

"Because we lived in the cities they built. They were not like us, Kaylin. You hate Arcanists. You wouldn't have a word for what the ancestors were. But it is believed that they were not possessed of single, true names, but complex phrases. When the ancestors were bored, they had options to alleviate that boredom that are undreamed of by the rest of my people now.

"One of them historically involved destroying the rest of us." At Kaylin's sharp intake of breath, Teela shrugged. "They did not see it as destruction; they wished to take control of the words that gave us life, and to remake them in some fashion.

"They attempted to do the same with the Dragons; if I am fair, they attempted to relieve the Dragons of their names first." Teela began to walk again, taking the hall to the right because the hall to the left ended abruptly in a lot of wall.

"I'm going to assume that failed, since we still have Dragons."

"It was not notably successful, no. It caused some difficulties with the Dragons."

"Were there Dragon ancestors, as well?"

"You will have to ask your Arkon," was the stiff reply. "The Barrani are not keepers of Dragon lore, except where it involves war."

Kaylin was silent for another long beat. Dragons did not require names to wake. They didn't require names to live. They just required true names to become their dual selves. She decided that if Teela didn't know this, she wasn't about to inform her. Then again, Nightshade was probably listening. Ugh.

He was diplomatic; if he heard, he said nothing.

"If they were that dangerous, how did you kill them?"

"We formed the war bands," she replied. When Kaylin

failed to respond immediately, she added, "You didn't think they were created just to fight Dragons, did you?"

Since the answer was more or less yes, Kaylin said nothing. "We don't have a war band here."

"No. You said there were two?"

Kaylin nodded.

"I'd really like to strangle Nightshade."

"How would Annarion feel about that?"

"At the moment? Sanguine. He doesn't, on the other hand, feel it would be easy."

"Easier than meeting the ancestors head on?"

"Definitely easier than that." Teela stopped. "Corporal? The halls have not materially changed since we entered them, and I dislike being roped together like human foundlings."

Severn nodded and unwound his chain. To Kaylin's surprise, he also released her. He didn't sheathe his weapons, and the visible scar on his jaw looked whiter and more pronounced than it usually did. The talk of Barrani ancestors had clearly raised the stakes.

Not that they were insignificant to begin with.

Nightshade, are the ancestors still guarding the Long Halls?

Yes.

Are they awake?

I am uncertain, Kaylin. The Castle is in flux.

Where are you, damn it?

I am at the heart of my castle.

And where is Annarion?

He is also at the heart of the Castle. Before you ask, we are not in the same place.

Kaylin *hated* magical buildings with a loud, multisyllabic passion. *Can you come to us?*

Not safely—for you. I am attempting to keep the Castle's defenses at a minimum.

Given the existence of Barrani that even Teela feared, this didn't seem like a great idea.

If the Castle's defenses are fully mobilized, it will attempt to exterminate all intruders. This is unlikely to harm the ancestors. It is, however, likely to damage you.

You don't seem that concerned.

No? I am unlikely to perish here, no matter what the outcome. You, however, are not guaranteed to survive. Do not look for me; look for the runes of the Ancients. It is there you will be safest.

She was silent for a beat, watching Teela's tense back. *The runes are in the heart of the Castle. We'll need to enter the Long Halls to even get there.*

In theory, yes. But remember: you are in a fief Tower now; geography bends to the dictate of will.

CHAPTER 7

The dimly lit hall seemed to go on forever, something Kaylin definitely didn't remember from her first visit to the statuary. She had been by Nightshade's side while traversing the halls; he had made it clear that she was not to leave him if she wished to move safely within the Castle.

This wasn't something Tara, the Avatar of the Tower of Tiamaris, had ever enforced. But Tara was awake, in a way that the Avatar of Castle Nightshade wasn't. She'd asked the fieflord once why his castle didn't speak directly to her; he'd replied that living within the folds of a sentient being was not one of his life's ambitions.

What his actual life's ambitions were, he'd never made clear.

"Teela, is Annarion talking *to* anyone? I don't think he's speaking to his brother at the moment."

Teela replied without looking back. "I believe he is speaking with…something. He isn't speaking a language I recognize or understand."

"Would he know if he was speaking to your ancestors?"

"We prefer *the* ancestors, if we must speak about them at all; it's not considered wise."

"Probably wiser than walking into a sleeping, sentient building that's having nightmares."

"If the building hears us, it is not guaranteed to end our lives."

"It might help preserve them," Kaylin replied.

"No, Kaylin. Your Tara—and I am making assumptions on hearsay, because I have not visited the Tower in Tiamaris—was, in some ways, emotionally corrupt. You cannot assume that the other Avatars are likewise compromised. If their mission was to halt shadow and its contamination, we are—in the best case—irrelevant."

Squawk.

"Can you hear Annarion?" Kaylin asked the small dragon.

Squawk.

"...Can he hear you?"

The small beast tilted his head to the left. All the way to the left; by the time he stopped, it was almost upside down, which made it hard to meet his eyes. He whiffled.

She would have pursued the line of questioning, but the ground beneath her feet—stone, and at that, rather plain stone—began to rumble. She looked to Teela and Severn; they'd both stopped walking. They hadn't stopped moving; they were now on alert, and they scanned the halls and the walls that enclosed it, hoping to see danger before it dropped on their heads.

The small dragon wilted. So did Kaylin, as the walls to the left and right began to recede. The stone beneath their feet didn't, but it expanded to fill the growing space. The ceiling above, however, faded from sight. In its place was something that didn't resemble normal architecture in any way.

It looked a lot like sky, if sky were full of storm clouds and edged in flashes of luminescent light that refused to remain one color. The clouds were gray-green; they weren't the roiling darkness of the shadows at the heart of the fiefs. Kaylin frowned; something was wrong—if you didn't count the disappearance of ceiling and the sudden enlargement of the halls themselves.

The clouds weren't moving; they were fixed. She revised her opinion of their composition; they looked like they were made of stone. She hoped there were support beams somewhere that kept them off the ground.

"Forward or back?" Teela asked, dragging Kaylin's attention away from the heights.

Kaylin shrugged. Reaching into a pocket, she flipped a coin, caught it, and laid it against her forearm. Her eyes narrowed as she looked at the result. "Forward."

"What's wrong?" Severn asked.

She grimaced and handed him the coin.

He held it up to Teela, trusting Barrani vision to show her what he could see up close. The coin had two sides—which anyone expected from a coin. The two images, however, were not the usual Palace and Emperor; they were the profiles of two familiar men. Nightshade and Annarion.

"Nightshade was forward?" Severn asked, as he handed the coin back to Kaylin.

"Nightshade landed face-up. There's no way he was responsible for changing the coin," she added. "Having his face on money is probably beneath him. If I had to guess, the Castle is making its opinion known." She glanced up. "In more ways than one."

Wider halls meant they could walk three abreast. Kaylin drew a dagger, although moving her arms made her skin ache. The small dragon was making his usual quiet noises; the rune that was glowing between his teeth didn't seem to inhibit his version of speech.

"You're thinking out loud again," Teela said.

"I'm just trying to remember how Tiamaris took the Tower in the fief."

"And you have to work *that* hard?"

"Very funny. The heart of the Tower in Tiamaris was covered in words. Very like the words on my arms—except that Tara could read them. I think, in total, they were meant to be the governing commands of the Tower; I'm not sure all Towers have identical words at their heart.

"But...there was one room—and room is a really *bad* description—that was also adorned with words in Castle Nightshade. It was where I first heard the word *Chosen*." She hesitated again.

Teela's exhalation was sharp enough to cut. Or should have been. "Out with it."

"I—does Annarion know that I know..."

"No. I am not a child; I understand how to maintain privacy of thought and action from those with whom I've shared my name."

Clearly implying that Kaylin didn't. "I would have been lost in that room if I hadn't had Nightshade's name as an anchor. I didn't take his name. I couldn't see it. He offered it to me."

"Why exactly did you require an anchor?"

"I don't know, Teela. I just—I'm not sure I could have come back from wherever it was I got stuck. I couldn't really *see* the Castle or the rest of the world clearly. I could see his name."

"That is far too much information. I'm amazed Calarnenne isn't screaming his lungs out."

I have some concern for my dignity.

"You weren't likewise trapped in Tiamaris."

"No. But Tara was there. She was trying—inasmuch as she

could—to guide me. I had to choose the words that would reaffirm her existence as a watchtower without the benefit of actual understanding."

"But you don't own the Tower."

"No. I didn't get a chance to fully finish whatever it was I was trying to do. Tiamaris kind of threw me out of the circle."

"And Nightshade is likely to do the same?"

"I don't think the situation's the same. We're not under attack here. By shadows," she added. "The Tower defenses kick in on their own in emergencies; they're open to suggestions—or commands—if the emergency isn't the one they were built to handle."

"You're still hesitating, kitling."

"I'm not sure we can all get to the heart of the Castle without passing your ancestors."

"*The* ancestors."

"Whatever."

She hadn't had to walk through the Long Halls to get to the forest at the heart of the Castle. Nightshade had opened doors which *should* have led to halls in any sane building; they'd opened to trees, instead. Kaylin had thought—for one long moment—that she'd stepped outside. She hadn't. The forest grew within the Castle.

She'd been afraid of Nightshade, that first time.

It was not fear, he told her softly, *but caution. Caution, when dealing with my kin, is not only wise, but necessary.*

A stray memory of Teela stretched, catlike, across Kaylin's narrow bed passed by; she made an effort not to grab it.

Even An'Teela. Perhaps, in her current situation, especially An'Teela.

I don't understand why you can't come to us.

I am not entirely mobile; the Castle itself demands most of my concentration.

Is Annarion aware that we're approaching him now?

He should be. If he is not, consider why.

Kaylin exhaled. *We need to bypass the ancestors.*

Yes, sadly, I believe you do. Be cautious, Kaylin. It is not in your nature, but try. I think the possibility that they remain bound to the Castle's environs during this upheaval is low. There is nothing in the Castle that presents more of a danger to you now.

She thought of him. He laughed; she could feel the warmth of his surprise and amusement. *Yes,* he replied. *But I am only a danger to you should I decide that your death—at this moment—suits my purpose. It is your preservation that is proving more challenging—but that is oft true of mortals.* The humor dimmed. *If An'Teela can communicate at all with my brother, she must make the threat the ancestors pose clear.*

I can't imagine she's not trying. Teela was unimpressed. Annarion would likely be less so.

Yes. But it may be enough to focus his fury; to narrow it. He... is still my brother at heart, but we have both changed in inexplicable ways—to each other.

"I do not think it wise," Teela said, when Kaylin hesitantly asked her to tell Annarion that danger times two was likely to pop up at any time.

"I know. But we don't have Nightshade with us. We can't circumvent the ancestors—if they're still standing guard at the doors at all." Kaylin slowed. She'd bypassed the ancestors on the way into the forest, the first time. They had had to walk through them to leave it.

Clearly it was easier to find one's way into the heart of the Castle than to leave it, even for Nightshade.

"I know you don't like the chain line," she began.

Teela waved her, imperiously, to silence. "I'll accept it. You think you can take us to where we have to go?"

"Yes. I should warn you that if I can, it's a one way journey; we get back the long way. Severn?"

He was already winding links of chain around Teela's waist. Kaylin was surprised: she'd meant to use the chain as a rope line. It didn't look like he could fight while they were bound together.

"You'd be surprised," he said, his smile slender; it was all edge.

"I've had enough surprises for one day. For," she added, with more emphasis, "one lifetime."

"I haven't," Teela interjected. "But I think I'm done with surprises for today."

"Fine," Kaylin replied. "You choose the door we take."

Teela turned to stare at her. "If you were any other mortal, I would assume your questionable sense of humor was at play. There's only one door."

Kaylin frowned. "There are doors on either side of us down this hallway. We've passed a handful; you've just been avoiding them. They're hard to miss, even given the width of the hall."

"Corporal, do you see these so-called doors?"

"No. I see the door at the end of the hall in the far wall. There are no halls to either side of it."

Kaylin glanced at the small dragon, who exhaled the sigh of the long-suffering everywhere.

"Is there any sign, from any of these doors, that whatever lies behind them is occupied?"

"No. You'd've noticed that."

"Because I noticed the doors in question, of course." Teela's eyes were blue. "Is there a reason to avoid the door we're being herded toward?"

"It's a *Tower*, Teela. How should I know? If the Tower is

determined, any door will lead us to where the Tower wants us to go."

"In which case, we can cut to the chase. Pick a door."

"Fine. I'll take the invisible door on the left." Teela turned toward the wall she'd mentioned. There was no door there.

Kaylin walked directly toward the blank stretch of stone; she placed her hand on the wall. It was distinctly warm beneath her palm, although the warmth was not as strong a sensation as the marks on her arm. "There's no door here," she told the Barrani Hawk.

Squawk.

"But...I'm not sure there needs to be. Nightshade's not driving a lot of the Castle right now."

Squawk.

"Yes. If you're going to get rid of the rune in your mouth, this is probably the place to do it."

The small dragon nudged Kaylin forward, if by nudge one meant swatting the side of her face and craning his neck toward the wall her hand rested against. Given she was already touching said wall, she found it annoying. She started to lower her hand, but he jumped down to her extended arm, and crossed it, shuffling sideways as if it were an unstable bridge.

When his snout was flush with the wall, he exhaled. A small, pearlescent cloud left his tiny jaw before Kaylin could speak; it folded itself around the rune in his mouth. Given what his breath had done in the past, this wasn't comforting. The rune absorbed the glinting white-gray and slowly melted into the stone face of the wall, as if the stone were a sponge.

"It's not that bad," Kaylin said, to no one in particular. Or herself. "Tara can rearrange the contents of the room you're sitting in." And she frequently did, if not reminded that some people found this lack of solidity disconcerting.

The wall began to thin. It didn't thin in the shape of a door; it thinned in the shape of a spreading patch of what seemed, on the surface, to be liquid—except thicker. It was unlike any liquid Kaylin had seen; glass was thicker and far more dangerous to touch when it melted—she hoped.

But as the patch spread, the stone beneath it became translucent, reminding her of the texture of the small dragon's wings. "Can you see this?" Kaylin asked softly.

"Yes," Teela replied. "From what you've described, though, it doesn't look like it leads to the Castle's center. Where does this lead?"

"I'm not sure," Kaylin replied, staring. "I can't actually see much. But I think this is where we need to go."

"I am not filled with confidence."

The small dragon crooned, the edges of squawk softened as he made an effort he generally didn't waste on Kaylin. She tried not to resent this.

"I think I prefer large dragons," Teela told him, without obvious resentment.

The small dragon gave a version of a shrug that would have been at home in the fiefs.

"Severn?"

"I'm not the resident expert on Castle Nightshade," he replied. Which more or less meant he was willing to leave it up to her.

"We have no resident experts." She sucked in air. "Let's go before I lose my nerve. If we're lucky, this is the Castle's way of telling us to get the hell out, and we'll end up butt first on the street."

Kaylin was never willing to bet on her luck. Stepping into what looked like unshaped glass didn't take her into the familiar—and far less changeable—streets of the fief. It took her into forest. Nighttime forest.

She'd seen forest in Nightshade before—but it wasn't quite this forest. A hint of moonlight touched branches; the air was still. "Teela, tell me this doesn't remind you of the forests surrounding the West March."

"I don't know why you complain about people who lie," the Barrani Hawk replied. "Because you generally demand that we do it."

"No comment." The forest had no obvious path, which was the first thing Kaylin looked for. It had no insects, which was a bonus, but also didn't appear to have any of the other noises she now associated with forest travel. She touched the nearest tree. "This is made of stone," she said, voice flat.

"The ground is packed dirt," Severn observed.

Kaylin nodded. Had it also been stone, she'd've felt—and probably heard—the difference. "I don't think this leads us to the center of the Castle. If I had to guess—"

"It leads to Annarion." Teela, untethered by Severn, chose a direction and began to walk. Her feet made no sound.

Kaylin and Severn followed her. They walked quietly— but speed made silence impossible for the merely mortal, and Teela didn't seem intent on proceeding with caution. Watching her back, Kaylin frowned.

What's wrong? Severn asked. Given Teela's proximity, whispers would reach her ears, and given the color of her eyes, discretion was necessary.

She knows where she's going. She's not just scouting—she recognizes this place. Or she recognizes the place it's modeled on. Kaylin bit her lip; the small dragon had settled around her shoulder like a shawl and couldn't be bothered to add commentary. By unspoken mutual consent, they closed the growing gap.

Teela was armed. Severn grimaced and unwound the weapon chain around Kaylin's waist, arming himself fully.

Kaylin's daggers remained in their sheaths. She knew that she was still within the Castle; she guessed that her current surroundings were the Castle's attempt to communicate with Annarion, and was grateful that the Castle wasn't attempting to speak with her. She'd had experience with that before; she didn't envy Annarion.

They didn't clear the forest; the forest continued. Kaylin touched the odd tree; she found that most were stone. But one or two felt like actual, living trees; the bark was rough in a different way. There had been living trees in the Long Hall; she wondered if some of them had been transported here.

"I will never get used to this," she murmured. "I want physical objects to remain static." It was impossible to get a grasp on the strategic value of layout if the layout arbitrarily shifted. Nor could she assume that the Castle was safe—given Teela's reaction to the ancient Barrani who served as door wards, the opposite was probably closer to reality.

But the small dragon wasn't concerned. If Kaylin was embarrassed to take cues from a creature the size of a small cat, it didn't stop her.

Squawk.

"Thanks a lot, small and squawky."

"Why," Teela said, voice drifting back as she continued to walk, "don't you call him by his name?"

"Because his name—at least the version I can say out loud, is 'Hope.'"

"I fail to see the problem."

"It just seems like—like too pretentious a name. Or something. I'd look like an idiot."

"That's never stopped you before."

"Very funny, Teela."

"I note that neither of us is laughing."

"Severn's grinning, does that count?"

Teela chuckled. It was a better sound.

"I don't think small and squawky cares, if that helps."

"Not much."

Given Teela's tone, Kaylin dared a question. "Are we heading toward Annarion's previous home?"

"The forest here is modeled on the lands that surrounded his home. I'm not entirely certain what we'll find. But before you continue to ask questions, let me remind you that Annarion is one of Calarnenne's brothers. It's not impossible that we'll find Nightshade instead."

"I don't think so."

"No?"

"I'm almost positive Nightshade is at the center of his castle."

"You're certain that this isn't it?"

Kaylin hesitated. "No. Not certain."

The forest continued, but Teela slowed as they at last approached what looked—at a distance—to be an ancient, gigantic tree. The Barrani Hawk nodded once.

"This is it?"

"This is the family home as it existed in Annarion's time."

"And not as it exists now."

Teela shook her head. She held out a staying hand, which meant she intended to take the lead and she wanted some distance to assess the danger. On the street, Kaylin would have obeyed the gesture instantly. This wasn't the street. It was a Tower, a building made by godlike beings who didn't really understand merely mortal architecture or the concept of fixed shapes. Her arms were glowing; she had a familiar on her shoulders who had a much better understanding of ancient, impossible buildings than any of the larger people around him—even if his communication skills were lacking. She was not going to be a liability, here.

When Teela approached the tree, Kaylin joined her. Dark, perfect brows rose; Kaylin jabbed a finger in the direction of the small dragon. He bit it.

"Point taken."

"You heard her. You can let go of my finger now."

He did. He unfolded and sat on her shoulder, looking curious but not especially alert. Kaylin approached the bark of what looked like tree. It wasn't. It wasn't stone, either. She couldn't immediately place the material beneath the palm of her hand; it felt as smooth as sword blade, but with a little more give.

"I don't suppose this came with a door ward?"

"No," Teela said softly. "It is like—and unlike—the Hallionne. Or it was. I assume that this building is at least externally a representation of home, to Annarion. Before you ask, Annarion was chosen as one of the twelve, just as I was. He was not eldest; he was expendable. Home does not have the same meaning for the Barrani that it does for you."

"I had no home for years, Teela."

Teela snorted. "You try to make small homes wherever you go. Small, mortal homes. We don't. We've learned, through bitter experience, not to trust the concept."

"But...does that mean you never wanted it?"

"What? A home?"

"In the mortal sense." She considered this carefully and added, "Or at least in my sense."

"We live. We breathe. We congregate. Of course we want it. But we are not strong enough to build it and believe in it."

Kaylin was almost shocked; she turned to meet Teela's gaze, but Teela was looking up at the heights of the structure.

"Your jaw is hanging open."

"Doesn't matter. Here, no insects will fly into my mouth. I'm just—I'm surprised that you used the word *strong* that way."

"Hope and belief are *risks,*" Teela replied. "And in the end, the Barrani *are* strong enough to live without them. Mortals have an adage: there's strength in numbers. And for mortals, there is almost no strength without those numbers. They band together in their odd, tribal clusters because it's their best chance of survival.

"The Barrani are not mortals. We *can* accrue enough power that we do not rely on numbers for safety. Numbers, among my people, are often the opposite. Only when we faced Dragons or ancestors did we feel numbers were necessary. We go this way," she added. "If there's any accuracy at all in the depiction of this home."

"If Annarion was expendable," Kaylin asked, "why does he care about home and what happened to it?"

"Some of us were willing sacrifices. Some were not. We were *young,* Kaylin. We were young, and we weren't raised the way mortals often are. The risk was acceptable if it accrued both personal power and prestige to the line."

"But you didn't—"

"If my father had not killed my mother, I wouldn't have cared about his choice on my behalf. I would have been disappointed. Possibly hurt—I was young, as I said. I would not have spent centuries planning his death. What he wanted from me was both power and prestige; it is what most of the Barrani want from their children. And had I not lived with my mother, I might not have cared at all. I was from an ancient lineage. My father was a Lord of the High Court. He was respected, admired—and feared. The safety of his children was all but guaranteed; no one would have dared to mark any of his children—or the children of his cousins—the way Nightshade marked you.

"But I spent much of my early life with my mother. The West March was considered rustic—a High Halls word for *weak* or *ineffective*. What she wanted for me was not what my father wanted. Did the power that became hers through marriage appeal to her? Yes. It would have appealed to anyone with any sense. Power *is* safety, of a kind. But it is not particularly warm; it is not particularly giving—giving and yielding are too much the same, among my father's kin.

"After I returned from the green, I was under a cloud of suspicion. No, not a cloud—a full-on storm. But among my kin, anyone with power is. I was considered a power simply because I had survived; I was considered a danger for the same reason. I used it, of course." Teela shrugged, that restless "I've been talking about serious things for too long" shrug, and came to a stop.

"Here."

Here was, to Kaylin's eyes, the same as any other spot on the bark of what looked like a tree. "Annarion," Teela said quietly, as if she were speaking to the surface of the tree she faced. But when the tree failed to respond, she continued. "He was, in your parlance, very straight-laced. He believed in the base nobility of our people. He was a warrior's son; he was not, however, a boy who believed that expressions of power were necessary to *be* a power. And, sadly, he all but worshipped one of his older brothers."

"Nightshade?"

Teela nodded.

"But...why?"

And chuckled. "Calarnenne is not what he once was. Although we live forever—absent the usual, violent death that awaits many of our kind—we are not static; we seem so to you because our changes do not occur at the speed of yours. I did not revere Calarnenne; if I had not been chosen, I would have held Annarion in wary contempt; my father did."

"What was Nightshade like?"

"When Annarion is less angry, you will have to ask him. Nightshade was, for a Barrani, more openly curious and far less cautious than is our wont when we are anything but children." She reached out to touch the tree; her hand had about as much effect as Kaylin's.

"Is he in there?"

Teela shook her head. "I don't know where he is. I can't see what he sees—and yes, kitling, I've been trying. Mandoran knows. I think everyone but me does. But they can't explain it to me, either." She hesitated and then added, "I think he *is* inside. I'm just not sure that we can safely or sanely be where he is now."

"It's a moot point," Kaylin replied, as she lifted both hands and ran them up and down the trunk of the nontree—or at least as far as she could reach in any direction. "If we can't get in, our survival on the inside's irrelevant."

"You're going to be disappointed, then," Severn told them both.

"No, only Kaylin," Teela replied. "I'm not bored, at the moment."

The side of the tree collapsed before she'd finished speaking. The tree itself didn't seem to notice the large, gaping hole that formed on its side.

CHAPTER 8

As doors went, it was about as welcome as the ruins of a collapsed hovel. "Please tell me this is not what his home looked like when he actually lived in it."

Teela shook her head, although she didn't look as surprised as Kaylin felt. "It didn't. It may, for all I know, look like that now. I'd guess—and you know I hate guessing—that this is how Annarion feels about his home as it exists in the present time; I'm certain it doesn't look like this in the real world."

"Can we get a bit of light?"

"I have no idea what Lord Sanabalis thinks he's doing," Teela replied, lifting a hand.

"Pardon?"

"He's teaching you rudimentary magic and you can't create a simple light?"

"I lit a candle," Kaylin replied, trying—and failing—not to sound defensive. Her arms, which were still glowing faintly, began to itch. Teela was using the branch of magic with which Kaylin—or at least Kaylin's skin—was most familiar.

"A candle, in my opinion, is about as difficult. If he was

going to torture you with the lessons you resent so much, he could have started with something that would actually *be* useful in investigative work."

"No argument, there."

Light grew in the palm of Teela's hand. "A word, however, to the wise." She frowned at her audience, and then turned to Severn. "The use of magic in buildings of dubious structural integrity and even more dubious intent isn't always safe."

"You couldn't have said that before you used magic?"

"I could have. I can see in the dark," she added. "You can stub your toes and curse like a Leontine, which might be just as unwelcome. Six of one, half dozen of another."

There were days when Kaylin vastly preferred that Teela speak in High Barrani; it didn't have as many useful—or mocking—phrases. But Teela was right: she couldn't see in the dark. Neither could Severn. He'd fallen silent as Teela chose to enter the forbidding, gaping hole, Kaylin almost glued to her heels. Teela kept the radius of light small; it was steadier than a torch or a candle, but its glow didn't fade the way natural light did; it simply ended.

If the outside of the tree felt like warm glass to the touch, the inside didn't; it was all building, and at that, building that Kaylin wouldn't have entered without rope, and possibly scaffolding. The floors were wood, but the planking seemed so worn she could practically see the basement beneath it. "Do we have to go down?" she asked.

"I hope not," Teela replied. "Understand that I was not in any way a frequent visitor. I traveled here a handful of times in the company of my father; we were treated like honored guests. No," she added, frowning as she held up the light, "we were treated like dangerous enemies meeting under a flag of brief truce. Any happy memories I have of those visits are overlapped with Annarion. His father was cut from the same cloth as mine."

"Did he meet the same end?"

A black brow rose. "You are becoming more perceptive."

"It's not perception, Teela. He was a Barrani Lord."

"A Barrani High Lord, yes. Calarnenne was not happy when he learned of Annarion's fate. He did not, I believe, bear the same resentment toward his father as I bore mine, but he was bitterly angry when all possibility of search—and possible rescue—was denied him."

"Is that why he's outcaste?"

"Not directly, no. I believe it played a part in the decision."

"Did he kill his father?"

"Ask him. I am certain he would tell you if you but asked."

"I'm not."

"I am willing to bet," Teela told her. "And I think we are meant to take those stairs. They go up," she added.

"I'm not sure up is any safer than down at this point." In Kaylin's opinion, they were probably the same damned thing.

"If you wanted safety, you should have stayed in the Palace. What *were* they arguing about anyway?"

"The definition of surveillance."

"Ah."

Stairs were a normal feature of most of the buildings Kaylin had lived in or visited. Even the Palace had them. But the Barrani Hallionne hadn't; they'd been single story dwellings inside. The Warden's home had had stairs, but the Warden's home wasn't sentient. Kaylin let Teela test the stairs because Teela carried the only source of light in what was a dilapidated hall. Its interior dimensions didn't match its exterior— which Kaylin could still see if she turned to look back. This was more of a comfort than it should have been.

"Can you hear him?" Teela asked, her hand on a tarnished rail which was missing parts.

"Annarion?"

The Barrani Hawk nodded.

Kaylin shook her head.

Squawk.

"Well, I can't. Sorry."

"Can Nightshade?"

"I have no idea."

"Ask."

Nightshade was amused. Kaylin, less so. *Tell An'Teela that I hear what she hears. If she asks you how, tell her that I am still Lord of this Castle. I cannot believe that my brother took such a careless risk,* he added. It took Kaylin a moment to understand what risk Nightshade referred to. He meant the giving of the name, of course.

You aren't surprised that Teela did?

Less so. She is not young, Kaylin, and she has never been at home among our kind. Her mother was weak and dangerously sentimental; in the end, it cost her her life.

There was a pause into which Kaylin shoved anger.

She serves the Emperor. Were she a lesser power, that choice would have destroyed her; it has not. It has not destroyed any of the Barrani Hawks who choose to do likewise, and that is significant; they do not have the power An'Teela has. She watches them all, although they have not explicitly sworn oaths to her. Just as, he added, *she watches you. No, I am not surprised at her choice. I expected better from my brother.*

Kaylin was an only child; her experience with siblings—or the expectations and effects they could have on each other—came largely through office gossip and complaint. People very seldom said warm, wonderful things about their siblings. Then again, they seldom said warm, wonderful things when they were annoyed.

He probably expected better from you, as well.

Nightshade didn't answer. Teela, however, swore.

"Nightshade can hear what you hear," Kaylin told her. She glanced at Severn, who shook his head. "Neither Severn nor I can."

If you chose to do so, Kaylin, you might hear what I hear.

The thought hadn't occurred to her.

No. It seldom does. You do not understand how to view people solely for the advantages they might bring you. Not even Annarion would be so squeamish; he is perfectly willing to see what any of the twelve see as it suits him.

They can shut each other out at need.

Can they?

She glanced at Teela. *Well, Teela can. The rest of them aren't my problem.*

Not yet.

Can you tell us if the ancestors are still sleeping?

Nightshade fell silent. After a long pause, he said, *No.*

No they aren't, or no you can't tell us?

The latter. It clearly didn't amuse him. It didn't amuse Kaylin, either.

Is that because Annarion is interfering with your control of the Castle?

That, Nightshade replied, *is the optimistic interpretation.*

"Can't you just *tell him* to stop speaking to the Castle?" Kaylin asked, as she hurried up the stairs, stepping exactly where Teela had stepped. The stairs didn't creak ominously beneath her feet. The floor didn't teeter. It still looked like it would collapse at any second.

"I've tried."

"And he said no?"

Teela's brows rose. "He's Annarion, not Terrano. He agreed."

Kaylin glanced pointedly at the stairs beneath their feet. "Let me guess. He doesn't understand what you mean by speak."

"The *Castle* doesn't understand what I mean, no."

Kaylin stopped walking. "If the Castle doesn't understand, how is *finding him* going to be helpful?"

Teela shrugged. "For you?"

"For anyone."

"I'll worry less."

"Bet?"

Teela snorted as she reached a landing and flat floors. Like the stairs, this floor seemed to be composed of wood; unlike the stairs, the wood looked relatively new. Or at least in good repair. There were walls to either side; the walls looked less finished than the floor. The usual adornments in halls of this size failed to materialize: there were no paintings, no tapestries, no mirrors. Kaylin frowned.

"Remember what I said about your face getting stuck that way."

"I remember Tain said it wouldn't look any worse, if that helps."

"I suppose he had a point. Why are you frowning?"

"The walls are made of wood."

Teela nodded. "And?"

"It's rough, or seems rough from here." Kaylin hesitated again. "It looks like the inside of a cheap coffin."

"What on earth makes you choose that particular metaphor?"

"It's not a metaphor, Teela." Kaylin looked up at the ceiling. It followed the design of the building, in that it was high—

probably ten or eleven feet off the ground. "It's a hunch. I think the Castle is trying to communicate with Annarion."

"Or lay him to rest?"

"Or that." Kaylin had to lengthen her stride to keep up with Teela as Teela began to jog.

Annarion was inaudible, but Kaylin didn't need to hear him to know that he was near. Small and squawky sat up on her shoulder, spreading his wings. He lifted his neck, drew his head back, and opened his tiny, perfect jaws.

"No, do *not* breathe here!"

He also smacked the side of her face with a wing. If this wasn't enough, the marks on her arms had brightened; she no longer needed Teela's light to see by. She wasn't terribly surprised when the marks separated themselves from her skin as they sometimes did; she was surprised, this time, to note that the shadows of their base shapes remained, flat and gray, against her skin. Had this always happened?

"The reason there are stairs," Kaylin said, to Teela's back, "is that Annarion is in a bedroom. Or a room. Someplace small."

"The Barrani don't separate rooms by level in that fashion."

"I know. Barrani don't require sleep."

"Neither do Towers, that I recall."

"The Hallionne have some memory of what they were before their transformation. I'm guessing the Towers of the fiefs do, as well."

"You're making the assumption that the Towers were created the same way as the Hallionne."

It was Kaylin's turn to shrug. "If you can think of other sentient buildings—"

"The High Halls."

"They don't change *shape*, Teela."

"You saw the heart of the High Halls." It wasn't a question. "In theory, the journey to it differs, depending on the word seen before it begins. What the High Halls contain is not content to be captive. It is not stupid, slow or weak. It has never ceased its attempts to escape. The jail itself requires flexibility and fluidity."

"And a Lord."

"A High Lord, yes."

"The Hallionne don't."

"No. But the Towers in the fiefs do. I do not think it a coincidence that the Towers and the High Halls are located in the same geographical area. Your assumption is that the Tower remembers...sleep?"

"It makes sense, given the layout. Which probably means that that's our door."

"And the coffin metaphor?"

"I don't think the Castle *wants* to be asleep."

Teela thought about this as she came to a stop outside a modest, single door. After a pause, she nodded, the set of her lips somewhat thinner than usual. "If the Castle is waking, what are the chances we see its Avatar?"

"Your guess is as good as mine. I'd be more interested in the chances that it will happily go back to sleep again." The small dragon bit her ear. "...or not." The runes that had lifted themselves off Kaylin's skin began to expand. They moved slowly, and came to rest when they filled a volume of space that looked like a translucent sphere. Kaylin stood at its center, but it also encompassed Severn and Teela.

The small dragon bit one of the words; Kaylin let him know, in terse Leontine, that this was not acceptable. He hissed. She rolled up her left sleeve to her elbow. The marks were still on her arm. But they were also brilliantly visible above and around her.

Squawk.

"He wants me to open the door," she said.

Teela's eyes narrowed. "You don't understand a word he's saying."

It was true. She had a history of lying to Teela—and Tain, if it came to that—but no history of doing so *successfully*.

"Honestly. It's not the attempt at a lie that I begrudge."

Kaylin grimaced. "I know, I know. It's the quality of the lie and the insult it does to your intelligence."

"Exactly. You can't possibly think much of me if you expect something that pathetic to be successful." She lifted a hand as Teela opened her mouth, and to Kaylin's surprise, the Barrani Hawk's eyes were a lighter shade of blue than they'd been all evening. They weren't green by a long shot, but you could imagine, looking at them, that they could be, some day. "But yes. In this case, I'll let you play point. I don't imagine the shield that surrounds you is that easy to penetrate—even for a Tower. I'll be right behind you," she added. "With apologies to the Corporal."

"I hate it when you call him that."

Teela chuckled. "I know. If I attempt to leave this shield, I'll try to give you warning."

"Don't leave it."

"I reserve the right to do so if it proves necessary. Annarion is in that room."

"You're certain?"

"Yes."

The small dragon added claws to his stiff, readied posture. They probably hadn't pierced her skin, but they weren't doing her clothing any favors, and clothing was more of a problem, since skin healed naturally and didn't cost anything. He didn't offer to cover Kaylin's face with his wing. She didn't offer to smack him.

Instead, she reached for the doorknob. It wasn't particularly fancy, but she was grateful it was there; she had no intention of touching any door ward found on the inside of this Castle. The handle turned. She heard a faint click, took a breath, and pushed the door open.

She couldn't see Annarion.

"Teela?"

When Teela failed to answer, Kaylin turned to look back over her shoulder. "You can't see him, either."

"I think your protections must be preventing it."

"That's not promising," Severn said, joining the conversation quietly as he sometimes did.

"No, it's not," Teela replied, staring intently ahead. "Because Annarion can see us."

"Why would the protections stop us from seeing him?"

"Think about the question you just asked," Teela replied, with just a trace of her familiar annoyance.

"I am. The only possibility I can come up with is—"

"Yes?"

"He's not in a physical form the small dragon considers safe for the more corporeal among our number."

Teela nodded. "Don't waste your breath asking me how he might be considered a purely physical danger, or what his current form is. I can answer neither."

"And the rest of your friends?"

"They can't answer it in a way I can understand." Her expression softened. "And to be fair, not everyone does understand it."

"Is this because they spent so long trapped in the heart of the green?"

"It's because they spent so long trapped there without the

anchor of their names, yes. There's a reason the ancients gave us the Lake, and the names."

"But they have names, now."

Teela nodded.

"The names they were awakened with."

"Yes. I believe your Arkon would find this fascinating."

"Not my Arkon, Teela." She hesitated. The Arkon had, in fact, left his library to offer her a warning about Annarion. She considered mentioning this to Teela, and decided against it. "Is Annarion even in control of the form he takes at the moment?"

"That would be the question."

"Does he understand that we can't see him?"

Teela nodded, frowning. Her eyes narrowed; her forehead creased. She was staring at a spot just to the left of Kaylin, and about two feet higher. Kaylin could see nothing but the room. The ceiling of this room was of a height with the hall's ceiling: high. Exposed, dark beams traveled from the left of the room to the right; curtains ran the length of the wall facing the door. There was no bed in the room, no closet; there was a chest of drawers against the left wall, and a large, plain cedar chest against the right. There were no chairs.

The only other piece of furniture in the room was a desk tucked into the leftmost corner. It wasn't particularly impressive—it was, in fact, the type of furniture that Kaylin would own. To her relief, it wasn't an exact replica of the desk she *did* own.

The small dragon hissed.

"He understands it now," Teela replied, her voice much softer. Soft in Teela was never a good sign.

The shield that surrounded them brightened as it grew— to Kaylin's eye—more solid. "Is he trying to change that?"

Teela nodded.

"He's Barrani," Kaylin said, voice flat.

Teela raised a brow.

"The problem *can't* be with him. Of course not. If he has the power, he has to rearrange everything *else*."

Teela surprised her. She laughed and slid an arm around Kaylin's shoulder. The small dragon hissed in the Barrani Hawk's face. "Oh shut up, you. How far can you extend this sphere?"

"I don't know." Kaylin frowned. She closed her eyes; she could still see the runes. She could no longer see the rest of the room. All the words hovered beyond her physical reach.

Squawk.

"I'm *trying*," she snapped.

He nuzzled the side of her face, muttering as he did. She was used to the squawking, the hissing, and the warbling. Mostly, they sounded like animal noises. Today, she heard the echoes of what might have been syllables in the thin, high voice. There was a very odd cadence to the sounds emitted by his translucent throat; it was deliberate and measured. It sounded, for the first time, like language.

It wasn't a language Kaylin could understand. But as she began to pick—and repeat—the syllables she heard—corrected by an indelicately applied wing when she didn't quite mimic the sound to the small dragon's satisfaction—she felt it was a language she could understand, if she really worked at it. And it was a language that hovered on the edge of the familiar: it felt like she *should* recognize it and should be able to speak it.

Then again, having a grammar teacher who didn't speak any of the languages she *could* understand would make learning really, really challenging. At the moment, it didn't matter. The marks that were so much a part of her skin she'd almost feel naked without them at this point began to brighten. And to move.

"What are you doing, kitling?"

"I told you. I'm trying to extend the sphere."

"I'm not sure Annarion is going to appreciate the attempt."

"Annarion can just learn to live with it. You know I'm not trying to attack him or injure him—he'll pick that up from you."

"Our communication is not perfect at the moment."

"It'll be good enough." Kaylin frowned and opened her eyes. "Is he speaking with the Castle now?"

"I believe it more accurate to say the Castle is in communication with him."

"Let's hope he can make it clear to the Castle that protecting myself isn't an act of hostility." She closed her eyes again. Teela fell silent. The only sound Kaylin could hear was squawky dragon voice; she joined it with her own. Each word had an associated sound. She was aware that there was more than simple sound to the act of speaking this particular language, just as there was more than simple sound when she spoke Nightshade's name.

But that hadn't always been clear to her.

Hearing the Consort call him *Calarnenne* had been a bit of a shock. Hearing the rest of the High Lords who were forced to address him do the same made clear that the sound of the syllables had meaning to those who spoke them—but the meaning was superficial. It was anchored to the speaker and not the person to whom they spoke.

The name Nightshade had revealed to her what felt like years and ages ago was part of *him*. When she spoke the name, the syllables contained more than sound, although the sound felt just as superficial unless she attempted to give him orders or force him to do something he had no desire to do. Attached to her understanding of the syllables was some hidden part of Nightshade himself.

These words were like that.

They were like Nightshade's name. Or Lirienne's. Or Ynpharion's. What she spoke was not simply what she heard: these words were rooted in her, part of her. They were like true names.

But...they weren't. If someone else spoke them, they sounded familiar, musical; their voices caught and held her attention. But they couldn't be used—as true names could—to control her. The binding went one way.

She had a freedom that the Barrani didn't.

And she paid for it by being mortal.

She caught the sounds of squawky voice and folded hers around it and tried, as she did, to match sounds to runes. Every time she managed this, the light the specific rune cast grew more solid. She reached out and the rune moved—forward or back—as if it were beneath her fingertips.

"Yes," she said to Teela. "But it's not perfect control."

"It's good enough." Teela's tone implied the opposite.

"He can see what I'm doing."

"Yes." Teela hesitated and then added, "He can hear it. I'm not sure he likes what you're saying."

"I don't even *know* what I'm saying."

"I'm trying to convince him that's true."

The air in the room dropped twenty degrees over the space of Teela's very curt sentence. "Try harder." Kaylin frowned, and added, "What does he think I'm saying?"

"I don't have words for it," the Barrani Hawk replied. "But it's protective and he's confusing protection with containment."

Kaylin frowned; Teela, concentrating, probably missed it. "I'm not sure it's confusion."

"I'm not sure I want to hear this."

"Lack of containment—for me—probably means death. I

don't have a convenient physical container I can hop in and out of at will. Neither," she added, "do you or Severn." Her frown deepened. "The Castle isn't contained the same way in its own space. Teela—is Annarion?"

Teela exhaled a couple of inches of height. "I don't know. My suspicion at this point isn't comforting. It's my belief that destroying his physical form would destroy him. Finding his physical form, on the other hand, would be difficult."

"Is Mandoran like this?"

"You'd have to ask him," Teela replied. "Or rather, you'd have to observe him. He's shouting a very loud no, at the moment. He's also shouting at Annarion." Her frown matched Kaylin's as an indicator of concentration, and then her brows rose. "Whatever you're doing, hold it right there."

Kaylin froze instantly. Teela had used the tone of voice she sometimes used in a stakeout that could go pear-shaped between one breath and the next.

"Can you see him?" the Barrani Hawk demanded.

Kaylin could see the room—and her own breath, the room had grown so cold. "No."

"He can see you more clearly."

"Do I even look like me, to him? Can he see Severn?"

Teela frowned. "He can see Severn, but not distinctly; he says Severn is out of focus, and nothing he does makes sight of him clearer. He can see me—but I think that's a function of my name. He can see the small creature on your shoulder."

Squawk.

"Live with it," Teela told him. Her eyes rounded and she turned to look at the small dragon. "But he doesn't see what we're seeing when we look at him."

"Is he seeing something dangerous?"

The small dragon stuck his chest out, puffing up.

"He considers it unsafe, yes." Teela muttered something

in Leontine and reached out to touch the small dragon; the small dragon caught her finger in his jaws. His teeth glittered as they rested against her skin.

The air in the room shifted. The wall undulated. The temperature dropped—and given that Kaylin's hands were going numb, she would have bet against that being a possibility. Something emerged in front of them. She heard Severn's sharp intake of breath.

"Teela—is that Annarion?"

Teela, hand still attached to small jaw, nodded. Her expression wasn't chilling in a room that was already too damned cold.

"Did he come here because you're in danger?"

"I believe so. I find it insulting, and it's clearly been long enough that he doesn't remember how unwise it is to insult me." She stepped forward, and the small dragon bit down. He didn't break skin, but it was now clear he could. "Kitling."

"He doesn't listen to me," Kaylin said in a rush. To the small dragon, she added, "Let go of her hand." The small dragon squawked around a mouthful of Teela. "I don't think he trusts you to stay within the sphere."

Teela said something in Aerian, a fallback curse the Hawks seldom used. To the small dragon, she added, "I am not your responsibility. Kaylin is. Let go."

The room beyond the sphere's boundary began to shift. It fell away. Or rather, it melted, as if it were a watercolor hit by rain. Unlike the detritus of her previous home, this left no architectural bits, shed no flying splinters, no chunks of glass, wood or the occasional bit of stone. The disintegration of the room itself was eerily silent as colors that had once marked chest, wall, curtain and door ran into what remained of the floor. The floor, on the other hand, seemed made of solid stone; it didn't absorb what were fast becoming puddles.

The colors began to seep into each other. For a moment, the resultant pool reminded Kaylin very much of the shadows that had attacked the fief of Tiamaris, seeping across the barriers that divided the fiefs from the darkness that lay at their heart. Kaylin took a step forward, because Teela did, and Teela was still attached by dragon mouth. Since Kaylin was at the center of the sphere, it followed.

The pool that had once been a room condensed as they watched. The strange, liquid surface caught the light Kaylin's barrier emitted, reflecting it. As they continued to watch, that light was absorbed, and the blend of darker interior colors brightened. The melted blob lost the look of Shadow.

"Please," Kaylin said, grimacing, "don't tell me that that's Annarion."

"If he cared what mortals thought, he'd probably be offended," Teela replied. She gave her hand a sharp tug, and the small dragon opened his jaw; to Kaylin's surprise, Teela stumbled. Just how much force could jaws that small exert? He hadn't bit *into* her. He had, on the other hand, added deeper runnels to Kaylin's shoulders.

"Teela," Severn said. "Don't. Just watch and wait."

It surprised them both; Severn wasn't given to making commands. Surprise held Teela in place as the puddle on the floor began to rise. Kaylin wasn't terribly surprised—although she was very disturbed—when the puddle developed eyes. Blue eyes.

Facial features followed as the puddle became a misshapen column; the eyes rose as the column did. A mouth formed beneath them, and a nose pulled itself out of what was now clearly otherworldly flesh. The patrician line of chin and cheekbones followed, as did ears to either side of the emerging face. Kaylin couldn't help it; she winced.

Teela, notably, did not. She might have watched flesh form out of random chaos puddles every day. Her arms hung by her sides, ending in loose fists.

Annarion—and it was, finally, Annarion—staggered. He was naked. He was bald. The bald didn't last; hair pushed itself out of the rounded dome of his head, like shoots of black grass; weight caused the hair to fall in a perfect drape around his shoulders. Clothing, however, didn't follow. He staggered as if the whole of his physical weight had returned to him in a rush.

Kaylin moved, then. The sphere moved with her, the light harsher and less forgiving. Annarion's blue eyes widened; his lips parted. But the sphere rolled over him and came to a stop only when Kaylin did.

And she did, because she was standing uncomfortably close to a naked male Barrani.

"What did you do with your clothing?" Teela asked. It was a remarkably mundane question, given the circumstances.

Annarion blinked rapidly. He then lifted his arms, turning his hands and flexing his fingers. He also flexed his toes. "Where is my brother?" His voice was hoarser or rougher than most Barrani voices.

"In the Castle."

"What did he do to me?"

Kaylin snorted. "He did nothing to you. As far as I can tell, you—"

"Kitling."

But Kaylin shook her head. "You understand that you're staying in one of the Towers that surround *Ravellon,* right?"

Annarion nodded slowly.

"The Towers are like—and unlike—the Hallionne. The Hallionne stop *all* their guests from fighting or killing each other if the guests are in the Hallionne's domain. Towers don't care what so-called guests do to each other. They *do* get defensive when they think their Lord is under attack."

"I did not attempt to kill my brother," Annarion replied. His eyes had shifted into the darker spectrum of blue, and the fact that he was stark naked didn't seem to affect his attitude at all.

"No, you probably didn't. I don't think Nightshade considered you a threat; the Castle clearly didn't agree with his assessment." She turned toward the door they'd entered; it was gone. The floor beneath her feet was stone—and it was familiar stone. "Teela, are we in the hall again?"

"Magic lessons, kitling," Teela replied. She lifted a hand, and a harsh, sharp light flared from her palm. Kaylin closed her eyes, opened her mouth for a couple of Leontine words, and opened her eyes again.

We found him.

Yes.

Can you take control of the Castle, now?

The answer was longer in coming. *There is a difficulty.*

Of course there was. All Kaylin had wanted out of the evening was to find a new place to live. A normal, slightly run-down apartment in a part of town that was relatively safe walking distance from work. Then again, all she'd wanted from the day job had been a normal, boring patrol through Elani, with the usual non-world-threatening irritations, Margot being chief among them. She should have known.

Can you control enough of the Castle that you can find Annarion some clothing?

The lack of clothing, Nightshade replied, with genuine amusement, *is unlikely to cause him harm.*

It's illegal.

It is not illegal in Nightshade.

Does the difficulty have something to do with the ancestors? she asked. The small dragon squawked, loudly, in her ear. Kaylin glared at him, and something beyond his lifted wings caught her attention: movement from down the hall.

"Teela—"

Teela's magical light shifted in place. Instead of a broad glow, it now emitted a beam. She aimed it carefully down the hall. Standing in its center, between two stone walls that continued into darkness beyond it, was a figure.

CHAPTER 9

In shape and form, he was a Barrani male. His skin was pale and flawless, his cheekbones high and pronounced; black, straight hair framed his face and fell past his shoulders toward the stone, blending with the robes he wore; at this distance, Kaylin thought them either black or a shade of blue that made no difference. He was of a height with Teela and Annarion.

Teela was tense. Annarion was as well, but at least his discomfort made sense: he was naked, and part of that naked included unarmed.

As the silent stranger continued to walk toward them, Kaylin frowned. There was something wrong with his eyes. They weren't Barrani in anything but shape; they were dark and vaguely opalescent. They were Tara's eyes.

I think I see part of your problem, she said to Nightshade.

Ah.

I don't suppose you've given the Castle a name?

I have. It is Nightshade.

Think of a better one, she replied. *Or things are going to get re-*

ally bloody confusing in the very near future. To Teela she said,
"It's an Avatar."

"You're certain?"

"I'm willing to bet on it."

"You're willing to bet the sun won't rise tomorrow; that's
hardly comforting."

Annarion had, in theory, spent much of the evening in
conversation with the Castle. It obviously hadn't been particularly pleasant, given the set of his jaw and the color of his
eyes. She started to tell him that the stranger was very much
like the Avatars of the Hallionne, but stopped. The Barrani
didn't care for the Hallionne when they were awake.

And the Castle was now awake. Or at least sleepwalking.

She reached up and poked the small dragon on her shoulder. He squawked.

The stranger froze, his forehead creasing, his eyes narrowing. The change in expression was exaggerated; it almost
seemed deliberate. Wilson and his various unnamed brothers
had had a similar grasp of facial expressions.

It was the only thing about the Avatar of Castle Nightshade
that reminded Kaylin in any way of the Hallionne's brothers.
Where Wilson had been unclear on the concept of physical
form, his experimentation—if disturbing, as limbs weren't
meant to shift in length or texture—had been almost playful.
Nothing about the Avatar that approached them now seemed
to imply the same curiosity, wonder, and innocence.

Squawk.

The stranger stopped. Kaylin almost laughed out loud when
the avatar responded in kind, his voice thin and grating.

On her shoulder, wings rose; claws tightened. Slender neck
elongated as the small dragon lifted his head. Clearly what she
heard from the Avatar—poor mimicry of small dragon—was
not what he heard.

The Avatar took three long steps and stopped at the outer edge of the sphere centered on Kaylin. His eyes reflected the light shed by the marks that comprised it, narrowing further.

"Bearer of burdens," he said. He spoke in Barrani—High Barrani. And he spoke to Kaylin.

She wasn't certain how to address him in response. She'd become accustomed to the word Chosen—although she often wanted to reply *for what*—but bearer of burdens was a new one. She was spared the need to carry her part of this conversation.

"You are mortal?"

Some instinct caused hesitation, which allowed the small dragon to reply instead.

The stranger reached out to touch the edge of the sphere. His fingers sizzled. This was so not how Kaylin wanted to make a first impression.

"Do not," Teela said, in a cold, flat voice, "even think of dropping your protections."

Kaylin glanced at her. Her eyes were midnight. They didn't reflect light the way the Avatar's did. She glanced at Annarion—or his face, at any rate—and saw his eyes were the same color.

She looked, again, at the Avatar. In the brighter light of her sphere, he was almost white, but his lips were a darker blush of color. He looked Barrani, to Kaylin, but she couldn't have confused him with any other Barrani she'd ever met.

Barrani really looked remarkably similar to one another; it was familiarity that made distinguishing the individuals possible—at least in Kaylin's experience. She found their voices more distinct than many of their physical characteristics, but the being standing in front of her with slightly smoking fingers was an Avatar, and Avatar's voices were unique.

The Avatar did not attempt to touch the sphere again. "You did not call me," he said, and turned to Annarion. His eyes shifted as Kaylin watched; she had seen Tara's eyes do the same thing. They became Barrani eyes in both color and composition.

"You did."

Annarion's eyes didn't change at all; they were about as dark as they could get. The stranger looked around at the stone of the halls and frowned. Kaylin tensed as the walls began to recede; she had some fear that the floor would do the same. Nor was she wrong—but the shield itself seemed to ignore simple things like gravity—if gravity in a sentient building was ever simple.

She waited for the landscape to return in a different form—for trees to sprout or a different room to coalesce.

"You may have heard me," Annarion said, in slow and stiff High Barrani, "but it was not my intent to disturb your sleep."

"You did not disturb my sleep," the Avatar replied. "My sleep was troubled. It is difficult to ignore the voices of those who should not be within my walls."

"The only things that shouldn't be within your walls," Kaylin interjected, "are Shadows."

A brow rose; he stared down a long, perfect nose at her as if she were an interesting, intelligent animal. "Oh? You claim to understand the whole of my imperative?" His smile was so lacking in warmth it seemed like a threat. "The burden you bear is light in comparison. And flexible." He turned his attention to Annarion again. "You should not be here. You have disturbed my kin, and they seek you now."

His...kin.

Nightshade.

I am speaking with the Avatar, he replied. *Just as you are. We are not having the same conversation.*

Is he going to try to kill Annarion?

Silence.

When the Castle talks about his kin, is he talking about the ancestors?

That is my belief. I have not interacted with the Castle in this particular way before. It is…instructional.

He's not like Tara.

No, Kaylin, he is not. I stand at the heart of the words that bind him. You stand at the heart of words that protect you from him. I do not believe there is anywhere else in the Castle that could now be considered safe.

But…

Yes?

Andellen is in the Castle.

Yes. And others of my men, as well. I do not know if you can find an exit. But if you can, take it. This is not the place for you.

What will you do?

I will continue my discussion with the Castle. The Castle understands that, on some visceral level, it accepted me as its Lord. Unless and until I die, I will remain Lord.

She didn't doubt him. But watching the Avatar, she wondered if his survival was guaranteed.

"You are not one of the echoes," the Avatar said to Annarion. "Nor are you one of my kin. What *are* you?"

"He is," Kaylin replied, when it became clear Annarion had no intention of doing so, "brother to your Lord."

The Avatar frowned. "I cannot hear you," he told Annarion. "Not as I did before." His attention refocused on Kaylin. "Bearer of burdens, he is not for you. Release him."

"I'm not holding him here. He's here of his own volition."

"I can barely hear him at all, and he is my domain. Release him."

Kaylin glanced at the sphere made of words. "He's free to leave if he so chooses. But he is also free to remain."

The small dragon squawked.

The Avatar's eyes narrowed. "What did you say?"

Squawk.

Eyes that now looked Barrani darkened.

"Maybe," Kaylin said to her companion, "now is not the time to antagonize him."

The Avatar opened his mouth on silence. But silence had texture; it had motion, it had temperature. Translucent wings rose and spread; claws dug in. Kaylin thought she felt a tail wrap itself around her throat. She didn't need to understand small dragon squawk to know that the Avatar was dangerous.

Severn unwound his weapon chain. He didn't set it spinning; in the sphere, packed as they were, there was no room. But if he meant to fight, fighting while anchored to anyone was a hazard for everyone concerned. Everyone except the Avatar. Severn gripped a blade in either hand, but said, and did, nothing else.

Teela didn't bother to arm herself, which was a sign of how useful she thought weapons would be here. Her eyes couldn't get bluer. She stepped partially in front of Annarion, as if in warning.

Squawk.

"Impossible."

Squawk squawk squawk.

Light flooded the hall. It was sharp as a blade, but wider; it pierced the darkness beneath their feet, stretching toward walls that could no longer be seen by the merely mortal. What it touched, Kaylin couldn't say, but she saw rock as it formed beneath her feet; it was a long way down.

"Teela—beneath the Castle there's a cavern. A series of tunnels. I think they're similar to the tunnels beneath the Heart of the Green."

"Were they made the same way?" Teela asked.

Kaylin glanced at Annarion and remembered the sudden, inexplicable storm in the heart of Evanton's Garden. Mandoran had tried to speak with the elemental water, and the elemental water had not been pleased. Kaylin thought, at the time, that the water had been enraged—and that was probably true.

But she thought, as she stood at the heart of a sphere that wouldn't let her fall, that the water had also been afraid.

Teela understood what Kaylin didn't put into words; if they didn't share the intimacy of the bond created by knowing a true name, they had almost a decade of lived-in experience together. Teela inhaled.

The small dragon exhaled.

Kaylin froze in near panic as a stream of smoke left his mouth in a conic plume. It wasn't steam; it wasn't the smoke that generally accompanied Dragon fire. It was opalescent, flecked with colors that caught and reflected golden light.

Severn and Teela knew what the small dragon's breath could do. Annarion probably knew as well, although he hadn't been there to see it in person at any other time.

"Do you honestly think to threaten *me?* Here? Do you not understand what I have *become?*"

Trust a Barrani—an ancient, powerful, proto Barrani—to argue with something that had a brain the size of a walnut.

Squawk.

The Avatar lifted both arms; the air cracked, as if it were made of glass.

"We'll risk the water." Teela's voice was low and urgent.

The sphere dropped. Everyone in it stiffened as gravity returned. Above their heads—inches above—the world exploded in something that felt like fire. It was white, and hot. Words— foreign and completely beyond her understanding—followed that fire. Kaylin didn't need language to recognize fury.

★ ★ ★

The sphere dropped; the rock bed that Kaylin had glimpsed when she'd stood at the level of castle halls grew closer between eye blinks. But the sphere itself didn't strike ground; it stopped abruptly a yard above impact, and hovered.

"Is this the same?" Kaylin asked the rigid familiar sitting on her shoulder. "Is this the shield you conjured to save us when the Arcane bomb exploded?"

The small dragon shook his head.

"It's not his shield," Severn said quietly. "It's yours."

"I can't reliably light a *candle*."

Severn offered her a pure fief shrug. "I paid attention in all the Arcane arts classes taught to the Wolves. This isn't a magic that the Imperial Order is capable of teaching."

"And lighting a candle is."

"Lighting a candle is a magic anyone who has magical power can learn. Apparently. It's a base test of both ability and focus."

"You know this how?"

He shrugged again. "Shadow Wolves are tested for a variety of aptitudes. If it helps, I couldn't light the candle. I couldn't," he added, as Teela opened her mouth, "make a simple light, either."

"I'm going to demand that Sanabalis teach me the light trick. It's got to be more useful than candles."

"It's theoretically more difficult than candles." He looked at the sphere. "Could you do this again, if necessary?"

"I don't know."

"Take that as a no," Teela helpfully told Severn. She had an arm around Annarion's shoulder. "The first principle of magical competence is repeatability. You have magical power, which makes you dangerous. You can't predictably use it, which makes you erratic. You don't control the way the power is expressed, which makes you dangerously erratic. There's a reason the Imperial Court wanted you dead when you first arrived on the scene."

"Is the Court composed of mortals?" Annarion asked.

"It is almost entirely composed of Dragons," Teela replied. "Why?"

"Dragons clearly don't feel immortality the way the rest of our kin do." Before Teela could speak, he added, "Immortals become weary with the passage of centuries."

"You're weary?"

Annarion shook his head. "I am reckoned old by my kin, but...I have not had the time to grow weary of this world; I have barely lived in it, after all. I have not seen all the changes wrought since we were first exposed to the *regalia*. I cannot understand how they occurred—I cannot believe it possible that we live peacefully in an Empire ruled by a Dragon. For what were we sacrificed? Why did our kin lose their lives in the wars that preceded that sacrifice?

"To become the tame Immortals that bow to a *draconian* Emperor?" He glanced pointedly at Teela, and although he could have spoken to her in the silence of their name-bond, he said, "I understand that ennui is inevitable. But the lengths to which our people have gone to avoid it almost beggars the imagination."

Teela snorted. "It was not about ennui."

"Oh?"

Above them, light shattered and fragmented. The Avatar roared like a Dragon.

"It was about the Shadows and the darkness that exists at the heart of this city. You will come to understand it if you take the Test of Name—but you will never understand it fully."

That stung Annarion, judging by his expression. Whatever

he said in response was fully private, which Kaylin guessed meant it was insulting.

"Oh, don't. Just don't." Teela spoke in Elantran. "The world is what the world is. Try to change it when you actually understand *more* of it. If I catch you anywhere near the border at the heart of the fiefs—"

"Yes?" Annarion's voice was very, very chilly.

"She won't have to do anything," Kaylin cut in, not liking where this was going given the ruckus happening above her head. "You'll probably attract the attention of every dangerous one-off in miles, and you'll die or get absorbed or get transformed. It's probably the latter she's worried about." It occurred to her, as Annarion drew breath, that she was in charge of where they were actually standing, because she was at the center of the barrier.

She began to walk.

Everyone—even angry Annarion—followed.

"The world is not supposed to be this way," he said, to no one in particular. Or to everyone.

"Tell me about it," Kaylin replied. "I grew up with no parents in the fief your brother is Lord over. We were hunted by his thugs, by his Ferals, and by the mortals who were strong enough to enforce their particular desires. We ate garbage when we could find it. We didn't have a stable home.

"I didn't particularly like the way the world was. I don't particularly like the way the world *is*. But complaining about it doesn't change anything, and charging into Nightshade or his thugs would have just guaranteed that I'd be a casualty. You can charge across the borders if you want—"

"No," Teela said, "he can't."

"—But it's not going to change the world in a way anyone who lives in it would appreciate. Probably not even you."

Annarion said, "Not while I'm naked, at any rate."

Kaylin surprised herself by laughing.

"What, exactly, is a 'one-off?'"

Kaylin glanced at Teela.

"No you don't," Teela replied. "It's not terminology my people use. If you want him to have an understanding of your imprecise nomenclature, you can explain it yourself."

"Your people being Barrani, not Hawks."

"I'm perfectly capable of multitasking."

Kaylin snorted. "You know about the Shadows, right?"

Annarion frowned. He said nothing but after a pause, nodded, his expression one of intent concentration.

"If rumors are true, they're concentrated in the center of the fiefs. No one crosses those borders."

"And the Shadows remain there?"

"Not willingly. There are Towers in the fiefs. Six that we know of for certain. Some people believe there's a seventh."

"In the center of the fiefs?"

Kaylin nodded. The light shed by her sphere was strong enough to illuminate smooth, worn stone. It was natural stone; it hadn't been laid in by masons. She closed her eyes as she heard the distant trickle of water. "The Towers are like the Hallionne. I don't know if they were created the same way. Given the Avatar, I have my suspicions."

"They sleep, like the Hallionne."

Kaylin nodded.

"And they wake the same way?"

She stopped. The Hallionne slept unless they were woken. Waking them wasn't simple. It wasn't a matter of shouting a few words or kicking the nearest wall. They woke to song—a specific song. Kaylin had seen and heard it performed by the Consort. The Consort and Nightshade, in harmony. By the end of it, the Consort looked as if she'd carried half her body weight on a twenty-mile forced march; she was exhausted.

"Clearly not the same way," she replied. "Have you heard the song of waking?"

He blinked. She might have asked him if he'd ever drawn breath before. "Of course."

Teela's glance was sharp. It implied a question, without vocalizing it.

"Is there a song to put them *back* to sleep?"

"No. They drift, if there is no one to converse with." Pause. "Sometimes you can converse with the Hallionne while they sleep. Their answers, then, are different."

"And you conversed with the Castle while it was sleeping."

"Not on purpose." He hesitated, and then added, "The imperatives of the Castle are not the imperatives of the Hallionne; the Hallionne were meant to protect anyone who dwelled within their walls. The Castle's imperatives are less clear to me."

"Less clear how?"

"It is listening," he replied, after a long pause and another distinct glare from Teela. "It is listening for one voice."

"That's not what I've been told."

"I do not know what you have been told. You have not spoken with this Castle before. Perhaps the Towers, like the Hallionne, are unique, and each has its own imperative." He frowned. "You have not spoken with the Castle, but the Castle knows your voice. It has listened, while sleeping. It understands what you are."

"Please tell me you're not talking with him now."

"No. I cannot hear him, not as I did before."

"Can he hear you?"

Annarion glanced at the translucent sphere of words that surrounded them all. "I...do not think so. If he is like the Hallionne, he will be displeased."

"He's not like the Hallionne," Kaylin replied. "I *don't* want him reading my mind."

"He will not hear anything that my brother's servants do not think."

"He'll hear a *lot* that they don't think." She continued to follow the rough stone tunnels as she spoke. They were wider than the tunnels at the heart of the green, and much taller. *Nightshade, we're leaving. I don't think it's a good idea to leave Annarion here.*

He will not thank you for his rescue.

I don't need his gratitude. I need to survive. I'm not sure I care if he does, but Teela won't leave without him.

Nightshade chuckled. *Neither will you.*

She said nothing, frozen for one moment in the fiefs of her adolescence. And then, grimacing, she shook herself free. No, she wouldn't leave him behind. She wouldn't kill him. Not unless her survival depended on it—and maybe, if she was honest, not even then. She'd lived a life of fear, and fear had become the whole of her life until her life wasn't worth anything to anyone—not even herself.

She wouldn't go back to that: fear living her life, instead of her.

She knew Nightshade thought of it as a weakness. He thought of it as an amusing weakness, a charming flaw. It didn't matter. Kaylin was not now, and would never be, Barrani. She had nothing to prove to Nightshade.

She hoped she had nothing to prove to Nightshade.

The sound of water grew louder as they walked. "Whatever it was Mandoran tried to do or say to the elemental water," she told Annarion, "avoid it. I think the water will carry us out of the Castle—but I'd really prefer not to be bashed against every bit of available rock on the way."

"My brother—"

"Is going to be insulted if you finish that sentence. He's Lord of the Castle; he has been for decades."

Centuries.

Whatever.

"And is he proof against the ancestors?"

"Your brother? No. The Castle, yes." She spoke with more certainty than she felt. It didn't matter. In Annarion's eyes, she was mortal—and at that, some variant of indentured.

"Don't ask me," Teela told him—out loud and in Elantran. "Kaylin's understanding of your brother far outpaces mine."

"But do you think he'll be safe?"

"If the ancestors are—as I suspect—awake? I can't see how he could be. But Kaylin's spent more time speaking with buildings, as well."

"I think the ancestors are here," Kaylin told them both, "because they're related to the Castle. Or what the Castle was before he became one of the sentinel Towers. I'm not as certain that he volunteered, the way the Hallionne did."

"Can Nightshade keep them here?"

"It would be safer if he did not," Annarion said.

Kaylin stopped walking. It hadn't even occurred to her that he wouldn't try. "Safer for whom?"

She felt Nightshade's laughter. He was genuinely, if bitterly, amused.

"Most of your kin are *in this city*," she told him, with more heat than she'd intended.

"He is one man," Annarion replied. "The High Court is many. And if he is outcaste, he owes the High Court nothing."

"You don't know why he's outcaste."

"No. No more, I am certain, than do you." Annarion's eyes were an oddly luminescent blue. They were not a familiar Barrani color. "I am certain," he said, voice low, "that there *is* a reason. I am certain that a mistake has been made."

He is young. He is...as I remember him. I am not, however, as he remembers me. I am a disappointment to him. It is...vexing. I should have known that he would react in precisely the way he has.

You couldn't have known that he could have this effect on the Castle.

No. But the effect, as you call it, is secondary. I am reminded, now, of how I would have viewed the man I am now, when I was his age.

Not well, I take it?

No.

Kaylin thought about what her thirteen-year-old self would think of her as she was now. The difference—at least in her case—was that she was certain her thirteen-year-old self would be wrong in every possible way. Except for the envy. She had the feeling that it wasn't as cut-and-dried for the fieflord. And it was actively painful for his brother.

Can you take control of the Castle?

Yes. It is not, as you suspect, trivial. But the Castle requires a Lord. I believe such requirement is fundamental to its existence.

And if the Castle prefers one of the two sleeping ancestors you have in your basement?

I hope to render that irrelevant, he replied, with more ice. *But I will owe you all a debt of gratitude if you preserve my brother.*

I think that's going to be more challenging than—

Yes. He is as I remember. He is the brother I worked, planned, and surrendered so much to save. I can remember the arguments we had in the past—now. For his part, they are similar to arguments we had with our parents. For mine, they are of necessity different. Immortals have the arrogance of assuming that nothing about them changes; he is proof that that is a lie we tell ourselves so thoroughly it feels like truth.

I didn't think the Barrani had a problem with lying.

A lie that is planned has intelligence, intellect, and elegance—

when used upon others. Preserve my brother, Kaylin, and I will be in your debt.

She knew how Barrani felt about debt.

Indeed. In this case I will discharge that debt with honor and gratitude. Anything less would be a severe disappointment to my brother, and I am uncertain that the fief would survive another such disagreement. You understand my attachment to Annarion, as does An'Teela. I believe the Consort has never doubted it. It is a weakness, Kaylin. A singular weakness. At the moment, I believe I could cheerfully strangle my brother—and I consider it my right. If I am not to have the satisfaction of destroying him, I will allow no others to do so.

He's not going to be happy if you don't survive this.

No. It is unusual for Barrani kin to form such strong attachments. Perhaps if he had lived as we had, he might be more pragmatic.

Kaylin stubbed her toe. Cursing, she said, *He's just as pragmatic as you are. If I understand what's happened, you spent centuries looking for a way to reach the brother you were certain was still alive when everyone else had given up on him. Don't make him do the same thing.*

It would, in mortal parlance, serve him right. Go. You are the only occupant of this Castle who can exit safely this way.

He fell silent. His words, however, would have failed to encapsulate what he felt. Annarion, altered or no, was the only surviving person for whom he was willing to risk his life. He was kin. He was family.

The Barrani made show of disavowing all such ties, but Kaylin never had. In the absence of blood-ties, she built family wherever she could. It was the only way she could feel at home, that she could feel home meant something. So she understood what Nightshade would never put into words, and she had the words for it.

She kept them to herself, but began to walk more quickly.

Stopped. *I don't suppose there's any way to get the Castle to make Annarion some clothing?*

I would not be willing to take that risk at the moment, was the dry reply. *I am certain your Tara could do it.*

She considered showing up at this hour of the night on Tiamaris's doorstep, and decided it could wait. The tunnel had finally opened up into cavern. She didn't need the light to know that they'd reached the river; she could hear its roar.

There were words in it.

CHAPTER 10

Without thought, she reached out and grabbed Annarion's left wrist. "I'm sorry," she said, voice low. "But—don't speak. Don't try to talk to the water." When he failed to answer, she looked at him. His eyes were wide, but the rest of his expression might have been carved of stone.

"Too late?" she asked Teela.

Teela's lips had thinned; where Annarion's eyes were rounded, hers had narrowed. "If it helps, he thought he understood Mandoran's mistake."

"So he needed to make a *different one?*"

Severn cleared his throat, loudly. Water rose.

It wasn't clear water; it didn't have the tranquil purity of the pond in Evanton's Garden. Small rocks, rounded stones and bits of debris Kaylin couldn't immediately identify given the speed of their movement, were contained within. But the swell at the water's height wasn't due to the speed at which it traversed the carved bedrock.

Roiling water took shape as it rose. It didn't splash; it didn't shoot up the tunnel to dislodge them. The small dragon hissed in Kaylin's ear.

She wanted to send the small dragon toward the water, but she was afraid of losing the sphere that protected them and granted them light. She knew that the power itself came from the marks that adorned her skin; she wasn't certain if she had been the one to invoke it. She had her doubts.

The small dragon didn't apparently share them. He pushed himself off her shoulder, squawking loudly enough to be heard over the water's roar. The water reached out to envelope him; he dived.

"Teela—hang on to Annarion." Kaylin handed his wrist to the Barrani Hawk. "Severn, hang on to me."

He sheathed his weapons. Against water, they weren't going to be much use. He framed Kaylin's waist with the palms of either hand. She walked toward the pillar of water that now stood in the riverbed.

The small dragon squawked and squawked; his voice resembled a flock of angry pigeons. Or seagulls. Maybe seagulls. The water lifted an arm to swat him out of the way. It would have been funny at any other time, but as the arm came down on dry rock, the rock cracked beneath it.

Kaylin couldn't help it; she flinched. She knew what storms could do to ships in harbor. But rain had never killed her. Water, when it struck her, never stung. And the water here had been her first introduction to the Tha'alaan. She couldn't be afraid of it.

But she was. She was afraid of its anger.

Fear or no, she knew there was a way through it. Like an elemental mother—like a loving mother, she silently corrected herself—the intensity of anger and rage had limits. She might scream at Kaylin in fury; she wouldn't try to smash her to a pulp. She wouldn't kill her.

She believed that. But she'd never been good at approaching her own mother when her mother's cheer had frayed and she had seen the anger and pain that lurked beneath it. That anger had terrified her child self.

Did people ever truly grow up? Or did they just get better at dealing with life as life became familiar? The fear was just as strong now as it had been when she'd last seen her mother's anger. But her mother's anger had been infinitely preferable to her sudden, complete absence. Kaylin inhaled, clinging to that certainty.

She lifted an arm, yards from the water's edge. She lifted her voice, as well. Although the Tha'alaan had no audible voice, Kaylin did. She used it, hoping to catch the Tha'alaan's attention. She managed. Water snaked out and fell in one thundering crash that once again cracked rock.

It cracked rock everywhere but the ground on which the sphere itself shed light. Kaylin reached up as the water fell, palms cupped as if she were still a child in the fiefs. Water pooled briefly in those hands, seeping between her fingers toward the ground in a way that wouldn't break anything.

And then it stopped falling, as if it could ignore both gravity and the fact that it was liquid. It grew warmer as she carried it; it felt like palms had been placed, gently but completely, over her own.

Kaylin.

She closed her eyes. *Tha'alaan.*

You did not heed my warning.

I did—this one isn't the same as the one who visited the Keeper's Garden. I wasn't going to bring him to the Garden.

Is he not the same? He feels the same. He looks the same.

Kaylin privately thought all Barrani looked the same, and would have considered this a perfectly reasonable opinion had she not known that it wasn't the racial characteristics the water was speaking about. *He's not the same. The last one was Mandoran. This one is Annarion.*

You are mistaken, Kaylin. Why have you brought him here?

To you? We're trying to get out of—

To the last line of defense.

I didn't bring him here. We're trying to remove him from the Castle—without killing him. He is brother to the Lord of the Castle, and he is precious to him.

He is, as I told you, a danger. You do not understand what he is.

No, I don't. But neither does he.

You said that before.

It was true before, as well. He's— Kaylin bit her lip because she could, and continue to speak. *He's young. He's like the young Barrani. I don't know if you see them or interact with them. He's not like the Lord of the Castle. He's not like the High Lord—or the Arcanists who summon some part of you and bend it to their will.*

He is a danger to you and your kind. If he believes he is like the others you have named, he is mistaken. If he cares about the people to whom he claims kinship, he must *leave these lands.*

These lands are his home.

No, Kaylin. They cannot safely contain him. You believe—I can feel your belief—that he is struggling to become what he believes he still is. If that is the case, tell him: until he achieves this, he is a danger to his kin. The water in Kaylin's hands chilled. It was not—quite—as bad as cupping ice, but it was damned close. *He is not the only presence who must remain contained and hidden. What has been done here?*

The ancestors, Kaylin thought. The ancestors weren't, as she'd feared, sleeping anymore.

Kaylin had never understood how the water knew what it knew. She didn't generally question it. But something about the sharp edge of the question—maybe it was the ice—made her hesitate. The water knew, of course. It could hear her—

when they were in contact—as if it knew Kaylin's true name. Or as if Kaylin knew the water's.

There are secrets, the water said quietly. *We do not keep them from you because we plan to use them against you; we have no easy way to explain what they are. Your Mandoran/Annarion is one such secret. I cannot explain what he is to you, because you cannot hear the explanation; you can hear only one part, and it is the lesser part.*

I exist as water, in this realm. I am part of the world into which you were born, and in which you will eventually die. But I am part of the green. I am part of the heart of the green. I am part of the Outlands. There is only one place I do not touch willingly, and only one place in which I surrender all dreaming and all sentience. Ravellon.

But—Ravellon *is part of this world.*

So, too, is your Mandoran. Your Annarion. If he cares—if they care, if they truly believe they are separate—he must leave. I will allow your passage from this place, she continued. *I will do what I can to preserve you all. But everything in me, daughter, wishes his absence, however that might be achieved. I will not sleep again while the ancestors wake. Go, now.*

Kaylin turned to Teela as the water once again bled through her curved fingers. "We can leave."

"You know where the exit is?"

"More or less." She glanced at Annarion and added, "You're probably not going to like it, but the water's promised to do her best not to destroy you."

He lifted one brow, the expression so much like Night-shade's Kaylin almost laughed. "I cannot believe a city that houses so many mortals can be so unexpectedly, unpredictably deadly. You could have warned us, Teela."

"It wasn't unpredictable in this particular way until the two of you arrived." Her knuckles, where she gripped Annarion's wrist, were white. "But if we're being fair, you weren't responsible for the Destroyer of Worlds, and you weren't responsible for the Outcaste Dragon. You weren't responsible for the tidal wave that nearly destroyed the city, either."

"You've forgotten the Shadows that tried—"

"If I make a list, it'll just remind me how much of a hazard *you* are."

"I think I prefer it when you speak High Barrani."

Teela snorted. "We're not walking out, are we?"

"No. The water will give us a lift."

Annarion's eyes went straight to the almost draconian gold of Barrani surprise. "You can't mean to jump *into* the water?"

Kaylin nodded. Annarion replied—in Leontine. Kaylin laughed.

Squawk.

"Sorry. I hadn't forgotten you."

Squawk. Squawk.

"Well, maybe just a little—but I was busy trying to keep us alive. Are you coming with us, or are you going to fly?"

Squawk. He hovered nearer to the cavern's height, and showed no obvious intention of descending.

"Suit yourself. We're getting wet."

Annarion proved himself to be younger than Nightshade or Teela in one regard. He was suspicious of the water—and given the water's attitude, with good reason—but he could not let Kaylin, a mere mortal, take a risk he was afraid to take. When Severn detached himself from Kaylin's waist and bound the weapon chain tightly around his own, sheathing both blades, Annarion inhaled, lifted his shoulders and walked directly toward the much calmer river.

He didn't jump in; Teela caught him before he could. Her eyes were blue. She wasn't surprised at all. Then again, she'd rarely been surprised by stupid feats of pride on the part of

Kaylin's younger self, either. She'd pretty much owned outrage, though.

"Let her go in first."

"She's mortal—"

"Yes. She's the mortal who talked to the water and *calmed it down*. She goes in first."

Kaylin turned to Annarion. "I'm mortal. I'm not a child."

"Not on most days, at any rate," Teela unhelpfully added. "She doesn't like to try new foods, and she's lazy when it comes to cleaning."

"Teela. Now. Is. Not. The. Time."

Teela laughed. It was the deep, sensual laughter that usually made her eyes go green—and they did. Annarion's were also a greener shade of blue by the time she'd finished, although he had the grace not to join her.

He didn't, however, attempt to stop Kaylin when she approached the water. The thought of sloshing her way home in soaked boots and clothing—where in this case home was the Imperial Palace—was the only thing that made her hesitate.

It didn't last long. She sat on the rocky outcropping and lowered herself into the rushing current, feet first. The water rose instantly and enveloped her. Kaylin trusted the water enough that she didn't flinch; she'd been carried by water before. She did hold her breath.

She heard the watery splashes as she was joined by her three companions; the sphere that surrounded them began to thin and fade. The last thing she heard as the water began to pull them along in the folds of harsh current was the squawking of a very discontent small dragon.

They came up through the old well. The water crested the top of the worn, stone structure, spitting them out as if they were poison. If the outer facade of the Castle had changed—

and no one could deny that it had—the well itself remained roughly where Kaylin had found it the first time. She pulled herself to her knees and noted that the dirt and debris that streets generally gathered were now clinging to her clothing.

It helped that it appeared to be clinging to some of Teela's. Teela's hair, on the other hand, fell in a straight curtain. It was wet, but it looked attractive. Kaylin was certain hers now looked like the side of a half-drowned cat. Annarion, however, was naked, and that was going to be more challenging.

As if he could read her mind—and technically, if he wanted to, he probably could—Severn removed his shirt. He spent a good five minutes wringing as much water out of it as he possibly could before he shook it out again and handed it to Annarion. They were roughly the same height, but Annarion was slimmer.

"Take it," Kaylin told him. "It's better than nothing."

"The cold—or the heat—that will kill mortals causes at most minor discomfort to my people."

"This isn't about the cold. People don't walk around the city streets stark naked unless they happen to be toddlers."

"We don't generally have the same taboos mortals have," Annarion replied.

"We *didn't*," Teela corrected him. "While resident within the city of Elantra, we adopt them."

"Why?"

"Mortal drool is unattractive?" Kaylin offered. "Yes, that was meant to be humorous," she added, because he looked uncertain, and uncertainty seemed so wrong on a Barrani face.

He took the shirt. He grimaced, but that made sense: it was wet, and it was probably cold. It was only barely long enough that it covered the relevant body parts.

"Where are we going?" he asked.

"I'm considering jail," Teela replied, in a tone that was only half-joking.

Annarion wasn't offended. "So...that would be Tain's?"

Kaylin laughed; Annarion grinned. He'd probably said it out loud because he thought it might be amusing to the two mortals who would otherwise be left out of the conversation.

Annarion sobered first. "You don't mean to take us back to my brother."

Kaylin shook her head. "He forbid it."

"He can't forbid—"

"You? He can, but you can probably ignore him. I can't ignore him as easily."

"You could if you were willing to learn how," Teela said. "It can't be worse than lighting a candle."

"That took me *months*."

"And your point is? Even in the span of a mortal life, a few months is not an onerous, life-consuming period. It took you longer than that to become competent at using daggers. It took you longer than that to memorize most of the Law. This is important; it's probably more important than competent use of knives. You should be more concerned with privacy."

Since Teela had insisted on having keys to Kaylin's apartment—when she'd actually had an apartment of her own—Kaylin thought this was ironic. Especially given how frequently she'd used said keys without giving any warning.

Annarion held up a hand.

"Yes?" Kaylin and Teela said, in unison.

"My brother?"

Teela said nothing. Kaylin, however, said, "I don't know what you did while you were arguing. Your brother's not certain, either. He's now attempting to exert his will upon a Castle that can think—and speak—for itself. He feels that your presence will make it significantly more difficult. And more dangerous. For him."

That is not what I said.

"That cannot be what he said," Annarion replied.

Kaylin wanted to laugh. "No, that's not the *way* he said it. But that's what he meant. He can't explain what you did, or why you had the effect you had—but it's destabilizing enough that he's going to have to work to bring things back under his control. And given the Castle is now awake, that control won't be what it once was."

Annarion looked torn. Teela grabbed his elbow. In Elantran, she said, "You can't just charge in and expect things will work the way you want them to work. While I have no personal objections to your punching your brother in the jaw, wait until he's outside of his fief next time." When Annarion tried to pull free of her tightening grip, she added, "You can't help him tonight. The closest you can come is by leaving the fief, and that's what we're doing."

Squawk.

Annarion looked up, exhaled, and shrank about three inches as the small dragon, who had appeared out of almost nowhere, flew circles around his head.

"You're worried." Severn accompanied Kaylin to the Palace; Teela took Annarion to Tain's.

She nodded. "Mandoran and Annarion are going to be way more of a problem than Teela thought." In fairness, while Kaylin had thought they'd cause trouble, she'd expected it would be trouble they *intended* to cause. "They seem to think they're Barrani."

"And you don't?"

"I did. I assumed that they were friendlier and more ready to laugh because they were young. The young don't come to this city. As far as I can tell, they live on their family estates in the middle of nowhere until someone decides they've got a hope of surviving outside of them. All the children chosen for the *regalia* in Teela's time were considered too young to be fully adult. So the differences made sense.

"But now? No. Evanton thinks they're a danger. The Castle thinks they're a danger. The *Arkon* thinks they're a danger, and he's never met any of them except Teela, who as far as I can tell doesn't count. She didn't spend most of her life in a space that didn't have physical laws and didn't require, oh, bodies. I hope Tain survives them," she added.

"Tain didn't seem to find them threatening. Annoying, yes. Irritating, yes. But not dangerous."

"I'm not sure they'll be a danger to him. Unless he really loses his temper." She then exhaled.

"More on your mind?"

"I know this is going to sound petty—but I want my own place. I'm going to walk through Imperial Guard checkpoints looking like a drowned cat. If I'm lucky, I won't have to explain *why* I decided to throw myself, fully clothed, into the Ablayne." She then gave a quick—and increasingly frustrated—rundown of the events of their very first apartment viewing.

"The Emperor doesn't want Bellusdeo to move out."

"No. And if I'm moving out and I can't tell her she can't come with me, my chances of finding even a *room* I can call my own are approaching zero. I know it's a problem that many, many people would be overjoyed to have. I'm trying to be reasonable, here. But—I hate living in a space I can never just relax in. I can't be myself in the Palace—there are too many people to offend. I feel like I'm offensive just by breathing."

Severn slid an arm around her shoulder, and she leaned into his chest. She was cold; wet clothing in the dead of night had that effect. "On the other hand," she said, lifting her head as they slowly approached the courtyard gates, "I think Bellusdeo has finally stopped shouting."

If Palace Guards caused stress just by existing, roommates sometimes had the same effect. Kaylin navigated the door ward she hated so much, and entered the room with numb left arm. Bellusdeo was curled up in the largest chair, waiting. Her hair was down and she wore, of all things, a bathrobe. She looked about as far from courtly as a rich, powerful Dragon could.

Her eyes, however, were a shade of orange. Kaylin didn't expect that shade to change much while they called the Palace home. Unless she swapped orange for red.

"Are you wet?"

Since there was no way to deny it, Kaylin nodded.

Dragon eyes narrowed.

"I had a little accident. It's fine."

"A little accident."

Kaylin nodded.

"So—nothing like the reason you were soaking wet this afternoon."

"Technically, it was yesterday afternoon." The small dragon squawked. A lot.

Bellusdeo's eyes did not shade into a friendlier color.

"How was your discussion with the Emperor?"

"I'd rather not talk about it."

Which was fine; Kaylin wasn't entirely certain she wanted to hear about it, either. Angry Dragons, other than Bellusdeo, weren't supposed to *be* her problem. She headed into the bedroom and began to peel clothing off her skin. A bathrobe hung in the closet that was really its own small room; Kaylin grabbed it, angry at herself. Yes, she'd had a crappy evening. Yes, some of that had something to do with Bellusdeo—but it wasn't Bellusdeo's fault, and truthfully, an obstructionist Emperor couldn't hold a candle to ancient, murderous Barrani ancestors and a Castle that seemed to be cut from their cloth.

She left the bedroom and headed back into the room that contained Bellusdeo.

"We can find a place," she said. "It's obviously going to be harder, but—we'll find something."

One golden brow rose. "Do you understand what the long sleep is?" she asked. It wasn't the question Kaylin had been expecting.

She'd heard the phrase before—but only from the Dragons. She had assumed that it was pretty much what it sounded like. Bellusdeo's tone killed that assumption. "No."

"Mortals don't sleep that way," Bellusdeo replied. "They wouldn't last five days; the dehydration would kill them. What *do* you know?"

"Good question. I know—I think I know—that the long sleep is a choice."

Bellusdeo snorted. With smoke.

"You don't think it's much of a choice."

"If you're offered the choice between painful, messy death and, oh, anything else, how much of a choice can that anything else be?"

Having made similar choices in the past, Kaylin found a seat. It happened to be on the table nearest the big chair, but given the furniture at her old home, this wasn't a stretch of etiquette. She reached out and caught one of Bellusdeo's hands in both of hers. "I don't want you to think about the long sleep," she said.

Bellusdeo stared at the place where their hands joined. "You don't even understand what it is."

"Then tell me. What I know is that you won't be here, anymore."

"If I'm not here, you'll be able to find a place of your own. You won't be subject to these odious, unfriendly guards and the whims of this equally odious Dragon Court."

Kaylin lifted her bathrobe and pulled up her sleeve. She was wearing the bracer; Severn had returned it on the way home. "I'm subject to the whim of the Court. The difference is that the Emperor doesn't care if I live or die. He'd probably be happier with the 'die' part. He's more subtle because—"

"Yes?"

"Well, actually, I don't really know. I'm assuming it's because of the not caring whether or not I 'die' part."

"I don't have that luxury."

"It's not generally considered a luxury," Kaylin reminded her, "...but I'm beginning to appreciate how it could be. Back to the sleep thing."

"It means more or less what it implies. If the sleep is a choice that is forced, there are places in which we might...rest. These places are protected; while we sleep we are at our most vulnerable in almost all ways."

"You don't get visitors in your sleep, clearly."

She laughed. It wasn't a happy sound. "No. No visitors. Perhaps there are dreams. Those who have woken from their long sleep have not said that the sleep is troubled by nightmare or vision; if it is, they don't recall it."

"You've spoken to Dragons who have awakened?"

Her gaze slid off Kaylin's face, to land somewhere around the fireplace. "Yes. In my youth. I was not, myself, considered fully adult; I had not yet unlocked my second form. I did not understand the desire to sleep—there was so much I wanted to see and do, the idea of great weariness was foreign."

"And it's not, now."

The Dragon's shoulders slumped. "I understand," she said, looking down at her hand, which was still held tightly in both of Kaylin's. "I understand why I'm important. I understand what the stakes are. I understand what my role is—and must—be."

Kaylin said nothing.

"Diarmat despises me," Bellusdeo continued, when Kaylin failed to add words of her own. "I can even understand why. But I—" She stood. "If there was *some* freedom, *some* sense that who I am, and not the physical reality of *what,* made a difference—" She closed her eyes. Opened them. Looked, for a moment, like a drowning girl. Kaylin had never been that girl.

But she'd been a girl figuratively drowning in different waters, and if the causes weren't the same, the sensation was. She tightened her grip. "You want him—you want them— to see you as you are."

Bellusdeo nodded, looking slightly embarrassed. "They see what I am: female. Dragon. They know that I am the effective Mother of the Race, if the race is to survive. But I could be anyone else as long as I possessed those characteristics. I could be any other person. I could have all the charm and wit of Diarmat. I could be a psychotic killer—is that the right word?—and all would be ignored. Not accepted, exactly, but ignored. For the greater good."

"The Arkon sees you as you are."

The smile which was almost a perfect expression of humiliation, shifted, softening. "Yes and no. He sees me as I *was,* but at least that's part of who I now am. And I'm being unfair. I think he marks the changes, but he hasn't seen them all."

"How much have you shown him?" Kaylin asked.

Bellusdeo didn't answer. After an awkward pause, she said, "So why did you enter the Palace sloshing wet?"

Because this was neutral ground, Kaylin answered. Given the color of the Dragon's eyes, she figured nothing she could say was going to make things any worse.

★ ★ ★

"Well," the Dragon said, when Kaylin was done—which, given the usual interruptions, took longer than it should— "your Teela was right."

"First of all, she's not *my* Teela, and second, about what?"

"You are never going to be boring. You might even make boredom seem appealing." She glanced down at their joined hands, squeezed briefly, and then gently extricated her fingers. "Even if I chose to sleep rather than serve, I'm not sure it would be allowed. And I *understand* why, Kaylin. If you're fomenting rage against the Emperor, don't bother; you can't come close to the rage I feel whenever he opens his mouth."

"What did he decide?"

"He decided that perhaps my complaints had some small value."

"Which means he'll interfere less?"

Bellusdeo snorted more smoke.

"It means Caitlin won't be vetting apartments before you view them. Emmerian will. You won't be humiliated by the Dragon Court because unless the accommodations meet with Imperial preapproval, you won't be speaking with any landlords." She swallowed. "If I choose to remain in the Palace, you will of course not be subject to this procedure."

Silence.

Kaylin could, at this moment, say two things and mean them both. The first: she didn't want a roommate. She was, and had been, happy living on her own. Yes, she had lived in a small space, and yes, it was a mess. The mess didn't bother Kaylin, but it annoyed the Dragon.

But the second: that she couldn't just walk away and leave Bellusdeo here. Kaylin didn't have a lot of friends, and because she didn't, she clung to them ferociously. Bellusdeo had none.

None, if you didn't include Kaylin, and Kaylin wasn't certain that she wasn't assuming too much; desperation wasn't exactly friendship. If Bellusdeo had been Queen in Elantra the way she'd been Queen on the world that she'd lost, she probably wouldn't have had the time of day for Kaylin. And to be fair, Kaylin would have avoided her like the plague; she had too much money, she had too much power.

But all her money was secondhand, and all her power was theoretical.

"I'm not leaving the Palace without you," Kaylin told her, and meant it. "And I'm not living here one minute longer than I have to."

The Dragon's smile was wan. "I don't understand you."

Kaylin shrugged. "Welcome to the club. Most days I don't understand myself—but I don't let it stop me."

"Maybe you should."

"Maybe. Not starting now, in case you were wondering."

Bellusdeo closed her eyes. "I feel so pathetic." She spoke in Elantran, which made sense—Kaylin wasn't certain there was a word for *pathetic* in Barrani that didn't mean mortal.

"Me, too—on the same 'most days' I don't understand myself. Go to sleep. Tomorrow will be better." She turned toward the bedroom and then turned back. "After my shift, I'm taking Annarion to visit Tara in Tiamaris, if you want to come."

CHAPTER 11

Mandoran did not appear in the Halls of Law the following morning. Neither did Annarion. Tain had taken a temporary—paid; Kaylin checked—leave of absence, which couldn't possibly be a coincidence. Teela did show up on time. For a member of a race which didn't consider sleep a necessity, she looked a lot like she could use some.

Then again, Bellusdeo looked about the same.

The Dragon wore simple clothing—for Court. The Barrani wore her uniform. They gave each other the heavy once over; it was Bellusdeo who broke first. "I hear you had an interesting evening."

Teela glanced at Kaylin, who shrugged. "*Interesting* is the most politic choice of word for it, yes. I hear you had a less eventful evening. But not less enraging."

"Rage is useful. It's often overrated, but it's useful." She smiled; it was edged.

Teela returned the smile, sharpness for sharpness. Kaylin decided that today was a day for good behavior, just to be on the safe side.

★ ★ ★

There was an absence of safe sides on the trip to Elani, because Teela joined them. This was not the usual arrangement of patrol beat; the Barrani Hawks tended to be given the rougher sections of town. The better sections bored them more.

"Why are you coming with us?"

"Because Tain is on leave, and Bellusdeo is with you. Apparently the Imperial Court has decided she's safer with me here."

"I don't believe you," Kaylin replied, voice flat.

Teela met her gaze and held it, before finally cracking a smile. "You win. I'm sure I could have sold you on it before the assassination attempt."

Kaylin shrugged; it was true. "Why *are* you tagging along?"

"I need to speak with Evanton."

Evanton was at home. Which is to say, the shop was actually open to the public. For someone who had a storefront, Evanton kept inexact, verging on inhospitable hours; for the most part he was closed to custom.

He seemed to be expecting theirs, today. Grethan answered the door. The best thing about the introduction of an apprentice was that he could answer the door quickly. Evanton creaked his way toward the sound of the bell at a speed that made snails look fast—if he decided to answer the door at all. If you made the mistake of ringing the bell while he was already on the way, he got angry. Kaylin had learned this early.

On the other hand, if he'd actually failed to *hear* the door when she was expected, and she failed to ring the bell a second time, he *also* got angry. It was very much lose-lose, with hope wedged in to add anxiety.

Since Grethan had appeared as apprentice, the stress of

standing on the outside of this particular closed door had lifted. He smiled hesitantly as he opened the door.

"Is he in a bad mood?" Kaylin asked, voice low.

"Not so far." His tone added, *please don't change that,* although he was too politic to put it into words. She could hear Evanton's voice as she stepped across the threshold. If he wasn't in a bad mood, he didn't sound like he was in a particularly *good* one.

"Is that Kaylin?" he shouted.

"Yes, Evanton. Kaylin, Bellusdeo, Corporal Handred and Teela."

The sound of something hitting the floor a room away wasn't entirely unusual—but it did mean Evanton had decided to hurry. He appeared in the door on the other side of the long bar in his customary apron; his hair looked like it had been exposed, when wet, to a lot of wind.

He offered Bellusdeo a bow. It was an almost perfect bow, something Kaylin could only appreciate after sessions with Diarmat, one of which was due to start in two days. The best thing about the West March had been the utter lack of Lord Diarmat. On the other hand, Diarmat was an oblique and unstated death threat; many, many things in the West March had been less diplomatic.

Bellusdeo offered him a perfect bow in response. Teela folded her arms and waited. Whatever respect Bellusdeo felt for Evanton—all of it genuine—was lost on the Barrani Hawk. Probably because she had vastly more experience with the curmudgeonly Keeper, who had never offered a similar respect to Teela.

"My apologies for the mess you find us in."

Since it was more or less the exact same mess it always was— which the cobwebs with their inches of gathered dust attested to—Kaylin's jaw momentarily unhinged.

He caught it, of course. "I'm willing to bet that you live in far more of a mess than I do, Private."

"You'd lose if you made that bet now."

He raised a brow, which changed the fall of lines across the better part of his face. "A poor choice of phrase on my part, but a fortuitous reminder of why I hoped to see you. You are, apparently, looking for a new domicile."

She frowned.

"A new place to live."

Ugh. "I haven't recovered from the last landlord interview."

"No?"

"We had a Dragon Lord as escort. Emmerian. He was almost actively insulting."

"Unfortunate—for the landlord."

"To be fair, Lord Emmerian is the least in-your-face Dragon I've ever had tag along."

At that, he smiled. It was slender.

"You know Emmerian." It wasn't a question. Kaylin's eyes narrowed.

"I have some acquaintance with him, yes. He shops here. And no, don't ask for what. I have *some* pride as a merchant."

"You work on Elani," she countered, with all the inherent criticism of long experience.

"The venue does not make the man. You are distracting me, and if you are going to do that, drink some of the deplorable tea I've made." He turned, turned back, and to Kaylin's annoyance, offered Bellusdeo his arm.

Since Bellusdeo hadn't been raised in Imperial Courts, this gesture might not mean much. But she *was* a student in Diarmat's despised class; she took the offered arm without even a whiff of hesitation or confusion. If it weren't for the rest of Bellusdeo's life, Kaylin would have envied the ease with which the Dragon fit into it.

★ ★ ★

"I hear you had some difficulty last evening," Evanton said, as Kaylin took the rickety chair she considered hers. She felt Teela's sudden glare as she reached for a cup—a full cup—of cooling tea. Since she had sensation in her mouth, she vastly preferred tea that didn't scald her tongue.

"I didn't tell him," she said, reaching for a cookie, as well. "I haven't had the chance." To Evanton, she added, "Is there some kind of supernatural flyer that the rest of the world sees that bypasses the Halls of Law?"

"Of course. You wouldn't read it; it would look too much like paperwork to your untrained eye."

"Very funny." The best thing she could say about Nightshade at the moment was that she'd gone there on her personal time and wouldn't be required to file an official report. "What did you hear?"

Teela cleared her throat. Loudly. This implied that she was sitting far enough away that stomping on Kaylin's foot under the table would cost too much dignity. Kaylin ignored this. She trusted Evanton. She didn't trust his *mood,* which could be changeable and unpredictable, but she trusted what he would do with said mood.

"That there has been an inexplicable change in the configuration of what was previously known as Castle Nightshade."

"I'm not sure the change will remain in force."

"Ah." Evanton cleared his throat and helped himself to a cookie. If he didn't care for tea—except when drenched and chilly—he did like the cookies. "The changes were not made by the fieflord."

Kaylin stopped eating. Notably, Severn did not. Then again, Evanton rarely grilled Severn. "No."

"Does he remain fieflord?"

"That's the question, isn't it?"

"I assume you have more ready access to answers. He will not, however, hear the answers you choose to share—not while you are here." He glanced at her cheek.

"He's still fieflord, for now."

"Good."

"Good?" She didn't ask whether or not he knew Nightshade.

"If he is not a man of whom you would otherwise approve— and he is not, I am not a fool—his reign has been stable. He is not Barren."

Kaylin stilled; she always did, when Barren was mentioned. But she didn't freeze, and the pause in conversation went unremarked upon. "No."

"An'Teela," Evanton continued. "You had something you wished to say?"

"To ask."

"Ah. From the cast of your expression, I'm going to guess you don't want to ask it of me."

"No. I want to speak with the elemental water in the Garden."

Kaylin inhaled crumbs, which made her cough. "I'm not going in there with you," she said. "I'm done with being a drenched, soaking sponge for at least a day." Frowning, she turned to Evanton. "The water told you."

His smile was indulgent. "Very good. Grethan. *Grethan!*"

Since Grethan had started moving practically the minute the first syllable of his name had left the old man's lips, Kaylin thought the shouting could have waited. Grethan appeared instantly in the narrow door frame.

"Take Teela to the Garden."

He froze.

"Is there something on my face, boy?"

"N-no."

"Good. She wishes to speak with the elemental water, and I have a few words to say to Kaylin and Lord Bellusdeo. I am willing to allow this, and you are perfectly capable of entering the Garden on your own. Teela doesn't," he added, "have all day."

Kaylin glanced at Teela, who shrugged in response. Her eyes, on the other hand, were the shade of blue-green that implied casual suspicion. She joined Grethan, who lead her away.

"How bad was it?" the Keeper asked, after the space of five minutes had passed. He was, of course, staring straight at Kaylin.

"Severn was there," she replied, throwing Severn under the carriage.

"Corporal?"

"It was, as you suspect, difficult. The water did carry us to the exit." Severn liked tea that was both bitter and hot. Evanton hadn't poured a cup for him, so he did this for himself as he spoke.

"Yes. The water, however, was not entirely pleased to be carrying one member of your party. Elemental water is *not* a person, but inasmuch as it can, it trusts Kaylin. Or it trusts Kaylin's intent. You asked?"

Kaylin hesitated. "Yes."

"This is another of Teela's lost friends?"

Severn nodded. Kaylin wouldn't have; she would have asked him why he bothered to ask a question to which he already knew the answer. "Teela sees both Mandoran and Annarion as young Barrani men. I believe they see themselves as Teela sees them."

"You understand that she is not entirely objective, in this?"

"Yes. But Evanton, I see Kaylin the same way."

White brows rose. So, for that matter, did dark ones.

"Do not glare at him like that," Evanton told her, although Kaylin wasn't exactly glaring. "He is illustrating a point, and he is doing it with characteristic grace. You are Chosen. What this means—to you, to the world—is imprecise. You are not what you were when you lived as a child in Nightshade. But you are also not what you were seven years ago, when you first darkened my doorstep.

"You are not, in my opinion, what you were a year ago. The essence of mortality implies constant change. The Barrani are not mortal, but they are distant kin—although I advise you to keep that to yourself. Be that as it may, the marks of the Chosen have changed you. They've changed what you believe you can—or can't do. They have altered what you have to offer the world." He nodded to Severn. "Your Corporal does not bear these obvious, distinguishing marks; he cannot make use of their power; he cannot shoulder the burden that comes with it.

"But he, too, has changed, and he has different things to offer." He turned his attention to Severn once again. "You believe that the two are similar, in some way, to Kaylin?"

Kaylin's eyes rounded so quickly they almost fell out of her head.

"They're nothing like Kaylin," was Severn's quick reply. "But...I think there's some similarity in their circumstances. They don't yet know what they are, so they cling to the comfort of what they were."

"Private," Evanton said, to Kaylin, although he was in theory watching Severn, "One of these days your face is going to get stuck like that."

"I wouldn't have called the 'what I was' part particularly comforting."

"That is because you have chosen to deliberately misconstrue the Corporal. Where you were is not all that you were;

where you are now is not all that you are. Ah, and I have allowed myself to be sidetracked. I don't have time to waste," he added, the implication clearly being that Kaylin did. "So I will come to the point. You are at the moment living at the Palace, but you wish to live elsewhere."

"Desperately. The longer I'm there, the less I care where that 'else' is."

"I will not quibble. Most of the residents of Elani street would be thrilled beyond words to live in the Palace; it would generate a fair amount of business." He had an elfin grin that he used rarely; clearly the idea of Margot in the Palace amused him.

It put Kaylin off her feed. Unless, she thought, the Palace did have dungeons.

"By a strange coincidence, an old friend of mine is looking to let a place in the city."

It hadn't actually occurred to Kaylin that the curmudgeonly old man *had* any friends who were still alive. It was a novel thought. "Who?"

"Pardon?"

"Who is this friend?"

He looked down the length of his nose. "I will pretend you didn't attempt to pry into my personal life."

"Evanton—"

He lifted both brows.

"If I'm going to rent a place, I'm going to have to meet with them anyway. They're someone you trust?"

"They are someone I would not like to offend, which is why I'm ambivalent about even making the suggestion. But in my experience, there are very few coincidences. They are looking for a tenant. You are looking for a home."

She wilted.

"You aren't?"

Bellusdeo, who had been as silent as the small dragon throughout most of this conversation, cleared her throat. She, like Evanton, abstained from tea; unlike Evanton, she ignored the cookies, as well. "She is. But she is saddled with a Dragon for a roommate, and at that, a Dragon the Emperor feels possessive about."

"Protective," Severn said quietly.

"There's no practical difference." She brushed invisible crumbs off her sleeve. "Because he does, our first viewing was an unmitigated disaster. It has been decided that we will avoid all future similar disasters by viewing only apartments that meet with the approval of Lord Emmerian. If he believes the quarters are—or can be made—suitably secure, we will be invited to inspect them." She lifted her chin. "We would therefore be wasting the time of the friend you do not wish to offend."

To Kaylin's surprise, Evanton chuckled. He really *did* like Bellusdeo. "Let me give you the address."

"And the name?"

"The name will not mean anything to either of you. The address will at least mean something to someone who's spent the better part of her life patrolling city streets."

"We need a name to mirror—" Kaylin began.

"If, by some small miracle, your mirror can make a connection, she won't answer. She hates mirrors, at least as a form of communication. If you wish to arrange an appointment, you will have to visit in person."

"How much is she asking?" Kaylin asked.

Bellusdeo simultaneously said, "How large is the space?"

"The answer to both of those questions," the Keeper said, rising, "is variable. If she is willing to let the place to you, she will not ask for more than you can reasonably afford."

"The Emperor has offered to pay the lease," Bellusdeo informed him.

"I believe Kaylin is about to turn purple," Evanton replied, his grin deepening.

"I don't see why he shouldn't," the Dragon said, although she carefully avoided meeting Kaylin's narrowed eyes. "Given that most of the difficulties caused are caused by his *ridiculous* demands, it should be considered compensation."

"I will not argue with you," Evanton said. "Nor will I disagree. Neither agreement nor disagreement will change Kaylin's opinion. If she is to live somewhere, she can't feel at home if she isn't responsible for her own upkeep."

"That is a luxury I do not have at the moment." Bellusdeo stood, as well. "But you are, of course, observant. If you believe that this is a space in which we could both feel at home, we will take the address."

"Oh, I'm not claiming that you're certain—either of you—to feel at home. Home is a very personal concept, and I'm not in the business of giving personal advice. If I were," he added, his voice sharpening, "I would have a few choice words to say to your Emperor. I believe Teela is just finishing up in the Garden, and she'll be with you shortly."

Kaylin was dying of curiosity. Bellusdeo, however, was not. The word *Emperor* set the Dragon's teeth on edge—even when she was the one who used it. When they found themselves on the street side of Evanton's door, she exhaled a couple of regal inches of height. "I like him," she said. She sounded pensive.

"You could probably visit him. He doesn't get much company except poor Grethan, and I think he'd be happy for yours."

"And not yours?"

Kaylin winced. "He met me when I was an angry, thirteen-year-old girl. He didn't throw me out of his shop—probably because I was with Teela. He certainly didn't bow when we were introduced."

"But he makes you tea and he bakes you...cookies?"

"He bakes those for himself and pretends he's doing me a favor," Kaylin countered. She began to walk, in the deliberate, slow stride the Hawks used on patrol. Bellusdeo fell in beside her. "Teela?"

The Barrani Hawk was quiet. It wasn't a murderous silence—Kaylin was familiar enough with those she wouldn't have uttered Teela's name if it had been—but it was a softer sort of grim.

"Yes, I spoke with the water. No, I'm not about to tell you everything that was said. It's complicated and—with luck— completely irrelevant to your current situation."

"You know what my luck's like."

"I do. I'm hoping, however, that it won't rub off on me any more than it already has. What did Evanton want to say to you?"

Kaylin considered withholding the information, since that's what Teela was doing. She decided it was unforgivably petty, as opposed to the usual kind of petty they both indulged in. "He gave us a possible lead for an apartment."

Because Teela was ancient and had the benefit of experience, she didn't miss a step. It was, judging by the shift in her expression, a close thing. "Where?"

"Somewhere on Ashwood."

She frowned. "Ashwood is a tiny street in the East."

"You know where it is?"

"Yes. You wouldn't be terribly familiar with the street; it's not heavily trafficked in *any* way. I doubt we have reports that even mention its existence, in the Halls. It's not as close to the Halls as your previous home."

"Is it much farther than the Imperial Palace?"

"Not much farther, no. Where, exactly, on Ashwood did he say it was?"

"It's number, umm—"

"Three," Bellusdeo supplied.

Teela's frown deepened. "Three." She shook herself. "When are you going to look at this place?"

The Dragon and the private exchanged a glance. "About that," Kaylin finally said.

"About that, what?"

"We have to *go* to the place to make an appointment to see it."

"What, this place doesn't even have mirror access? How old *is* it?"

"Well, the owner is a friend of Evanton's, if that's any clue."

Teela pursed her lips. "You're going tonight?"

"We're going to drop in to make an appointment to see it—but we won't really have time to do more. We'll probably try to inspect it tomorrow."

"Why won't you have time?"

"I was hoping…" At the moment, she kind of hoped a large hole would open up in the middle of Elani to swallow her. Given that she was in front of Margot's, it would kill two birds with one stone.

"I am not sure I'm constitutionally capable of listening to your explanation without a large inflow of alcohol. Unfortunately, you're working. What, exactly, are you planning?"

"I was going to ask Annarion if he wanted to…well… never mind."

"No, please, continue. Given the success of Annarion's last outing, this might be the one instance in which a suggestion of yours, no matter how outrageous, might not be an unmitigated disaster." Teela was in a mood.

"I was hoping to take Annarion and Mandoran to meet Tara."

She half expected Teela to shriek. In public. Her brows certainly rose; her lips thinned. She even opened her mouth— but the words that fell out were not the ones Kaylin expected. "Have you consulted Tiamaris about this?"

"...No."

"Given what happened at Nightshade, taking them to Tara without prior consultation is like suicide, only more painful."

Kaylin shook her head. "Tara's awake. She's in full control of herself and the land she inhabits. Whatever Annarion did, he did it with the Castle's subconscious permission. Tara's not sleeping. I don't think either Mandoran or Annarion can cause trouble there."

Teela snorted.

"Well, not accidental trouble, at any rate. I don't think Annarion would try."

"You're forgetting one important fact."

"What?"

"Tiamaris," Bellusdeo said, before Teela could, "is a Dragon."

"Well, yes, but— Oh. Right."

"I have noticed that Mandoran is not particularly fond of my people," Bellusdeo continued.

"He's not," Teela agreed. "But Mandoran didn't attempt to assassinate you. We live with Dragons. We are, in theory, ruled by them. But we fought a few wars between my friends' departure and their return. They'll get used to it—and if they agree to visit Tara, they won't antagonize Tiamaris."

"I've noticed you have an odd custom in the Hawks," Bellusdeo told them both; it sounded like a change of subject. It wasn't. "Betting?"

"Kaylin's fault."

"I would like to make a bet."

"No thanks," Teela replied. "I wouldn't, sadly, touch that one."

Kaylin, however, asked, "How much?"

Annarion, it turned out, didn't want to visit Tara. Mandoran had recovered enough from his visit to Evanton's that he was game.

Teela agreed, grudgingly, to argue *for* the visit—in person.

"Why don't you just argue now?"

Teela grimaced. "Annarion, Mandoran, and the rest of my cohort have lived with the constant flow of each other's thoughts for almost as long as I've been alive. They're accustomed to merging all thought and all experience; they sometimes forget whose experience it actually is, or was." She exhaled for a long moment. "I lived with them for years, but our shared experiences—for me—ended at the Heart of the Green.

"I mourned. You cannot imagine how much—or perhaps," she added, voicing softening, "you can. But I could either destroy my life or *live* it. I learned to live it. I learned what other High Lords learn. I do not trust easily or often, and if I trust intent—which is rare—I seldom trust competence."

Kaylin had personal experience with this. About seven years' worth.

"I have allowed no one into my life the way I allowed my cohort into it. I learned to guard and hide my thoughts; I learned to control my emotional responses. Again, these are all traits the High Lords learn; if they fail, they fall. I therefore have a different set of choices when dealing with my friends: to join, or to stand back." Her smile was slight. "I would not have said that I would choose the latter, if I were ever to find them again. I've changed. They've changed in a different way.

"It's...awkward."

"So...this request in person is a way of preserving your privacy?"

Teela nodded. "You can speak with Nightshade any time you want. How often do you choose to do so?"

Almost, but not quite, never. "It's different."

"How?"

"I had no idea what he was giving me, and I've never trusted him. I lived in the fief he ruled for most of my life. I know what he's capable of. I know what's beneath his notice—and that would be almost every *other* person in the fief. When you made the choice, you offered your name to people you both loved and trusted. It's safer for me to argue with Nightshade in person than it is to argue...that way."

"You place an inordinate weight on the love and the trust given by children—which is what we were."

So do you, Kaylin thought. She didn't say it out loud, and Teela couldn't hear *her.*

"I'm only barely willing to go to Tiamaris. I've listened with some interest when you speak of your Tara, and I'm willing—barely—to let curiosity override common sense. Annarion is against it. If he has the same effect on Tara as he did on the Castle, he'll be facing an enraged Dragon and the possibility of a breach in the Shadow defenses. If he understood what he'd done to cause Castle Nightshade to react so strongly, he'd be willing to take the same risk I am. He is," she added, "one of three of my cohort who generally prefers common sense.

"Given his concerns and their validity, I hope to make clear that Tara is a personal friend—of yours. She is fully awake, she is bluntly honest, and she is likely to be able to explicitly explain what he did to rouse Castle Nightshade. If he knows, he can take conscious control of the action, which means he *might* be able to visit his brother without immediately being a threat to his brother's existence."

Severn brushed hair out of his eyes. "Have either of you considered the possibility that Tara will instantly recognize the two as a threat and will refuse to allow them entry?"

Kaylin hadn't.

Teela, however, nodded. "I think your idea is solid. I admit that it would not have occurred to me." She waited for Kaylin to pick up her jaw, which had fallen open and was hanging there. "Why are you looking so pensive?"

"I just—I remember the first time I entered the Tower. I remember what I saw there. It was every single thing I had ever done wrong. Not small wrong, but big, self-defining wrong. It made me relive the horror of my own life, and my own bad choices."

"You're rethinking your suggestion."

Kaylin shook her head. "She wasn't trying to force me to live with my guilt. She was trying to show me that she understood the worst of my pain. And, you know, she *did*. She understood it completely. She knew every single thing I hated myself for. But she wasn't trying to make me suffer *more*. I don't think she really understood the way time works for mortals. I think of her as childlike. The best parts of childhood. The curiosity and the openness and the joy.

"But...that's not all she is, and that's not all she knows. I think she'd like Mandoran and Annarion."

"Why, exactly, do you think that?"

Kaylin frowned. "They grew up in a Hallionne. They could go where they wanted, moving between the Hallionne and the green. They understand sentient buildings in a way I'm certain *I* never will. And I think they'll understand Tara in a way that even Tiamaris can't."

"You think she's lonely?"

"Not anymore, no. But—there's something about someone who's shared your experiences. I love the Hawks. I love all of you, even Joey's mother."

"Who is not a Hawk."

"I probably know more about Joey's mother than I know about my own."

"Fair point."

"I'm aware that we've built seven years of history, working together. I hated Barren. I hated my life in the fiefs. I would kill before I went back to it. Or die. But...I feel close to Morse *because* of that life. Because she understands it in a way that—"

"That I don't?"

"Yes. To be fair, you probably don't understand my happy life, either."

"I am content with that particular ignorance—beyond a desire to see that life continue. You are not boring, remember?"

"Neither are Mandoran or Annarion, and I don't see you dancing a jig about them."

CHAPTER 12

Bellusdeo was not, technically, given permission to accompany Kaylin to the fief of Tiamaris. Kaylin, aware of whose neck was actually on the line, mirrored the Imperial Palace Library. She got a face full of orange-eyed, annoyed Royal Librarian for her trouble.

"Is this an emergency?" the Arkon demanded, tufts of smoke leaving the corners of his mouth.

"Yes?"

"You sound doubtful."

Bellusdeo stepped into the mirror's view. Her eyes had tinted toward bronze, but she never went full-on red in the Arkon's presence. "Lannagaros."

"Bellusdeo," he replied—in an entirely different tone of voice. Even his eyes brightened to gold. "My apologies."

"Apologies to me are never necessary, Lannagaros—but I find you a touch hard on Kaylin."

"Private Neya is like a particularly bright kitten," was his unselfconscious reply. "I find it best to set hard boundaries, and police them ferociously; she is perfectly capable of demanding inordinate amounts of my time, otherwise."

Dragons.

Kaylin cleared her throat. "I'm about to head down to Tiamaris. We want to speak with Tara. Bellusdeo hasn't seen Maggaron for a few weeks."

The Arkon frowned. "When you say 'we', Private, do you refer to yourself and Bellusdeo exclusively?"

The Dragon and the private exchanged a glance.

"I will assume that is a no." More smoke escaped the corners of his mouth. He would have looked like a sage out of a story if he'd actually bothered holding a pipe. "You are taking Teela's friends?"

This time, Kaylin kept her eyes firmly on the mirror; she felt Bellusdeo's gaze smack the side of her face. "If they'll agree, yes. They're having a bit of a problem adjusting to the new world paradigm."

He surprised her. He chuckled. It was dry enough to light paper. "I imagine they are. I would appreciate the opportunity to meet and speak with them, in future."

Kaylin thought it would be far easier to get them to visit a Tower in the fiefs, even one owned by a Dragon, than it would to get them to visit the Palace, since the Dragon in the Palace ruled the Empire. She didn't have to say this.

"I would not, of course, invite them here." Which would have been a relief, but he was the Arkon. "I hear that you visited the Keeper today."

Bellusdeo's smile froze, although it still remained on her face. Somehow. "Lannagaros—"

"I consider him a wise choice of acquaintance. I meant no criticism. The Emperor was concerned about the outcome of your last visit, but as you did not emerge on a second visit in full armor, he is somewhat mollified. Was the visit interesting in any way?"

Bellusdeo's eyes narrowed. "You are not, I hope, interfering?"

"I would interfere in a heartbeat if you but asked," was his formal reply.

Her smile unfroze. It was pensive. "Did I ever ask for help in the Aerie?"

"Not when you actually needed it, no. A request for aid was always a sign of trouble to come."

At that, Bellusdeo did smile; it made her look much younger. "You were always so stiff and proper," she said, with obvious fondness.

"It has not, generally, worked to my detriment."

"No, I don't imagine it has. It rarely worked to mine, either. Yes, we had a peaceful visit with the Keeper. He reminds me a little of you, you know. Don't make that face."

"He's mortal."

"He's the Keeper. Mortality is his weakness, but it has not yet killed him. I don't believe he'll allow it to kill him, either, until he's fully trained his replacement."

"And the private mirrored me to ask if you might accompany her to Tiamaris, did she?"

"The private," Kaylin pointed out, "is right here. You could ask me."

"Or you could fail to be offended, and answer."

Kaylin snorted, without the smoke. The small dragon, however, batted her cheek with his head. "Yes, that's why I interrupted you. Bellusdeo would like to accompany us."

"You consider it safe?"

"I'm not convinced that what I consider safe is the deciding factor here, but yes, I consider it safe."

"There is something you are not telling me."

"You usually don't like it when I—as you put it—chatter endlessly."

A white brow rose. His eyes, however, remained the gold they'd become in conversing with Bellusdeo. "Very well. I will inform Lord Emmerian. He may choose to join you."

Bellusdeo said nothing.

"In different circumstances, you would like Emmerian. Of all the young Dragons, he is the least likely, in my opinion, to find his hoard. He is easily contented."

This didn't mean much to Kaylin; it clearly meant something to Bellusdeo. "He is not," she conceded, "Diarmat."

"No. There is only one Diarmat. We are lucky to have him," the Arkon added, as if trying to be fair, "but he requires tolerance."

"Spoken like a man who doesn't have to take his infernal etiquette lessons."

"Indeed. He is very hierarchical, and I am above him in that hierarchy. In different circumstances, Bellusdeo, you would be, as well."

"I am unwilling to leave Kaylin to suffer his odiousness alone."

"And Kaylin," Kaylin added, "appreciates her presence immensely. We have a lesson tomorrow night."

"Do not remind me. Very well, Lannagaros. Inform Emmerian if you must. We will be heading almost directly from the Halls to the fief."

Kaylin took the time to mirror Tara to tell her that she was arriving with an unspecified number of guests.

"You don't usually mirror before you arrive."

"I don't usually know exactly when I'm arriving," Kaylin replied, hesitant. "But—you always know before I get there."

"Yes. I know when you cross the Ablayne. Who are your guests?"

"Bellusdeo."

"I will inform Maggaron."

The Dragon thanked her.

"...and Lord Teela of the Barrani High Court. She's a Hawk. Tiamaris knows her."

Tara's face, in the mirror's surface, went blank for a moment as she consulted with the Tower's Lord. "He is surprised."

"Yes, well."

"He is suspicious."

Bellusdeo chuckled. "And not without reason. I'm not sure if you've heard, but Teela has visiting...relatives...staying in the City."

Tara frowned. It wasn't an angry or even disapproving frown; she frowned when something confused her. "Teela," she finally said, "has many relatives staying in the City."

"Yes, but these two are new to Elantra."

"And she wishes to bring them here?" Her face went momentarily blank again, and it remained that way for much longer. When it cleared, Tiamaris was standing in the mirror's frame beside his Avatar. His eyes were a lovely, lambent gold, and he smiled when he saw Bellusdeo. His smile dimmed when he turned his attention on Kaylin. She felt very underappreciated.

Without preamble, he said, "There was some trouble along the Nightshade border last night."

"...Trouble."

"Yes."

"What kind of trouble?"

"There was a small, localized shadow storm. Some of the buildings on my side of the border were damaged; the border zone itself is, at the moment, untraverseable." His eyes narrowed. "Given your expression, I assume this is not a complete surprise to you."

"Oh, it's a surprise," Kaylin replied, shrinking a few inches. "There was some difficulty in Castle Nightshade last night."

"Was it resolved?"

"He still holds the Castle."

"And now, coincidentally, you have decided not only to visit my fief, but to bring at least one guest who would not, in my opinion, willingly visit had she many other options. And she is bringing strangers with her. They are Barrani?"

Kaylin chose the safe reply. "More or less."

It was only safe when used on someone other than a Dragon.

"She means to say: they were, once," Bellusdeo said, stepping in to rescue her from the growing orange of Tiamaris's eyes. "They believe themselves to be Barrani now."

"Were these friends guests at Castle Nightshade last night?"

"One of them was, yes."

"Absolutely not."

Tara, however, placed an arm on Tiamaris's sleeve. He glanced down at her—her Avatar form was shorter than his mortal form—and snorted. There'd been a lot of visible smoke in this series of conversations. He fell silent as Tara turned toward Kaylin, her expression troubled.

"Lord Nightshade is not known for the risks he takes with his castle."

Kaylin nodded. "The visitor was his brother. His younger brother. He—" she hadn't intended to tell Tara what happened. She'd hoped Annarion would, and that Tara might understand, without prejudice, what no one else could. Given Tiamaris, that wasn't going to be an option. "You know that Castle Nightshade was sleeping. I mean—you're awake. Castle Nightshade wasn't."

Tara nodded slowly.

"Nightshade and his brother got into a bit of an argument."

"Did the younger brother attempt to kill the Lord of the Castle?"

Kaylin shook her head emphatically. "He—the younger brother—is upset and disappointed in Nightshade and what Nightshade's become. They haven't seen each other for, oh, centuries."

"But he did not attempt to harm Lord Nightshade?"

"No."

"The Castle reacted to the presence of the younger brother." It wasn't really a question, but Kaylin nodded.

"The younger brother—his name's Annarion, by the way—somehow spoke *to* the Castle. He's not sure how. No one is. But the Castle...woke."

"Annarion woke the Castle?"

"I think it's more accurate to say the Castle woke itself. And...it's not really a Castle, anymore."

To Tara, for whom architecture was fluid, this wouldn't necessarily mean much. Tiamaris's eyes, however, widened. "And you want to bring this Annarion *here?*"

"Because Tara's *already* awake. I met the Avatar of Nightshade. Awake, he's...nothing at all like Tara. I'd be happy if I never saw him again, anywhere, for any reason. Tara's already awake. Annarion can't accidentally wake her, and if he *does* somehow speak to her in a way that he can't speak to the rest of us, she'll know exactly what he's doing. She may be able to tell him how *not* to speak with Castle Nightshade in future. He's very attached to his brother," she added. "Knowing that he's thrown the entire fief—and the Tower—into a state of chaos is probably killing him."

Tiamaris said, "I dislike this intensely."

But Tara's grip tightened briefly.

"You wish to do this?"

The Tower's Avatar nodded. "Kaylin wouldn't bring people whom she knew to be a threat."

"Kaylin is blessed by a profound optimism, one that frequently stems from equally profound ignorance." He exhaled. "If Tara considers the risk worthwhile, I will allow it. But I do so with reservations."

If Annarion and Mandoran were no longer Barrani in the strict sense of the word, they were considered Barrani by the average person bustling from one place to the next, where most of those average were mortals, and most of those mortals were human. Given that it was after-work hours, Kaylin's tabard was in the mess of her locker; she wore her normal clothing.

So did Teela. Bellusdeo brought the average up; if her clothing was simple, it was simple for Court. Most of the people who passed her by didn't recognize her for the Dragon she was; she was simply a tall, attractive woman. There may have been flirting.

The bridge across the Ablayne to Tiamaris was not heavily traveled in the evening. A pair of guards stood on the far side—that was new. They had apparently been informed that guests were expected. They weren't Swords; they radiated nervousness when they stopped the party to ask their business, eyeing the three Barrani. Since it was nervousness due to perfectly reasonable fear, Teela chose not to take offense.

Neither did Annarion or Mandoran.

"I will never understand how you can live in such a crowded, noisy place," the latter said, when they were well out of the guards' earshot. "And the smell!"

"You get used to it."

"I don't see how." The Barrani clearly didn't bet as a pastime, because if they had, Mandoran would have been laying money on the figurative table, given his expression. Since the streets of Tiamaris weren't as crowded or noisy, he subsided, although his outrage at the crowds and the smell were more entertaining than the slightly sulky boredom that surfaced in their place.

Since Mandoran could whine in the privacy of his thoughts, Kaylin assumed this was passive-aggressive criticism on his part. Given the tenor of rants in the office, it was mild; she didn't particularly feel offended on behalf of Elantra. She did feel offended on behalf of mortals, but that was pretty much business as usual when dealing with Barrani.

Mandoran opened his mouth—again—and Teela glared. Annarion chuckled. His smile froze as he caught sight of the Tower of the fief of Tiamaris.

It was a white tower; something reflective at the heights caught light and scattered it across the rooftops of the much shorter buildings surrounding it. Kaylin wasn't a student of architecture; she knew what she liked. What she liked mostly consisted of a roof that wasn't leaking and walls that were more or less straight. Doors that actually opened and closed without getting stuck in their frames were good, too.

But she liked this tower. She liked the Lord who ruled it, and through it, the fief that bore his name. Barren, which is what the fief had been called before Tiamaris's arrival, had been her home for six months. Jail would have been both safer and less soul-destroying. But if Tiamaris had been fieflord when she had arrived here, she would probably never have left. She might *be* one of the guards at the foot of the bridge.

Or one of the guards who patrolled the streets when the sun set. With luck—and plans to visit a residence on the sleepy street of Ashwood—they'd clear the fief before then. The evening streets were patrolled for a reason: Ferals hunted in them. Even with guards and a Dragon captaining their various squads, people still got unlucky.

A lot fewer of them, though.

"That is your Tara?" Mandoran asked, poking Kaylin in the ribs. "Don't frown like that—this is the third time I've asked."

"The frown comes with the face," she told him. It deepened. Mandoran was not looking up. He was looking ahead. Ahead into what were, to Kaylin's eye, empty streets. The streets were under construction—or at least two of the buildings were. She started to answer and fell silent as two people turned a corner and headed toward them.

She recognized them instantly. One was the Tower's Lord, and one, the Tower's Avatar.

Tiamaris was in full Dragon armor. Kaylin had seen him like this only a handful of times. She glanced at Bellusdeo, whose eyes had both narrowed and shaded to a copper-bronze as she caught sight of the Dragon Lord. Given the arrival of three Barrani—who were not by any stretch of the definition "frequent" visitors, she could almost understand why: he was trying to make a statement without stooping to inevitable threats or warnings.

As statements went, given the darkening eyes of all three of the Barrani, it was effective. It wasn't Tiamaris's natural armor that made Kaylin so uneasy, though. It was Tara's dress.

Tara generally wore gardening aprons, and as she did the actual gardening, they were usually smudged with both fingerprints and dirt, especially around the knees. Today, all signs of the woman who insisted on growing *food* on her front and back lawns so that she might contribute something useful to the citizens of the fief were gone.

She wore a dress that would be at home in the Barrani High Halls. It was, as the Tower itself, ivory in color, and if it wasn't made of stone, it looked about as friendly. The reflective material of the dress was gold thread, gold embroidery and beads of some sort. Two months ago, Tara was still getting the hang of the significance of nonmartial wear; she understood the use of armor in all its forms, but couldn't quite grasp that dresses such as this one *were* the equivalent of armor in a more subtle battlefield. Even Kaylin had not been that naive.

The small dragon sat up on her shoulder and squawked.

Tiamaris stopped. He lifted a brow, and before Kaylin could clamp a hand over small and squawky's big mouth, he replied. The large Dragon's reply, on the other hand, shook the streets. If they'd been empty as a natural consequence of the time of day before, they'd be empty for other reasons now.

The only person—for a value of person that really needed work—who was not put off was the small dragon. He flapped wings once or twice—hitting Kaylin's nose without apparent malice—and replied.

Mandoran said, out of the corner of his mouth, "Can you get him to *stop?* We're going to be deaf before we reach our destination at this rate."

The Dragon ensconced in the middle of the visiting party snorted, a reminder that apparently Mandoran needed. "If this will deafen you, your ears are fragile."

"Pardon us for being created with vocal chords designed for actual speech," Mandoran shot back.

"I consider it a design flaw; it is not, however, your fault," was Bellusdeo's equally friendly reply. Kaylin wanted to kick herself for even thinking that putting Bellusdeo and Mandoran in the same fief was somehow a good idea.

Clearly, she wasn't the only one. Teela lifted a hand to pinch the bridge of her nose. Mandoran fell silent.

The small dragon squawked and squawked and squawked. It sounded like he was delivering a lecture. Given Tiamaris's approaching expression, he probably was.

Tara, however, laughed.

Teela looked at her, her eyes narrowing. Annarion and Mandoran, however, were almost gaping. Kaylin cut the distance between the Tower's Avatar and herself by jogging ahead. Tara opened her arms and caught the Hawk in a hug.

"I'm very glad you mirrored," she said, in perfect Elantran.

"So you could prepare a welcoming party?" She glanced pointedly at the armored Dragon who was still staring at the Barrani as if they were a very tiny war band.

"Yes," Tara replied, missing the gallows humor in the question entirely, which Kaylin found comforting. "Are you going to introduce me?" she asked without apparent guile. She held out a hand and very gently scratched the underside of a small, squawky chin; Kaylin's constant companion not only allowed this, but seemed to somehow feel it was his due.

"This is...Hope," Kaylin said, her voice dropping into the whisper range on the last word. Only Tara could fail to find the name maudlin or inappropriate.

"An interesting name. When did you choose it?"

"When I was in the West March. It's a long story, but semirelevant—that's where I first met Annarion and Mandoran. I'm stuffing this up; I'm terrible at formal introductions. Let me start again from the top. You know Bellusdeo."

"Of course."

Arm still locked around the Avatar's, Kaylin turned to face the rest of her friends. "I don't think you've met Teela?"

"You are correct. I've heard a lot about her, though."

Teela, being Barrani, had Barrani hearing. She shot Kaylin The Look.

"She has not said anything bad," Tara then told Teela directly. "She looks up to you."

Annarion and Mandoran raised brows at each other; Mandoran grimaced. "That is not generally a terribly good idea," he told Kaylin. "She can be a bit headstrong, and she likes to show off. If she knows she can impress you, she'll—" He stopped speaking abruptly. Teela had not noticeably stepped on his foot.

Kaylin resumed introductions in a rush to stave off any further embarrassment. "This is Teela. She's a Lord of the High Court, but we don't call her Lord Teela at the office."

"But she calls you Lord Kaylin at the office."

"Yes—but only to embarrass me."

Tara now looked confused, and Kaylin wanted to kick herself all over. "Being a Lord of the Barrani High Court is not generally considered embarrassing. Is it?" she asked this of Teela.

Teela's lips twitched. "For those who are mortal, it demonstrably is."

Annarion and Mandoran, on the other hand, wore expressions of full-on, dumbfounded outrage.

"It's not embarrassing," Kaylin told them both. "But—I don't deal well with the stuck-up rich. The Hawklord—my boss—won't send me out on any investigations that require, as he calls it, diplomacy. So—being *called* Lord Kaylin in the office...makes me look like a hypocrite. Which is why Teela does it. Most of the other Barrani don't."

"None of the other Barrani Hawks are Lords of the High Court," Mandoran said. The statement tailed up a little at the end, as if it were a question.

"Not that I know of. But I didn't know Teela was, either, for at least the first six years. She didn't exactly demand to be called Lord—and none of the Barrani Hawks do it."

"The Hawks, if Tain is indicative of their general demeanor, are slightly unusual," Mandoran said. He turned, then, and offered Tara a perfect, elegant bow; it looked almost like a dance move, not that Kaylin had seen many dances. "None of them are Towers. I am Mandoran," he added. "Of—"

"The Line of Casarre."

Kaylin held her breath; she expected Mandoran to be slightly put-out or defensive. He wasn't. His smile was brilliant and open. "Yes. You know of my family line?"

Tara nodded. "It is old enough that I am familiar with it. It was a prominent Barrani family in my distant youth." She turned to Annarion. "Your family was no less prominent; it was more unusual."

Annarion was not Mandoran. If such a thing as unfettered joy existed in his life, he was far too careful to visibly expose it. He didn't seem suspicious of Tara, on the other hand; his caution was almost entirely due to the Dragon who ruled the fief. Bellusdeo caused Annarion far less annoyance than she did Mandoran.

Tara now offered Bellusdeo an obeisance that was as perfect as Mandoran's to her, if a little stiffer. "Should I tell Maggaron that you've come to visit?"

Bellusdeo considered this for all of five seconds. "Yes. It is possible that you will have much to discuss with your new guests, and they might find my presence stifling."

"Oh, they're not too worried about you," Tara replied. "It's Tiamaris that's unsettling them." As she spoke, she smiled. The smile was an unusual one on her face; it had a bit of an edge. "If it makes you feel at all comfortable, my Lord was not notably *happy* that you chose to visit. He is at his most cautious, now. You understand that the fief is his hoard?"

Mandoran nodded. Annarion said nothing. Teela, however, snorted. "We absolutely understand that, but even if we did not, we are aware of the import of the Towers; we understand their function. Not even as a Lord of the High Court could I openly interfere with that function without censure. We mean neither disrespect nor harm."

Tara nodded. "I believe that without reservation. You are

Kaylin's *kyuthe*." She had slipped into High Barrani. "But your companions are not."

"We understand why Teela is fond of her," Mandoran offered.

"Even were you to be as fond of her," Tara replied, "you are not what Lord Teela is."

Both young men stiffened.

"And you, Mandoran, must learn how to be silent. Beyond my interior borders, the Shadows are waking at the sound of your voice."

That fact, Kaylin thought, in the silence that followed Tara's genial advice, would pretty much explain the armor and the color of Tiamaris's eyes; it pushed Bellusdeo's and Teela's further into their orange and blue range as the information settled and took root.

Tara said, to Bellusdeo, "He is not, of course, attempting to communicate with the Shadow deliberately; I was concerned when he first crossed my border. He believes he is exactly as he appears."

"And you believe him to be what?" Teela all but demanded. Mandoran had lost about four inches of height, and the easy good humor had shriveled. His eyes, quite dark blue, looked bruised, and he cast his glance toward the stones beneath his boots as if they were anchored.

"Mandoran," Tara replied. She turned to Tiamaris. "I believe we will be much safer if we are in the actual Tower; I can only partially limit the range his voice carries while I am in the streets."

"Very well." Tiamaris shot Kaylin a glare—which might be deserved, given Tara's observation, but still felt entirely unfair—before he turned to lead the way to the Tower of the fief he had claimed as his personal-reason-to-continue-existing.

By the time they had arrived, Tara had shed her exquisite gown for a familiar apron. Annarion walked to her left, Mandoran to her right, and if they were conversing in a private, silent way, the conversation Kaylin *could* hear was on Tara's favorite subject: farming.

To her surprise, it was a subject to which both men took readily and completely, and entry into the Tower took about forty-five minutes longer than it should have, given the rest of them were practically standing at the front door. Tara lead Annarion and Mandoran into carrots and onions and potatoes, and then from there into things that grew on trees.

Only when they were entirely out of immortal earshot did Tiamaris turn to Teela, who had also remained behind. "What are they, An'Teela?"

"They are children," she replied, weighing her words with enough care that she spoke slowly, "who were exposed too early to the *regalia* of my kin."

"A true tale?"

She nodded. "You have some familiarity with the power of those tales. I believe the Arkon is capable of speaking some small part of the tongue of the ancients."

Tiamaris grimaced. "He is—but not even the most curious of his acquaintances asked to hear it more than once."

"Oh?"

"It exhausted him. The Arkon, when exhausted, is a particular and special type of foul. Enduring it is not worth the satisfaction of what is, after all, idle curiosity."

Bellusdeo chuckled. "At least that hasn't changed."

"You find it amusing?"

"I do. Lannagaros never visited his foul temper on me or mine."

"An advantage to being female I had not considered," Tiamaris replied.

Kaylin frowned. Bellusdeo, seeing her expression, laughed out loud. "Remember, Kaylin, that the Dragons as adults have dual forms. The females of the species are born into an almost mortal frailty; the males are not. What could kill me, as a child in the Aerie, could not kill Tiamaris as a child in a similar Aerie. Our laws are therefore quite strict. This does," she added, laughter fading into a smile that still clung to her lips, "mean that his mood when exhausted must have been as foul as Tiamaris says—otherwise, we would have actually *seen* some of it."

"I am unaccustomed to having my word doubted."

She raised a brow; her eyes had shifted to an almost natural gold. "How dangerous are they?"

He didn't even blink at this sudden shift in conversation. His eyes had remained orange, but Bellusdeo's levity hadn't annoyed them into a darker shade. "If Kaylin had not mirrored ahead, Tara would have done everything within her power to close the borders when they crossed the bridge.

"Everything within her power," he added softly, "would cause notable destruction in parts of the rest of the fief. What she observed, when she met them—and you—in person must have mollified her somewhat."

"Meaning she knows what Kaylin knows."

"Exactly that. Kaylin is not Tha'alani, but for the purposes of Tara, she might as well be. It doesn't occur to Kaylin that she *can* hide anything, so she doesn't even try. Tara now understands as much as Kaylin does about the events that occurred in Nightshade. But those of us who border Nightshade felt something, regardless."

"I would guess," Teela said, glancing at Kaylin, "that Tara now understands far more than Kaylin does."

Tiamaris nodded. "Kaylin has no experience being a Tower."

"Whatever happened last night, Annarion didn't intend. I'd bet my life on it," Kaylin said quickly. She didn't particularly care for the color of his eyes.

"You may have already done that. I would not, however, be willing to bet my fief on it."

"Yet you chose to do so, in the end," Teela said.

"Tara is certain that she can contain the difficulty, or I would not have taken the risk." His eyes narrowed. "You did not think that Tara would be in danger?"

Kaylin's brow creased. "I would never have brought them here if I thought that was even a possibility."

"And if your experience was commensurate with your certainty, I would find this a comfort." He exhaled a small stream of smoke. "I am not pleased." He didn't turn her to ash, which was not technically illegal in the fiefs. Instead he offered Teela a nod. "My apologies. My concern has compromised my hospitality, and it is seldom indeed that we have Barrani as guests."

At her silence, he offered her an uncharacteristic fief shrug. In Elantran he said, "I'm happy you dropped by."

This surprised a laugh out of Teela. Given the color of her eyes, Kaylin would have bet against her sense of humor.

"Tara is ready to join us. Is there any other warning you care to offer?"

"They are kin to me. The last time they walked among us, the Dragons had just embarked upon their war."

"The first war?"

Teela shook her head. "The second."

"I assume they have been informed of the events that unfolded in their absence?"

"Yes. I invite you to imagine your reaction should you voyage from the city and return to find the Barrani High Lord ensconced in the Imperial Palace as Emperor."

"Understood."

"Mandoran finds it particularly difficult; his family lost much to the wars. He did not resent the loss until now. Now, all the sacrifices and all the deaths amount to nothing. Less than nothing; a Dragon is now the undisputed ruler of these lands."

"If it helps, we number so few because the Flights would not consent to being ruled by a single Dragon."

"It won't help him. As for me? I lived through the history that is hearsay to them; I understand where we currently are. I have no advice to offer. I admit that my curiosity is not idle." She hesitated and then added, "I am aware of the honor you do us."

"I doubt very much your companions consider it an honor."

"Not yet," was her calm reply. "But they will. If they survive."

"I am callous. It is not their survival that now concerns me."

CHAPTER 13

Annarion and Mandoran looked both bemused and far more relaxed as they came round the Tower, following its Avatar. Tara herself looked far less intimidating. It was easy to forget how terrifying and intrusive she could be when she talked about growing food.

Or maybe it was just in Kaylin's nature to forget.

The doors of the Tower rolled open in silence.

"I ask you not to touch anything unusual without asking first," Tara told them. "There are protections within the Tower; they are so much a part of what I am I am not always consciously in control of them."

"What are they meant to defend against?" Annarion asked.

"Corruption."

"Corruption of what?"

Tara frowned. She spoke the word in at least three languages that Kaylin understood, and probably a dozen that she didn't. When Annarion failed to look enlightened, she turned to Kaylin. "Am I using the wrong word?"

"It's probably too general."

The frown deepened. "Would 'bad transformation' be better?"

"That's slightly more exact—but the Tower transforms pretty much at your will. Maybe: changes that I don't institute or control."

"Not all change is bad," Tara said, without much conviction.

"No. Some change, as we've both seen, is necessary and good—if painful to start." She turned to Annarion, who was following the conversation as if it were difficult higher mathematics, his brow creased. Mandoran paid attention without the obvious signs of struggle. Whatever they heard, it wasn't what Kaylin was hearing.

"No," Tara agreed, as she entered the large hall that hunkered behind apparently modest doors. "You hear the sounds that I make, and you call it speech. But your friends hear the things that cannot be resolved into simple words."

"Then why don't they understand it better?"

Tara tilted her head. "What makes you think they don't?"

Towers.

Teela stepped forward. "I do not hear what they hear."

"No. You are like Kaylin or Tiamaris. Words are…like a very narrow alley. I have a very wide carriage; it is the width of the alley exactly. Without careful and precise driving, I cannot get the carriage through the alley; it is a long alley, not a short one. Your languages are like that alley, but I am not trying to drive a carriage through it; I am trying to sail a ship."

"You can't sail a ship through an alley, Tara. No water, for one." Kaylin clasped her hands loosely behind her back.

"Exactly."

Towers had never been particularly good at constructing metaphors.

"No; it was never required. Only when speaking to those

who cannot see or hear all we attempt to show or tell them do we make use of metaphors at all." She frowned. "I do not consider you pathetic or inferior."

Since Kaylin was getting pretty damned tired of just that attitude—which she assumed was behind the words—she had the grace to redden.

"The Towers require Lords. To the Towers, there is very little difference between Barrani, Dragons, or you. You age and you die, it is true; I will miss you when you no longer come to visit us. But my Lord hears what you hear. Yes, even when I speak to him in the fashion Annarion and Mandoran employ between themselves, he hears as you hear."

If Tiamaris found this insulting—and it was clear that Bellusdeo was a bit put out—it wasn't obvious.

"He is not less important or less significant because he does not think like a Tower," Tara said quietly. "He is, to me, far more important because of that fact. If he cannot hear all I say immediately, he listens to what he *can* hear. So do you. The fact that I am not as you are does not make me less valuable or less important to you."

"It should make you far more valuable," Mandoran pointed out.

"Value, to Kaylin—and to my Lord—does not mean what it once meant to the war-bands of the Barrani or the Dragon flights; it does not mean, in the end, what it meant to my creators. They are not simply interested in the power invested in me; nor are they interested in how they might gather and use that power in their own interests. They attempt to understand what *I* want and how I feel. They know that I am bound to my duties. They understand that those duties cannot be simply abandoned at their whim.

"Nor have they ever asked it." She frowned. "You *know* the Hallionne are sentient; could you possibly imagine that that sentience is entirely without personality? You lived within the heart of one for most of your lives. Did you do so without actually seeing him?"

"One is not necessarily concerned with the personality of one's jailor," Annarion replied.

"Yet the Hallionne was concerned with the personality of his guests. And their safety. And you were his guests."

"Are you asking us," Mandoran asked, with obvious incredulity, "to love a *building?*"

Kaylin stiffened. Before she could open her mouth, Teela stepped on her foot. Kaylin chose to ignore this, which didn't always work out well unless one *wanted* bruises. "She's asking you to treat her with the same respect and consideration you'd treat any other person who was *doing you a favor.*"

"What, about our behavior, implies a lack of either respect or gratitude?" It was Annarion who asked. His confusion seemed sincere.

"You are talking about Tara as if she were a—a—"

"Building." Teela supplied the missing word.

"But she *is.*"

"That's not *all* she is. She is a *person*. She probably started life *as* a person. I think all the ancient buildings *did*. She is capable of loneliness, of regret, and of fear. She is capable of love and loyalty. Which of these things are required in a building?"

"I would guess none," Mandoran replied. "They're not always considered useful in people, either. Does the private always talk about you like this?" he asked Tara.

Tara smiled. "Not always. Sometimes she complains. Kaylin is very good at complaining."

"You can say that again," Teela told her.

"But...her complaints are often entertaining. And also, impossible."

"The solutions to her various complaints are often impractical, yes." Teela's eyes had lost the tint of midnight; they were a blue-green that was normal for Barrani. She looked around the spacious hall, toward the very wide doors facing them. Tiamaris, noticing her gaze, said, "Yes, I can fit through those doors in my Dragon form."

"Do you, as Kaylin calls it, go Dragon often?"

"Mostly in the evening; I fly above the street patrols. We have not completely recovered from the difficulty the former fieflord created, but it has been some time since we lost any of my citizens to the Shadows." As he spoke, the doors rolled open. "Welcome," he said, addressing the three Barrani—and the small dragon on Kaylin's shoulder, "to Tiamaris."

Maggaron was waiting for Bellusdeo. She almost ran down the hall to meet him.

The *Norannir* were almost eight feet in height as adults, and most of the fief's native buildings couldn't easily accommodate either Maggaron or his people. Construction work was therefore occurring along the border. This worked because no one else—even the truly desperate—wanted to live in a building that was literally across the street from the heart of the fiefs, or more accurately, the Shadows that lived within it. The deaths and losses that had occurred because of a breach in the Tower's defenses were far too new.

Maggaron, however, was a special case. He was Bellusdeo's Ascendant, which had once been more than a fancy word for bodyguard. The Imperial Palace *could* house him, but Bellusdeo had not chosen to bring him there.

Kaylin had asked her why half a dozen times before she'd chosen to answer.

"It will only upset him. This Palace is not my palace, and his role in it is nonexistent. I am no longer bound to him as a weapon; he is no longer bound to me as my wielder. I would like—if at all possible—for Maggaron to return to what remains of the *Norannir,* and build a life there."

"You were his life."

"I know."

"He was happy."

"He was happy because he knew what his role was. He was completely committed to it. But he wasn't trained to be a steward or a page or even one of those humorless, dreadful Imperial Guards. What he needs to do now is to find a place for himself and a cause that will require his commitment and dedication."

Kaylin understood Bellusdeo's desire, but privately felt the Dragon was being unfair to her former Ascendant.

"Kaylin, do not give me that look."

"What look?"

"The I-feel-sorry-for-the-puppy look. He is almost double your height; he could snap you in two without breaking a sweat. If he decided to pick you up and use you as weapon, he wouldn't even notice your weight."

"It's just that what he did *was* useful, and he was raised *to do it*. You can't expect him to just throw it away and find some other random thing to replace it."

"Oh?"

Kaylin often felt she should just shove her foot in her mouth and let it stay there; it was certainly better than letting some of the actual words she said leave it.

"I have nothing to offer him. I am not leading the *Norannir* against the Shadows. I am not responsible for protecting *this* world and the people it contains from extinction. Were I, I would not have the support I required when I did so in lands that no longer exist. I have no power, Kaylin. I have no authority."

"He doesn't need you to have those things."

"He doesn't need me to have them for the gratification of his own ego, no." She smiled. It was both fond and sad. "But he needs me to be respected. He needs me to be treated as if I matter. Yes, you can argue that I matter a great deal to the Emperor and the Dragon Court. But not in any way that would count for Maggaron. He will be upset, confused, and eventually enraged. I would spare him that. I would," she added with a grimace, "spare myself that; he is not easily dealt with when upset."

"He's not violent—"

"Of course not. But his mood is a great blanket of gloom that it takes work to alleviate." She grinned, clearly thinking of some of that past work. Kaylin winced on Maggaron's behalf, even if Bellusdeo didn't elaborate.

"If we find a place that's larger—"

"You mean, a place you can't afford unless you accept Imperial funds?"

Kaylin had fallen silent, then. She liked Maggaron. She wasn't certain she liked him enough to go begging at the new Exchequer's, but she probably wouldn't do that on her own behalf, either.

She watched Bellusdeo leave. When the Dragon was with her Ascendant, she looked younger and seemed happier. Kaylin had walked away from her old life; she never, ever wanted to go back. Having the life she'd built in Elantra torn away from her would probably kill her. Bellusdeo, on most days, didn't look dead. But on most days she didn't much look like she cared all that much for her life.

"She does," Tara said quietly.

Kaylin blinked. "Sorry. I was just thinking—"

"About Maggaron and Bellusdeo, yes. Maggaron is not

happy; he endures. It is harder for me to read Bellusdeo; she is cautious. She has asked me to refrain from speaking of what I do hear. I think, if I understand Maggaron correctly, that he would be happy to be her...butler?"

"I'm not sure that would work out well. The Palace has standards that don't make sense to most of the rest of us. I'm fairly certain that an eight foot tall giant wouldn't meet them. If Maggaron was unappreciated in the Palace, Bellusdeo would be angry. If Bellusdeo got angry I'd be incapable of hearing anything other than Dragon roaring for days afterward. If she ever stopped." Kaylin hesitated, thinking about the possible lead into a new apartment.

Tara froze. "Where is Ashwood?"

"I'm not completely certain. It's not a street I've encountered on any of my regular patrols—but Teela says that's because it's a quiet, small street that never causes any legal troubles."

Tara said, without pausing, "Records."

Given that they weren't in the room with the large pool that served as a mirror, and were not in fact in the presence of an actual mirror, this was surprising. Annarion and Mandoran stared, but for other reasons; Mandoran found mirrors and mirror technology fascinating. It seemed—to Mandoran— that the mirror networks were built on an assumption of trust that was foolishly unwise, at best.

Light that was a blend of red and white filled the space in front of Tara. It had dimensions; it was like a flat sheet of translucent cloth, woven of, and anchored by, unseen magic. Kaylin's arms itched, but only slightly. The small dragon sat up and tilted his head until it was at right angles to the rest of his neck.

He squawked.

Tara, however, was absorbed in the creation of this standing mirror. "It is not a mirror. It is what a modern mirror contains. I require concentration because it has none of the usual anchor points. Do you recognize the image?"

Kaylin nodded slowly. It was a map of the fief, with lines for streets and the occasional square, rectangle—or in the case of the Tower herself, circle—to mark significant buildings. "It's Tiamaris."

Tara nodded. "Beyond my own borders, I must rely on the information transmitted between my Lord and the court." As she spoke, the map shrunk in place, the lines of red-tinged white expanding and ending; it was like watching a crack in ice. "My Lord feels the information is reliable."

"You don't?"

"It is not exact, and it is not always current. I do not understand this."

"The city isn't like the Tower; there's no single sentience behind it. The Emperor doesn't rule it the way a Tower's Lord rules. If the Emperor wants complete information, he has to send out people who can gather it accurately and convey it to Records. He can't simply close his eyes and feel both the streets and whatever's walking *on* them. But these are good enough for the Halls of Law." She frowned. "These *are* the records we use."

"Yes."

"I mean—they're the exact same."

Tara looked confused. "Yes."

"I am not even going to ask how you have permission to access our Records, because I don't want to know."

"You don't?"

"She does," Tiamaris interjected. "But if she does know, and she is ever asked, she will surrender that information, to her regret. She is not wrong," he added.

"I do not understand your city," Tara replied. "I do not understand your Emperor."

"It is perhaps best that you do not." He smiled down at her with affectionate indulgence. The expression—on a Dragon's face—looked entirely wrong; it was almost embarrassing.

"Why?" Tara asked.

"Ashwood?" Kaylin replied. The very last thing she wanted to do was discuss the relationship between Tara and Tiamaris when Tiamaris was actually present. In response to the single word, a section of the city began to glow. A tiny section. Teela hadn't been joking; the street was small. It was tucked away in a small cul-de-sac behind homes that belonged to the rich and the powerful; she recognized three of the streets that bounded Ashwood. None led directly to it.

"That's it? That's the entire street?"

"Who gave you this address?" Tara asked. When she looked away from the standing map, her eyes were obsidian; she'd become so absorbed in her Tower thoughts she'd forgotten to maintain some part of the illusion that made her look more human.

"Evanton."

"The Keeper?" Brows rose in chiseled lines.

"Tara, what exactly is wrong with this street or this address?"

"Why did the Keeper give you this address?"

"He said an old friend was looking for a tenant. He knows I'm looking for a place to live, and he thought—"

"He did not."

Kaylin exhaled. "He did."

"Why can you not just remain in the Palace? It is almost as safe for you there as it would be were you to live here. And I," she added, "would be happy to house you."

Tiamaris coughed, which caused Tara to frown, although her eyes rounded, rather than narrowing.

"Oh," she said. "My Lord does not feel the Emperor would

be happy if I offered to house Bellusdeo. I am uncertain why this would be a difficulty."

"Tiamaris is a Dragon," Kaylin replied.

"Yes? So is Bellusdeo."

Reddening, Kaylin said, "Tiamaris is a *male* Dragon."

"So…you think the Emperor would be *jealous?*" The last word was almost incredulous.

Mandoran began to cough; if he'd been standing closer to Kaylin, she would have kicked him. Since she couldn't with any subtlety, she didn't—but it was close.

"Wouldn't you be?" Bellusdeo surprised Kaylin by asking. She had returned at the mention, no doubt, of her name; they were speaking quietly, but quiet human voices were no protection against Immortal hearing. "If I came to stay, if I lived within your walls, wouldn't you be jealous or worried?"

Tara shook her head. "I would not have offered when Illien was Lord. Then, I think I would have been afraid. Illien was looking for something, always, and I could not give it to him, no matter how hard I tried." She smiled at Tiamaris. "Tiamaris was looking for *me.* If you lived here, we would shelter you. We would defend you. We would keep you safe. But you are not, and could not be, me."

Bellusdeo was silent for a long moment; she then offered Tara a brief bow. "I believe you. The Emperor, however, is not looking for *me,* either. He would be, if not jealous, proprietary."

"But you are not his property."

Bellusdeo grimaced. So did Tiamaris. "No. Nor has he laid claim to me in that fashion. But Tiamaris is, of course, correct; it would not be appropriate for me to remain here. Kaylin, however—"

"Kaylin won't stay here if you can't," Tara told her. "She

doesn't want to abandon you. She thinks you are already lonely enough."

Bellusdeo looked both embarrassed and irritated. The irritation, she shared; if looks could kill, Kaylin would be a small, smoldering heap of ash. She said nothing for a long beat, and given the orange shade her eyes had adopted, no one else did, either. Tiamaris was carefully studying the map, as was Teela. Mandoran was staring at Kaylin as if he couldn't believe how incredibly stupid she'd been—and given Kaylin hadn't actually *said* any of this, she thought it unfair.

But life wasn't fair on most days, and she'd managed to survive it so far.

"What," Bellusdeo said, changing the subject pointedly, "concerns you about our destination?"

"You are *certain* that you are to go to Ashwood, and that this is the only Ashwood in your city?"

"I am reasonably certain," Bellusdeo replied.

"I'm completely certain," Teela said, at the same time. "And I now feel some qualms about it. I would be happy," she added, with emphasis on the two syllables that somehow implied the opposite, "to know what your concerns are."

Tara said, after a very long pause, "The house on Ashwood is as old as I am."

Mandoran was the first person to speak. He perked up. "That *does* sound interesting. Can we come along?"

He really did remind Kaylin of some of the foundlings: he could go from crushing depression to wild enthusiasm in the space of a word or a heartbeat. Kaylin had never been that emotionally flexible. She glared.

He smiled brightly, like a puppy. Exactly like a puppy. Given what had happened at Evanton's, Mandoran was about the last person she wanted to take with her. If the rooms were halfway decent, and they *somehow* met the strict demands of the bloody Dragon Court, Kaylin needed to make a *good* impression on the landlord.

She opened her mouth to say as much, but the puppy eyes defeated her. She couldn't kick him in the figurative face.

Tara, however, said, "I think that is a very bad idea."

Mandoran's brows rose.

"I wouldn't have let you cross the bridge if Kaylin hadn't asked it as a favor. I wouldn't happily let you wander the streets of the fief, now, although I am comfortable having you as a guest in the Tower itself. Because you *are* here, and because you are speaking with me in ways that Kaylin and Teela can't hear, I understand that you have no ill intent. But Mandoran—and Annarion—I could *hear* you from the bridge. And there are things that can hear you from farther away."

"You haven't explained *how* we're talking," Mandoran finally said.

Tara looked troubled. "I don't understand how you can't understand it," she finally said. "But I think...you are used to speaking with your friends in a very specific way."

It got a lot quieter.

"Your friends are used to hearing what you say or think. They see what you see and hear what you hear, even if they cannot otherwise see or hear it themselves. You, in turn, hear what they think of your experience; it becomes part of what you individually believe."

Mandoran snorted.

"Not all your responses are verbal. Many of them are conscious; none of them are what would normally be considered speech among the rest of your race." She turned to Teela. "The Lord of this Tower was, for centuries, a Barrani High Lord. He, like all of you, possessed a True Name. Unlike the three of you, his hatred of this weakness was so vast, he all but de-

stroyed himself in an attempt to be rid of it. He would not—
and did not—make the choices that you made. The existence
of the name itself was anathema to him; he would not have
shared it, even to preserve his life. You did. You did so willingly, and I believe it brought you joy."

"I was very much younger," Teela said, as if in her own
defense.

"Yes. It is not a choice you would willingly make now. But
that is not true of your kin. I will," she added, "call them kin,
unless you object."

Sarcasm drifted in and out of Teela's expression; she leashed
it because she was talking to Tara, who often took things literally. "I have no objection."

"You alone of the twelve were not part of this continu-
ous conversation. You did not adopt their habits; I do not
believe, given the differences in your living conditions, that
you could."

"I couldn't reach them—"

"We tried!" Annarion and Mandoran said, in one breath.
Kaylin had the suspicion that they were not the only ones who
did, but she couldn't hear the others.

"It is not an accusation. For whatever reasons, you did not
develop the same communication paradigm as your kin. You
hear them now as you would hear anyone whose name you
were given. For the most part, you converse as Barrani converse; with words, and in speech.

"The others were transformed by their early appropriation
of a language not meant for your kind. In the formative years,
they had no other ways of speaking, if I understand their situation correctly. They did not learn silence; they did not learn
to guard their thoughts. When they felt anger, confusion,
resentment—or love—it did not occur to them not to share it.

"I believe the Hallionne Alsanis heard their voices. They

were the only voices he might hear, given his self-imposed isolation. He understood what they had lost, and in some fashion,
I believe both Alsanis and the Heart of the Green attempted
to protect the core of what they had been before the *regalia*.
But what they protected existed outside of your friends for a
very long time. They were connected to it—but it was not all
that they were. It is not all that they are now." She turned to
Annarion. "Were you trapped within the Hallionne?"

"Yes. For centuries. Only toward the end of our imprison-
ment did we find ways of slipping outside."

"You are outside, now," was Tara's almost serene reply. "But
you do not yet fully understand what exists outside of the Hallionne. When you left the Hallionne, you did not walk the
roads that led you there in the first place. You entered spaces
that were not meant for your kind. Many of the Barrani have
come to these places—but they come from their own lands,
and return to them quickly. They cannot remain beyond without changing, and they cannot control the changes.

"You approached the other worlds from within one of them.
The paths that eventually led you to some small amount of
freedom were not paths that your Teela could walk without great effort and intense magical preparation. Even were
she to do so, she could not live on them; she would starve to
death, in time.

"This was not true for you. Not until now. You have come
home, but home is not the place you imagined it would be.
You are not familiar with your physical bodies; you are not
familiar with the limitations under which all of you exist."

"But—"

"Yes, Kaylin?"

"They're alive. They live *in* their bodies."

"They do, yes. They do now. But Kaylin, so does your familiar. It is not the only place he exists, and that is not the only shape he either knows or has."

The small dragon squawked.

"He believes you know this already," she told Kaylin. "And perhaps he is right. But knowing something and understanding it are not the same. You don't consider the small dragon a threat. Most of the Barrani consider it dangerous. Most of the Dragons have difficulty seeing danger in it; I believe the Arkon both knows and understands. But there is more, always, than danger or risk." She smiled brightly, which was at odds with the obsidian of her eyes. As Kaylin looked at her face, the eyes adjusted. Of course. Tara could hear every stray thought that escaped Kaylin's mind.

Annarion said, "Can you teach us to be quiet?"

"I don't know. I don't think I can teach you to be so quiet that a Tower can't hear your voice. I'm sorry," she added. "Until Lord Nightshade has completed his accommodations with his Tower, it is not safe for you to visit. Or rather, it is not safe for your brother. You cannot hurt the Tower. You can, however, demand its attention."

"Am I demanding yours?"

"Yes. But I am not uncomfortable paying attention to you."

"And if you were?"

"You would not be in the Tower." She exhaled. "Come with me. No," she added, as Kaylin moved to follow. "Not you. What we discuss will either bore or upset you." Teela, notably, had not moved an inch. Tara transferred her attention to the Barrani Hawk anyway. "I understand all the reasons why it is not comfortable for you to be here, but if Mandoran and Annarion intend to remain in the city, it is best that you either allow them to stay here, or bring them here frequently."

Tiamaris cleared his throat. Loudly.

Tara, however, merely tilted her head. "It is within the purview of my responsibilities," she told him firmly. "If they are not here, they cannot be in the fiefs at all. But I suspect that the city itself is not safe. They will not harm the citizens of the city," she added, as Kaylin opened her mouth to protest. "But the things that hear them will be drawn to their cries. They are like lost children."

Still.

"Not all those that are drawn to them will mean them harm, but harm is the outcome that is most likely to occur. The elemental water attempted to remove Mandoran."

"...Yes."

"Did she attempt to destroy him?"

"I don't know." It had certainly looked that way to Kaylin. "She didn't feel that Mandoran belonged in the Keeper's Garden."

"No. But neither do you or Lord Teela. Mandoran was as much a guest as any of the rest of you. His voice, however, and perhaps some part of him, exists in spaces which none of the rest of you can easily touch at will, if at all. No, not you," she added, as the small dragon elongated its neck, lifting its chin and glaring. "You understand the spaces you occupy and you are courteous when you enter them; nor do you enter without permission."

Since he hadn't exactly asked to be allowed through the doors, Kaylin thought this inaccurate.

"They must learn how to ask that permission; failing that, they must learn not to occupy or enter spaces that are forbidden them. Because they are unaware of the spaces they occupy outside of the world they now see, they invade spaces which were never meant for Barrani. Or mortals. I will teach them as much as I can, for your sake."

"The obligation," Annarion said, "would be ours, not Lord Kaylin's."

"Actually," she said, as she offered both men an arm, "it wouldn't. It's my chance to discharge an obligation of my own—to Lord Kaylin. My Lord says that obligation is fraught and onerous and should be discharged at the first available opportunity. You, however, may both feel obligated to Kaylin."

This left Teela, Bellusdeo, Tiamaris, and Kaylin standing in a large hall. Tiamaris relaxed, although this was only evident by the color of his eyes; he couldn't exactly remove the Dragon armor without causing a different kind of problem. "If half of what Tara suspects is accurate, I do not envy you," he told Teela.

"You probably never did; Dragons aren't notably given to envy."

"You are, of course, mistaken. What will you do?"

Kaylin found the question confusing. Teela didn't, but judging by her eye color, she didn't appreciate it.

"I will, with your permission, continue to visit your Tower."

"You have it; I don't think Tara would be content, otherwise. She likes to help." He glanced at Kaylin. "She is not the only one."

"No." Teela relaxed. "I understand why you like her. I can't, I admit, see why she serves you, but love has always been almost inexplicable when it involves other people."

It wasn't *exactly* an insult. To Kaylin's surprise, given the gravity of Teela's tone, Tiamaris's eyes shaded into gold. "I no better understand it than you," he replied. "But I am more than content, An'Teela."

"I envy you. Having acquired a long dreamed-of goal, I find it unexpectedly dire." But she smiled as she said it. "It is good to know that not all dreams are so fraught when they become reality."

"Oh, even these have been fraught. For one, there is far more to lose," he replied. His eyes were still gold.

With the apparent change in atmosphere, Maggaron felt it safe to approach them. At a distance, he looked like a young, earnest man. Up close, his size kind of swamped the sweetness of that expression. He wasn't wearing armor, and he wasn't carrying an obvious weapon—although at his size in this particular city, obvious weapons were probably overkill. Kaylin tried to imagine what it would be like to live in a city built for and populated by the *Norannir;* she failed.

He bowed to her, the bow temporarily bringing them to almost the same height. "Thank you," he said, as he rose, "for keeping Bellusdeo safe."

"It wasn't me," Kaylin replied. She had a natural aversion to compliments—and a raging aversion to either insults or condescension. "It was this guy." She indicated the small dragon, who elongated his neck to its full extension, which didn't bring it much closer to Maggaron's face.

Maggaron clearly had some difficulty accepting this at face value; the small dragon was the size of a bird—and when he spoke, and he did, he made pretty much the same noises. But Maggaron was well-mannered enough not to snort or disagree. Instead, he changed the subject. "Bellusdeo said you were going to inspect possible new living quarters."

Kaylin nodded.

"He wants to accompany us," the Dragon said, poking her Ascendant in the ribs.

Kaylin wasn't particularly looking forward to rooming with a giant. But his expression reminded her of a foundling's. She couldn't bring herself to say no. She *really* missed the days when she'd lived on her own. "No problem," she said.

Bellusdeo lifted a golden brow in obvious skepticism, but

Maggaron couldn't see it. "Are we actually taking Annarion and Mandoran with us?"

Given that Maggaron was coming, Kaylin thought the tone of her question unfair.

"Absolutely not," Teela replied, before Kaylin could. "Given Tara's reaction to the possible location, we'd be courting disaster."

"Given what's occurred so far when they're left to their own devices?" Bellusdeo replied.

Kaylin was still stuck on the use of the word *we*. At this point, she considered canceling the outing and sneaking to Ashwood on her own. Given Bellusdeo and Teela, she decided against it, but it was close. "Tiamaris?" she said, turning to the Dragon with the suspiciously golden eyes.

"Lord Kaylin?"

Bellusdeo snickered.

"Can I borrow a mirror that has access to the rest of the world?"

CHAPTER 14

"...And then, Teela invited *herself* along. I swear, we're going to outnumber the entire neighborhood at the end of this!"

Severn was, post work, toweling his hair dry while he listened to Kaylin rant. "So, let me get this straight," he said, draping the towel across his shoulders. "You're going to one of the posher districts, off-duty, with a Barrani, a *Norannir,* and a Dragon for company."

"With *three* Barrani."

"Put in a brief word with Jared." Jared was the Caitlin of the Swords. He was rounder than the Hawks' office den-mother, and about a foot taller; he had a voice like sandpaper, the disposition of a friendly version of the Arkon, and the patience of a saint. "If the Swords get complaints about your small group, he can handle them without sending Swords to investigate. Trust me."

"Let me add it to the list," Kaylin muttered. She hadn't quite finished, but had run out of steam. The small dragon squawked. "Oh, right. I forgot someone. This will probably be the only time he's not the subject of interest."

"And you're mirroring because you've decided you're outnumbered and you want company?"

Kaylin blinked. "I was mirroring," she replied, "to whine and complain where it won't hurt anyone else's feelings and won't make me look like I'm as cranky as I *am*. I don't suppose we could change places?"

Severn chuckled. "I don't think it's me Bellusdeo wants as a roommate."

"I think, at this point, anyone who *isn't* the Emperor will do."

"I'd take that bet if you were stupid enough to make it."

Kaylin fished around in her pockets for change. "We're waiting for Tara to finish with Annarion and Mandoran."

"Let me go get changed," Severn replied, cutting the connection.

Severn arrived at the Tower before Annarion and Mandoran arrived in the large, parlorlike room that everyone else now occupied. He was seen into that room by a frazzled Morse, who was no one's idea of a steward or butler, unless the point of either was to scare away any potential visitors. She nodded to Kaylin, but didn't ask for introductions; given Morse, she probably didn't want them.

"We've got a problem," she told Tiamaris, without preamble.

Tiamaris's eyes shaded to orange. He rose.

"It's not sundown, but the Ferals are gathered across the border. The old lady sent word. I went to check it out."

"And?"

"I've never seen a gathering of Ferals like this one. They must number two dozen—it's hard to count them; they're not exactly standing still."

"They aren't attacking each other?"

Morse shook her head. "Any idea what's going down?" Tiamaris glanced at Kaylin; it was a brief flick of eyes. Morse noticed anyway. "This have something to do with you?"

"No."

"Right." She didn't press the point because Tiamaris hadn't, and Tiamaris was the boss. "I'm calling all my reserve out," she told him. "The *Norannir* are out in full force along the border."

"I will join them. The Lady is with guests; I will ask her to truncate her visit."

"These guests have something to do with the shit going down?"

"Not intentionally."

Morse made clear what she thought of intentions. She looked as if she was going to make that clearer, but managed—to Kaylin's surprise—to bite back her words. "Are we leaving by the side hall?"

"Yes."

"Great."

Tiamaris headed out the doors of the suddenly silent guest room, but Morse turned back. "I hate flying," she told Kaylin, looking slightly greener. "I have no idea why you were so obsessed with it when you were a kid."

"I obviously came at a bad time," Severn said, to the quiet room.

"I'm surprised to see you here at all. I should have guessed," Teela replied. "You were feeling outnumbered, kitling?"

Since Kaylin hadn't actually *asked* Severn to come, this wasn't exactly fair. "Severn is calmer than any single one of us."

"Speak for yourself."

"—And I figured we'd need some calm, given none of the rest of us are contributing much of it."

The small dragon squawked at Severn; Severn nodded in his direction. He didn't take a seat, which turned out to be smart. The doors didn't so much fly open as disappear. Tara stood in the frame; her eyes were obsidian—but at this point, so was the rest of her skin. "I do not think it wise," she told Kaylin, "for either Annarion or Mandoran to travel with you tonight."

Kaylin had difficulty finding her voice. Black wings rose in arches to either side of Tara's face. "I have made some contingencies when they walk within Tiamaris. I will not be able to shield them while they move outside of it. Wherever else you allow them to wander," she added, speaking sharply to Teela, "do not allow them to traverse any other fief at all until they are better able to control their shouting." This would have been harsh no matter when it was said; given that the two were actually standing just behind her, Kaylin almost felt sorry for them.

But Tara didn't turn herself into battle gear just for Ferals. Something else was up.

"I will see you out," Tara told her. "And yes, you are correct. The Ferals are not the only things that are moving on the edge of my borders."

"Should we stay?"

The obsidian version of the gentle gardener blinked. "Unless you intend to remain behind *these* walls, no. It is best that you leave before the sun fully sets." Her voice softened. "It is an emergency, yes—but it is one we can handle. I am not certain that your presence in the current situation will aid us." She turned to Annarion and added, "Kaylin taught me that intent matters. I do not blame you for what has occurred. But I believe you are, however unintentionally, the cause of it—and deliberate or no, in emergencies of this nature, people die. My people."

She wasn't speaking of the Towers.

Nor did Annarion assume she was. He was ashen, for a Barrani; so was Mandoran. Kaylin had never seen either of the two look so uncertain.

"I do not think it wise that you have the two accompany you this evening."

"Would it be wiser to leave them on their own?"

Tara was silent for a beat. "I cannot say. But that is not, now, my problem." Her dark, stone lips moved in something that resembled a smile. "I am happy to have met you both. Accept my apologies for our poor hospitality."

Mandoran's jaw dropped. Annarion's didn't. But neither of them had the implacable neutrality of Teela.

"Come on," Kaylin said, moving toward the now doorless frame. "We're leaving." She paused in the door, and then impulsively hugged Tara—who felt as much like stone as she looked. Being hugged in return by stone wasn't entirely comfortable. Or it shouldn't have been.

No one spoke a word for four city blocks. Bellusdeo's cheerful expression had evaporated, and Maggaron was looking around for exit routes, in case they were necessary. Kaylin recognized the look, because it often haunted her own expression. She was generally good with other people's silences. Today, not so much.

"Did Tara tell either of you why she was concerned about the house on Ashwood?"

"Not directly," Mandoran replied. Of course it would be Mandoran. "Oh, don't give me that," he added, although no one had spoken out loud. "It's clear that Tara hears every word Kaylin's thinking. She answers the questions Kaylin's trying to be smart about keeping to herself—out loud, where anyone can hear them.

"She's concerned because the building itself is as old as she is. In mortal terms, it probably shouldn't be standing. Annarion pointed out that the Keeper's Garden is probably *older* than she is, and it's been here in one form or another all along."

"It has had other Keepers," Teela observed.

"Yes, but the Garden itself?"

Since he had a point, Kaylin nodded. "She thinks the home on Ashwood is like she is."

"Not exactly like she is, no." This was said in the wrong tone of voice.

"How did she feel it was different?" Severn asked, after a long, awkward pause.

"The Towers were created to be helmed or captained. They were meant to be tactical weapons in a time of war."

"That is not—"

"All that they are? We know. Believe," Mandoran added, with wry emphasis, "that we understand that now. But Tara herself said this. She's not you. She doesn't find facts offensive."

"Because she understands they're *selective*. When she says it, she's not assuming that's all that can be said about herself!"

"Kitling."

Kaylin shut her mouth. The small dragon squawked quietly, and rubbed her cheek with the side of his face. "...Sorry."

Mandoran shrugged. He had taken the presence of Maggaron in stride, as had Annarion, but he kept throwing side glances at Bellusdeo. She didn't return them; she was quietly conversing with Maggaron, who was leaning in attentively to catch her words. This dropped a few feet from his height.

"The house on Ashford wasn't meant to be a Tower."

"What was it meant to be?"

"Tara's not certain."

"Is she worried because she's uncertain?"

"She's worried because she knows most of your kind live in hovels," was his cheerful reply. "You don't know how to

cut wood or quarry stone in a way that preserves the life inherent in it."

Stones weren't, by any definition of the word, alive. Kaylin
failed to point this out, but only barely. She alternated between
finding Mandoran charming and charismatic, and finding
him annoying and condescending. "Fine. We're primitive
mortals. We're incapable of turning any building—sentient or
otherwise—into a raving danger to life." The minute the
words left her mouth, she wanted to claw them back. *This*
is what happened when she let annoyance do the speaking.

There was a block of fast, silent walking. This time, it was
Annarion who spoke. "This is far more complicated than we
thought it would be."

"Less boring," Mandoran added, but with less humor. "And
yes, clearly the elemental water at its purest doesn't attempt to
drown you, either."

"It didn't attempt to drown me," Teela pointed out—purely
for Kaylin's sake, as she had no need to verbalize with the two,
otherwise. "And Bellusdeo—a Dragon—was treated like a
welcome guest. Look, I understand that this is difficult for
the two of you; it's difficult for *all* of us. But we're heading to
Ashwood now, and if we could concentrate on the possible
difficulties *there,* I'm sure we'd all be more appreciative." As
an invitation to truce, it looked a lot like a club. A big, heavy,
Barrani-wielded club.

"As we were saying," Mandoran began again, "the Towers were created to be captained. Their creators depended on
their own knowledge of Shadows and their abilities; they built
the Towers to withstand encroaching attacks. They were *also*
aware that the nature of Shadow was not, and could not be,
fixed. That they melded and transformed the living, in ways
their creators had not intended to be possible. The Lords of
the Towers were meant to be their eyes; they were meant to

give instructions where their current knowledge superseded the initial knowledge built into the Towers themselves.

"The Towers, however, were built to be proof against subversion."

"And the house at Ashwood?"

"Tara is uncertain. She knows that it was not meant to stand as a bulwark against the Shadows; that was neither its design nor its intent."

"What was it built for?"

Mandoran shrugged. "Which part of uncertain wasn't clear?"

"Does she think it's possibly dangerous simply because it was created at the same time?"

"Yes," Mandoran replied.

"No," Annarion said. They spoke in unison. Sort of.

Kaylin turned to Annarion. "I'll take the no for five silver."

He frowned at Teela, to indicate that perhaps he had not understood the Elantran he heard. Teela, however, laughed, which caused him to flush. "Tara does not believe that any building was created for its own sake. Buildings serve a function. The Hallionne were created to keep the peace between factions who might otherwise murder each other in their sleep—if they bothered with the pretense of sleep or rest at all.

"Tara was created to keep the fief free of the contaminant of Shadow, and to find a Lord who would share this responsibility. She does not understand what the purpose of Ashwood was; if she understood it, she would know what we faced."

"Not *we*," Kaylin told him. "*I'm* looking for a new place to live. *Me*."

If Teela had second thoughts—and given Teela, she was probably well into fifth and sixth by now—she kept them mostly to herself. She was as good as her word; she knew where Ashwood was, and knew how to reach it. She was comfortable in any of the streets of this city; Kaylin wasn't. The minute they hit the large, perfectly maintained roads with the very fancy magical lighting, her shoulders began to tense.

"You did mirror Jared?" Severn asked quietly.

Kaylin nodded.

Teela walked like she owned the street. Bellusdeo, sensing Kaylin's discomfort, drew herself up to her full height and did the same. Neither Mandoran nor Annarion had fully recovered from their visit with Tara, and if Mandoran rallied from time to time, it was clear he was unsettled. He didn't, however, walk as if nothing on these streets could possibly be of interest; stray elements of streetfront fences and architecture caught his attention. Kaylin wasn't certain if Annarion was likewise engaged; he had adopted Teela's stance and expression.

"You did tell Lord Emmerian that we were going to inspect possible living quarters?" Kaylin asked, quickening her pace to keep up with the two women who had taken the lead.

Bellusdeo shrugged.

"...You didn't."

"You were with me the entire afternoon, except within the Tower. No, I did not think to do so. It may come as a surprise to you, but I dislike the constant, unwelcome interference."

Kaylin winced. "We don't have portable mirrors here," she pointed out.

"No. I understand that they are possible."

"They are—but they're finicky; we cart them around in emergencies, with full departmental approval. Full departmental approval requires a cartload of paperwork."

"Ah. Your Sergeant is well-known for the regard in which he holds that paperwork."

"Yes. Very well-known."

"I did, however, ask Tara for a list of known previous residents of the house we will visit this evening."

"When? She was with—"

"She's a Tower. I asked, and she answered. She is perfectly capable of holding a dozen conversations simultaneously; she understands that most of us find this perplexing, and attempts to confine herself to one Avatar. She does not, however, do so because she lacks the ability to be in many places at once. I know you're fond of her," Bellusdeo added, her voice gentling. "I even understand why.

"What I didn't entirely understand was that she is just as fond of you. If you asked her, she would allow you to move in before you'd finished making the request. She doesn't have door wards—anywhere—because she knows how much discomfort they cause you. She doesn't have multiple Avatars—which would be more efficient—for similar reasons. I feel this unfair," Bellusdeo added, "but she pointed out that you've never said anything; she intuits it because you are, to use an Elantran phrase, an open book. She doesn't want you to feel unhappy or uncomfortable when you visit her, because she's afraid you will visit even less than you do now."

Kaylin said nothing. She felt...guilty. She was effectively telling Tara to be *less* herself—in her own home. "I think I could get used to it," she said, in a much quieter voice. "She shouldn't have to change herself because she's afraid of what *I'll* think."

"Why not? Isn't it what you yourself do?"

Kaylin was at a momentary loss for words. Teela, being Teela, filled the gap. "She has you there, kitling. You spend an inordinate amount of time thinking about the opinions of other people as they relate to yourself."

"I don't—"

"You do. You dislike old, judgmental men. In the past, you

made yourself so obnoxious they were bound to dislike you on principal. Why do you think you did that?"

Kaylin said nothing.

"Because then you'd be in control. You'd *know* what they judged, and why. You've improved greatly over the past few years," Teela added. "You don't assume that every authority figure in the city will automatically assume you are an ignorant, venal wretch from the fiefs. What Tara does is vastly less offensive—but Tara makes no assumptions of the kind you did. She knows what you think; you hide nothing. You don't even try. She's aware that she caused you pain in the past, and she regrets it; she is determined never to make that mistake again."

Kaylin said more nothing, as Teela glanced at Bellusdeo. "Were there any names on that list?"

"Yes."

"Any recent names?"

"No."

"How would Tara even have the early names?" Kaylin asked.

"That," Bellusdeo said, "was the important point. Your Imperial Records are an echo of the communication and collective memory of structures such as Tara, the Hallionne, and apparently places like Ashwood. Before you ask, the Keeper's Garden is not part of what Tara considered an array."

"Did Tara know any of the previous occupants?"

"Not personally, no." She glanced at Kaylin, and then continued to watch the road.

"What?"

"It is nothing."

"It's not nothing. What?"

"It does not appear that you fully understand that Tara, like any sentient being who can speak and think, is fully capable of lying when it suits her purposes. You," she continued, "are an *incompetent* liar. This does not mean that you do not, from time to time, make that attempt. It's my suspicion that, were it not for the emergency on her borders, Tara would have asked Lord Tiamaris to accompany us."

Kaylin wasn't of a mind to feel grateful for the type of emergency that Tara and Tiamaris now faced—but it was close.

"He would have, at this point, been more welcome than Emmerian."

"He's still a Lord of the Dragon Court."

"Yes—an independent Lord of that Court, with a fief that operates as a small, separate country under his command." Bellusdeo exhaled heavily. "His existence—his continued existence—is possibly one of the only things that gives me hope for my own future."

"You said you mirrored Jared?" Teela asked.

"Yes."

"Good. There's a rather unpleasant amount of activity at the various windows we're passing; he's probably cursing the existence of mirrors—at all—at the moment. Pick up the pace. I happen to like Jared."

Ashwood did not, in Kaylin's opinion, live up to the word *street*. It appeared, as they made their final right, to sport no sign that declared its name in precise, Imperial lettering, for one; it was short, for another. There were two manor homes— one to the right and one to the left—and they were very much in keeping with the general style of this neighborhood—the front doors were as far from actual pedestrians as it was possible to be while still facing the street; there were heavy, ornate fences, and there were gates. Very closed gates. There didn't appear to be gatehouses, on the other hand.

The road itself led to a third residence. It was also fenced in. It was gated. There were no other homes.

"The one at the end is number three?" Kaylin asked their native guide.

Teela nodded.

"It looks a lot like one and two."

"Which says more about mortal vision than it does about either of the three manors. You're certain you're expected?"

Kaylin stared at the back of Barrani head. Teela turned slowly. "I'm certain we're not."

"Given Tara's concerns—"

"If I'd known that Tara had some sort of connection with Ashwood, I'd've asked to use *her* mirror. Evanton said the owner of the house is off the mirror network."

"The owner of the house," Bellusdeo added, "is off the Tower network—if such a thing exists—as well. Tara has no ability to communicate with the building here."

"But she did in the past."

"Yes."

"Did she tell you how or why that changed?"

"No. I did, however, ask." Bellusdeo now approached the front gate. "She was concerned. You are important to her. But she understands that you—and myself, if I am being honest—are desperately unhappy living at the Palace. She is not certain that Ashwood is a danger; she is only certain that it can be. I, on the other hand, am a danger. Were it not for my presence in your life, you would not now be searching for another place to live. Teela is a danger. Were it not for Teela—"

"I get it, I get it. She thinks Ashwood is more like you or Teela than Shadows, which have intent to harm?"

"Yes, I believe so. She doesn't have a finer understanding of either diplomacy or tact—"

Mandoran snorted.

"—but she has, with Tiamaris's help and instruction, learned much in the past few months. She does not feel that you have learned *as* much."

"She has a better teacher," was Kaylin's glum reply. She joined Bellusdeo at the very closed gate.

"She asks me to remind you that tact and diplomacy can be used without dishonesty."

"Oh, I'll be tactful."

This time it was Teela who snorted. "The gate is closed."

"Locked?"

Teela carefully attempted to open the gate. "Yes."

"And there doesn't seem to be a gatekeeper," Bellusdeo added.

Which meant Jared was getting a faceful of "concerned" citizenry for no reason. Kaylin muttered a few choice Leontine phrases, shoulders sagging.

"Tact, remember?" Teela chuckled.

"It's not like anyone's listening. Tact is the thing you use when people can actually hear you." She reached out, grabbed a bar, and rattled the very, very solid gate. "I feel like I'm in jail," she said, to no one in particular. It had been a damned long day.

No one was more surprised than Kaylin at the sharp sound of metallic click. She yanked her hand away as if burned, although the metal was cool and solid to the touch. The gates, however, began to roll in toward a lawn that was neither wild nor precisely tended. Grass rose on either side of a deliberate stone path; the stones were flat and even—wide enough to accommodate even the most fussy of Imperial carriages. Certainly wide enough to accommodate the diverse party that now stood at the foot of that path.

★ ★ ★

"Did I miss a ward?" she asked, although she knew the answer.

"You couldn't have. You aren't whining enough," Teela replied. "Do you see magic here?"

"I see evidence of magic."

"Very funny."

The small dragon yawned. He draped himself across Kaylin's shoulders, mimicking a very bored cat. He did not, however, attempt to speak to the moving gate. Kaylin took this as a good sign.

"How did the Keeper know that his friend was looking for a new tenant?" Mandoran asked, as Kaylin took her first hesitant step up the drive. "If neither he nor the Ashwood building are part of the mirror system?"

"Don't ask me."

The front doors were not as intimidating as the open gate, because they weren't actually open. Doors were a little like people, in Kaylin's experience; they told you a fair amount about what to expect on the interiors. The door to her old apartment building had been finicky; it was wider on the street than the interior doors. Getting furniture into—or out of—the apartment had been a nightmare that had only been resolved by removing that door from its hinges, and even then, the door frame was narrow. No one who lived in the apartments, the doors implied, could possibly have much of value or size to move either in or out.

In Kaylin's case, that had been true. Even the closet had been a gift—of sorts—from the Hawks in the office.

These doors, however, could easily accommodate the same carriage that the drive could if it weren't for the stairs; they were steep and narrow, as if they belonged at the front of an entirely different—and much smaller—building.

"This place is going to be out of my pay range," she said, as she reached the top of the stairs. "Unless it's a rooming house."

Bellusdeo snorted smoke. "There is no way there would be a rooming house in a neighborhood like this."

"It's not illegal."

"Legality is only one form of social pressure. Have you spent much time with the humans who claim wealth and power in the city you police?"

"Remember that tact and diplomacy I appear to lack?"

"Ah, yes. Well. This is not a place for the less well-off to either live or gather."

"Bets on the door opening on its own?"

"Define on its own."

Severn however said, "You're betting it won't?"

Kaylin snorted. "No."

"This, kitling, is why you lose money. That is not a bet anyone would take."

"I'd take it at high enough odds," Severn countered.

Mandoran said, "I do not understand the purpose of this 'betting.'"

"Teela hasn't explained it?"

"She's done more than explain it—but it still makes no sense."

"You need to spend more time in the office," Kaylin replied, before she actually checked the words leaving her mouth. "You'd pick it up in no time. I'm not so sure about Annarion, though."

The door did not roll open as they approached. There were no obvious door knockers, no pulls that might ring interior bells; those would probably be found at the trade entrance—

the doors regular people were expected to enter. Kaylin had personal experience with this, as a Hawk.

There was no glowing door ward, either, but this wasn't unusual in the larger manor homes. Door wards were considered inferior to actual, working guards—and the wards were generally cheaper. Only in the run-down, older buildings was there a similar lack of wards, but for the opposite reason: door wards were *not* cheap.

"Ready?" Kaylin asked Bellusdeo.

"I am uncertain," she said, after a long pause.

Surprised, Kaylin looked toward the Dragon. The Dragon was watching Mandoran.

Mandoran was the color of milk.

Annarion was nowhere near as pale; to Kaylin's surprise, he stepped in front of Mandoran; his hand fell to the hilt of a sword Kaylin would have sworn he wasn't wearing when they entered this district. She physically turned to face Teela, whose eyes were predictably blue, raising her brows in question.

"Someone's coming," Mandoran said.

Before she could ask how he knew—and she probably wouldn't have, as she had a suspicion she wouldn't understand any answer he'd care to give—the doors began to roll open. Standing between them was a withered old man.

Sadly, withered was not a figurative description.

CHAPTER 15

Kaylin started forward immediately. So did Severn. Even Teela moved.

They were Hawks. They had training. And they had some experience recognizing death when they saw it. They didn't *usually* see a dead man standing between open doors as if his very last act had been opening them—but this was a big city. Stranger things happened.

Kaylin caught him as he toppled—and he did topple; he didn't crumple.

The small dragon lifted his head as if he were bored. He also yawned, to drive the point home.

Severn immediately checked for vital signs as Kaylin, grunting, lowered the man to the ground. In this particular case, she chose to stay on the safe side of the threshold. Teela came to stand on the other side of the two Hawks. She didn't ask for the man's status. "Is this work for Red?"

"Hard to tell," Severn replied. "He didn't just open the doors and drop dead; he's been dead for a while."

"How long?"

"Less than a couple of days. There are no obvious signs of violence; no visible bruising, no bleeding; there are no obvious bumps on the back of his head." There weren't any on his forehead either.

"He's mortal?" Annarion asked.

Kaylin was surprised. "What else could he be? He's *old*."

Annarion joined them, kneeling by Kaylin's side. The small dragon whiffled in his ear, but he ignored the sounds; he seemed fascinated by the corpse. Fascinated, Kaylin thought, not repelled. "He aged to death."

"Yes. It's pretty much how most of us are going to go—if we're lucky."

"And age means weakness."

"Well, *this* age does."

"There are no signs of violence," Severn finally said. "None that I can see. He's not emaciated enough to have starved to death."

"Oh, he didn't," Kaylin replied. She was the one who'd caught him as he toppled. "He certainly couldn't have been poor, given where he was living. And his clothing is a little on the odd side, but it's not cheap."

"You are certain," Bellusdeo asked, keeping a respectful distance from the Hawks at work. "He lived here?"

"Well, he either lived here or he wandered in through the trade entrance and died on the way out. There's no sign of struggle; there's no sign of anything obviously wrong. To know more, we'd have to send him to Red." Before Bellusdeo could ask, Kaylin said, "Red doesn't examine every corpse in this city; he barely has the resources to examine the bodies that are obviously murder victims."

"We can't just leave him here."

"No, we probably can't." Kaylin rose. "But we're short a wagon or a carriage, and even if we did have one, we'd have no destination." She grimaced and added, "I hope this wasn't the landlord." Her expression softened. "And I hope he didn't die alone."

"No, of course not," a new voice said. They looked up. The light on the interior of the manse was bright and even; it seemed to wrap itself around a woman who now stood in the doorway, her toes touching, but not crossing, the threshold. "He hoped," she added softly, "to be able to meet the new residents."

Kaylin rose. The small dragon rose as well, although he didn't leave her shoulders. She expected him to squawk; he was silent. His wings were high, but he hadn't yet extended them.

"Did you know him?"

"Yes."

"Do you know if he has family in the city?" Kaylin blinked. They had examined the body in the light from the foyer, but the light—at the time—hadn't been so harsh. She couldn't clearly see the speaker's face. She could see her height, and the shadowed outline of her body; her voice was strong and clear, but it didn't imply youth.

"No. He has no remaining family in the city. There is a plot of land at the back of the manor; a small, private graveyard."

"You're going to bury him here?"

The woman nodded. "I would appreciate your help in this; I am afraid that I am not quite up to the task of digging a grave these days."

If someone had told Kaylin that she would be digging a grave in a rich person's bloody backyard under the moons' light, she would have laughed at them. Well, no, she would have made a bet. Sadly, she would have lost. There were shovels of varying widths in a small shed at the corner of what was, indeed, a private graveyard. The graves were adorned by markers—all stone. The prospective landlord had offered them lamps. The Dragons and the Barrani didn't require lamps, given moonlight; Severn and Kaylin did.

The landlord had used a rich person's version of "help." She wasn't the one lifting shovels or making the hole in the ground; she wouldn't be the one filling that hole, either. "Do you think she can even leave the house?" Kaylin asked, as she tossed dirt into a growing pile.

"I note you didn't ask her," Teela replied. She tossed a larger amount of dirt into the same pile. "You don't think she can."

"No."

"Do you suspect she's responsible for the man's death?"

Did she? Kaylin shook her head. "…No. I think she genuinely cares that he's laid to rest here. I think she was waiting—or hoping—that someone would stop by who *could* operate outside of the manor. That just happened to be us."

Maggaron was using a shovel that looked, in his giant hands, like a spade. If they finished this job inside of an hour, it would be because he was helping. On the other hand, his first suggestion had been instant cremation. Kaylin explained that instant required magical aid, which they didn't happen to have on hand—and his brow had creased. Multiple times.

Bellusdeo's chuckle made clear why. "It doesn't require magic at all. I could breathe on the corpse. You still aren't used to being surrounded by Dragons, are you?" She exhaled a small cloud of smoke, to make a point.

"I don't think that's a good idea," was Kaylin's uneasy reply.

"Of course you don't," Teela said. "It's the practical solution."

Maggaron, having been raised and trained in a world where corpses could be utilized by Shadows to the great detriment of the living, would have argued; Bellusdeo shook her head, and he subsided. He did, on the other hand, insist on a pit that was at least twelve feet deep. Bellusdeo nixed that, as well.

And so they dug a grave for an old, dead stranger. Kaylin thought the landlord looked on from one of the windows at the back of the house, but those windows—when she glanced at them—remained stubbornly empty.

The Barrani and the Dragons felt that something ceremonial should be said, once the corpse had been placed—with surprising care—in the open grave. Kaylin thought this was a waste of time, and was forced to say as much when they deferred to the two mortals present. "He's dead. The dead don't care. We don't know him, and the only person who did isn't actually here." When this was met with silence, she added, "We mostly threw corpses into the Ablayne, in the fiefs. Or we left them out in the streets overnight."

Everyone looked appalled, which Kaylin found grating. "If you have something you want said, you can say it. I've got nothing. We're not leaving him to rot. We're not leaving him as food for the Ferals so that they might—just might—not add to the body count before morning. We're not dumping him in the river—"

"Which is illegal, as you well know."

"I know he didn't die alone. If we believe the landlord, he didn't die in pain. He was healthy until he died. He wasn't hungry, he wasn't cold, wet, or in need of shelter. For many of the people who grew up where I did, he was *already* blessed."

Silence.

Kaylin attempted not to feel resentful, but that left her feeling guilty. She'd spent a couple of days in the company of Immortals. She *knew* they had their own problems and their own crises, and she could usually empathize, because when it came down to it, she *did* feel for them. They were her friends.

But they weren't like her. They never had been. The similarities didn't erase the differences.

She closed her eyes, exhaled, and said, "Sorry." It was true—the differences would always be there. But Severn had lived the life she'd lived, and Severn wasn't snapping and snarling.

"Why did you agree to bury him?" Teela asked. Maggaron was busy putting away the shovels—which, given his size, proved difficult. The shed was not large.

"Because she wanted us to bury him. He's dead. He doesn't care. But she's not—and she does."

"You are certain?"

"Yes. No. Yes."

No one asked her to make up her mind. Teela, however, slid an arm around her shoulder. "Let's head back, then. If the landlord wants to say a few words, she can say them in private. I think she's waiting for us."

When they once again climbed the narrow stairs, the doors were still open. Kaylin glanced up to the height of the foyer, expecting to see a chandelier—or four. There wasn't one. The foyer itself was not quite palatial. The ceiling was high, and the floors—marble—caught and reflected light. There were doors that faced the front doors, and smaller doors to the right and left; there were also staircases—and these were wide—that curved from a recessed second story on both the right and the left; they wound their way down, pointing to the foyer's center.

What there wasn't, anywhere in sight, was the landlord.

"Hello?" Kaylin said, squinting slightly as her eyes adjusted to the difference in ambient light. "Helloooo!" She could swear her voice echoed. She glanced at Teela, who shook her head. She then turned to Mandoran. "Is the landlord still here?"

"She is somewhere in the building; she's no longer in the foyer."

Kaylin exhaled. "Fine. Why don't we try this tomorrow when there's more light and less dirt wedged under our fingernails?"

"Speak for yourself," he replied, lifting his hands.

Barrani. Maggaron, on the other hand, looked worse than she did. She was grateful someone did.

"There might be a slight problem with that suggestion," Teela said.

"Please don't tell me the doors are shut."

"Not exactly."

Kaylin turned to see what not exactly meant. Technically, Teela was correct: the doors weren't shut. This would be because they no longer existed.

"Teela was definitely right about you," Mandoran said, in the long beat of silence that followed.

"This has nothing to do with *me,*" Kaylin snapped. "You'll note that the *rest* of the excitement we've suffered had nothing to do with me. I caused no problems in the Keeper's Garden. I didn't cause Castle Nightshade to wake up in revolt. I also, for the record, didn't destroy my previous home."

The small dragon bit her ear. He didn't draw blood.

Kaylin exhaled. "And I know you didn't mean to cause trouble, either. I'm sorry. I would like—just once—for things to work out the *normal* way."

"What is normal?" Mandoran asked, apparently with genuine curiosity, rather than bored derision.

"Other people manage to find new places to live that don't involve corpses, burying bodies, or doors that disappear the minute you cross the threshold."

"Do they?"

"Every *other* person who works in the office has. Even Tain."

"Tain," Mandoran replied, "is doing his best to guarantee that our stay here is dull and pointless."

Teela cleared her throat. Loudly.

"Next time," Kaylin said, "I'm going to ask Caitlin to help. It worked out fine the first time. Things like this don't happen to her."

"How impressed would she be if they did?"

"They wouldn't."

"How would *you* feel if you got her involved in something like this?"

"You win," Kaylin said. "And yes, I'm whining."

"And it's not attractive."

"Neither are dirty fingernails. Yes, okay, the whining is worse. Just—give me a sec." She removed the stick from her hair, shook it out, and put it back up again. Looking at her reflection in the reflective, smooth flooring, she said, "This is why I need a place of my own. I want my own home."

"Home," Mandoran began, frowning, "is not—"

Teela had stepped on his foot. "Home has different connotations for mortals. They do not use the word the way we do, and if some mortals are ambivalent about their homes, the ambivalence is likewise different. Kaylin feels safe in her home."

Annarion and Mandoran stared at Kaylin.

"If you had been safe in your home, we would not now be looking for a new one."

"*We* aren't looking." She folded her arms. "There's no absolute safety in *any* of our homes. Yours or mine."

"We have no expectation that there will be," Annarion replied. Teela was silent and expressionless. "Home—for those of us who choose to claim one—is tied to our bloodline. It is not something that we singly own or claim. It is the seat of political power. For that reason it is the least secure of our possible residences."

"Our homes aren't your homes, as Teela said. I lived in what you'd consider a large closet. I didn't own anything you'd consider valuable."

"You wear the ring of the Lord of the West March."

"Fine. I own *almost* nothing you'd consider valuable. Home's not a fortress for most of us."

"Then the safety is illusory, and you are aware of this fact."

"It's not *safety* I want."

"What, then, do you seek?"

"Privacy. I have had a long day," she continued, spacing each syllable evenly as if it were a sentence of its own. "It hasn't been fun or productive. If I had a home of my own, I'd be there now, whining at the walls, which have the advantage of not caring. I could be in as foul a mood as I want. I could curse in any language I know. I could give up on being responsible for one night and crawl under the bed and try to sleep. I could do it in any state of dress. I could *be myself* for a couple of hours without having to worry about offending anyone else. Or hurting them. Or caring whether or not I've got dirt under my fingernails. Dirt happens when you bury people.

"Maybe other people are capable of living without that— I'm not. I want to be self-indulgent enough to feel sorry for myself for an hour or two, even if it's not justified. I *like* having friends. If I don't have a place of my own to go to sometime soon, I'll probably drive them all away." She had to pause for breath, she'd been talking so quickly.

"Kitling, the only person who mentioned the dirt was you. You're probably the only person here who cares."

Kaylin muttered one of the milder Leontine curses, which meant, roughly, *I hope your claws get caught in your blankets.* It was only used on family.

"Even the landlord appears to consider it largely irrelevant."

"I'd like to know what the landlord considers relevant," Kaylin replied. She considered the words only after they'd left her mouth. "Actually, I'll take that back." Not only was she dirty, she was achy. Digging graves at the tail end of a stressful day did that. She turned around to face a windowless—and yes, doorless—wall. Exhaling, defeated, she said, "Up the stairs or into the manor? I've had enough of basements for a long damn time; we're skipping all the stairs that lead down."

The general consensus—which mostly meant a lot of watchful silence—was up the stairs. Neither Mandoran or Annarion seemed overly troubled by the change in the architecture; they were the only ones who weren't. Maggaron looked like he expected shadows to emerge from the floors; Severn had unwound his weapon chain; Teela's eyes were blue, and Bellusdeo's, orange.

Kaylin turned to Mandoran. "You're sure you have no idea where the landlord went?"

He frowned. "I didn't say that."

"Tell me what you did say, but in shorter words. Shorter, Elantran words."

"I'm not certain I can lead *you* to the landlord." This time, he put the emphasis in a different place. "But I'm fairly certain we could find her."

If the building itself was in any way like Tara, the landlord could hear everything anyone was thinking. Kaylin chose Leontine as her language of choice, but kept sliding into tired, frustrated Elantran. Given Teela's expression, she kept as much of it to herself as she possibly could; given her mood, it wasn't one hundred percent.

"Hello!" she shouted, as they began to climb the left set of stairs. With the single exception of the doors, none of the rest of the building had undergone radical and immediate change. The stairs felt like stairs beneath her feet. The rails were cool to the touch; they were metallic. The chandelier did not magically become the type of lampstand that would have graced Kaylin's old apartment when she could afford the fuel.

"I swear, I'm going to strangle Evanton myself."

"I wouldn't advise it," Teela replied. "It'll make what happened to your old place look tame and insignificant in comparison, in the end."

"Why did he even make this suggestion?"

"You're asking the wrong person. If we find a way out before you expire of old age, ask him in person."

"Oh, I will." She glanced at the small dragon, who was yawning. If he'd had a voice, he would have been complaining—loudly—about boredom; he had other ways of making his feelings known. But he didn't look nervous. He didn't look worried. He didn't look angry.

"Do not use your familiar as a weather vane," Teela told her. Teela knew her well enough she didn't *need* to be a mind-reader. The stairs joined a landing; Kaylin paused to look over the railing at the ground below; she had to squint because the chandelier was closer. The doors had failed to emerge.

"Bets on getting out of here before dawn?" she said to Severn.

"Or at all?" Teela added.

Severn, blades in hand, grinned. "I'll take it."

"Odds?"

"Even for Kaylin's bet."

"And mine?"

"There's no win condition."

"Fine. Make it: before the mortals perish."

Severn chuckled. "You won't be able to collect."

"Oh? That's a nice weapon you have there."

Severn's answering smile was slow and deep. "I'd like to see you try to pick it up."

All three of the Barrani laughed out loud.

A golden Dragon brow arched. "The weapon was originally meant for Barrani use?"

Teela chuckled. "It was. Or rather, every wielder prior to Corporal Handred was one of my people. Weapons, however, are like friends or lovers; they form attachments that objective observers cannot predict, and they reject attachments that seem—to all outsiders—to be the most advantageous."

"And if you attempted to wield the weapon?"

"Now? If I were lucky, I would have a burned and blistered hand."

"Lucky," Bellusdeo asked, "or powerful enough?"

"Both. I have been accused of many things; stupidity is not among them."

"Not anymore," Mandoran murmured. "If we find this landlord, do you want anything other than escape at this point?"

The obvious, smart answer was no. For some reason, it wouldn't leave her mouth. The small dragon butted her cheek with the top of its head.

"That's not a no," Mandoran said.

"It should be," she replied, finally turning to face the hall beyond the balcony. "But—" She shook her head.

"Share," he said, grinning.

"I don't enjoy finding corpses, and I definitely don't enjoy digging graves for them. But—it seemed clear to me that the landlord cared for her former tenant. And cared about what happened to his body. My guess is that she doesn't just kidnap new tenants off the street. I don't think the manor is a prison. Well, not usually."

"Based on what evidence?"

Kaylin shrugged.

"It's entirely possible her tenant was only allowed to leave because he was dead."

When Kaylin failed to answer, Mandoran looked like he wanted to pull his perfect hair out by the roots; he was frustrated. "I told Teela I wanted to give you my name and she nearly bit my head off. But this way of conversing is *tiring*."

Kaylin was appalled, and she wasn't even Barrani. "You *do not* go around giving out your *True Name* because you find speech tiring!"

"Add a few colorful phrases, quadruple the length, and you have Teela's speech. You're *certain* your eyes can't change color?"

"Yes."

"Other mortals have normal eyes—" He glared at Teela. "What? It's true. Leontines. Aerians. I haven't met the other races—but I'm told they all have normal eyes. She's not offended."

"And you know that how?"

"She's not exactly reticent, Teela. I'm not sure why I'm not supposed to ask about the differences. They're there, and she understands them better than I do."

"It's not her job to explain herself to you."

"It is if she wants me to understand her."

Bellusdeo had sidled up to Kaylin. "Should I have Maggaron throw him over the rails?"

"No. I don't think Maggaron's guaranteed to succeed, and I think Teela would take it badly."

"She wouldn't," Teela said.

Kaylin exhaled. Again. She didn't remember inhaling. "Leave it, Teela."

"Why?"

"Because *I* asked *you* similar questions when I first joined the Hawks. And you answered them. Were you offended at the time?"

"No. Mostly amused. A little surprised, but mostly amused. You don't look particularly amused."

"I've had a crappy day. If I were in a better mood, I wouldn't mind being talked about as if I were a really clever pet."

Bellusdeo snorted. "You're never going to be in a mood that good."

"I was the official mascot for the Hawks for a number of years, and I survived. I even liked the Hawks enough to want to become one."

"*Mascot?*"

"Don't ask. We might as well look for the landlord. I kind of feel like this is a game of hide-and-seek."

"Are you any good at seeking?"

"No. I suck at hiding, too, if that helps."

There were doors on either side of the hall—three each. They were not as tall as the doors that opened into the foyer—but they couldn't be, at least not from this side; the ceilings were a normal variety of high. The hall was well lit. Too well lit. It implied sunlight, with no obvious windows to let it through.

The doors were rectangular in shape, which pretty much described doors throughout the city, with a few notable exceptions. But these doors had carvings as ornamentation. They looked like very rough impressions of people, at first glance; they reminded her of the mud figures Marrin's children made, but with a lot less dirt.

They were, however, part of the door itself; they hadn't been carved and nailed or glued in place. And if they were simple—and they were—there was a bold certainty to the shapes that implied expertise, rather than the exuberant play-fulness of overconfident foundlings.

She frowned and glanced at Severn.

He nodded. "The figure on the door farthest down on the left has what might be wings."

"And on the far right," Teela added, "I think I can make out the hint of pointy ears. These are more like silhouettes given solid shape than actual carvings."

"Are we meant to enter the door appropriate for our race?" Bellusdeo asked. She didn't sound particularly pleased by the prospect.

Kaylin wasn't, either. If the body of the previous tenant hadn't been obviously mortal, she'd—she'd…do what? Storm out of the manor in a huff?

"I think this is supposed to be us," Mandoran pointed out. He'd stopped at the first door on the right, in front of the raised outline of someone tall and slender. There were no distinguishing physical characteristics in silhouette, because hair was apparently not included. Kaylin had never seen a bald Barrani.

"You can open it if you want," she told Mandoran.

Teela cleared her throat.

"Fine." Kaylin crossed the hall and reached for the large, brass handle that would—in a normal building—be used to open the door. "I'll open it."

The small dragon yawned and stretched a wing across Kaylin's face. He didn't leave it in front of her eyes, so he didn't mean for her to look through it. "You *could* be a little more helpful." Yawn. *Squawk.*

"I believe he's attempting to tell you that there's nothing to fear," Mandoran suggested. He'd come to stand by Kaylin's side, his long, slender hands clasped loosely behind his back.

"You were joking about giving me your name, weren't you?" she asked, as she depressed the upper part of the handle.

"No."

"Mandoran—"

"You've already seen my name." His tone was uncharacteristically serious. "You've carried it. You've spoken it."

"I haven't."

"You have. You've only spoken it once, but Kaylin, I heard you. Had I not heard your voice, I could not have come back. You already know my name."

"I don't." The door clicked. "If I did, you could speak to me the way you speak to the rest of your kin."

"Yes. I cannot; I've tried. We have all tried. It's strange. We've discussed it," he added. "Sedarias decided that you were not enough of a threat that we need be *too* concerned."

She pushed the door open, fully aware of what the need for concern probably entailed, given they were all Barrani.

"Teela," Teela added, "was *quite* definitive on the subject." She paused as she looked through the open door, and the pause became silence. "This was the Barrani door?" she asked, when no one stepped in to fill it.

"The only two distinct doors were the Leontine and the Aerian doors."

"There is also one that heavily implies Tha'alani," Severn added. "But yes—there is very little to differentiate the Dragons, the Barrani and the humans."

"The differentiation appears to be on the interior," Teela told him, moving through the doorway so that Severn could see the room. "And I would guess that this was, indeed, the Barrani room."

The interior reminded Kaylin almost instantly of the rooms in the High Halls—or in the interior of the Hallionne. The ceilings were high, but rounded at the corners; the floors were a warm, unstained wood. There were rugs, yes, but they didn't demand immediate attention; the plants did that. The door opened into a hall; it was small, but not narrow. There was no rug at the front to keep the usual bits of tracked in dirt in one easy-to-clean place—but dirt avoided the Barrani, as if it were smart enough not to piss them off.

There was a mirror to the left of the open door; trailing ivy grew around its frame, as if it were a window. Mandoran had frozen for a second in the doorway, which made it hard for anyone who wasn't preternaturally graceful to move past him. He shook himself and entered, pausing at the mirror to touch the frame and to rearrange some of the leaves.

He was silent as he left the small hall for the room at the end of it; he passed the two open archways to either side. Kaylin glanced in; she wasn't surprised to see two very large, very spacious rooms. One was definitely a bath—a bath very like Teela's in the High Halls. But even here, there were flowers that floated on the surface of the water.

But the room at the end, which in theory should have been a bedroom, wasn't; it was almost an enclosed balcony, and it opened to sun and breeze. It reminded Kaylin very much of the Warden's perch, although she couldn't exactly say why; the floors were not branches, and the whole platform didn't appear to be part of a growing, living tree. There were chairs, a round, pedestal table, and beside it, a small font.

Teela glanced at Mandoran, who had walked to the edge of the enclosure and was now facing out—or down. He hadn't said a word, or not a word that Kaylin could hear. But the balcony did open up to a city view—albeit a view of mostly the tall trees that lined the streets in this district. It was both peaceful and quiet. City quiet.

Annarion joined Kaylin, to her surprise. He drew her almost gently to one side as Bellusdeo and Maggaron joined Mandoran. Severn remained in the arch that separated the room from the short hall.

"You don't recognize this room," Annarion said.

"Should I?"

"No. But Mandoran does. Or rather, he recognizes the style. Teela will, as well."

"But not you."

"No, I was raised in a different environment, until I was chosen as one of the twelve."

"This building is like the Hallionne," Kaylin said, the last syllable trailing up as if it were a question.

"There must be some similarities. I don't think the building is trying to segregate us into our respective races, though."

Kaylin didn't either, although she wasn't certain why. "What do you think it's trying to do?"

"I think it's trying to figure out what our preferences actually are. I'm not sure I'm willing to enter the room with the Dragon symbol," he added.

"Why?"

"I don't like caves. They're too enclosed."

"Bellusdeo—and the entire Imperial Dragon Court—do not live in caves."

"No. Not now. But Mandoran doesn't live in a modest apartment like this one anymore, either."

They retreated from the room after their inspection, some of which was magical. The magic was subtle, but present; Kaylin's arms were tingling and achy. "Teela?"

"Yes, it's me."

"Find anything suspicious?"

The Barrani Hawk laughed.

"Okay, that was a stupid question. Find anything obviously dangerous?"

"No. There are no door wards. There does seem to be some rudimentary mirror network connection, but the mirror is currently inactive." She hesitated and then added, "I like the rooms."

"They're too open for me. Especially the one at the end. I was kind of hoping to find a place with either real windows—"

"Out of your price range."

"Or at least shutters that stay shut when it rains. Or at all. But other than that, I want about as much magic as my old place had."

"Which is almost none."

"Except for the mirror."

CHAPTER 16

Annarion wasn't wrong. Kaylin chose the next door, and she chose one of the figures that looked essentially human; it was stockier than the figure on the Barrani door, but had no distinguishing characteristics. Kaylin thought this unfair; if it was a Dragon room, a Dragon-form silhouette would have been helpful, and much harder to mistake for anything else.

The door opened into much dimmer, ambient light. The floor on the other side of the door frame wasn't wood with a bit of carpet for protection. It was solid, flat stone. The stone itself was pristine; it might have been newly laid; it had none of the subtle wear that the stones that girded the Palace did.

It did not, however, suggest cave or cavern. Kaylin glanced at Bellusdeo. "Is this something that speaks to you?"

Bellusdeo was not Mandoran, but there were some similarities; she'd spent a chunk of her life as a sword. A literal sword. She was, on the other hand, more guarded than Mandoran. If she chose to let her emotions loose, she was usually angry and felt there was no advantage to be gained by hiding it.

The hall that led from this door was longer; it was made of

right angles. It didn't quite suggest dungeon to Kaylin; it almost suggested jail. The small dragon stirred and squawked.

"Is he complaining?" Kaylin asked Bellusdeo, as the Dragon leveled a less than amused expression at her left shoulder.

"He does that. A lot."

Kaylin shrugged, which got another squawk. "I probably set a really bad example."

"You do," Mandoran agreed, from somewhere in the hall. "But at least your complaints are amusing. I definitely like the first rooms better," he added.

"I'm not sure our preferences are relevant." The hall led to stairs, and since the stairs went up, Kaylin was willing to climb them. She hadn't been kidding about basements. Bellusdeo said very little. She paused once to examine the two posts that fronted the stairs; there were no rails, because they were framed on either side by walls.

The walls banked to the right and left as they reached the landing. To Kaylin's surprise, it was well lit; there were windows here. The lower edge of those windows was at the height of her nose. They weren't open. In fact, Kaylin wasn't certain they could be. The center portions of each of the three windows were clear, solid glass; those sections were surrounded on all four sides by panels of colored glass. None of the public areas of the Imperial Palace boasted windows like these; if the private areas did, Kaylin hadn't seen them yet.

She glanced at Bellusdeo again. Maggaron was hovering, but he said nothing.

"Severn?"

He understood what she wanted him to do; he had both height and reach. He peered out the window and said, "It's a city view."

"Ours?"

Teela snorted. "Ours."

Kaylin noted that neither the hall nor the landing forced Maggaron to crouch. The same couldn't be said of most of the buildings in the fief he now called home, the exception being the Tower—Tara's Tower. Newer buildings were being constructed for the use of the *Norannir* on the borders of Tiamaris, but Maggaron spent most of his sleeping hours in the Tower.

Kaylin could read nothing from Bellusdeo's expression. Maggaron's, however, was almost painfully hopeful. He turned to the left, abandoning Bellusdeo to the windows through which she absently gazed. He approached a very tall door; there was one on the right of the stairs, as well.

He had no difficulty moving the door. Looking at it, Kaylin thought she might; it was thick and the hinges creaked. He entered what looked, from a brief glimpse, to be a small room, or perhaps rooms. She started to follow and then turned back to Bellusdeo; Teela had come to stand on her right. The Barrani Hawk said nothing; nor did Bellusdeo.

But Mandoran and Annarion kept a distance that seemed almost respectful.

Severn slid an arm around Kaylin's shoulder; she stiffened and then, slowly, leaned into him.

They've all lost their homes, she told him, not daring to speak the words out loud, because Immortal hearing was so damned good and Immortal pride was…prickly. *All except maybe Teela.*

Severn said nothing.

Do people always lose their homes? I mean, we did. He knew Kaylin; he knew the question was rhetorical. She was thinking it through and had no easy answer, but expected none. *Maybe home is something we have to make, and remake, over and over. But it's hard to make things when you're afraid—or you're certain—that they'll just be broken.*

You try.

Yes. And it kills me every time. Even thinking about my old place makes me feel like I'm falling. But—I was happy there. I was so surprised when Caitlin took me to find a place of my own. I thought she was just trying to get rid of me. But—she gave me dishes, and the old rug. She told me I could make my own home be whatever I wanted.

She didn't tell you not to give out keys.

Kaylin snorted, and glanced at Teela's back. *Wouldn't have made a difference.*

No. You didn't really want to shut her out.

"Kitling, if you're worried about *me,* don't be. I've had just as long a day as you have, and I don't have the patience for it."

Bellusdeo glanced at Teela's profile, and then at Kaylin, one brow lifted. One brow and the corners of both lips. Her shoulders relaxed as she turned to face the mortal Hawk; she moved away from the window.

"You recognize this place."

"I recognize the rough layout, yes. You'll note the height of the doors and the windows? This isn't the Aerie of my childhood."

Maggaron came out of the door; he walked immediately toward the only other door on the landing, and opened it. It was just as creaky. He disappeared into that room, and again, no one followed.

"Is this where Maggaron grew up?"

"It is not exact, of course—the windows are not enchanted, and they are far too ornate." Her smile faded. "Maggaron was sent to the Ascendancy as a child. He wasn't raised by his tribe; too many of them had died. He didn't love being a child there—but I don't imagine you would have, either. Tara offered to recreate his rooms," she added.

Kaylin hadn't heard that.

"He said no. If she asks again, I'm going to kick him in the shins until he says yes." Her smile was sad, but very affectionate. "Look at him. Let me drag him out of here."

Kaylin almost told her to leave him be. But they still hadn't found either landlord or exit, and it made more sense to stick together as a group until they did.

There was no cave in this hall—but it wouldn't have surprised Kaylin to see one. There was a series of small, rounded rooms, with apertures very like the one in the Hawklord's tower, although they were shut. There were rooms in which the Tha'alani could be at home, and rooms which resembled Marcus's residence—the only doors there were the ones that separated the rooms from the main hall.

The most run-down apartment was, of course, the apartment marked with an icon that was probably meant for humans. The ceilings were significantly shorter; Maggaron had to crouch to get through the door, and he couldn't quite straighten up to his full height. The floorboards were worn; the shutters to the windows were open. It was a larger space than the one Kaylin had lived in—it had a separate bedroom, for one—but it wasn't in any way upscale.

Kaylin exhaled. She turned to Mandoran and said, "Are we any closer to the landlord?"

He glanced at Annarion, who said nothing. Mandoran nodded.

"What do you suppose her rooms look like?"

"Anything she wants them to?"

"It's not a trick question. Or a test."

Mandoran laughed. "All life is a test—weren't you taught that? All a test, and you only get to fail once."

"Oh, I'm certain you're capable of failing far more often than that—as long as you survive." Teela looked down the hall to the only doors they hadn't opened. "It's not failure or success that's defining: it's whether or not the tests are interesting."

The small dragon yawned.

"Shall we?" Teela asked.

Kaylin nodded.

The stress of discovering a dead man—and the physical work of actually burying him—had diminished as Kaylin had inspected the rooms that lay beyond the various doors. She had no doubt at all by the end that the building was similar to the Hallionne or Tara, but the windows in the various rooms opened to Elantra. The view was roughly what she'd expect, given the orientation of the doors. She thought the apertures in the Aerian rooms would probably open to the actual sky, rather than an amorphous, shifting otherworld.

The size of the rooms themselves was unpredictable. Kaylin was fairly certain they didn't line up with the shape of the actual building as seen from the street—but at this point, she didn't expect it. What did she expect?

She glanced at Severn; he was alert. Although he was still armed, he no longer looked as if he expected attack from any quarter. There'd been a quiet about the rooms they'd seen so far that suggested peace, not death. They were empty, but they didn't feel impersonal. They felt almost like a greeting.

"Are we looking for a way out, kitling, or a way in?"

Kaylin blinked. "Sorry, I was thinking."

"And given the rarity of that, I shouldn't interrupt you."

"Very funny, Teela. I want to run Records through Missing Persons to see if we can identify the man we just buried."

Teela nodded. "You want to know if he remained missing."

"I want to know if his absence was ever reported, yes. I want to know if, when he walked through those doors, he just elected to stay here because he had no choice. I want to talk to his neighbors—"

"Not a good idea."

"Fine, I want *someone* to talk to his neighbors to see if any of them were aware that he lived here. I mean, the grounds are in decent repair and the external building—in evening light—doesn't appear to be falling apart, so the building looks occupied."

"All of which requires that we exit the building."

"I know."

"You just had an evil thought."

"Not *exactly* evil."

"Share."

"I'm imagining what the Dragon Court will say if they insist on the right to inspect the building as part of Bellusdeo's security detail."

Bellusdeo snorted. Her eyes, however, did shade to gold. "Can we send Diarmat instead of Emmerian?"

"I wouldn't wish Diarmat on *any* building of my acquaintance." Kaylin came to a stop in front of the only double doors in the hall. They were also the only doors whose center section was composed of plain panels of thick wood.

She caught the left handle in her left hand, out of habit; since door wards at their best sent a shock of pain up her arm that tended to make the hand useless for half an hour, she avoided using her dominant hand just to open them. These doors, unlike the others, failed to open.

Kaylin grimaced and tried the right handle, to the same effect. She then thought about how she approached her previous landlord on the rare occasions she needed to do anything but pay him, and she knocked.

When the doors rolled open—without any obvious help—she had the grace to redden. In no other prospective residence would she have just opened up random doors and done a walkthrough. Then again, in most other buildings, the doors would have been locked, and there would be understandably alarmed people on the other side of them.

The room on the other side of the doors was only barely a room, in that it had a door that led to it. The floors were not wood, they were stone; the ceiling was not roof, it was sky. The sky at the moment held a very familiar two moons—and they were the same two moons that had illuminated the sky on the trek here. It was not, however, an exit.

There were pillars where walls would generally be; the door appeared to be framed by two. This was more in line with her expectations of the interior of a sentient building. She liked it a lot less—but understood as she entered that these rooms weren't meant for her. She very much doubted that the dead former occupant had lived in them.

But given the quality of the clothing he'd been found in, she doubted he'd lived in the nominally "human" rooms, either.

Annarion and Mandoran entered the room less cautiously than anyone else, except Kaylin. She was fairly certain they saw what she saw, but it didn't surprise them; if anything, they seemed to relax.

"Lord Kaylin," Annarion said, ignoring her cringe. "Can you hear her?"

Since no one besides Annarion was speaking, Kaylin shook her head. "You can?"

He smiled. The smile was shorn of anxiety and guilt; it made him look young. "Yes. We can hear her—but it's not to us she wishes to speak. She will be present shortly."

But Kaylin guessed that. The stones beneath her feet began to emit a pale light, and the light—like faint starlight—could be caught more readily from the corners of her eyes. She couldn't *see* words engraved or painted on the ground, but she sensed they were there.

This was, in part, because her arms began to tingle—or at least the skin that bore the marks did. One day, she thought, as she began to roll up her sleeves, she was going to accept that they were a permanent part of her body, and she'd give up on trying to hide them.

On the other hand, *most* landlords would find them the opposite of impressive or appealing.

As the tingling deepened, the light on the floor brightened. Severn held out a hand; she fiddled with the magical studs on the bracer she wore by Imperial fiat, and the bracer clicked open. She handed it to him, since the bracer's sole purpose was to dampen the magic she could—and did—draw from the marks themselves.

Bellusdeo's eyes were orange; Maggaron was hovering, and she clearly found it irritating. Given his height, Kaylin thought she was being a bit unfair; at eight feet, he couldn't really stand beside her and *not* hover.

Then again, Maggaron was so earnest and so straightforward, he probably hadn't learned the art of hovering protectively without appearing worried. Severn, she noted, had. He didn't stand between her and possible danger; he didn't throw backward glances to make certain she was still safe.

Severn started to speak; she shook her head. The hair on the back of her neck was now standing pretty much on end—but that didn't mean danger; it meant magic of a fairly particular type.

The stones beneath Kaylin's feet were now bright enough they shimmered; the floor looked almost like the surface of a vast, still pond. It didn't, however, reflect moonlight.

Nor did it reflect anyone standing on it except the two young Barrani men. She could see both Annarion and Mandoran in the floor. She glanced up to make certain they were still standing near Teela; they were. If they noticed their reflections at all, it didn't show.

I don't see their reflections, either, Severn said, speaking, as he seldom did, internally.

"Teela, does the floor cast any reflections that you can see?"

"It's stone, kitling."

"I'm aware of that—I'm standing on it."

"It's not polished stone; it's stone."

"I'll take that as a no."

Both of Teela's friends looked at Kaylin, then. Mandoran spoke; it was almost always Mandoran who spoke first. "We can see the floor glowing." He indicated Annarion with a slight nod in his direction. "The room is brightly lit."

"Can you see the moons?"

He lifted his chin, exposing the perfect, flawless lines of his throat. Teela would never have taken that risk. "Yes."

"And they look like the same moons we saw on the way here?"

"I believe they are the same moons, yes."

"Teela?"

This time, the Barrani Hawk nodded. "I see the moons, as well." Her eyes darkened as she added, "And we have a visitor, I believe."

"I think we're the visitors," Kaylin replied, and turned in the direction that Teela was facing.

The woman—and it was a woman who approached— looked frail, to Kaylin. She was delicately built, her face and neck lined; she seemed to be almost as old as the man they'd buried. Kaylin wasn't great at guessing the age of the elderly, not correctly. The woman was dressed in a style similar to the man's, although something about the way she wore clothing seemed more formal.

Annarion and Mandoran offered her court bows; they extended those bows as she approached. In Diarmat's class, Kaylin had learned that the length of a bow indicated respect, unless one was prostrating oneself in front of the Emperor, in which case, it indicated utter obedience. Kaylin had been told, repeatedly, that the Emperor got to choose when that obeisance ended, not the person stuck holding it.

Clearly they didn't consider this woman the Emperor—but they took their time straightening out.

"You have such clear voices," she told them, as they rose. "Perhaps a little on the loud side, but I have lived in silence for decades."

No one else made haste to bow so completely, although Teela did offer a less exaggerated version.

"It has been many years since someone has come to my doors."

"Our years?"

The woman smiled. "Yours, dear," she said to Kaylin, in almost exactly the same tone that Caitlin would have used. "What brought you here?"

"Evanton," Kaylin replied. She knew she should be on her guard here; everyone except Annarion and Mandoran now were, and given their adventures in the past few days, following their lead was probably suicidal. But it was hard. The woman wasn't tall. Her eyes were normal eyes—brown, in this case—and nothing about her implied danger.

"Thank you, dear. It is kind of you to say so."

Since she hadn't, she reddened.

"Evanton. Evanton. Ah, you mean the Keeper?"

"We tend to call him Evanton," Kaylin replied. "But yes, the Keeper."

"I am not certain I've had the pleasure of making his acquaintance. Oh, but my manners are atrocious. Do please follow me; I've tea and refreshments waiting." She then turned and walked toward the pillars on the left. Teela and Bellusdeo exchanged a silent glance; Teela shrugged. Mandoran and Annarion had already fallen in behind her.

★ ★ ★

Manners in general dictated an exchange of names, or at least titles. The elderly woman had, so far, avoided either offering her own or asking for anyone else's. Since "hey, you" had been a prominent part of Kaylin's childhood, she couldn't take offense. She followed the two Barrani men, Severn by her side. The small dragon, who had been alternately lazing and yawning, forced himself into a polite standing position on her left shoulder.

Bellusdeo and Maggaron followed her; Teela pulled up the rear. The moons and the night sky gave way to the underside of a pavilion; lamps had been polished and lit, and a rectangular table, with chairs tucked under its surface, lay waiting.

The woman's idea of refreshments would feed the office for a day, but that was no surprise. If Caitlin were thirty years older, she'd probably be almost exactly the same.

The two Barrani men were first to sit at the table. Kaylin joined them; they were speaking to each other, but not with actual words—or at least not words any of the rest of their companions could hear. Seeing Teela's pursed lips, she revised that thought.

Eventually, when they were all seated at the table—except for the small dragon, for whom a place hadn't been set— the older woman joined them. She didn't sit at the head or the foot; she chose a chair opposite Kaylin's, in the middle. "Please, help yourself," she told her guests. "I will pour tea, but I'm afraid I'm a bit clumsy at the moment. Young man," she added, speaking to Severn, "if you could carve the meat, I'm sure we would all be grateful."

Severn did as she asked. The entire meal was so unexpected and so unpredictable, Kaylin quietly pinched her thigh.

"Why would you think you're dreaming, dear?" the old

woman asked. "Perhaps this isn't the right venue for a meeting?"

Kaylin hurriedly said, "No, no, it's fine!" in part because she didn't want the food to vanish. But she noticed that Teela wasn't eating. Neither were Bellusdeo or Maggaron. Severn, raised in the streets of Nightshade, would have started had he not been responsible for cutting the meat. The landlady didn't, however, look at any of the other visitors; only Kaylin.

Kaylin swallowed. The food didn't make her arms ache; there was nothing magical about it that she could see. Possibly because at this point, she didn't want to. She just didn't want to. Food had always been a blessing. Any food. Hunger made it all seem good. She hadn't gone hungry for years, but she'd never reached a point where food, freely offered, didn't seem like a gift.

"I'm pleased to meet you all," the landlord told them, folding her hands in her lap. "Let me introduce myself. I'm Helen. This is my home. It's a bit large, as you've seen. I used to live alone—but it was so easy to get lost in the emptiness."

Kaylin chewed and swallowed. "I'm Kaylin. Kaylin Neya. I work at the Halls of Law, with the Hawks. The young man is Severn Handred; he's a Hawk, as well."

Helen beamed. "And your friends?"

"Teela is the Barrani woman at the head of the table. She's a Hawk; that's where I met her. The two men on either side of her are Annarion and Mandoran."

"Ah, yes. They're new to the city?"

"Very. This is Bellusdeo, and her Ascendant, Maggaron." Maggaron sat at the foot of the table, towering over the food. Kaylin noted that the chair in which he was sitting was actually the right size—for him. He looked extremely uncomfortable in it anyway.

"And what brings you to my door?"

Since she'd already mentioned Evanton—with her mouth closed—Kaylin hesitated. Clearly the question didn't refer to how she'd found the place. "I've been looking for a new place to live."

The woman frowned. It was, like everything else about her, a delicate frown, but for the first time, it implied displeasure or disapproval. The food, however, didn't disappear; the lights didn't gutter; the garden didn't suddenly rear up in shadow tendrils.

"Of course not, dear!" Helen replied, looking shocked.

Teela and Bellusdeo now looked much, much more guarded; Annarion and Mandoran, more cautious. Severn, however, continued to eat. He'd glanced up at the small dragon on Kaylin's shoulder, who was upright, but not terribly interested in his surroundings.

"Do *not* bite that," Kaylin told him, trying to rescue the stick that kept her hair in place before he yanked it out. "I'm sorry. I forgot someone. This is—" She winced. "This is Hope."

The small dragon's name was clearly not as embarrassing to Helen as it was to Kaylin; nor did she seem to find it snicker-worthy. "Hope. Such a simple word, to hold so much. I like it," she added. "I think it's appropriate. There is never a guarantee, where hope is concerned; hope touches the edge of dream, but it is not a simple dream. It wants work, and sometimes it is bitterly painful—but no life is lived for long without it."

The small dragon had given up on the stick; he favored the old woman with his unblinking attention. "Did you choose her?" she asked him directly.

He squawked. A lot.

"I see."

Kaylin was torn. She couldn't understand the small dragon's words—to her, they resembled angry crows. But she was going to have to learn, somehow, because so many other people did.

"Oh, I see. Isn't that a bit extreme?"

Squawk.

"Well, then." She smiled at Kaylin. "I'm sorry, dear. I didn't mean to be rude. It has been a very long time since I've spoken with your friend. He does find the lack of clear communication frustrating; I have reminded him that you are mortal, which he knew before he chose you. It's not reasonable to expect people to grow extra arms just for the sake of one's own convenience. But I interrupted you."

"I'm looking for a new place to live."

"And you came here?"

Kaylin exhaled. "I won't be living here alone. Bellusdeo would be my roommate."

"She would be part of the arrangement?"

"She'd be living with me—but the place would be mine. I'm not sure—neither of us are sure—how long she'd be staying."

"And the *Norannir?*"

"Most of the buildings in the city are too small for him, but if—yes. If we seemed like an acceptable risk to you, he'd be living here for as long as Bellusdeo does."

Bellusdeo was surprised. Kaylin noticed only because she'd lived with the Dragon for weeks; it didn't change the color of her eyes much. Maggaron, however, had practically swelled two feet in height.

Helen smiled. "Is there something you're not telling me?"

"Yes. But you've probably heard it by now anyway." Kaylin's appetite finally deserted her. She looked up at the frail old lady and felt like one of the criminals she spent her life discouraging. "We need a new place because my old place was destroyed."

CHAPTER 17

"Destroyed?"

"I don't know how familiar you are with *our* version of magic, but my former apartment met an Arcane bomb. It was meant—we think it was meant—for Bellusdeo. It didn't destroy her. It did destroy my apartment."

Kaylin always tried to be pragmatic. She tried to be practical. She tried—and most days it was a real effort—not to take life personally. But it was *still* hard to think about the loss of what was, stripped down, a slightly run-down room with warped shutters and creaky floorboards. The bed and the armoire that had been a secondhand gift were splinters and shreds. The basket Severn had given her that kept food fresh had likewise been destroyed. The clothing she'd owned—and there hadn't been a lot of it that had still been in one piece, because she was hard on clothing—was gone.

The paintings Caitlin had brought to put up on her walls, and the scarf—scratchy, rough wool in Kaylin's opinion—that Caitlin had knit for her. The mirror she'd partially paid for.

The chair that served as the closet on long days. Oh, hells, on *most* days.

All of them, gone.

Teela had a key. She still had a key. Tain had a key. Caitlin had a key. Any of them could walk in and out of her apartment when they felt like it, although Caitlin had always mirrored ahead if she was coming. The keys still existed; they just didn't open anything anymore. There was no place that Kaylin could be found at home. There *was no home.*

The apartment had been the first home she'd chosen, and the first she'd really had since her mother's death. She couldn't even hate the man responsible for its loss because most of his mind had been destroyed and what was left was…pathetic and hopeful and naive.

"Kitling."

She swallowed and blinked. To her surprise, Helen was blinking as well, which made Kaylin rise in near-panic. "I'm sorry!" she said, almost knocking her chair over as she ran around the table.

Helen rose as well, and held out both of her hands; Kaylin took them almost without thinking. "My dear," she said— and tears trailed down her lined cheeks, "you do realize that *home* is the place that ties you down?"

It wasn't what Kaylin expected to hear. Then again, she wasn't certain what she'd expected. She swallowed again. "Home," she said, her voice less steady than she wanted it to be, "is the place you return to. It's the place that's waiting. It doesn't have to be perfect—mine wasn't. But…it was mine. I could offer my friends a place to crash. They could eat with me, or sit with me, or—"

"Listen to you complain?" Teela asked.

"Or that. In my space."

"Go on, dear."

"It's not that home means safety—if it did, I wouldn't *be* looking for a new one. But—if it's my space, I can be myself in it. I can be—be at home."

The hands that were holding hers tightened, but not in a way that was uncomfortable; they were too frail for that. "You are looking for a *home,* then?"

Kaylin nodded. She wanted to weep—and hated herself for it. This was *not* the way to impress a possible landlord.

"Not another landlord, perhaps," Helen said. "Do you know what *I* look for, dear? Here, give me back my hands and let me pour; I have been shockingly remiss." She returned to the table, leaving Kaylin with empty, but warm, hands. There, she bustled in place, pouring tea which seemed at odds with the plethora of dinner foods.

"People look for places—as you called them—to live. It is considered, by most, a necessity. They want different things from those places, of course. You are not the first person to enter my home since my last tenant passed away. You *are* the first to remain at the sight of his body. You surprised me, dear. You laid him to rest. It is not, I'm certain, an activity you undertake often.

"He fretted terribly in his final days and hours. He did want to meet the tenants who would replace him. He wanted to give them his advice, you see. To explain what he considered my eccentricities. He didn't want to leave."

"You didn't want him to leave."

Her smile was gentle, now. "No. It is always hard when someone leaves home for the last time. I wanted to find tenants before he died because it would have given him peace— but that is not, sadly, the way I am built. There are many people who would choose to live here if they could. Not all of them can reach me; not all the people who can are suitable. There are people who would like to rearrange my grounds and change my fences and open up my drives and renovate my exterior. They want to live here not because I am me, but because I am in the right place.

"There are people who are fleeing—sometimes from your Hawks, dear—who are looking for a place to hide. There are people who are looking for a change of venue—something more exciting or interesting to spice up their lives.

"None of these are innately bad." At Teela's lifted brow, Helen smiled. "Yes, dear, perhaps running from the Law would be considered bad in present company; that was not a well-chosen example on my part, but if you'll forgive it, I'll continue.

"These people have their eyes upon their futures, whatever those futures might be, and they will not be tied down by an old woman. Nor should they be. They need a *place*," she continued, frowning at the word—just as she'd frowned when Kaylin herself had used it. "I'm sorry, dear. I understand—I truly do—that this is simply one part of your brief, mortal lives.

"And often, the people who do want a home have a dream of home that is ideal. It is perfect. I am not, perhaps, as worn out as your previous home—but I am far from perfect. Nothing living can be. I do try," she added, slightly self-consciously.

"Why—why do you choose mortal tenants, then?" Kaylin asked. "If you *find* the tenant that's perfect for you, he—or she—is going to die. And you won't."

"Ah, now that is a good question. It is rather a long answer, though. Your tea might get cold."

"Believe that the rest of us are quite interested in the answer," Teela—who had not touched her tea—told her.

"Well, then." Helen smiled. "I suppose an interview does work in both directions. You have answered—perhaps unintentionally—the questions that are closest and most important to my own heart. I will try to answer yours.

"Immortals—like your fellow Hawk—do not use the word *home* the way you do. What they own, they own."

Kaylin frowned. "Tiamaris—"

"There will be exceptions, of course—but I could not be home to a Dragon unless he had chosen to dedicate himself to me, as your Tiamaris has done with your Tara. His Tower *is* his hoard. He owns it; he claims it; he protects it. But—he treasures it, and defers to it, and speaks with it; it is not a simple place into which he has moved and over which he presides. It is not something that denotes hierarchy or personal power. The Tower—to Tiamaris—is alive. He owns it *and* is owned by it. It is not a simple exchange. Yes, he is Lord of the Tower. Yes, if he chose to do so, he could enforce every single one of his desires. It is, in part, what a Tower is designed to allow of its Lord.

"I was not built for mortals," she continued, her gaze growing distant, her voice losing some of the frailty that her appearance all but demanded. "But I was aware of their fragile existences. They seldom spoke with power; it was very easy to lose track of their individual voices. My Lord was often away; in those days, the wars were fierce, and they transformed the landscape. I was, of course, safe from such transformations—but many, many things were not.

"Immortality is not invulnerability; Immortals know death. One day, my Lord did not return. I was left empty for a long passage of years, before another came to take his place. There was so much danger, dear, so much transformation and contamination. I was sensitive to it in a way the Lord was not, and within my confines, there was safety of a type.

"For him and his people."

"Not for you?"

"I am old, as you know. I was created by the Ancients in a bygone era; the reasons for my creation are lost to history. The Towers may know; I do not."

"Did you ever know?"

"Yes, once."

Kaylin fell silent.

"The Lord was a man of power. I am not sure what you would call him now." She looked to the left of Kaylin's face, and a squawk made clear that she'd been speaking to the small dragon. "Ah. Sorcerer, perhaps. He was not an Ancient, but he envied their power; people often envy the powers they perceive they do not themselves possess. I had power. I had been constructed with power. He understood that words lay at the heart of my foundations—and the words themselves allowed me almost limitless control over my own form.

"He thought, if he could deconstruct some parts of me, he could learn to harness that power and use it outside of my walls."

"You didn't agree."

"No. I didn't. But—he was powerful, Kaylin. I protected what I could of myself; I injured him. In the end, he was destroyed—but not by my hand alone."

"By whose?" Teela asked.

"I was still, in those days, in contact with the Towers that you speak of now. Before I took the most severe of my injuries, I asked for their help."

"But they—"

"Yes. They did not have a mandate to protect each other. Or me. But they conferred with their Lords, and in the end, their Lords chose to leave their Towers to come to my aid."

"They probably wanted the power—" Mandoran began. He didn't finish. Teela's look implied that he would be if he kept talking.

"Was he killed?"

"No. But he was driven out; I do not believe he remained in this world. There were portals at one time that opened onto other vistas. They are lifeless now—a consequence of his work. I had done what I could to protect my core functions—at least, that's how I considered them at the time. I do not know what the other functions might have been; they are lost to me, the words riven and destroyed.

"Yes," she added, glancing at Mandoran although he hadn't spoken. "I was left crippled and adrift. I had no Lord, and none would take me; it would mean abandoning their necessary posts at the outskirts of the sphere. I expect they thought someone would come who would. And men did come. Men of power," she added softly. "But they came to find the Sorcerer's research and the artifacts of possible power he might have left behind."

"We call those thieves," Kaylin said.

Teela chuckled. "Don't call them thieves in their hearing, and understand that their hearing is far superior to yours."

"Searching the interior, as it had become, was not a simple task; nor was it safe. They discovered that they could not command me; that I did not conform to their desires as either guests or Lords. They were, in short, quite rude."

"If they'd had better manners, you'd've given them what they asked for?"

"I'm not entirely certain, dear. What I was certain of at the time was that they offered me nothing in exchange."

"You mean...like rent?"

"Very like that, although perhaps not in the way that you think. Where was I? Ah. Yes. It was not a trivial task, and it was not short. They came, somewhat as you did, dear, with retainers."

Teela coughed. Bellusdeo coughed louder.

"They're not my retainers," Kaylin said; she didn't need the dramatics as a prompt. "They're my friends."

"Ah, then perhaps they were different. They did not gather friends; they had servitors, servants. Possibly slaves. They had to spend the time here, and as I did not approve, they were forced to feed themselves, and to clean the quarters they'd chosen. They did not," she added, with a slender smile, "choose to maintain quarters here for long. Only the powerless were left as witnesses, should I choose to change the environment." She fell silent for a long moment, and then, to Kaylin's surprise, drank the tea she'd poured herself.

"It was during this time that I became acquainted with mortals. I knew of them, of course, but they had never been relevant to my existence in any practical fashion. One of the servants was mortal. Ah, no, three were. But there was one. She was an older woman—older than you, dear—with gray hair; it was quite, quite long when she let it loose, but she always bound it and kept it off her neck. It got in the way of her work, she said.

"And it was such *odd* work. She swept the floors. She washed them. She washed the mantels—where they existed. I once put a small statuary in her way—and she cleaned that as well, although perhaps her language was a little on the colorful side at the end. She often said, 'I'm not young anymore!' while she worked.

"She came with flowers and branches and leaves; she came with small things—carvings, mostly, but sometimes small blown-glass figures. I broke some of them to see what she would do—I was younger myself, and less civil—and she swept up the pieces and removed them. Only once did she show some reaction. She was very, very quiet. Very still. She gathered those pieces by hand, one at a time."

"What was it—what was the figure of?"

"Another mortal, I think. A child." The woman said, "If you would like to see it, I kept it."

"You said you broke it."

"Yes. I did. But—her reaction made me look at it more closely. I could see no discernible merit to the figure; it seemed much of a style with the rest. But for some reason, it was personal to her. And one day, in apology, I gathered the broken pieces, and I fixed them. And then, in case the figure should happen to break again, I made more. Many more." She smiled as she spoke, her eyes that kind of faraway that meant memory. "I left many of them in the room in which she slept. It was a small, dark room, with a single high window and a very narrow door; it was meant as a closet, at one point.

"When she returned to her room after a day's work, she found the room changed. I didn't think the lack of light would make my gift clear enough, so I altered the window. And the window itself was so flat it almost seemed like a prison window; I changed that. I did not change the size of the room, or otherwise alter its shape—I didn't want the changes to be noticed easily by anyone but her.

"Her name was Hasielle."

"What did she do when she saw what had happened?"

The smile deepened. "She froze in the door and stared at the window. I think it took her a while to notice the small figures that were on the sill, the light from the window so captivated her. She was not used to living in light—only working in it, always. She told me later she didn't mind the dark, because in the dark, there was silence and peace. But—yes, she saw the figures after she managed to take her eyes off the window, all of them. She covered her mouth with her callused hands. She might have cried—I am really not allowed to say."

"She's dead, isn't she?" Mandoran asked. If Kaylin had been

sitting beside him, she'd have kicked him. He'd have the most bruised shins in the *city*. "What? It might be relevant!"

"She's protecting the person's *privacy,* idiot," Kaylin said. "She doesn't mean Hasielle is going to threaten or hurt her if she talks."

"She lived here. I did nothing for her for years. I made her life harder, rather than easier. But...she didn't tell her masters about the figures—or the window. She kept the place clean; she cleaned up after them if they'd been particularly destructive. She was here for years before she injured her shoulder and her back." The smile faded. "And then, she didn't come for months. The others came. New people. New mortals. They were not like her. They didn't bring me things. They didn't bring their flowers and their curtains and their small, fragile figures. They didn't hum while they worked.

"I was...sad. Not angry, not enraged—but sad. It was not a new feeling; I understood it; it was familiar. But I had no memories of feeling it before. I was particularly unfriendly during her absence—it was really unfair to the people who replaced her, because they had no choice in their work. They were terrified, by the end of two days; they had to be forced to enter the building at all.

"But their masters had mishaps as well, and of a kind which made the fears of their servants more relevant. I thought they would give up. I wanted them to give up. I wanted them to *leave.*" The last word was spoken with a force that none of the other words had contained; it caused Kaylin's skin to tingle.

The small dragon rose, wings lifted; he roared. Sadly, it came out as a longer, louder squawk. Kaylin reached up and put a hand over his mouth. "You are going to deafen *me,*" she said, pointedly. He bit her hand, but not hard enough to draw blood. "There's nothing wrong with wanting intruders to leave, either. Just—stop." She turned her attention back to the landlord, whose eyes had shifted into a decidedly non-mortal appearance.

"I'm sorry, dear," she said.

"It's all right. Tara has problems remembering her eyes, too." There were a lot of questions Kaylin probably should have asked next; the landlord seemed to expect some. But at the moment there was only one question she wanted answered. "Did Hasielle come back?"

The landlord smiled. Her eyes had once again become normal human eyes; at this distance they were an indeterminate shade of brown, lighter than Kaylin's. "Yes. But she came back after I was no longer anyone's responsibility. I was so surprised to see her," she said, her voice softer. "I knew she was mortal. I thought she had died of her injuries."

"Injuries don't always kill us," Kaylin said.

"No. She looked much older, and her gait was so changed I almost failed to recognize her. She was afraid. Fear is so strong it taints the air; if someone is afraid of me, it's often the first thing I hear. And she *was* afraid. But...it was a different sort of fear. She was anxious; she kept looking back over her shoulder—at the perimeter of the property. I could hardly believe it was her.

"And I knew—I thought I knew—what she was looking for. I moved the earth, for her—literally. I changed the front doors. I changed the stairs—they became a ramp, with a rail, so that she might walk up more easily. I unlocked the doors. I knew—I knew she would hate the rubble and the splinters that I'd allowed myself to gather, to become—so I swept them away.

"And the entire place had become a bit of a maze. It was only suitable for vermin, really—but that had been deliberate on my part. I considered all the visitors vermin, at that point.

They were carrion creatures. They considered themselves, of course, somewhat differently. People always do.

"But—for the first time since Hasielle left, I saw myself as she would see me. She had always taken some pride in my appearance, no doubt for her own sake. She had such odd notions about tidiness, cleanliness, and order. I had never spoken a word with her. I felt that I couldn't. I was not her master, but neither was she; she owed loyalty to the men and women who searched for the remnants of the Sorcerer's research.

"So what she knew of me was slight, indirect. I had to rearrange everything before I could open the doors to admit her. But there was one room I hadn't changed. I sealed it off when it became clear to me it would no longer be lived in. And it wasn't. I would not allow the others to use it, you see; nor would I allow them to take anything from it. Anything at all. I wanted to preserve her things. I wanted to preserve them until she returned.

"I think—I think she must have known. I think they must have told her what I'd become—if I'd had the time to think it through, I would have realized this. But I didn't, of course. I was excited. I was…happy. I was in such a rush to get everything *done* before the door was opened.

"And I finished. She opened the door. She walked in. She could see my front hall—but it wasn't truly mine, by then— do you understand?"

And Kaylin did. "It was hers. It was the hall she cleaned and tidied. The rooms—they were her rooms. She left flowers in them. She changed curtains. She didn't *know,* until the glass figures, that there was anything special about you, but she did all those things anyway. Until she was injured. How was she injured?"

"I don't know. She fell, I think—but it was outside. Outside where I can't go. It didn't occur to me to resent my lack of mobility—and I didn't. Not immediately. But they brought me no word of her. And she did not come.

"You can imagine what her reaction was when the doors did open."

But Kaylin shook her head. "Actually—I can't."

"What would you have felt, dear?"

Kaylin met Helen's gaze.

"If you opened the door to the home you thought destroyed, what would you have felt?"

Kaylin closed her eyes. "Suspicious," she said, quietly. "Because it would be impossible." But...she had opened a door in the heart of a Hallionne which lead to the apartment which she knew she'd never enter again. And suspicion hadn't been her first thought; it hadn't even made the list. She opened her eyes. "I don't have words for it, Helen."

Helen smiled. "I didn't coalesce; not as you see me now. She had never seen me. I was her home, but I wasn't part of the way she viewed it. But I was waiting. I don't think I've ever been quite so nervous. I have, of course, been worried; I have known fear, and anger, and even rage. But this type of nervous? No.

"But—she was nervous, too. I could almost *see* her straighten her shoulders as she entered my hall. She had the frown she wore when she was certain there was work to be done. I think she might have been disappointed to see everything so tidy. But—it was her tidiness. It was her order. I didn't have flowers for her, though. I had the vases but they were empty. Flowers are difficult, for me.

"I had her small glass figurines. I put them everywhere she might have left flowers. I didn't write her letters—although I could have. I held my breath. Hasielle held hers. And then she closed the door firmly behind her and marched toward the small room she'd occupied when she was my caretaker.

"And when she opened that door, and she saw her room—with the windows I'd given her on that day—she cried.

"I didn't know what to do with her tears," Helen added, lips folding in a fond smile that held a touch of pain. "She was happy. But she was not happy in a way I'd experienced before—not from any of the many masters of this house, and not from their guests. It was so strange, so odd, and so entirely like her.

"I wanted to talk to her, then. But—I may have mentioned I was nervous. She'd been gone so long, and I knew that she could just turn around and walk out the door again."

"You could have prevented that," Annarion said quietly. It was the first time since Helen had started that he'd spoken.

"Yes, of course. I could also prevent any of you from leaving." She frowned, and then added, "Perhaps not you and your friend. But the rest, yes."

The dragon squawked.

"Yes, dear, I know. But you know I wasn't referring to *you*."

"Imprisoning her wouldn't give you what you wanted," Kaylin said. "Because then you wouldn't *be* a home. You'd be a jail."

"Yes, dear." Helen smiled. "I didn't appear to her. I watched her, of course. I was worried. She was older and frailer. I made certain everything was solid enough that nothing would hurt her. I was almost afraid to *have* stairs." The nervousness, of course, had long since faded, and she recalled it with affection.

Kaylin, recalling her own nerves and their often catastrophic results, wanted to be old enough that she could look at them the same way. It was an odd thought.

"But she was there in the morning, in her bed. She woke early, as she always did. She made the bed. She cleaned the room. She headed into the kitchen, and she fussed about, cleaning things that didn't really require cleaning. She was very quiet. She had never done any cooking on her own before—and none of her masters lived on the premises. Cooking for one, she later told me, was not really cooking.

"But she worked. I thought she might inform her masters that I was safe again. She didn't. I'm not sure she knew quite what to do with herself. I certainly didn't understand what to do for her. I wanted her to stay.

"And she wanted, in the end, to stay. I am not quite like your Tara. I think I was damaged enough in the wars that I do not always see clearly or understand what I see."

Given Tara's interpretation of the thoughts she could easily read, Kaylin thought Helen was wrong.

"Within a few weeks she was less hesitant. And she started to sing while she worked. I didn't clean everything for her, because she liked to have something to do. I did clean things that required too much lifting or too much crawling. She settled into her routine here. She would go out and come home with food. But she began to work in the garden, as she called it. It was not so much of a garden at that point. I don't know if it's because I didn't leave enough for her to do in the house— but I think she liked to help things grow.

"And she grew flowers, that first year. She brought them into the house, as she had before. They made her smile. They made me smile. I remember the night she first placed them on the table—the dining room table, which she never used. She was expecting a guest. She didn't have clothing suitable for a dining room, in her own opinion. But she wore the best clothing she had, and she made dinner—for two. She used the plates that were used by her masters—never for herself, of course.

"And she served her first course, and water, and wine— which she herself couldn't abide, she found it so bitter. It was all so very strange. I watched the door. I knew she expected someone important—but no one arrived. I had never asked her if she had family; she had never once thought of them where I could hear her.

"But no one arrived. The candles burned, wax melted; I kept the food warm while she waited. And she did wait. I think two hours passed while she waited, and then she rose. I thought she would leave. Instead, she turned to the mirror and said, 'I know you're here. You've been here all along, haven't you?' There was nothing in the mirror but Hasielle's reflection—that, and the table, the candles, the flowers she had brought. She wasn't looking at herself.

"'You were here when I served the Sorcerer and his subordinates. You were here while they searched. You were here when I fell. I thought you'd left. I heard about the difficulties the Sorcerers began to face in my absence. They replaced me, of course—I couldn't do the work. And the building fell to ruin—stairs broke. The chandelier in the front hall. The stairs that lead both toward the tower and toward the basements. The floors themselves wore; the boards thinned. Windows shattered.

"'I was certain you must have left,' she continued, for I didn't know how to respond. 'And I grieved. I shouldn't have. You never showed yourself to me, after all. You made me no promises. You weren't like me; the Sorcerers spoke of you with respect. Well, with what passes for respect from their lot. But…you understood that my small glass child was important to me. When I broke it, you somehow fixed it. I couldn't believe that you would let the house fall to such ruin in my absence, but the women they hired to replace me spoke of all that had happened.

"'And I had to come back. But—you were here. You were waiting. My home was waiting for me. I was so afraid when I walked through that door. I didn't want to see ruins and destruction and neglect. And I didn't. We've never talked,' she continued. 'And I would like to. I am told that if you wish it, you can speak to me as if you were *like* me.'

"And she was right, and that night, I did."

CHAPTER 18

"She was my first tenant," Helen said, when no one spoke. "And if that first night was awkward—and oh, dear, it was— it was only the beginning. And I have learned that no matter how much we desire beginnings, all beginnings have awkward moments. Fear makes us awkward. But trust dispels fear, in the end.

"You meant to ask, when you arrived, to see the apartment I had for let; you meant to ask me how much I intended to charge you, and how I wished to be paid. Is that not true?"

Kaylin nodded.

"And were I a more traditional landlord, I would have answers to that question. I would, of course, have some flexibility. I would ask you in turn how you intended to pay; I would ask you about your place of employment. I might, as a matter of course, ask for references. But as you see, these are not meaningful questions, on either of our parts. You are, clearly, someone who can give me what I require. If this is an interview, you have impressed me with your suitability.

"What questions do you now have for me?"

Kaylin hesitated. The small dragon did not. He squawked enough for an entire flock of birds—when they were fighting over the same crusts of bread.

Helen's brows rose, although her eyes retained their more-or-less normal appearance.

"He would be living with me," Kaylin said quietly, when the dragon paused—probably for breath—and Helen had failed to speak.

"Yes, he's made that quite clear."

"What is he saying?"

"You are really going to have to do something about your linguistic difficulties," Helen replied. "At the moment, he is asking about my rules."

"All that was one question?"

"He is informing me of his. They are interesting. I am not entirely certain they are in keeping with what *you* would expect of a home."

"I'm not sure *I'm* in keeping with what you'd expect of a tenant. I don't keep regular hours. Gods know I've tried, but it doesn't generally work out as planned. I'm not particularly tidy; I don't let food rot in the open air, and I don't track mud—or worse—in through the door, but I'm not exactly a gardener, and I'm really not a flower person. I also don't own very much at the moment, and I don't have any furniture or other useful things.

"Bellusdeo would be living here, as well. She is, as mentioned, a Dragon. In case you don't get out too much, her gender is significant to the *rest* of the Dragons. It's significant to those who don't want there to *be* any more Dragons. She's—"

"The reason your former home was destroyed. Yes, dear, I know."

"Would she be safe here? Emmerian—"

Bellusdeo cleared her throat.

"*Lord* Emmerian, who is not present at the moment, is responsible for signing off on the security of any building she chooses to live in. He has a list of demands that are taller than I am. I'm not going to list them all because frankly, I don't remember most of them. But they kind of all mean the same thing: Bellusdeo must be safe."

"And not her roommate?"

"They don't give a rat's ass about her roommate."

"I," Bellusdeo cut in, "on the other hand, *do.*"

Helen nodded. "There is no need to glare at me like that, dear. I've been aware of that since you entered my front hall. I am sorry to say that if Kaylin chooses to live here, she will not have an entirely free run of guests."

Kaylin blinked. "Pardon?"

"You will be as much my home as I will be yours," Helen replied. "No one who means you harm in any way will be allowed through my doors. If they somehow manage to enter, they will not be allowed to leave—not the way they arrived."

"So...no thieves?"

"It depends on the reasons for their theft."

"It does?"

"Well, dear, it does to *you.*"

Kaylin flushed. "I know what it's like to be hungry," she said. "And desperate. I just don't think many hungry or desperate people are going to make it all the way to Ashwood. Not where it's currently situated. And I'm a Hawk, so randomly killing people who intend harm without causing it first would be really, really career-limiting. And yes, it'll still matter if it's you and not me."

"Yes, I would accept Maggaron as well, if that's what you desired."

Since that hadn't been the question Kaylin was struggling with, she reddened.

"You are worried about your marks?"

"Yes."

"You needn't be, dear. The marks reflect the Chosen, after all. There is nothing that you would do with them here that would threaten me."

As she spoke, Kaylin rolled up her sleeves. The marks were glowing a faint, luminescent gray. She hadn't noticed because they didn't hurt.

Teela noticed; so did Severn. The silence around the table shifted.

It was broken by the distant sound of howling.

Helen was the first to stand. She still looked like a delicate, frail old lady, but she moved like a Barrani. At her sudden, two handed gesture, the food on the table vanished. So did the cutlery, the dishes, and the teapot. "I think," she said, gazing past them all into the evening sky, "it's time we went indoors."

Severn had drawn his weapons, unwinding the weapon chain; Kaylin had drawn two knives, balanced for throwing. These were not her ideal fighting conditions. They were, on the other hand, the ideal conditions for the Ferals.

And Kaylin had no doubt at all that the howls she heard were the voices of Ferals; they had haunted her nightmares for years. One of the things she loved best about visiting Tiamaris was the existence of his nighttime Feral patrols. She loved that Morse headed out with the earnest and dedicated to kill those Ferals before the Ferals could kill any of the fief's residents. She loved that they didn't have to cower in terror or run until they dropped—and died.

She was side by side with a Dragon, a *Norannir* and *three* Barrani. She had no reason to cower or run.

"The Ferals," Teela said, "don't always hunt alone." She didn't have to read Kaylin's mind; she knew her well enough by now to make a really educated guess. "We're not in Tiamaris or Nightshade," she continued. "We're across the Ablayne and beyond the fiefwalls. There's no way there should be Ferals in the streets." She drew her sword—the sword which she wasn't allowed to carry while on active duty. "Mirror Jared," she said. "And mirror the Hawklord. This may be major trouble."

Kaylin turned to Helen, and then turned back. "We don't have a mirror connection here," she said, voice flat.

Teela grimaced. She glanced at Severn, in his civvies. "Corporal? One of us has to go to a neighbor's and mirror in to the Halls."

"There is a slightly faster way," Bellusdeo said.

Teela glanced at her, and away.

"I can go," Annarion volunteered, as if Bellusdeo hadn't spoken.

Teela said nothing, at least not audibly. Given that Annarion was waiting for a reply, Kaylin guessed she'd said nothing privately, either. "You can't," Kaylin told him. "Neither you nor Mandoran would be a good choice. If there are Ferals in the city—if they somehow crossed the border in the wake of something more powerful—they're probably heading here. For you two."

She glanced at her arms. The glowing soft gray of the marks had given way to traces of color; it made them vaguely opalescent.

"We *really* need to go inside, Kaylin," Helen said. "All of us."

Kaylin hesitated for one long moment.

"If you are correct," Helen continued, "and something is coming for your two friends, it is best not to meet them outside."

"We're halfway prepared compared to most of the city,"

Kaylin replied. "We've *got* weapons; we've got experience. If they're left to wander the streets—"

"They are not wandering. They are coming here. I doubt that they will pause in between to slaughter the citizens it is your sworn duty to protect. I have not attempted to engage with the mirror network of your city or your Emperor before—but I will make that attempt now if you will return to the house."

"Living in the city for less than half your life has really had a profound effect on your attitude," Teela said, as they followed Helen at an almost martial pace from her grounds to the main body of the house.

"I was *thirteen*, Teela."

"And you've become so much more powerful in the intervening seven years that you can rush out into the streets and stand against a Shadow of unknown capabilities?"

She's right, Severn said. *You are not the only Hawk in the city. You have access to magic that most of us don't—but you don't have control and you don't have knowledge. If Helen's right, they're coming here.*

And if they leave a trail of bodies behind them in their so-called straight path?

Then people die, same as they always did. You can't save everyone, ever. If you think only about the deaths you didn't *prevent, you'll break.*

She was silent.

I'm not saying that you shouldn't care. Your interference saved the Norannir. *It saved the city. But you could* interfere, *there. Here, I don't see it.*

I don't want to be a coward.

Severn said nothing.

And I'm terrified.

I know.

But I don't have a better way of not being a coward.

Yes, you do. You can work with and through the fear—but letting it make you stupid will only get you killed. It won't save other people. It'll just mean you won't be around to deal with the guilt. Silence for a beat; the back doors opened and Helen held them, waving everyone through. *I've spent a lot of time living with guilt.*

She stared at him for one long minute, and then turned on her heel and marched into the house.

The doors they entered were not the same doors they'd left by. Those had been bedroom doors, in theory. These were glass-paneled dining room doors. Behind them was a dining room table, with the large lighting that fancy houses boasted.

Helen gestured at Mandoran. "Boys, do come away from the windows."

Teela's brows lifted and her lips tugged up at the corner. Annarion glared at her, which caused her to laugh out loud. "They are not terribly biddable," she told Helen, when she could speak again. The boys, as they were, did come away from the window, although Mandoran had to be dragged.

"You're certain we're safe here?" Kaylin asked.

Helen was silent for a beat too long. "I am certain that you are safer than you would be if you were outside. I am not, as I told you, what I was."

"You can change your structure."

"Yes, of course." She glanced pointedly at Kaylin's left shoulder, where the small dragon was doing his imitation of a gargoyle. The small dragon yawned, displaying teeth that were remarkably solid given the rest of his translucence. "They are almost here."

Kaylin moved toward the window that the "boys" had been gently forbidden; Helen said nothing. The moons were not quite full, and the street, given the trees on the grounds and the fence around the property, were at best obscured. She couldn't see anything—but she could hear the howls of the approaching Ferals. She wasn't Morse; she didn't feel a surge of reckless excitement at the prospect of hunting—and, face it, butchering—the hunters.

No, she still felt the stiffness of fear. And, damned Severn anyway, guilt. She'd escaped. *She* had. But she'd been beyond desperate; when she'd crossed that bridge on the night that her life changed, she hadn't expected to survive. Hadn't really wanted to.

And now the fiefs were coming to her city. To the city she policed; to the streets she patrolled. She glanced at Helen, and prayed that Helen was right: they were coming here.

"Or the High Halls?" Helen asked.

Kaylin reddened as Teela arched one brow. "Ferals in the High Halls wouldn't last a minute."

"They wouldn't," Teela added, "last ten seconds. It's not the Ferals I'm worried about." She lifted an arm, but Kaylin now saw what Teela saw. The moons were fading from the night sky.

Helen spoke three words Kaylin didn't recognize. They weren't magical foci. They were spoken softly and quickly—and they didn't cause Kaylin's arms to break out in a rash.

"Kitling, can you reach Nightshade?"

Annarion stiffened.

Kaylin frowned. She didn't generally make the attempt to speak to him by the name that bound them both; it was never an entirely comfortable experience. But as she looked up at where the moons had been, she understood exactly what Teela was afraid of, and she tried.

Nightshade.

Silence.

Calarnenne.

Silence. Kaylin turned to Teela. "He's not—he's not answering."

"Is he alive?"

"How the hells should I know? He's not—"

"If he were dead," Annarion replied, "you would know."

She wasn't nearly as confident—but she was mortal. Maybe True Names—or at least their knowledge—didn't affect mortals the way they affected Barrani; mortals didn't have True Names.

Except Kaylin did.

"Helen, can you see the moons?"

Helen frowned. "Yes."

"Because we can't. Bellusdeo?"

"I'm part of 'we', in this case. The sky is dark; I assume that something large has come between us and our former view."

Helen frowned. "It is a seeming," she said. "The moons are still there. You were worried about the Ferals."

Kaylin nodded.

"You are not concerned about them now."

"Not *as* concerned. What's coming with them?"

Helen's frown deepened. "They are not," she said, shoulders sagging, "Shadows. They are not of the Shadows, but they can utilize some of the chaos of their substance."

"They."

"Yes. There are two. But Kaylin, one of them is not coming here."

Kaylin had prayed to nameless, faceless deities for most of her life—they never answered. Now was so *not* the time for them to start.

"Which direction is that one headed in?"

"I cannot be certain. My awareness of the city external to myself does not extend very far at all these days. All information comes—in the end—from my occupants. I don't suggest that you attempt to discover the information now, because one of them is almost upon my gates."

"How can you see them?"

"They are not, in their entirety, part of this city; I am not, therefore, subject to the same informational limitations. It is how I sensed the two boys. It is," she added, voice softening, "how *they* sensed them."

"Helen—what are they?"

"I believe your Teela knows."

"She's not *my* Teela."

"And I believe you have some suspicion yourself. You have encountered them while they slept."

Teela was now the color of bone; white-gray. Kaylin caught her by the forearm as she began to move away from the window. "You are *not* going out there."

"Says the woman who wanted to run into the streets with her *daggers* to confront Ferals."

"Fine. I accepted that it was stupid. What you're thinking is *way* worse."

She caught Mandoran and Annarion exchanging a brief glance—and it was comforting, somehow. Even if they could practically think each other's thoughts, they were looking for normal, visual confirmation of what they probably already knew.

She glanced at Severn. He shook his head. There was no way he was going to take her place as Teela's living shackle.

"Helen." Teela's voice was ice. "Have you established mirror connections with the rest of the city?"

"No, Lord Teela. It is not, at the moment, safe to do so. I am not a part of the mirror stream as it currently exists; I can slide into it and communicate through it, but to do so I have to open channels internally that are not completely secure." The implication was clear: this was a very poor time to attempt to massage known vulnerabilities.

"I'll have to go now. In person."

"I cannot open the gates."

"If I understand what is happening now, the gates will cease to exist in minutes—if they survive that long. Word must be sent—any advance warning at all—to the High Lord." Her eyes were the color of midnight; her voice was the temperature of winter. She started to leave, but Kaylin was still attached—firmly—to her arm. Teela was Barrani; she was strong enough to drag Kaylin from here to the High Halls without breaking a sweat. But she wouldn't move *as* quickly.

"You want word sent to the High Halls—I can do that, Teela."

Teela stiffened. "You're certain."

Kaylin grimaced. If she hated to call Nightshade by use of his name, it was purely a matter of personal discomfort. For reasons of his own—reasons she had never tried to penetrate—he didn't wish her harmed. Or dead. Neither did the Lord of the West March—but he was nowhere near the High Halls, and she wasn't entirely certain her voice would reach him from the heart of Elantra.

"Yes," she said, straightening her shoulders and clenching her jaw.

The third Barrani name she held had not been willingly given. She had seen it, in the heart of the space defined by a Hallionne, and she had reached out—literally—to grab it. She had spoken the name, and in speaking, she had anchored it.

There was no way to release it; not according to Nightshade or Lirienne. Only if the Barrani died would she be free of his anger, his humiliation, and his hatred. It had gotten so bad at one point in the West March she had seriously considered forcing him to walk off a cliff. Unfortunately, there hadn't been a conveniently placed cliff, and by the time she'd found one, she'd calmed down.

The return from the West March had not been nearly as difficult. She'd learned to compartmentalize his background resentment; when she couldn't, she would speak to the Lord of the West March; his presence drowned out the other.

Ynpharion.

She felt an instant, sharp pain, as if a spike had been driven behind her eyeballs. Resistance. Fury. Suspicion.

We. Do. Not. Have. Time. For. This.

The sharp pain increased. Kaylin looked up at Teela and managed to unclench her jaws long enough to say, "What do you need said to the High Lord?"

The tenor of Ynpharion's struggle shifted from resentment and rage to stillness. Kaylin stumbled; it was almost as if she'd been fighting a literal tug-of-war, and he'd suddenly dropped his side of the rope. *What is happening?* he demanded.

I don't know how old you are, she replied, as Teela began to speak. *But we have a problem. Well, the High Halls are about to have a problem, and it's not small.*

"Tell the High Lord that An'Teela sends an urgent message." She lifted her hand and raised her palm. Kaylin's entire body crawled in response to the wordless gesture, although she saw no obvious use of magic on Teela's part. "Two of the ancestors that once almost destroyed our kind have escaped the shadows and the fiefs. One, at least, is on its way to the High Halls."

And the other? She blinked as she saw the interior of the High Halls superimposed across Helen's dining room. Ynpharion was on the move. Kaylin didn't recognize the halls themselves, only the style: the height of ceilings meant to remind visitors of their lack of stature, the statues and small founts that adorned the passing walls. *You said there were two.*

Teela said there were two.

Where is the other if it is not on the way to the High Halls?

Oh, in our backyard. If you're lucky, you'll have your freedom soon.

I would not trade my freedom, he said, cold fury adorning every mental syllable, *for the lives of my Lord and the Lady.*

Do you understand what Teela's talking about?

Frustration warred with humiliation; frustration won. *No. But she has made clear that she considers this to be as much of a threat as the Dragon Flights once were.*

Bellusdeo said nothing for a long, long moment. She then turned to Helen. This was not going to be a banner night. "I will retreat. Can you arrange a different exit?"

Helen frowned.

"I will not walk out into the contested streets, Helen."

Helen's eyes brightened. Literally. "You will fly."

Bellusdeo nodded.

"You take a risk, Bellusdeo. There is a reason that the moonlight is obscured, at least for those of you who stand upon the ground."

"I am not particularly fond of the denizens of the High Halls," the Dragon replied. "But I have become fond of this city. I will call upon the Dragon Court, and we will attempt to head this creature off before it enters the Halls."

"But not," Teela asked, "before it reaches them?"

"The Halls themselves are protection against invaders that the rest of the citizens of Elantra do not have; the Emperor will not risk a fire fight in those streets unless there is no other option. Our fires are unlikely to melt your stone halls; they are likely to raze any other building."

Kaylin let Ynpharion go, inasmuch as that was possible. "If anything happens to you, the Emperor will turn me to ash."

"Yes."

Kaylin opened her mouth; Bellusdeo raised a hand. This one didn't cause Kaylin pain. "If this creature stops to destroy parts of the city on its walk toward the High Halls, I have the greatest survival chance of all present. I would say Helen has greater, but she cannot move. I can. It is not to the aid of the Barrani I fly, Private Neya."

Kaylin closed her mouth.

"I will take Maggaron with me."

And opened it again in a rush. "Maggaron is *mortal*."

"Yes. But he will not remain behind, and it would pain me greatly to injure him by throwing him off the heights of a tower." She turned, once again, to Helen. "I assume there is a tower."

"Yes, Bellusdeo. And yes, I will lead you there if you are determined." She turned to the three Barrani. "You will not last long against him once he breaches the walls; not in your current state. You have advantages—well, you boys do—that are unusual. Do *not* listen long to his speech if he makes the attempt to speak."

Without another word, she turned and left the dining room. Bellusdeo and Maggaron followed.

"Do you two have *any* idea what she's talking about?" Kaylin demanded, when the door had closed.

"No," Teela said, before either Annarion or Mandoran could answer. "They don't. And for the record, neither do I. I wish I had brought my sword."

"You have a—"

"My real sword. This is for mortal play, at best. It is not without use, but it has no true power. When Helen said 'walls', did she refer to the fence?"

"I think so."

"Hardly comforting." She glanced at her two friends. "Are you going to hide behind me," she asked, "or prepare your-selves?"

Mandoran snorted. Annarion failed to acknowledge the question, but he drew a long blade. It looked out of place in the cheerful, large dining room. He didn't join Teela as she stood by the window, looking out. "Kitling?"

Kaylin nodded. She turned to the small dragon; he snorted, but obligingly lifted one wing so that it covered her upper face—and, most important, her eyes. The howls of Ferals were so close Kaylin knew they were less than a block away. But that was a fief block.

All right, Helen, she thought, as she moved to stand beside Teela, *let's see what you've got.* She turned to look out the win-dow and froze.

The translucent, dragon-wing mask revealed what Kaylin's normal vision couldn't. The grounds of the Ashwood Street house seemed as wide at the front as they had when she'd walked up the path.

"Hey, watch where you swing that," Mandoran snapped.

Kaylin almost turned, but didn't. She'd found what looked—and felt—like a fence from the outside of the prop-erty, and she was certain, if the small dragon withdrew his wing, it still would. At the moment, it looked like a glowing, pale wall of thick glass. The wall was taller at its height than the fence had been, and although she thought of it as glasslike, she could not see the streets she knew lay beyond it.

What she could see, clearly, were the Ferals. It was a full hunting pack; she counted six. Seven. Eight. When the Ferals hunted, their voices could be heard across the fief. Only when they fell silent was it safe to risk a glance out of a window—and only then if you happened to be high enough above the ground. She had never stayed in the window long enough to count eight.

They weren't running, now; they stood in a line on the other side of the wall, visible, their eyes oddly luminescent; they turned their heads toward the center of the line, as if waiting on the actions of the pack leader.

She looked as well, because it was impossible not to. In the strange glow cast by the fence, stood a Barrani man.

Barrani sometimes walked the streets of Nightshade; they were Nightshade's men. They didn't patrol the streets to keep them safe; Kaylin had no idea what they did on those forays from the Castle, or if they did it at the fieflord's command. The Barrani were, like Teela, unimpressed by the Ferals; they didn't consider them a danger. To the Barrani, the Ferals were very like dogs gone wild.

They did not, however, command them; where the Ferals were not cautious enough in their choice of victims, they died.

"Teela—"

"What do you see?"

"I see Ferals. They're standing in a line; there are eight. Four to each side of a single Barrani male."

"He is not Barrani."

"His hair is longer than yours. Longer than Nightshade's. It's—darker, somehow. And his skin looks white." She hesitated, and then continued. "White like alabaster. He doesn't look alive, to me."

"He looks dead?"

She shook her head. "No. He looks like a sculpture."

"A statue?"

"Yes—like the statues that serve as pillars across the entry to the High Halls. He's like—like an artist's interpretation of a Barrani man. There are no flaws."

"Sounds boring," Mandoran said.

"Stay away from the window," Teela replied.

"I wanted to see this paragon of unearthly beauty."

"Why? Jealous?"

"Skeptical."

Annarion grabbed Mandoran's right elbow; Mandoran laughed. The laughter banked abruptly because Bellusdeo *roared*. The man standing before the wall in the center of a line of Ferals looked up at the sound of her Dragon voice. And then he smiled.

The smile stopped Kaylin's breath. "Helen!"

He lifted an arm as if in graceful, lazy greeting, and black shadow gathered around his fingertips in a nimbus of anti-light.

"Helen!"

CHAPTER 19

"Helen!"

"Kitling—" Teela fell silent.

Everything Kaylin knew about Towers she'd learned from Tara and the Hallionne. They'd been built for different reasons, and operated by rules that served the builders' purposes; those rules were their foundations. She had no idea what Helen could—or could not—do. But she was certain the wavering, thick barrier was an extension of Helen's body.

"Helen!"

Light traveled through the undulating, thick barrier, drawing to a white, bright point in front of the stranger who seemed, for the moment, occupied with Bellusdeo's aerial escape.

"Be prepared," Helen's disembodied voice said, "for difficulty. This will not be without cost."

"We'll deal with the cost—save Bellusdeo!"

The wall fell on the ancestor, moving like a tidal wave, and landing with enough force that it crushed the four Ferals closest to him; Kaylin could practically hear the sound. It didn't crush the stranger. It didn't seem to *hit* him. But he brought his arm down as the wall heaved most of itself on his head, raising a palm as if to catch its weight.

He did. He caught the weight that would have turned him into a dark smear on the street, in the center of the other dark smears. That left four Ferals and one significantly more dangerous creature. Who did look, to Kaylin, like the idealized paragon of Barrani power.

"You'll need to be very careful," Helen told them. She still hadn't appeared. "Only at the height of my power could I contain one of his kind. I could not destroy them without causing irreparable damage to myself."

"How could you destroy—"

"She let them in," Mandoran said.

No one but Kaylin turned to stare at him, and her gaze bounced back to the window. Her arms began to glow.

The small dragon squawked.

"No, I need your wing where it is. You can drop it if the bastard breaks through."

He bit her ear lobe; she cursed in Leontine. Raising a hand to provide a less delicate target, she stopped. Her arms were glowing; the light could be seen through the fabric of her shirt. But the light was solid, and as she watched, her sleeves began to bulge.

Cursing increased as she rolled her sleeves up, shoving them into crinkles above her elbow. Runes were, once again, lifting themselves off her skin. This time however, it was only a few. She desperately hoped that something similar wasn't going on with the marks on her legs or back; she couldn't afford to replace the clothing she was wearing; it was pretty much all she had, if she didn't count her uniform—and she was not about to strip naked before a fight.

"You're worried about replacing cheap rags at a time like

this?" Mandoran demanded, his brows vanishing into his beautiful hairline in outrage.

"Unlike *some* people, I have to buy my own clothing!"

"Now is not the time," Teela told them both. She was right. It wasn't. But until the Barrani either broke through or gave up—and she wouldn't have taken a bet at any odds on the latter, which said something—they had nothing else they could do.

Mandoran, however, fell silent, giving Teela the last word. He was staring at the marks that had risen to the level of Kaylin's eyes. There were six in total, and they cast no reflection in the glass panes of the window. Since it wasn't normal glass, Kaylin wasn't too surprised.

The small dragon squawked loudly.

"Do *not* bite me again; I'm paying attention." She gazed through a gap in the runes to see that the Barrani ancient was staring—at her. Or at the words; at this distance it was hard to tell.

He lifted a palm and slammed it into the barrier; the barrier undulated. She heard him speak—how, she didn't know, but she assumed Helen was somehow facilitating—and this time the rest of her body responded; her skin went from tingling, which could be ticklish and uncomfortable, to pain of the sandpaper-on-skin variety.

Without pausing to think, Kaylin threw herself into Teela; Teela had a size and weight advantage, but she wasn't expecting danger from her right side. Both women tumbled clear of the windows just before the glass shattered.

Severn's weapon chain began to spin.

The small dragon's wing dropped; he looped his tail around her neck. The tumble hadn't dislodged the runes—but it seldom did; they were stationed just over her head, like a wreath made of lines, squiggles, dots. She rose and glanced at Teela.

Lord Kaylin. Ynpharion's voice. *Tell Lord Teela that the High Lord has been informed of the danger. He asks only one question.*

"Teela—do you recognize the guy attacking the house? I mean, recognize him as an individual, not as a general threat?"

Teela hesitated. "No."

Ynpharion didn't believe her. To make matters worse, neither did Kaylin—but given what she'd said in Castle Nightshade, there was no possible way she could actually recognize the individuals. *Tell her what you told me,* Ynpharion said, in disgust. *Now is not the time.*

She hasn't seen either of them close-up. That's probably going to change real soon. It was her turn to hesitate; he caught it. He didn't have time to push for more, and to her surprise, didn't attempt to take advantage of the rest of the distractions. The Ferals were howling right beneath the window, at least by sound.

What are the Dragons doing?

I'm not anywhere near the Dragons at the moment, Ynpharion.

Not even your Bellusdeo?

No.

Where is she?

I'm not going to answer that question.

Listen to what I hear, Lord Kaylin. It will not take much effort or time; I will not fight you. Just—listen. It was almost a plea.

It wasn't just sound; the Ferals were beneath the windows. They had always been better jumpers than dogs.

"Helen—the barrier—"

"I let the Ferals in," she replied. "To better focus my defenses on the actual threat. Please deal with them."

"Done," Teela replied.

"My power extends to the edge of my property—but the only exceptional defenses I have are within the walls."

"Meaning, don't just jump out the window?" Kaylin asked. Helen failed to respond.

Lord Kaylin.

Kaylin closed her eyes. She didn't like and didn't trust Ynpharion; the feeling was mutual. She wanted to spend as little time as possible being made aware of his existence. If there were *any* way short of killing him that she could release his name and all knowledge of it, she'd do it in a heartbeat.

But that wouldn't have been at all helpful tonight, because he was the only way she had of getting a necessary message to the High Lord.

I also appreciate the irony, Ynpharion surprised her by saying. *I have spent the whole of my life attempting to gain power and to prove my worth to those that have more of it—and I have, in one evening, done more to advance my cause than in the rest of the centuries combined. And all because I am in essence your slave.*

She drew closer to him as he spoke. Close enough to feel the burning edges of his shame and humiliation; it was not nearly as suffocating as it had been when she first made contact with him, even this evening, but she understood how much effort it took on his part. Everything in him screamed to fight; everything except the reason he had made contact with her.

Her eyes blurred as her vision shifted to the familiar audience chamber—which was mostly forest and a bit of clearing—in the High Halls. She could see the High Lord; he was not seated; she could see the Consort.

It was the Consort who looked directly at Kaylin. She could hear the formal tones of High Barrani, wrapped in the urgent pragmatism of a war band. For now, for tonight, all bitter political rivalries and plotting would be set aside, as if they were of no consequence.

"Lord Kaylin," the Consort said. Kaylin froze. She could hear and see the Consort so clearly she might have *been* Ynpharion for that moment.

She didn't speak, but realized suddenly that she *could*. Ynpharion had moved aside; he had opened himself up entirely to her intrusion. The Consort spoke again, but her words were drowned out by the roaring of a Dragon.

No, Kaylin thought, freezing in place. Not *a* Dragon. More than one.

Where are they? she asked Ynpharion.

They have not yet arrived. Do you—

Yes. Bellusdeo is definitely there. I bet she flew straight from here. She was with you.

Yes. We're in—we're in as safe a spot as we can be, given the danger. The High Halls are not like the Hallionne or the Towers in the fiefs; we weren't certain what the—the Barrani ancestor could do. Bellusdeo flew out to rouse the Dragon Court; my guess is she didn't bother to land. There is no *way the Emperor would have allowed her to fight for—and in front of—the High Halls. Not after the assassination attempt.*

She is not alone.

No—she's not. I don't understand Dragon speech; I can feel it more than I hear it. If she's flying around the High Halls roaring for aid, the Emperor will probably send the entire *court. He'll probably join them. Whatever you do, don't attack her. Don't let* any *of the Lords attack her.*

You will not tell the Consort yourself.

…No.

Even if she is aware of your presence.

No. Because then everyone *will be aware of it. I know* this *is bad for you. It looks bad. It's a mark of inferiority. All that crap. But she has to understand your mettle, here. Yes, in theory I could have forced you to carry word. I could have used your name against you.*

But…I didn't have to. You were willing to risk the loss of everything you've struggled to build in order to save your people.

You seem surprised.

I am. Tell her what I've said. Bellusdeo will not harm you; the Emperor will not. But—

Lord Kaylin? Lord Kaylin!

The wall cracked and a section the width of two men toppled inward.

Kaylin was on her feet before the dust had settled, daggers in hand, small dragon around throat. Severn's chains were now a sheen of translucent circles, although he held the end blade in his left hand. The Ferals had no need to try to leap in through the shattered window's frame; a path had just been made for them.

The Ferals were no threat to Teela. The man—who definitely would be—hadn't followed the Ferals in through the gaping hole he'd made in the building's side, and Kaylin risked a glimpse out the jagged opening. He was still on the street-side of the fence. The fence, without dragon wing to translate the visual image, was battered and dented; the tops of the tines which were well above Barrani heads had been damaged enough they now curled—or dripped, which was disturbing—toward the ground.

The buildings beyond the street—which Kaylin could now see much more clearly—had not been harmed—but where the four Ferals had been crushed flat, pools of shadows were growing.

She could hear the Dragon court at a distance. The entire city probably could. The sound of their roaring didn't distract the Barrani ancestor; Kaylin wondered if the Draco-Barrani wars had been much after his time.

She ducked as Teela's blade whistled an inch above her

head; it connected with the neck of a Feral. Teela was in a foul mood; giving her something to kill was no doubt an unintentional kindness on the part of the attacker.

Annarion killed two of the four, which left one; Severn dispatched it. Teela hadn't broken a sweat. Blade slick with blood that looked black, she raised her sword arm and brought it down as if she intended to cleave the air in two.

"Corporal?"

Severn nodded. Teela stepped back and to his left. Annarion, in silence, moved to take up a similar position on his right as Severn moved to stand in the gap that had once been wall. The chain didn't cover the entirety of the hole as it spun, but covered enough of it; there was no convenient wall to stave in to crush Severn's weapon.

The small dragon squawked and batted one of the runes still attached invisibly to Kaylin's head. She had no idea what they were meant to do, but she felt safer while they were there. The dragon squawked again, and then screeched, which was piercing.

"Fence is almost done for," Kaylin said, while trying to cover her ear.

"I think," Mandoran said, "your familiar is trying to *tell you* something." He pointed at the runes. "You're standing in a building that's confessed it's quite diminished. The building is under attack; its defenses are not what they were. She *told you* this. Were you not listening?"

"I was—"

"Your familiar feels that your crown of words might help to heal the damage done. Now," he added more urgently. "There has to *be* something left to heal." He looked past Severn. No, Kaylin thought, watching his expression; he looked *through* Severn. "Teela—"

"Yes, take her and go. But Mandoran—"

"I won't kill her."

"Don't *get her* killed."

Mandoran snorted. He turned, caught Kaylin by the arm, and dragged her out of the dining room, leaving by the same door that Helen had taken. Helen, Kaylin was certain, had gone up. But she was also certain that up wasn't the way to go if they needed to reach the heart of the building.

"It's not," Helen agreed. "I am about to lose the outer wall."

"How long do you have, Helen?"

"Perhaps five minutes. He is not yet at his peak power; he is using borrowed power."

"I meant, how long do you have once he does enter the house?"

"That will depend on your friends, dear."

Kaylin noted that Helen wasn't giving Mandoran directions, but he didn't seem to need them. He entered what might have been a large kitchen in other homes, and found his way to what looked like a small supplies closet. Instead of buckets and brooms, there were stairs. The stairs were not well lit. They wouldn't have been lit at all were it not for a crown of words; those words shed an even, ivory light—enough so that Kaylin could see that the stairs were a descending spiral around a central column of some sort. The curve was gentle; it was not a small circumference.

It must be the tower. From the streets, no such tower had been visible.

"Is there anything in the basement we should be worried about?" Kaylin asked.

It was Mandoran who answered. "Yes."

She didn't ask why he was so certain; it was clear that he was. Nor did Helen contradict him.

"Shadows?" she asked, when the silence after the bad news had stretched on too long.

"Not exactly. Follow me when we reach the bottom. Or an exit. Either will do. Step exactly where I step. *Exactly.* Your feet are smaller than mine; they should fit within the same space." He grimaced. "I don't think anyone's been here in centuries."

The stairs suddenly shuddered. Mandoran cursed—in Leontine. He tightened his hold on her arm as the walls moved away from the staircase—in both directions. "This is bad," he said.

"In what way beyond the obvious?" Barrani balance was better in general than mortal balance, but Kaylin had walked narrower stretches, higher above the ground.

"Whoever he is—he's speaking to Helen. And Helen is responding."

Down continued for at least five minutes; Kaylin was counting seconds as she moved, knees slightly bent. The stairs shuddered twice more; on the third iteration, the tower once again expanded to fill the gap created when it shrunk. Kaylin kept one hand on the stone, increasing her pace to match Mandoran's; she was aware the tower might once again change shape, and kept her touch light. The walls on the other side— to the right while descending—did not magically reassert their existence; there was a drop here, and Kaylin couldn't see how far it was.

They didn't reach the bottom. A door opened to Kaylin's immediate left; it sprang out and almost knocked both her and Mandoran off the stairs. She had to admit she liked the way Mandoran used Leontine: as if he meant it.

The door didn't slam shut after it had been very narrowly avoided.

"Helen?"

"She can't answer you—not in a way you can hear. Not now." Mandoran's next breath was sharp enough to cut. "Now we understand why Teela was so pissed off."

"You've got each other's names—didn't she explain it?"

"Yes. But her explanations lack immediacy. And detail. And substance. Let me go first. Remember what I told you."

"Step exactly where you step."

He didn't look back. The small dragon squawked, and Mandoran appeared to be considering something. "Not yet," he finally said. The small dragon snorted.

"Shouldn't you be upstairs?" Kaylin asked him. "The heavy lifting is all happening there. Or at least we hope it is."

In answer, the crown that wasn't quite touching her head began to rotate, which made as much sense as most answers about magical battles did. The familiar, still anchored to her neck by his tail, didn't budge as Mandoran moved to stand in the door frame. He had to release her arm to do so; she grabbed a handful of tunic just in case she needed to haul him back.

"The heavy lifting—as you say in Elantran—is meant to be a distraction. Can you hear those words?"

"Which words?"

"The ones you're carrying."

"No."

"Figures. Teela can't, either."

"Can anyone but you and Annarion?"

"...No."

"Can you tell me what they're saying?"

"Lord Kaylin—they're right in front of your *face*."

"You're calling me that to be irritating, right?"

He laughed. "Annarion feels it inappropriate. You're going to have to let go of me, or we'll be standing here until the ancestor arrives."

"He's not coming here."

"Where else would he go? You have some understanding of the buildings the Ancients created; you know they have a core, and the whole of their power resides there."

"She does," Helen—who had been largely silent through-out their descent—said. "She understands possibly more than you do."

Mandoran snorted. "She's mortal, Helen."

"She's Chosen."

"Yes—but she's not particularly perceptive. Or bright."

"If you don't want me to knock you over, you might consider taking that back."

"I didn't say *I* was perceptive or bright, either."

She let go of his tunic and braced herself in the door frame.

"You'll want to be careful here," Helen told them.

Kaylin, looking at a floor that seemed to be made of solid, if worn, stone, glanced at the small dragon on her shoulder. He didn't lift his wing until she cleared her throat. He took the hint—but he batted the side of her face first.

The floor, seen through translucent wing, looked exactly the same. "Fine. Sorry." She looked back to Mandoran and froze—because Mandoran didn't.

He had the same height, the same shape, the same features—well, seen from the back, at any rate—but he was translucent. Not as much as the small dragon, but she could see stone walls through the contours of his back. He was also glowing faintly. Strands of his hair moved back and forth as if caught in a cross-wind, and as she watched, the trails of gentle light they left in their wake formed a weave, a pattern of some kind.

"He's right," Helen said, as Kaylin considered walking across the floor. "You *can* walk through this room, but it will not lead you to me."

"Where will it lead me?"

"Quite possibly a laboratory or a library. There are many rooms that I chose to absorb during the time of difficulties, and their contents remain scattered throughout my... basement."

"Are they safe?"

"No," Mandoran said sharply. "They're not." He had started to walk, and he moved slowly and deliberately; he didn't follow a straight path, but at this point that wasn't in his character. "I'm finding this more difficult than it should be. Probably because of the noise."

Squawk.

Kaylin followed in Mandoran's footsteps, because she could see where his feet had touched stone; he'd left a mark that was a gray blur in his wake. She was pretty certain the mark would be invisible without the veil of dragon wing, and she moved quickly. She had always been steady on her feet, and she had learned to step lightly, to make as little noise as possible.

She could therefore walk where Mandoran lead without falling behind. But there seemed to be no pattern to the path he was following.

"He isn't following a path," Helen told her. Mandoran cursed under his breath. "He's making one."

"And you're letting him?"

"Yes. It is challenging, I admit."

"Could you not just open a path we could both walk across now?"

"No."

"But the Hallionne—"

"And your Tara, yes. They could—and did—lead you into the heart of their power. I could have done so once—but I surrendered that ability to protect myself."

"From what?"

"I did not wish to be forced to serve a master not of my own choosing."

"But if you're willing to let *me* live here—"

"Yes, Kaylin, I am. But you are not my master. And you've no desire to be." The floor shook; Mandoran swore in loud Leontine as Kaylin put both of her hands on his back to steady him.

"Someone does," he said, and he began to move more quickly.

He walked toward the door on the far wall. To Kaylin, the door hadn't changed; it looked older, but solid; it was of scored wood, but the frame, like the rest of the room, was of stone. To her eyes—even given dragon wing—it looked as if he'd just chosen a very circuitous route instead of marching across the floor in a direct line.

When he reached the door, he stopped. He didn't touch the handle; he didn't try to open it. Instead, he placed both palms flat against its surface, at the height of his shoulders, and bowed his head. His hair rose in swirls, long strands twining and thickening around his shoulders, until they formed three distinct braids, which moved like rope snakes. It was disturbing.

It really didn't help when the hair—with no visible help—rose above the height of his shoulders and drove itself—in three spikes—through the wood of the door. The door *cracked*.

"What are you *doing?*"

Mandoran didn't answer; his hair did; it seeped between boards and through splintered wood, pulling more and more of what had been door apart. The small dragon hissed when wood bits bounced off his wing, which didn't make Mandoran any happier.

But Kaylin understood why; the floor was shaking almost constantly. She bent into her knees, her hands still on Mandoran's back. The door they'd entered slammed shut; Kaylin turned her head to look back at it. She hadn't closed it; neither had Mandoran.

"I did," Helen said. "Tell your friend he has to *hurry*."

"Helen—"

"Your friends are still alive," she replied, before Kaylin could ask. "They are fighting as we speak. Because Annarion is present, the enemy is forced to fight on two fronts."

"He should be fighting on three."

"On two. One is the small, physical world you inhabit. This would be much more difficult for all of us had you not brought them with you; as it is, the enemy can do far less damage while being engaged. Annarion can attack him on the same plane that Teela and Severn can. He can also attack in a different way. If Annarion were not here, there would be very, very little we could do to counter the damage he could do in that dimension."

The closed door they'd entered shuddered. Once. Twice. Kaylin thought she heard the crack of wood.

Mandoran's door came down first. He turned and grabbed Kaylin by the waist; before she could react, he lifted her off her feet as if she weighed nothing, and tossed her through the jagged opening. "Go!" he shouted. "I'll hold the rear!"

CHAPTER 20

Kaylin scraped skin off her elbow as she rolled to her feet. Turning, she looked back at Mandoran to make clear how much she appreciated this.

He wasn't there.

Neither was the doorway.

"Helen?"

"I'm here." Or at least her voice was. Kaylin looked around the room and discovered that *room* was the wrong word. It was, or it looked to be, a cave. A cave composed of alabaster, gold, and marble. The ceiling was high and rough; it rounded gently at its height. The walls closest to Kaylin were the same; if not for their color, they wouldn't have been out of place in the average cave.

She found her footing and began to walk. The words that adorned her brow were her only source of light, but at least they left her hands free. As she headed toward what she assumed was the center of the cavern—by height of ceiling—the light began to change.

At Tara's heart—if *heart* was the right word—Kaylin had

seen words. And she had seen the Shadows that had slipped between the cracks of defenses that mortals couldn't even *see* attempt to rewrite, revise, or destroy the words that had been written there. At the time, she had had the Tower's Avatar by her side as she attempted to halt the damage; she had had Tiamaris, who could, if not read the words, at least recognize the shape and form they should have, without interference.

And she had spoken the words, grouping syllables that should have been gibberish into sounds that Tara, at least, could acknowledge.

The words written here were very like the words written in the Tower of Tiamaris. There were, however, far fewer of them. As Kaylin walked, her feet passed over great, black scorch marks. In places, the floor was pocked and uneven, although the stone wasn't cracked; it looked, to Kaylin, as if it had both melted and cooled. There had once been words here.

"Yes," Helen said.

Kaylin turned, but Helen's Avatar was not beside her.

"I can't be, anymore. I can only be in one place at a time. I am almost in the dining room now; the ascent and descent of the tower are more difficult. I do think the two boys could travel at greater speeds."

"Is Mandoran still alive?"

"Of course. I do not think they will be able to drive the enemy away—but he cannot kill or absorb them without power—which he is expending as we speak. I am sorry," she added, her voice softening.

"For what?" The glow in the center of the cavern resolved itself into words, as Kaylin had expected. There appeared to be a central stone; the words that had not been destroyed ringed it in rough, concentric circles. There were far fewer words than Tara had contained; far fewer than she had once glimpsed in Castle Nightshade. Seeing the unoccupied scorch marks that occupied most of this cavern, Kaylin suspected that Helen had once had as many.

She knew what the words she carried as a crown were meant to do.

She didn't know *where* they were meant to go, and wasn't even certain their position was important.

Squawk.

But she suspected, given the noise the small dragon was making, it was. She closed her eyes. Eyes closed, she could still see the words—all of them. She could no longer see alabaster and crystal and cavern, but they were just distractions; she needed to concentrate on the words she couldn't, without a lot of coaching, even read.

The small dragon squawked again; this time his voice was softer.

"I wish you could tell me what these said. I think I recognize one or two of them—but there are a lot more than one or two."

Squawk.

The ground shook. In the distance, Kaylin could hear roaring. It wasn't, sadly, Dragon roar—and this is probably the only time she would miss *that* sound.

"Helen—"

And I *said NO.* It was Mandoran's voice. She heard it almost the same way she heard Ynpharion's, Nightshade's or Lirienne's—and that was disturbing. What she couldn't hear was who he was shouting *at.*

But the ground shook again, and this time—this time rubble fell from what Kaylin assumed was the ceiling. She opened her eyes, then; the last thing she needed was a chunk of much larger stone landing point first on her head.

Squawk! Squawk!

The wall on the far side of the room—where Kaylin had

entered—cracked. Loudly. Around the fissure that had appeared in white stone, she could see sparks of lightning.

"Yes," she told the small dragon. "I don't think you're much help here."

He bit her ear.

"Go help Mandoran."

He pushed himself off her shoulder, spun once around her head, and then flew off toward the damaged wall. Kaylin turned back to the words and the gaps between them. The spaces on the outer periphery were all empty; she let those be. The absence of those words had clearly not killed Helen, and she'd probably lived without them for a long time.

The absence of the words in the center hadn't killed her, either. But there was a lack of symmetry or a lack of balance in the central cluster that felt off, or wrong, to Kaylin. Clearly, Helen could live without all the words that had once transcribed her power. But Mandoran and the small dragon thought she couldn't defend herself the way, say, Tara could. And that she should be able to. It made sense, then, that if Kaylin was to surrender marks in Helen's defense, they be placed here.

She reached up to touch one of the floating runes; she felt its warmth, followed quickly by its surprising weight. She lifted a second hand to catch the word before it toppled.

She then carried it as she began to thread her way around Helen's words, which still glowed with the luminosity of the blood of the ancients. She wondered, as she began to head toward the center of the cluster, how single words could contain so much information. She knew a number of languages, and knew as well, that she'd barely scratched the surface; she could probably spend a decade learning a single word in each language which in theory meant the same thing.

Even if she did, it wouldn't mean she could communicate

the concept; people used the exact same word to mean different things. So these weren't really words; they were like containers. Somehow they contained enough information that they could be understood without context—if they could be understood at all. Kaylin had her doubts.

But she had her doubts about a lot of the Imperial Laws on the books as well, and it didn't stop her from gritting her teeth and obeying them.

"Helen?"

Silence.

"Helen!"

"I'm here," came the disembodied voice. It was quieter.

"Can you read these words?"

"Yes. But I can't explain all they mean to you. It's not because I think you unintelligent. You exist in a very precarious space. You are not the boys," she added, meaning, of course, Annarion and Mandoran, "and you are not a scion of the ancients in the strictest of senses. You can see—and hear—true language, but only with the limited senses available to you.

"You have seen paintings, yes?"

Kaylin desperately wanted to tell her that now was *not the time* for this. Instead, she said a terse, "yes, of course."

"You have seen paintings of buildings—castles, cathedrals, towers?"

"Yes."

"What you see—or hear—when this language is spoken is analogous. You see the painting; you cannot see the *building*. The painting can be evocative; it can give you a sense of the whole—and possibly your own intuition builds on that. But it cannot ever describe the actual, physical truth of the building itself. Your understanding is limited to the painting. You cannot enter the building."

"And they—the 'boys'—can?"

"Yes. They are, at the moment, confined to the foyer or the parlor, but yes."

"Can Teela?"

"No, dear."

"And the Barrani that's attacking you now?"

Silence. After a long pause, Helen said, "He—or his kind— could on occasion destroy the building. They could not *build* it. They could not *create*. But they could forage from the ruins of the things they destroyed, taking the stones and the glass and the lumber for their personal use. I'm sorry," she added. "I realize this is a poor analogy, but it is the only one I have."

"It's better than anyone else has offered."

"Yes, well. I've had some practice over the years."

"Can you tell me where the words should go?"

The hesitance was marked. "Not definitively, no. You are, if I understand correctly, Chosen. It is your responsibility to use the words given you to…finish things. To resolve stories that have been left hanging; to offer closure to the things abandoned long ago.

"I have too much of a personal interest in what you are now doing to be objective."

"Then don't *be* objective," Kaylin replied, with a little more heat than she'd intended. "Look—you want a tenant. *I* want a *home*. And if tall, broody Barrani ancestor has his way, there won't be enough of either of us left to get what we *both* want. *Yes,* you have an interest in this. So do I. But you *get a say*. This *is* about you. I don't know what I'm doing. I don't want to screw up because I'm ignorant—and if I'm doomed, by birth, to *be* ignorant—you're not. Help me. Help yourself. We're in this together, and I'd like it to stay that way."

"It's not as simple as that," Helen finally said. "I am the words at my heart. But I cannot separate them. You cannot see the inside of your hand without removing your skin, and causing possible permanent damage; you cannot look at your own heart beating without risking death. It is the same for me, Kaylin. It is the exact same."

"But Tara—"

"Yes. I can see what you think you did for the Tower. It is not, however, what you *actually* did. I can tell you what the words you carry mean; I cannot tell you how they will preserve me, because I cannot actually believe they will. Something about the interaction of you, those words, and the words that remain to me, work in concert, the sum greater than the parts, although the parts are all true.

"And we are running out of time."

"Tell me one thing, then."

"What do you need to know?"

"What happened to all the other words? How were they destroyed?"

"As I told you at the tea table, I destroyed them," Helen replied.

"You destroyed them." When confronted with something that made no sense, Kaylin often fell back on repetition.

"Yes."

"But—but—why?" Repetition, on the other hand, probably sounded more intelligent.

"Perhaps you will understand. You said 'you get a say.'"
Kaylin nodded.

"That was what *I* wanted. I wanted a say. I wanted to choose who I served, and what I did in that service."

"But the Towers choose their Lords."

"Yes. But I was not a Tower."

"What were you?"

"I don't know, Kaylin. Much of what was destroyed took memories with it. I attempted to preserve my knowledge internally; I am certain I did not fully succeed. As I told you, I cannot precisely see the internal workings of what I will call my own heart. I could not, then. But I could see the general shape of things, and I...amputated?"

"If you mean cutting off a limb, then yes, amputated."

"I destroyed the portions of my inscription that forced me to behave in ways I no longer wished to behave. I did this in part to keep the information I contained from the hands of those who would pillage graves."

"Did it matter?"

"Yes. I wanted to serve Hasielle. She gave things *to* me. She brought light. She *lived* here. Even as a slave. I thought they would kill her—probably unintentionally, although they were not particularly careful—and I did not want that. I was damaged somewhat before their arrival, and I completed that damage so that I could not be compelled."

"And the Barrani upstairs is trying to compel you as if you'd never been damaged?"

"He is not Barrani, and yes. He is confused. And angry. He seeks to give orders, to invoke words and phrases that will turn all control of my interior over to him. He cannot, now."

"But if I somehow repair you, he might?"

Kaylin could practically hear the frown she couldn't see.

"I highly doubt that. What is more likely, in my opinion, is that such repairs will give *you* the ability to control me."

"But I don't want that."

"No. You don't. The only risk I take—and I choose to take it—is that the next mortal who crosses my threshold, the next tenant, will not have your aversion to such control."

Kaylin closed her eyes again. The sounds of battle receded. The small scattering of pebbles and rocks didn't. She now ignored those, trusting Helen to give her warning if larger chunks were to follow. It would have been a trivial job if there were only six scorch marks in the center; there were over a dozen. Given the trembling of the stone beneath her feet, dropping words into random empty spaces seemed smarter than it had five minutes ago.

But it wouldn't work, and she knew it.

She threaded her way between the carved words until she stood in their center. There, she discovered a rune that did not glow; it was flat, dull, and lifeless. She opened her eyes. Beneath her feet, the stone was smooth. No lines had been carved into its flat, pristine surface.

She closed her eyes again.

The rune was there. But she could only see it with closed eyes. She regretted sending the small dragon back to Mandoran, then; she wanted his wing.

And she wasn't going to get it any time soon.

The rune, to Kaylin's closed eye, looked engraved. She knelt and touched the surface of the stone, tracing the long underscore with two fingers; she could feel the indentations in rock, even if she couldn't see them with her eyes open. She thought, as she stood, that this was the center-piece of Helen's heart, for want of a better word; it wasn't active.

She rose and scanned the runes that surrounded this one, noting their placement, and marking the positions of the absent words. The stones into which they had been engraved, unlike the central stone, were scorched or melted. "How much time did you say we have?"

"I didn't. I am uncertain."

Kaylin looked at the word in her hand. It seemed to her— with her eyes closed, and how wrong was that?—to be made of glass; the light that filled it wasn't an essential part of its form. But she knew if she broke it, the light would be lost.

She exhaled. In the West March, she had chosen two of

the words on her skin based entirely on the way they made her *feel*. This was not, in daily life, a good bet—but she had nothing else to go on. And she knew—as she had known in the West March—that the words would not now choose their intended destination. They were waiting to be chosen.

The usual fear of making a mistake was heightened by the stakes. The closest friends she had in Elantra were in this building, and if it fell, they'd die. Or worse. She had no expectation of mercy from the intruder. She was betting their lives on the placement of six runes, and it was a bet she would never have taken otherwise.

Breathe, she told herself. *And think.*

The words failed to speak to her. She hadn't the time to fly around them, examining them from all angles, as she had done in the West March. She hadn't the time to touch them all.

Think, Kaylin. Think fast.

What Helen wanted was what anyone wanted: companionship. Home. She couldn't *be* a home if she was empty. Home was a place where people lived. Home was a place where they belonged. Helen wanted that sense of belonging—and who didn't? Home couldn't mean, to Helen, what it meant to Kaylin—and yet it did.

Helen had been afraid that no one would come to her. No one who wanted to stay. It was a particular type of loneliness— and Kaylin realized that she held it in her hands, almost literally. For Helen, home was people. It wasn't the shape she presented; it wasn't the color of her walls or the type of wood that formed her floors. It was people.

Emptiness meant something very literal to Helen; it meant something metaphorical to Kaylin. Both of the meanings were enclosed in this rune. What Kaylin couldn't understand was *why*, of all words, this one was meant to have a place here.

Helen didn't need it—she had lived it. Kaylin considered attempting to reattach it to her skin.

Instead of wasting her time doing something she was certain wouldn't work, she began to walk toward one of the scorch marks. It was perhaps three rows back—although the words hadn't been written in neat, precise rings—when she stopped. She looked toward the rune in the center. Given the light shed by the runes that now surrounded her, she could no longer see it.

She stared, instead, at the words that surrounded the scorching. They were, for the most part, rounded and curved; the lines were delicate in their construction, and dots were more central. But they didn't speak to her the way the word she held did; she had no sense of meaning from them. She *hated* time. Or time's passing.

She hated the limitations of her own mortality. Had Mandoran actually come through the door with her, he'd probably have an opinion that was worth something. Then again, they'd probably also have some part of the intruder in the place most vulnerable to his attacks.

Tiamaris had told Kaylin that the words themselves were ordered; that they had a correct shape, a precise form. He couldn't assess their *meaning,* but he could see when something was off or wrong; he could see, for instance, if a word had been riven and was now incomplete. Although all these words were complete in and of themselves, Kaylin attempted to apply Tiamaris's advice to the shape of these words as a whole.

Because if these were words, she was making sentences, and the sentences had to be completed; they had to make sense.

Even if it was only visual, harmonious sense.

This word did not belong among the rest of them, if that were the case; it was too heavy, too bold, too thickly written. Yes, there were curved lines and dots—all the words had those—but not in the same way, and not to the same extent.

She moved, walking slowly, examining only shape, form, and composition, until she came to an empty space at the outer edge of the active words.

Here.

This is stupid, she told herself, adorning the spare sentence with Leontine. But stupid or no, she knelt to set the word down. Nothing happened. The word, however, did not return to the loose formation that adorned her head.

She reached up to take one of the remaining five. Gravity came with touch; the rune fell into her hands. Although she had chosen to place the words into the general pattern of the whole, she studied the word that lay in her palms for more than just shape and composition. This was the opposite of the first word; not loneliness, not the yearning that came of it, but contentment. She felt the warmth of Marcus's hearth fire, and the certain sense that she was welcome there. She didn't know what this meant for Helen—but she thought she could guess; if she was welcome, Helen was welcoming. If she accepted the gifts offered her as gifts, not entitlements or obligations—and she did—Helen was content.

No, it wasn't contentment. It was gratitude. And this was the problem with identifying true words: she only had mortal words to describe it, and she wasn't very good at it. She wasn't always good at telling other people how she felt or why she felt that way and if she did, they interpreted those feelings in ways she hadn't intended.

Even thinking, Kaylin had continued to walk; to study the shape of the form and the way it blended—or didn't—with the other words. This search took less time because the first had taken her far enough from the center that she now had a sense of where the patterns were laid out. Gratitude. That one, she could understand.

She wondered if one of the lost words had been this one; if

some part of Helen's make-up meant the same thing. It didn't really make sense that it would—why would a building require either gratitude or, worse, the concept of loneliness?

And yet, the Hallionne experienced both. Tara certainly did; the desire for companionship and understanding had almost driven her to the building version of suicide. Kaylin frowned. The Hallionne, at their core, had not started their eternal lives as architecture; they'd started as Immortals. Or possibly mortals. They'd started from the foundation of personhood, and they'd agreed to become what they did become: almost gods, in their own small domains. And prisoners, as well.

Were these the words that Helen had destroyed?

Kaylin found the space in which gratitude looked to be at home. She set it down. Once again, the rest of the words didn't react—but had she honestly expected they would? Shaking her head, she reached up for the third word. This one was harder to understand; she walked the third circle staring at it. The outer lines of the rune were solid; they looked almost utilitarian in the form they took: a straight rectangle. The interior was less rigid, and the rectangle appeared to be standing on far more graceful curves—but the external curves were bold, thick lines, as well.

It took her some moments to understand that this word spoke of protection. The lines of the rectangle implied either a room or a house—a simple house—that kept the interior separate from any other interference. The interior, however, wasn't empty. She frowned. Protection, of course, was too simple a word. The one that followed it was safety. Safety, in any real sense, didn't exist. It was a hope, a dream, a goal—but like immortality for mortals, it was always out of reach.

She *knew* this, but it didn't stop her from yearning for it. Protection was a thing you offered or accepted. Safety was a thing you felt. Maybe the word meant security. The meaning of the word didn't exist in isolation; it couldn't. Words.

To Kaylin's surprise, the only space that suited the composition of the word was the scorched, black mark closest to the center. All the words there had similar shapes, and similar hard, definitive strokes. She set the mark down with far less doubt than she had the first two, and she reached, as she did, for the fourth.

The fourth was like gossamer. It seemed impossibly delicate. She could imagine herself chiseling—badly—any of the first three; the fourth would defeat her before she'd started. The lines seemed to both cross and curve into one another; it was hard to tell, looking at the writing, which element had been laid down first, and which had followed. There were just too damned many parts. She had no sense at all what this word meant, even as she carried it, searching for its place. It was so complicated in appearance, she thought it must mean something that made sense to a specific type of Immortal— the type that got turned into buildings.

It reminded Kaylin of the words she had once seen that were, in total, the name of a world, an entire world; she could study it for the whole of her life and never truly understand the entirety of its meaning. Hells, she could barely find the meaning in her own life on a bad day.

She didn't have to understand. She told herself this. But there was no place for this fourth rune; it seemed to match none of the spaces that had been created when other words had somehow failed or been destroyed.

She frowned and returned it to its orbit, and it went. She dealt with the fifth and sixth runes first.

The fifth felt like responsibility or duty or honor or something similar; it shone. Even in her palms it seemed to rest above her touch, as if it were meant, always, to be a little bit out of reach. It almost made Kaylin feel uncomfortable—as if, somehow, the word itself was judging her. But it didn't mean judgment, not exactly. Kaylin understood the whole being judged thing.

It wasn't the judgment of *others*. It was her own judgment. It was comprised of both the harshness and the forgiveness that one aimed at oneself. None of her Elantran words encompassed it until she set it down and began to walk away.

Self-respect.

This entire endeavor had become surreal. Not that most of Kaylin's encounters with true language had ever been anything else. But she had an ambivalent relationship with self-respect, and understood why it had hovered just out of the reach of her palms. She couldn't imagine that Helen needed whatever the word would give her—but she often couldn't imagine that anyone else did, either; everyone else seemed to have the self-respect that Kaylin struggled so hard to reach.

She held the second to last of the words in her hand; she was walking along the second circle of carved, glowing runes. The word was smaller and tidier than any of the others; it was simpler, as well. It reminded her of Maggaron's name—the name that he no longer possessed.

It meant honesty. Or truthfulness. Or truth. And truth was such a personal thing, in the end. As a Hawk, she'd come to understand, very early, that no two people experienced an event the same way; witness testimony differed. Sometimes the differences made you wonder if the witnesses had even been standing on the same damned street—but the witnesses believed that their version of events was the only version.

Kaylin, who had believed at age thirteen, that everyone lied, wasn't offended at what she assumed were lies—but she was almost shocked when the Tha'alani made clear that they

weren't lying. The witnesses were attempting to fully coop-
erate with the Hawks; their testimony was true—to them. It
just didn't match the testimony of other witnesses.

Which made police work much more difficult.

Kaylin had come to truth the hard way. Truth was what
you offered when everything else had been stripped away. It
was a bet with stakes so high even the fieflings would have
steered clear of it if they had any other choice.

Or it had been. But time spent with the Hawks had reminded her that not all truths were dark and shameful; not
all truths were so large they threatened to crush the rest of
life with their weight.

It was true that given the choice, Kaylin would rather help
people than hurt them. It was true that she would rather be a
Hawk than one of Barren's enforcers. She would rather be a
Hawk than anything else. It was also true that she wished the
pay were better—but it was money she'd earned, and it put
a roof over her head, and she had enough left over to give to
Marrin and the Foundling Hall.

It was true that she loved her friends. It was also true that
the word *love* was so embarrassing it wasn't used often in the
office, except by Caitlin when she was maudlin. It was also
true that no one resented it when Caitlin used it, although
Marcus did growl.

All the little truths existed, side by side with the hidden
ones. And if they weren't large and significant in the same
way, she'd built up enough of them that she could shoulder
the weight of the past without breaking.

And she could see why Helen might need that. Kaylin
couldn't wrap her head around the Ancient's concept of a
building. But maybe everything in the ancient world had been
sentient and immortal. In the end, she wasn't here to judge;
she was here to find a home.

But if this was just some kind of near-suicidal game, she was going to be pissed off.

"It's a little extreme, even for me," Helen replied.

"I'll quibble with your use of the word *little* later," Kaylin said, kneeling to fit the last, stark word into the spot she'd chosen for it. Nothing changed, of course.

She reached up to the light that adorned her brow; there was only one word left, a word that could be the entire name of a world, but in miniature. This mark had risen from her skin. She'd *seen* it. But no runes on her skin had ever looked like this one. She was fairly familiar with the runes themselves, thanks to the modern miracle of Records capture—and playback.

Without giving herself time to doubt her decision, she strode decisively toward the center of the room—toward what was, she suspected, the center of Helen. She knelt, the tips of her toes overhanging a word or two as she positioned herself, and set the last word down.

The lights went out.

CHAPTER 21

Kaylin froze in place. Without the light cast by the words, the room was completely dark; there were no moons and no stars because the sky was a rounded curve of white rock. Even the marks that adorned the visible portion of her arms shed no light. She was alone with the sound of her breathing—when she started to breathe again.

Cursing followed breath, as if one was a consequence of the other. There was no way for Kaylin to retrace her steps and rearrange the words she'd set down; the best she could possibly hope for was that she could walk around those words without knocking them over or stepping on them.

It was easy to doubt herself in the darkness—always had been. It was easy to doubt that she'd done the right thing because she had *no idea* what the right thing was supposed to be.

"Helen," she whispered.

Silence.

Lord Kaylin.

Of all the voices she'd expected to hear, Ynpharion's was not one. She was, however, grateful—for about two seconds.

Lord Kaylin.

I'm here. We're having a bit of difficulty at the moment.

As are we. The Dragon Court emerged from the Imperial Palace; they joined Bellusdeo. The Lady says the Emperor ordered her to retreat.

She can understand Dragon?

Some of it. I did not understand the spoken words—if they can be called words at all—but the meaning was unmistakable. If it is at all possible—

I can't leave. I'm in a large cave with no exits. In the dark. I mean, pitch-black dark. Lord Teela and her friends are holding off the other non-Barrani ancestor, and he's not dead yet.

She felt Ynpharion's fear. It was not for, or about, himself.

The High Halls can't be in danger from one man—I don't care how powerful he is.

We are not directly in danger at the moment; the arrival of the Dragon Court diverted the enemy's attention. But—Lord Kaylin— he fell silent.

It was a bad silence. *What? What's happened?*

We cannot leave the High Halls.

Pardon?

The exits are blocked.

By what?

Magical barriers. They are not, however, inert. We have made three attempts to bring the barriers down; we have made two to circumvent them in other ways. There has been one death and two moderately severe injuries. The High Lord is now consulting with the Arcanists who were within the bounds of the Hall themselves when the barrier was erected. Given the events after the assassination attempt on Bellusdeo, that is almost all the extant Barrani Arcanists. We have attempted to lend aid to the Dragon Court in other ways—but we are stymied.

Ynpharion paused; Kaylin could almost hear a shouted Barrani order. She recognized the voice that conveyed the command; it was the Consort's. *The Lady has asked that you observe the streets.*

Given the darkness of this isolated chamber, Kaylin nodded; Ynpharion sensed assent, but even if he hadn't, he would have obeyed the command he'd been given.

"Lord Kaylin," the Consort said. Kaylin concentrated until she could see the platinum-haired woman who had the sole responsibility of waking the newly born. She saw her, of course, through Ynpharion's eyes. Once again, Ynpharion didn't fight her intrusion.

"She is listening, Lady."

"Come to the mirror, Ynpharion."

Do the mirrors work?

Yes. We can relay messages to—and from—Elantra. No one can enter the High Halls; no one can safely leave. There is one possible avenue that is even now being attempted. He didn't seem to be confident of success. Ynpharion, while speaking to Kaylin, had crossed the polished marble of an interior room; he joined the Consort in front of a tall, oval mirror, resting upon the clawed likeness of taloned feet.

The reflective surface of the mirror had already parted. A line had appeared in the mirror's center, traveling from top to bottom; on either side of that line, silver undulated and retreated. What was left in the mirror's view were the very familiar and upscale streets that led to the High Halls. They were not often traveled by any but the rich and the powerful; this close to the High Halls, even the Swords didn't bother with perfunctory patrols. No one outside of the Barrani themselves would be stupid enough to attempt to steal or vandalize anything behind the significant fences that marked Barrani property—and Barrani had their own ways of dealing with their troublemakers.

"Lord Kaylin," the Consort said. "Do you recognize all

the Dragons present?" The mirror view shifted, streets giving way to sky.

Tell her that Dragons don't remain one color. Having said that, she added, *I recognize Tiamaris. And Bellusdeo—she's the large, golden one. What are the spikes on her neck?*

I am not a Dragon, Ynpharion replied. *But in general they would indicate distress or fury.*

Fury, Kaylin told him. *I think the blue is Emmerian. No, not that one—the blue on the left. The larger one is probably Diarmat. If you're repeating these to the Consort, can you add 'Lord' in front of all the names?*

He was almost disgusted with the pettiness of the request—which was fair. The mirror's view continued to pan the sky, pausing as Kaylin identified the draconian forms of the Dragon Court. In the night sky, Sanabalis looked almost silver; she was certain that he was actually gray.

When the mirror's eye reached a Dragon she didn't recognize, her ability to form cogent thought paused for a moment. He looked black, to her eye—black and larger than any of the others, except perhaps Bellusdeo. Even thinking of her would-be roommate seemed to shift the mirror's view; it pulled right back, framing the Court as it moved. Kaylin could now see all the aerial Dragons—and her jaw dropped when the golden Dragon suddenly roared and flew—at full speed—toward the black one, knocking him two body lengths across the sky.

Before words could frame her shock, lightning did. It drove skyward from the ground, clipping one golden wing.

Bellusdeo roared. The mirror made the sound small; Kaylin's imagination and experience enlarged it. The golden Dragon tumbled toward the ground; the great black Dragon caught her, roaring, as well. Kaylin realized that she'd been wrong about his color; he wasn't black. He was a very, very deep indigo; the gold of Bellusdeo's scales brought blue highlights out of the darkness.

If Kaylin had entertained any doubts at all, she had none now. *It's the Emperor,* she whispered. *And Bellusdeo's been hurt.*

And she was. She flew toward the ground—the ground beyond the fence. She had, Kaylin thought, saved the Emperor.

And the Emperor, damn him, was going to be a raging berserker *because* of it. She was stuck in a windowless, doorless, dark *cave* and she could practically feel his rage. Had she been close enough in person, she would have smacked him.

Which was probably the fastest route to suicide known to Elantrans.

Ynpharion—what's on the ground? Is it the—the Barrani ancestor?

Yes. He has destroyed half the street; the Dragon Court has destroyed the other half. Their fires do not kill him; his protections are too strong. His magicks on the ground are much, much stronger; it is the reason the Court has remained in the air.

Kaylin frowned. *How do you fight him, then?*

In number, Kaylin. In great numbers. The Dragon Court could— we believe—destroy him. But it is not a certainty, and they will not all survive the attempt. We have weapons in the High Hall that have some effect against their sorcery—but we cannot leave the High Halls to join the Dragons. We have tried.

One of the Dragons is missing, Kaylin said. Ynpharion passed this on, and the Consort looked into—and past—his eyes. "The Arkon," she said.

Kaylin nodded; Ynpharion nodded. For a moment, they were almost one person; she found it uncomfortably disorienting.

"Will he come, Lord Kaylin?"

"Yes. Yes, he'll come."

"He doesn't leave his library often."

"No. But for Bellusdeo, for his Emperor, he will."

"You are certain?"

Kaylin nodded. She was.

"Good. I believe your Arkon is our only hope. I understand that you face one of these creatures now."

"Not me. I'm in the bowels of an ancient building trying to rebuild its defenses so the much less significant force stationed here doesn't die."

"Which building, Lord Kaylin?"

"I don't know how well you know the city, but we're on Ashwood."

The Dragons in the mirror disappeared as the Consort gestured; they were replaced by a map of the city. "The Halls of Law are mobilizing," the Consort said, as the map solidified. "I believe the Swords and the Hawks are being called up, en masse."

Kaylin stopped breathing for one long moment; it took that long for the words to make sense.

"You are here?" the Consort asked, as if the information she'd just relayed—which amounted to the probable massacre of everyone with whom Kaylin had *ever* worked—was of passing, casual interest. Ashwood, as seen by city Records, loomed into view.

Tell her yes. Please, she added.

"One moment, Lord Kaylin. If possible, please retain the connection."

Kaylin would have been furious in any other circumstance—but she was sitting alone in a dark cave with no entrances and no exits; she had nothing better to do. It occurred to her that the Consort was likewise trapped within the High Halls, although in much posher surroundings. Men in armor appeared closest to the mirror. Kaylin recognized one of them immediately.

The High Lord. He frowned, his eyes narrowed to indigo

edges. "What is this?" he asked the Lady. His tone didn't imply that she was wasting her time—it implied suspicion and grave concern. Kaylin decided irritation would have been preferable.

"You recognize it?" the Consort asked, voice cool. Her tone implied that not even the High Lord was allowed to speak to her with open suspicion; not in front of witnesses.

"Yes." He turned to the side and said, "Summon Lord Evarrim immediately."

Great. Just what she needed: to be a passenger in the mind and body of someone who mostly wanted her dead, listening to Evarrim while the Hawks and Swords crowded into the streets as fodder.

"Lord Kaylin," the Consort said. Her voice was far less stiff than it had been when she'd addressed her brother. "This may be of import. I understand it is difficult for you."

For *me*, Kaylin thought, with a sudden rush of guilt. What must it be like for Ynpharion?

It is...bearable, to my considerable shock. This is not the way I would have chosen to serve the High Lord—but I believe it is necessary; no other could do what I have now done.

But they know.

Yes. But you are much in the Consort's favor, and the High Lord owes you a debt. I can almost believe that they will not look at me with the utter contempt I would have expected. I am oddly grateful at this moment.

It won't last.

She felt a hint of bitter amusement. *Gratitude seldom does. Ah, Lord Evarrim is here.*

And he was. He had replaced the burned out ruby that adorned his forehead at the height of a slender tiara; his eyes were as dark a blue as everyone else's. As he caught sight of the mirror, their shape shifted into something more round.

"What is this?" he all but demanded. "Is this where the enemy originated?"

"No. It is our belief that the enemy came from the fief of Nightshade."

"So. The rumors were true."

"Indeed. It is possible I owe my father an apology; it is fortuitous that I will not be forced to tender one." The High Lord's father, Kaylin knew, was dead.

"You are certain?"

"Yes."

"Why, then, is this section of the city now under observation?"

"It is where the second of our enemies has traveled. It is under attack now."

Evarrim said something in High Barrani that Kaylin had never heard; she was almost embarrassed by the speed at which she committed the syllables to memory. Ynpharion was, once again, disgusted. "He must be stopped."

The Consort lifted platinum brows. "We are willing to entertain suggestions for how that might be achieved, given that we cannot, at the moment, leave the High Halls. The Dragon Court does battle at the edge of our lawn—and while none of the Dragons have fallen, neither has our enemy. I would suggest your demand is slightly ambitious." The black humor that informed her tone dissipated. "What do you know of this building, then? Why do you fear it?"

"It is as old," Evarrim replied, "as the Towers that gird the fiefs. It is not a Tower; it is not, therefore a necessity. Research has been done in ages past, upon the building."

"In what sense?"

Evarrim shrugged. "We wished information that the building was rumored to contain. That information was never found. It was almost found," he added, gesturing at the mirror. The image banked abruptly, turning into clouds of smoke and nothing. "With your permission, Lady?"

"What do you attempt to access?"

"The archives of the Arcanists. You will not," he added, "be able to peruse them at your leisure; they will respond to me—and only to me. I will, however, accept your commands."

He must be desperate, Kaylin thought. Ynpharion agreed; they were both uneasy and deeply suspicious.

The High Lord and the Consort conferred; Kaylin wanted to scream. She wanted the mirror to *go back* to the streets and the aerial combat; she wanted to *see*. The ground beneath her feet shuddered; she couldn't immediately tell whether it was the marble floors of the High Halls or the carved rock of the dark cavern.

It is the High Halls, Ynpharion told her.

"You have our permission," the High Lord told Evarrim. "But the Consort is concerned; this is one of the few windows we have to the outside world at the moment, and we cannot afford to have it compromised or broken."

Evarrim then took control of the mirror. The mirror responded sluggishly; the images were unclear. Ynpharion made it clear they were just as vague to him.

"Include Lord Ynpharion in your search," the High Lord said—without looking away from whatever the mirror showed him.

Evarrim was not a fool; he obeyed the mild command without apparent concern. *That's going to cost you,* Kaylin said.

Yes. But as even you have noticed, everything is costly at the High Court.

The image of a building sprang—almost literally—into view. It did not remain contained by the flat surface of the mirror, but grew out of its surface as if it had dimension. It was a tower. The peak was so high and narrow it looked like a spear's head, but the base was wide and blocky. It wasn't rectangular; it wasn't circular. Kaylin couldn't divine its shape in this view, but she wasn't an architect.

It has six points, Ynpharion told her, *if it is symmetrical.*

It looks nothing like Helen.

Helen?

Damn it. *The building's name is Helen.*

Ynpharion coughed. Sadly, the cough was not entirely on the inside of his mouth. *It is your influence,* he told her sourly. *And of course, I will bear the consequences.* He dropped into an instant bow. "Apologies, Lord."

"There is very little that is either amusing or outrageous occurring to my knowledge," the High Lord replied. "You will, of course, explain."

Ynpharion didn't want to explain anything in front of Evarrim—and Kaylin didn't want him to, either. It was the second time this evening that they were in lock step. *Evarrim is less of a concern than the displeasure of the High Lord.*

Kaylin didn't believe it. *I'm not going to stop you. I'm not going to try. But—I don't trust him.*

Of course not, was his impatient reply. *The miracle of you is that you trust anyone at all, and survive.* "Lord Kaylin believes that the building's name is…Helen."

She tried not to feel defensive at the looks she received. Or the looks Ynpharion did. *That's what she calls herself,* she said. *I didn't name her.*

"That is not how the building appears now."

"That is not," Evarrim replied, "how the building appears from the street; it is, however, the material space the structure nonetheless occupies. To our knowledge, the building has remained unoccupied since well before the founding."

The building hasn't been unoccupied.

"The building," Ynpharion said aloud, "has been occupied intermittently."

Evarrim's lip curled, reminding Kaylin of all the reasons she detested him. As if he knew she was listening, he said, "When mice or other rodents find their way into the cracks of a building, are they said to be occupants? They are vermin, no more."

Kaylin brought both fists down against the floor and let out a volley of heartfelt, furious Leontine.

He is trying to annoy you, Ynpharion said, with discernible contempt.

Well, he's succeeding.

Yes. That is why you should feel ashamed.

She left off the cursing, because the only target who could hear it probably didn't deserve most of it.

"The Tower was damaged in the wars against the ancestors," Evarrim was saying. She'd missed anything else he'd added after his gratuitous insult; Ynpharion was, of course, right. "Much of its control mechanisms probably took the brunt of the damage; the commands we were able to retrieve did not have the desired effect. We know the Tower was occupied," he continued, gesturing. The Tower faded; a Barrani Lord appeared in its stead, standing almost as tall as Evarrim. Barrani never looked friendly, with one or two notable exceptions; this man looked like the personification of the gallows. Even the expected, unearthly beauty did nothing to quell the fear he invoked.

He's not Barrani.

No, Ynpharion replied.

"This was the Tower's first known occupant."

"One of the ancestors."

"Yes."

"Did he fight against us?"

"He could not have," Evarrim replied. "We would not now be standing in this city—even ruled by a Dragon as it is—had he chosen a different side. We have very little information about him; he is believed to have perished during the long war."

"You are certain that he was the Tower's Lord?"

"Yes. His image—with a suitable, dire warning—appeared when the first of the researchers attempted to enter the Tower."

"Did they survive?"

"There were deaths," Evarrim said, in about as bored a tone as he had spoken of vermin. "But the method of death was not considered dangerous enough that the attempts were instantly abandoned. The first Lord of the Tower had conducted research, much of which was locked within the bowels of the building; some small proof of this was uncovered, but the Tower itself proved resistant to excavation. If it was damaged, it was still active.

"Our belief was that the previous Lord's commands still held sway; the Tower could not functionally accept the Lord's absence as death. Attempts over the next century were made to circumvent the Tower's functional protections—to little avail. In the end, the Tower collapsed. Much of the secondary research was lost, and the project itself abandoned as the Dragons were proving difficult.

"The research itself was never resumed. The building has stood fallow in the meanwhile."

That is not true, Kaylin snapped.

There is little point in venting fury at me, *Lord Kaylin. I am not the one tendering the opinion.*

You don't disagree.

Ynpharion chose not to reply, and Kaylin, aware that he had already put his reputation on the line in service to the High Court, didn't press. There wasn't any good point in asking more of people than they were capable of giving—not in an emergency.

The image of the ancestor or sorcerer or whatever it was the Barrani called them faded.

"Why," the Consort asked, "did the researchers feel they could circumvent the Tower's innate protections? We would not take that risk with the Hallionne."

"The Hallionne are distant cousins to the Towers; were it a Hallionne, we would not have made the attempt. But the Hallionne would not allow the research to be conducted within their domain; there would be no reason to excavate."

"That is not an answer."

Kaylin held her breath. She understood, suddenly, that the Consort was attempting to help her. The Consort had probably recognized the building about which she claimed ignorance.

"My apologies, Lady," Evarrim replied. His expression was glacial—but that was its default state. She thought he suspected what Kaylin herself now suspected. Regardless, he gestured again. The image that formed was smoke or mist to Kaylin's eye; it was, given the Consort's frown, no clearer to her; the Consort, however, didn't curse. She waited.

Since Kaylin couldn't be heard by anyone else, *she* cursed.

"It is difficult to discern," Evarrim said, gesturing again. The mist moved, rotating in place, and as it did, Kaylin could see that it had a form. The form itself seemed abstract; it didn't solidify into a known shape, the way Evarrim's previously recalled records had. But in motion, it had a discernible shape. It was like the ghost of a true word.

A complex, dense word.

The Consort saw it, as well. Her familiarity with the shape and the function of true words was second to none among her kin; she couldn't fail to see the significance of Evarrim's discovery. She did, however. "I am not certain how this would lead to the exploration involved. Exploring the area known as the fiefs is all but forbidden. Would this Tower, as you call it, not fall under the same prohibition?" She shook her head; the white spill of hair shimmered. "We are not a people who take well to such prohibitions, as history has shown. Were I curious, I might venture to the building on Ashwood—but such an image would not invoke that curiosity in me."

"What do you see in it that I do not?"

Evarrim clearly wanted to reply "Nothing." He didn't. "I see the shape and form of language. A hint, no more."

"I see that, as well. What, in this rune, gives you pause?"

"It is not, as you can see, a true word."

She nodded.

"But it is our belief that it once was; it is, if you are inclined to the fanciful, a ghost; it is what remains when the essential force of a word itself is consumed."

Kaylin had seen words consumed. The Devourer had consumed the marks that had risen from her skin for, she thought, just that purpose. And the small dragon had done the same—although admittedly he was a lot cuter about it. She didn't have the visceral reaction the Consort did to Evarrim's pronouncement. Then again, neither of the two, devourer or familiar, had left even a trace of those words behind.

But the words on Kaylin's skin didn't give *Kaylin* life; Kaylin wasn't a Tower.

"Where," the Consort asked, after a long pause in which her eyes had shifted to a blue so dark they looked black, "did you find this?"

"In the Tower itself." Evarrim said, "We were not surprised; is it not the reason that the ancestors attempted to destroy us? They wished to utilize the names at the center of our beings to create new sentences and new races."

"They wished," the Consort replied, in a voice that pretty much defined icy, "to empty the Lake of Life."

Evarrim immediately folded—literally; for a moment Kaylin thought his forehead would hit the ground. "It is not beyond possibility that they thought to do so with the Towers themselves; the Towers—like the Hallionne—have long been known to be built on a foundation of words such as these."

"And your interest?" Oh, the cold in her voice.

"It was not purely academic on the part of the initial exploration. It was felt that if the method of extraction were better understood, defenses could be built specifically to resist it."

He lied like a rug. The resentment Kaylin felt at this amused Ynpharion.

If no one present believes the lie—and the liar does not expect to be believed, is it a crime? It merely shows his willingness to expend social effort to be plausible; it shows his concern for his position.

"We were not alone in our interest. Very few of the researchers could even see the remnants of the word, and it could not, of course, be moved; attempts were made, some of significant power and planning. The word itself in some essential nature was wed to the Tower. In time, the researches were abandoned. Some attention, however, has been paid to the house itself over the passage of centuries. There have been visitors who have both arrived and left the premises intact; they have not, to our knowledge, removed anything of value.

"One of those visitors would be the current Keeper. He is not considered a threat. I consider that unwise—but if the Keeper constitutes a threat, there is very little anyone can safely do to contain him."

"Other visitors of significance?"

"In the past three centuries, very few; four in total. Three of these four were Dragons; one was a Barrani High Lord."

Nightshade.

"They did not remain long. One of the Dragons spent almost a month in the Tower, but survived."

"Which Dragon?"

Evarrim's smile was unpleasant. "I do not believe he is a member of the Dragon Court; he is outcaste."

Why, Ynpharion demanded, *do you insist on cursing so constantly?*

Why, she countered, *don't you?* She could figure out who the other two Dragons were: the Arkon and Tiamaris. Tiamaris, who had spent a good deal of time exploring the Towers and the Shadows in the fiefs before he'd claimed one of those Towers for his own.

She didn't bother asking what they'd discovered; there was no way that information would be given to Evarrim. The other members of the Dragon Court might know—but it didn't help Kaylin now.

The Barrani had found the ghost of a word. Kaylin hated the description; she wanted something solid and factual in its place. But true words didn't lend themselves to solid facts. They never had. And she was sitting in the dead center of Helen's heart; she presided, in utter blackness, over the words that the researchers had attempted to reach—no doubt to pillage or destroy for their own purposes.

They had been full of the light she associated with them when she had started her attempt to heal Helen. They had guttered the moment she'd placed the last of the six words down. Before she had put the last rune in place, nothing had changed. She couldn't understand why the last one drained all light out of the rest.

And she could not ask Evarrim for advice or explanation. She would never, ever be rid of the bastard if she did; Helen would always be at risk.

"We consulted with sages," Evarrim was saying. "We consulted with those among our people—and outside of it—that might give us some clue to the meaning of this rune; some clue to its function and the ability to call that function."

"That is not how true words generally work," was the Consort's cool reply.

"It is not how true *names* function," the Arcanist countered. "But there is general agreement that the words that serve as names are almost linguistically distinct from the words that serve as ancient descriptors. Over time, the researchers gleaned what they felt was enough information to at least begin; they assembled a reasonable force and entered the Tower.

"They attempted to speak the word itself. It is possible their conjectures were entirely in error, but I have seen some of their work; I do not believe it was."

"They attempted to speak the word at the center of the Tower?" the Consort asked.

"They could not," Evarrim replied, with barely concealed impatience, "reach the Tower's center."

"So they spoke this word within the confines of the Tower to no effect?"

"Indeed."

"Thank you, Lord Evarrim. I believe you are wanted in the upper reach."

Evarrim looked as if he wanted to argue.

Lord Evarrim is not the most controlled or measured of Barrani Lords. He is not unlike you in that fashion.

Kaylin knew Ynpharion meant no insult, but was insulted anyway. She watched as Evarrim left the chamber. He was escorted by two of the High Lord's men; only the High Lord, Ynpharion, and the Consort remained. That, and the ghost of a complicated word.

The Consort did not likewise dismiss Ynpharion. Instead,

she turned to face him. "I know," she said, in weary Elantran, "that this isn't your fault. Had you been responsible for waking the ancestors, you would already be dead."

"I'm in the Ashwood Tower's heart."

"Of course you are. Where else would you be? I don't understand your affinity for buildings. At the moment, I'm trying to be grateful for it."

"Can we go back to the Dragons?"

Ynpharion helpfully added, "I believe Lord Kaylin refers to the mirror's view."

"No. What I do here may be the only aid I am able to tender anyone in this fight." She raised her chin and said, to her brother, "I'm sorry. But I must ask you to leave."

"Lord Ynpharion will bear witness to anything that is discussed."

"Yes. But his presence is a necessity; he is the only conduit I have to the Chosen." She exhaled and added, "If I cannot trust you, my Lord, there is no purpose to trust at all. But our best chance of escaping to join the fray is in the upper reach; the power of the ancestor does not seem to be as concentrated above the ground. There is a reason that the Dragons have not chosen to land."

The High Lord reached out to touch his sister's cheek. He then turned to Ynpharion. Kaylin was certain he meant to threaten his Barrani liege, but he did not speak.

Does this mean he's going to kill you later? Kaylin asked.

Probably.

Then maybe you shouldn't stay.

We are not faring well against one of these ancestors, he replied. *If you do not succeed in whatever you now attempt, we will face two. I would not grieve at your death; it is not for your sake that I am willing to take this risk.*

"I don't want Ynpharion to die for this," Kaylin told the Consort. She spoke, of course, with Ynpharion's mouth.

"If you were willing to actually take control of him, Lord Kaylin, if you were willing to *use* the power of his name as any one of my people *would,* it would not be necessary; I would not have to trust Ynpharion; I would only have to trust you. But you are not immortal; he is. Even if you gave me your binding, blood oath, it would last only until you died. And then, Ynpharion—with this knowledge—would be free."

"Then don't give him the knowledge. I'll work it out on my own."

CHAPTER 22

White brows rose. To Ynpharion, the Consort said, "You understand the difficulty Lord Kaylin poses?"

"I would not have believed that she would be difficult in this precise fashion had I not experienced it so completely. But yes, Lady. I am willing to take this risk. Lord Kaylin, however, does not consider it a risk; she feels that she is demanding— or rather presiding over—my execution."

"She is naive; she is not a fool."

Kaylin, for the first time since this fight had begun, attempted to force Ynpharion to move. To move toward the doors that lead out of the chamber and away from the secret that the Consort was willing to share—with her.

She cursed him in four different languages when he fought her for control of his body; pain blossomed behind her eyes. Had she not been crouching, she would have fallen. In the dark. Onto stone.

The Consort chuckled. "She is trying to force you to leave."

"Yes," Ynpharion replied, through gritted teeth.

"And you are fighting her for the chance to serve—and die."

"Yes."

"She does have that effect, even upon the Lord of the West March. Her touch is light, Ynpharion—but if she is determined, you will both suffer. I am not entirely certain that she will win—but I am not certain that she will not. With Kaylin, incentive changes everything."

"She despises me," he replied, his voice far less smooth than it had been.

"Yes. And you despise her. But she is a Hawk, and she has learned that even people she despises are worthy of both life and the protection the Laws grant.

"Lord Kaylin, let me make this easier for you. I can read this word."

Kaylin froze.

Ynpharion, unhindered by the driving force of her will, turned once again to face the Consort. She felt his surprise. No, it was more than surprise; it was shock.

"Its form is not clear *enough* that I can read it with certainty; there is some chance that I am in error."

"You can—you can *read*—"

"Yes. It is a truth that is never acknowledged. Were it, I might be master of every single child that I chose to waken. Every one. You understand why Ynpharion's life is now in danger. Why I sent even the High Lord from this room."

Kaylin did.

"Understand, then, that there is a reason that it is a difficult and arduous process to find someone who might replace me. Any man or woman of power can rule. But to wake the children, to give them life, to let them go without binding or constraining them—no. To *see* the names and the meanings, to *choose* them, and to return them to their parents without ever speaking the words that will bind them forever in servitude and slavery, is no simple thing for people of power.

"Not among our kin. I am not certain that even among yours it would be so simple—but your births and ours are not the same. You can stop attempting to assert your will, now. Ynpharion knows."

"It has long been suspected." Ynpharion's voice was soft, hushed.

Does she know all *your names?*

Do not ask, Lord Kaylin.

"I do not know all the names," the Consort continued, as if Kaylin had spoken. "To speak a name, to absorb the whole of its meanings and workings, is not the same—for the Consorts—as choosing one. It gives us intuition; it gives us hope. But if you are afraid that I might look at any of the children who have left my arms and speak their names, it is both a reasonable fear and unfounded.

"And Evarrim is correct. True words are not true names. There is a difference in their function. When words such as the words at…Helen's…heart have served their purpose, they do not return to the Lake, wherein they might, in the fullness of time, wake to life again. I will tell you the story of this word."

"Is it a name?"

"No. No, and yes."

The ghost of a word rotated. Kaylin squinted, as if squinting would make the trailing strands of mist more solid. Ynpharion was predictably unimpressed.

"You have done this before," the Consort continued.

I haven't.

Ynpharion didn't repeat her disagreement. *What you can do with almost unforgiveable impunity, I cannot.*

"I haven't."

"Yes, you have. If you had not, Ynpharion would not be in

this room, and I would have no way to reach or speak with you. Ynpharion did not surrender his name to your keeping."

It was true. He hadn't. Kaylin had physically *grabbed* it. She had reached for it, in the strangely metaphysical interior of the Hallionne Orbaranne. She had held it in her hands, and she had spoken what she held without ever deliberating on *how*.

"This is not a true name—not in the Barrani sense."

"Dragons have—" Kaylin bit back the words.

Ynpharion was shocked anyway. *How is that you have managed to survive thus far?*

"If you are correct, and you are standing in the heart of the Ashwood Tower, the Tower itself is—or was—willing to allow you entry. She will not work against you deliberately; she may have defenses that will act without conscious intent. You will not have *time*."

"And if I—if I speak this word the way I spoke the other names—"

"Yes. If you speak this word in that fashion, you will invoke it. I do not think you will have control over what you have invoked—not in the way names give control—but you may have access to them. Or you may give the building itself access."

"The building was damaged—Evarrim is right about that."

The Consort lifted a hand. "No more. Listen, now."

And Kaylin did.

She didn't expect to hear singing, but the Consort sang, lifting her arms as she began. She adorned syllables with length and depth, elongating them and extending them. Kaylin had seen her do exactly this on their journey to the West March. She had, once, joined her in song at Nightshade's behest. But he'd been singing harmony, and she'd been following it; his voice was much, much stronger than hers.

Pretty much anyone's was; the best Kaylin could say of a good singing day was that she'd mostly stayed on tune. She understood what the Consort wanted. Reaching out—carefully—she cupped a word she could no longer see between the palms of her hands. To her relief, it was physically there. What she couldn't see in this darkness, she could still touch.

She closed her eyes to listen; Ynpharion's, however, remained open. The word in the mirror didn't shift or change—but it wouldn't. It was a Records capture of a moment in time. She wanted to know *how* the Barrani Arcanists—they had to be Arcanists—had found it at all, but didn't ask; she concentrated, at last, on the song, and the way it made her feel.

Ynpharion was surprised—or outraged. He attempted to mostly keep this to himself. He kept this distaste for her very, very inadequate mimicry of the Consort's song to himself as well, although she could sense its edges. This was the worst thing about having his name: no one wanted to feel self-conscious on the inside of their own head.

And she couldn't afford it. The ground shook. The tremor beneath her legs told her it wasn't the High Halls this time. She could hear Mandoran's raised, furious voice: it held desperation, and a touch of fear.

What she heard, his enemy could hear.

And she needed to focus, now. On the song. On what the song said to her. On what she made of it on the inside of her thoughts. She needed, nasal, off-tune voice notwithstanding, to *sing* it. To sing it as if she meant it.

She hadn't done this with Ynpharion. She hadn't done it with Nightshade or Lirienne. Bellusdeo, and the recreation of her name hadn't required it either, although she no longer even knew what Bellusdeo's name was.

But the Consort had sung a similar song to the Hallionne, and it was the song of their awakening. Helen was a building. Helen was not, as the Hallionne had been, asleep—but the Hallionne Kariastos had been theoretically asleep when he'd lifted the water from the riverbed and taken the form of an elemental Dragon. Making dinner for a handful of guests was probably nothing in comparison.

Kaylin sang. Yes, her voice was thin and scratchy, and yes, it didn't have the fullness of the Consort's—but she was alone in a dark cave. No one was going to throw stones at her to get her to shut up. She had Mandoran's voice for company, and it was dangerously intermittent. She hoped the small dragon was helping. Somehow.

And then she gave up that hope for the song that she now sang. It had words, but she knew that she would never understand them the way she understood any other language she'd been forced to learn. And it didn't matter. She understood that this song was part plea, part pain, and part desire—not as Bertolle's song had been; it was less earthy but, for Kaylin, more felt. She spoke *to* Helen; she sang *to* Helen. Because in some ways, Helen *had* been sleeping.

But Helen had chosen sleep.

Helen had destroyed parts of her physical self so that she could continue to sleep: so that she could live with Hasielle, and all the mortal tenants who had followed. Helen had remained sleeping—in the way the Hallionne did—while she waited for Kaylin to find her.

Kaylin needed a place, but she *wanted* a home. She had wanted a home since her mother's death. She had found only one, and it was gone. Evanton had sent her to Helen. Helen had opened the door.

And she would be damned if some ancient, ancestral, bloody Immortal closed it in her face—because Helen didn't want her to leave, and at the moment, Helen's was the only voice that counted. Helen wanted from Kaylin what Kaylin wanted to give; Kaylin wanted what Helen offered.

The marks on Kaylin's arms began to brighten. The marks on the ground didn't. Kaylin sang. She caught syllables; she held notes. Into the extended ones, she let loose with the force of all the things she didn't have words for, because she *didn't* have words.

The single word that she had chosen to place at the heart of the rest grew warm against Kaylin's palms. She held it as if it were Helen. Something this size and this shape she could carry—and had. She could protect it, if it was necessary.

But she couldn't give Helen back what Helen herself had destroyed. She could probably empty her skin of marks, and they wouldn't cover enough ground. Helen had chosen, long, long before Kaylin's birth; what she was *now* had come from those choices, good or bad. Kaylin couldn't judge her—how did one even start to judge a building?—and didn't try.

This word was *not* the word the Consort sang. It was almost that word. It was as dense and finely written. But this word was of Kaylin, and this word was for Helen. Kaylin had songs of her own, half-remembered. Song made her emotional; it always had; you could say things in song that no one in their right mind would ever put into words—not unless they were four years old.

The word, however, was glowing faintly. It wasn't gold— it was a pale gray, which was one of the colors the marks on Kaylin's skin often took.

Give the Lady my thanks, Kaylin told Ynpharion. *I think—I think I can handle it from here on.*

Handle it quickly, was his curt reply. He withdrew, or allowed Kaylin to withdraw. He really didn't enjoy being in contact with her. She didn't blame him. Then again, she didn't, as he pointed out, have time.

★ ★ ★

The songs she finished with were not songs she would have sung had anyone but a child been present. No one else was here. This room—this vast cavern—was Helen's, and if Helen slept here, if she slept as buildings slept—this was the equivalent of the small rooms that foundlings occupied in Marrin's halls.

Kaylin sang. She sang softly, because that was how these songs were always sung. It didn't matter if the parent—or guardian, in Marrin's case—was terrified and facing imminent death; the only fears that leaked into these songs were the quiet, unspoken fears *for* the child. Fear of what the future held. Kaylin could still remember—dimly—the feel of her mother's arms and the sound of her voice.

When she offered these songs in the Foundling Hall, she offered comfort, because it's what she'd taken—and still took—from the memories. She offered Helen, at the end of the Consort's song, this song of her own; the thunder and strength of Kaylin's attempt at the Barrani voice dwindling—but not dying—into the end of the day. Into Elantran words and a vocal range that anyone who could speak could manage.

But that was a lie: it wasn't a song of her own. It was a song her mother had sung. And a song that her mother's mother had sung to her, when she had—impossible though it had been to believe at the time—been a child herself. There was history, in this song. It wasn't ancient; it didn't come from a time when gods—if that's what they were—walked the world. It wasn't a song to waken sentient buildings to prepare them for war. It was a quiet song. A child's song.

But she remembered that the Hallionne had sung to the Consort—and that song, in the end, had been very like the one she sang now.

She even lifted the rune that she had placed as she sang,

forgetting—for just one minute—that it was *not* an infant, not an orphan, not a child abandoned on the steps of the Foundling Hall.

The gray light began to pale as it grew brighter. It passed from ash-gray to brilliant white, and from that almost blinding white to blue—blue edged in the gold that the marks on the floor had originally shed.

The cavern remained dark; the light from this single word illuminated only Kaylin and the stone directly beneath her. The ground shook.

Any time you want to do something, *Kaylin!* Mandoran shouted. He wasn't, of course, in this room. She didn't hear his voice as she heard Ynpharion's, or any of the voices that she knew because of a true name; she heard it as if he were standing in the vicinity of her shoulder. And shouting. In her ear.

She resisted the urge to shout back; she was certain *her* voice wouldn't reach beyond the cavern.

Squawk.

"All right, all right, I'm coming."

One word. One word at the heart of a building that had once been a Tower. Helen had made choices that Tara had not. She had learned to live; she had learned to become home to people very like Kaylin in what they were searching for. Maybe she couldn't go back. Given the damage she'd done to the runes on the outer periphery of this giant circle, there were things she could no longer do. Kaylin wasn't certain what those things had been.

But it didn't matter. This was Helen as she was. And *this* Helen, unlike the original one, had offered Kaylin something she desperately wanted.

She understood Tiamaris, she thought, although she knew her understanding was a tiny, tiny echo of his—a whisper in comparison to Dragon roar. She wanted a home that was *hers*.

And she wanted to be able to protect her home. She wasn't doing this out of a misplaced sense of responsibility—or worse, guilt. If she had to make a final stand—for any reason—this is where she wanted to do it.

Home had once been her mother. If her mother moved, home moved with her; she was always at its heart. And maybe Kaylin had been looking for a mother, in some ways, all these years. She was twenty. She was almost twenty-one. She was old enough to have children of her own.

Ynpharion was both astonished and disgusted at the very idea. In his opinion—his elderly, condescending opinion—Kaylin was a *child*. Children did raise children.

She knew she could push him out; she could wall herself off. She was too surprised at the intrusion of his thoughts to immediately lash out. He was listening. He was better at listening than Kaylin was.

You do not guard yourself against displays of weakness.

You're wrong, Kaylin told him. She drew the single word away from the cradle she'd made of her arms. *I do. But I don't consider this weakness.*

She set the rune down, afraid that its new light would once again gutter. It didn't.

Kaylin—idiot!—get out of there! Mandoran shouted. The ground shook; she wasn't certain, given the timing, that it wasn't because of the force of his voice—he could have been a bloody *Dragon,* he was so damned loud.

And there was really only one thing to do when a Dragon was screaming orders in your ear: obey. Her legs were already in motion before thought could catch up; she was racing—in the dark—toward the nearest wall. Which she couldn't see.

The farther away she got from the center of the room, the more the ground trembled. She was afraid, for a moment, that large chunks of ceiling that she couldn't see would crush her. The floors had curved slightly in toward the center—but they'd been smooth; there had been nothing to trip on, and nothing that required coordinated jumping to clear. She hoped. She hadn't really bothered to take a good look at any part of the cavern that hadn't once contained engraved words.

She reached wall, walking the last few yards. When her palm was against rock, she turned toward the one source of light in the cavern; the gentle glow of her own marks had faded while she'd sung.

Inhaling and exhaling for three breaths, she eased her shoulders down her back. "Helen!" she shouted, her voice—for the moment—as loud as Mandoran's beneath the curved ceiling of the cavern. "Helen." Her voice softened. "It's time to wake up, now. We're waiting. We need you."

Light.

White erupted in a sphere that expanded outward to engulf the room, obliterating the cavern's natural darkness. What light touched, it transformed. Words that Kaylin no longer recognized caught fire and retained it as the floor itself was remade, yard by yard.

Kaylin forgave Mandoran for the damage he'd done to her ears, as she flattened her back against the wall. Words radiated golden light, but a trace of blue at their cores implied clear sky. Boundless, clear sky.

She was holding her breath, and realized it only when she needed to exhale—or pass out. Beautiful, yes. But deadly.

Everything unnecessary was gone: the scorched, empty spaces, the melted, deformed stone, and the outer edges of the pattern that had been composed entirely of one or the other. What was left was golden, shining stone. It looked molten, but she felt no heat.

Kaylin could see no gaps in the placement of the words at Helen's heart.

She could no longer see the words she had chosen to place in the gaps that had existed, and she knew she could search for hours without locating even one of them. All but the one at the heart.

That one was shining a clear, strange blue, ringed, by the gold shed by all the rest of the words. The gold continued to brighten; the stone floor began to rise, as if to lift that one blue rune toward the heights of the cavern.

Kaylin pressed herself farther into the wall as the golden light changed the composition of the floor. No, she thought; the ceiling itself was changing, as well. Everything was.

Kaylin understood that change was part of life. Good change, bad change—it was just life. Until the change was bad enough that there was no life left. She knew everything that now occurred was necessary for Helen.

But if she couldn't find a way out, she'd change with it. And die. Gold inched toward her feet as she watched, while pressing herself farther into the wall. Next time, she was keeping small and squawky with her. She could now see the entirety of the room. There was no door anywhere, and no convenient arches that at least hinted at exit. In a few minutes, it wouldn't matter; if a door did open, she wouldn't have time to reach it; there'd be no path.

"Helen?"

No answer. She wasn't even certain that Helen could hear her, because she wasn't certain that the Helen who was looking for someone to make a home for was the Helen that these words now described. Everything had changed.

She was very surprised when the wall at her back fell over. She went with it, toppling out of the boundary encircled by stone and filled by words.

"What," Mandoran demanded, as she spilled across the floor, "did you think you were doing? No bloody wonder Teela always worries about you!"

She blinked. The room she was in was much darker than the one she'd just involuntarily left. Not that she was complaining about the leaving. She sat up; there were splinters and shards of rock clinging to her legs and tunic.

"Where's the small dragon?" she asked.

"He went off upstairs. I think." Mandoran offered a hand up, and she took it. His hands were winter cold.

"Mandoran—you're bleeding."

He shrugged. "Nothing's broken."

"You are also lying."

"Oh, that's right—you're a healer. I almost forgot. Teela says to tell you it'll serve you right if you try to heal me."

"I don't try to heal Barrani who aren't dying. Well, or aren't being transformed by chaos into something that will kill me. It just pisses them off."

Mandoran's smile was a shadow of its usual, cheeky self. "What were you *thinking?*"

"I was thinking I could use some of the marks grafted onto my skin to heal Helen."

He snorted. "And water is wet. I'm not talking about *that*. Why were you standing in the center of the maelstrom? Are you an idiot?"

"I didn't expect that to happen." In an effort to change the subject—her stupidity never being one of her favorites—she said, "What happened to the ancestor?"

"You'll have to ask Helen. Upstairs," he added. He hadn't let go of her hand.

"I can stand. I can walk—or run—better without the anchor."

"He's not doing it for your sake, dear," Helen said. Her

voice was still disembodied. But it sounded both stronger and younger, to Kaylin's ear. "He's doing it for his own. I tried to explain what Mandoran and his friend are."

"The painting analogy."

"Yes. Mandoran is now at the entrance to the long hall— he's gone past the front rooms. He needs to find his way back."

"But I'm still looking at the outside of a building I can never enter."

"Yes."

"And he's standing beside me."

"Yes. That's the trouble with analogies; they only convey the general sense of the truth. The specifics—I'm sorry—are beyond you. And he knows this. Your Teela is terribly angry— at Mandoran, and at herself—and it will make things very, very difficult for her."

"I got it." Kaylin shifted her grip on his ice-cold hand, entwining their fingers. "I won't let him go until he's back." Even, she thought, if she wouldn't be able to tell the difference. "Did you get rid of tall and ugly?"

"If you mean, is he dead, the answer is no. He is not, however, here."

"...Is he in the city?"

"No, Kaylin. I understand that the city is important to you. He is not, at the moment, in your world. If he returns, it will not be the way he left."

She recognized the room she was standing in; it was the room that she'd left in order to reach Helen's damaged core. There was no door, but a slab of rock that was approximately door-shaped now lay against the floor.

"Do you know how to get back?" she asked Mandoran.

"Same way we arrived."

"Great."

★ ★ ★

As it happened, the stairs were pretty much where they'd left them, but they seemed more solid; they were certainly wider and the incline less steep. They were bound on both sides by wall, but the inner wall didn't shrink in an attempt to pitch them off the stairs. They were also well lit, for which Kaylin was grateful; she'd left her only source of portable light in the big room.

Leaving the stairs deposited them into a familiar, narrow closet. It was well lit this time round. So was the kitchen. Mandoran's grip was tight enough, Kaylin's fingers were turning purple. She didn't let go. She wouldn't, until she could dump him properly on Teela.

In the light of the dining room—which is where they finally met up with everyone else, Mandoran's arm was hanging at a very awkward angle. His left side was bleeding; he'd taken a wound that had probably barely missed his lungs.

"Don't give me that look. He put part of the door through me; it wasn't a sword."

"Sharp door."

"It was moving quickly, with a lot of force."

The small dragon, who was in the dining room, as Mandoran had more or less stated, hurled himself toward Kaylin's face, stopping short at her shoulders. He twined his tail around her neck and flopped across them. Kaylin didn't have time for him at the moment.

She saw the blood trickling out of the corner of Mandoran's mouth. He didn't appear to notice.

Aside from Kaylin herself, everyone looked like they'd been in a very close fight; Mandoran's wasn't the only wound taken. "Are you back yet?" she asked him.

"I don't know. Am I?"

Kaylin looked up at Teela, and noted that she was also holding on to Annarion. She was doing it with less obvious force. Then again, she could snap a mess-hall table in half and look casual and calm while doing it. Kaylin had seen it happen.

"No," Teela said, obviously answering Kaylin's question. "He's not."

Severn's forehead was gashed and bleeding.

"His skull's too thick to take anything but superficial damage from a glancing wound," Teela informed her. She exhaled. "Well done, kitling."

Kaylin, however, shook her head. "The ancestor here wasn't the only one."

"I know."

"The other one is outside of the High Halls."

"There is a lot more power in the High Halls than in Helen's dining room."

"Yes—but the High Halls *aren't* like the Towers. Or Helen." She swallowed. "No one can leave the High Halls. There's some kind of wall across every exit."

Teela's eyes, which had shaded to their usual blue, instantly darkened.

"The Dragon Court's in the air; they're fighting the ancestor now. But they can't land; he does way more damage at close range."

"I am not going to ask how you know this." She looked at her hand—or at the hand that Annarion clasped. Then she looked at Mandoran.

"The Emperor's there."

Teela cursed in quiet Leontine. "Has Bellusdeo been hurt?"

"Yes."

Louder Leontine followed.

"She's alive. I think her injury's equivalent to Mandoran's— or it was. I don't know what's happening there now."

Ynpharion.

Lord Kaylin.

One down, one to go.

"The Halls of Law have called out the full force. All reserves. The Swords and the Hawks are mobilizing."

Teela's jaw dropped. Which was fair; Kaylin's had done the same. "They can't *do* anything but *die!*" She glared at Annarion and Mandoran. Annarion, whose arm wasn't broken, lifted his free hand.

"We're fine. We're not going to turn sideways and slip into the otherworld. We're not going to transform into something wretched and unfamiliar."

"More wretched and more unfamiliar, at any rate," Mandoran said. His Elantran was far smoother and far more natural than Annarion's. Kaylin suspected this was all down to personality. "Helen?"

Helen appeared at the far end of the dining room. "If they remain here, I believe I can contain them. You, however, don't wish to stay."

"No."

"Kitling—"

"Yes, there's nothing I can do." She poked the small dragon. "But I have friends. Hey, wake up. We need a bit of help here."

Squawk.

"I mean it."

"You'll want to leave by the Tower, I expect."

"If *someone* is cooperative, yes."

CHAPTER 23

"What, exactly, do you expect him to do?" Teela asked for the third time as they followed Helen up another endless set of stairs.

"Fly."

"Yes. Fine. If you wanted him to fly to the High Halls—" she stopped. "We're near the top."

Helen nodded. "You can hear the Dragons?"

"Yes."

Kaylin couldn't. But as she continued to climb, the voices that Teela could hear became audible for the merely mortal. The Dragons were roaring. Dragon roars never sounded like speech to Kaylin's ears; up close they mostly sounded like pain.

"I'm surprised the Emperor didn't choose to wait until after the ancestor had entered the High Halls."

"I don't think he could."

"Oh?"

"Bellusdeo flew straight there."

"The small dragon, as you call him, could have flown

straight there from the front door, which is much, much closer."

Kaylin said nothing.

Severn, however, said, "Are you certain you want to attempt something new? The little guy looks exhausted."

"*All* the Swords and *all* the Hawks."

Helen opened the door at the end of the stairs, and night rushed in. She stepped past the staircase and into what Kaylin suspected was the only room at the tower's height.

The walls curved; the room was circular. It reminded Kaylin of the Hawklord's tower. This room was wider across and appeared, from the height of the walls, to be taller. It was hard to tell; the ceiling was, at the moment, nonexistent. Kaylin saw the folds of roof that implied aperture. "You opened this for Bellusdeo."

"Yes."

Kaylin plucked the small dragon off her shoulder. He rolled over and played dead in her hands.

"Look—I don't care if you have to eat my *entire* arm if you need the marks for power." None of the miserable things had risen to offer themselves as food.

"*I*, on the other hand, *do*," Teela told him. "I'm going with her and I'm not in the mood to listen to her whine about blood loss and pain, neither of which she takes well."

Kaylin chose to ignore this. "We need to get there by the fastest direct route, and we need to be there *now*." She set the small dragon on the ground. He squawked like an angry gull.

Helen, after a pause, replied. Kaylin couldn't understand a word that left her mouth. "If you understand a word either of them are saying," she said to Teela, "I quit."

Teela chuckled. Her eyes were still a very dark blue, but her sense of humor hadn't been extinguished. This was unusual. "Helen, you're certain you can keep the boys occupied safely?"

"I am certain I can prevent them from harming themselves. I can certainly prevent them from being harmed, now." She smiled at Kaylin. "Thank you."

Kaylin was all for taking credit where it was due. But she had to feel that she'd *earned* it. She nudged the recalcitrant small dragon with her toe. He flopped over onto his belly. And complained. "I wouldn't have known what to do without the help of the Consort—who's currently under attack. I would never have reached your heart without Mandoran's help; I probably wouldn't have survived long enough to make a difference. Hey, you, cut it out," she added, to the small dragon.

"I'm beginning to think all the fuss about Sorcerous familiars was, as implied, childish story," Teela told him.

"Good public relations," Kaylin countered. "...Or bad, as the case may be." She knelt by the splayed-out familiar. "I know I wouldn't have made it this far without you. Mandoran might not have survived without your help.

"But Bellusdeo's in trouble. And if the Halls of Law are fully mobilized, everyone I've practically grown up with is going to head to the High Halls and die there. I think you can help. If you want, you can leave *me* behind. But I need the ancestor to be dead or gone before the Swords and the Hawks hit that street."

"I'm not sure what you expect something that limp and exhausted to do, kitling. From what I've observed so far, all he does is add to the problem; he doesn't exactly alleviate it."

Kaylin's cajoling had gotten nowhere.

Teela's dismissal, apparently, was what was needed; the small, transparent rat lifted his neck. The rest of his body, however, hugged the cool stone of the floor. He hissed.

Teela, not to be outdone, hissed back.

Kaylin was too far from a wall to bash her head against it; she was close to Severn's chest, and used that instead. He winced.

"You broke a rib." Her tone was all accusation.

"I didn't break a rib; a rib might be fractured."

"Fine. You let someone else break your rib."

"Jealous?"

Squawk. Squawk. SQUAWK.

"What did you *say* to him, Teela?"

Teela shrugged. "If you weren't paying attention, that's hardly my problem." She took a step back as the tower floor began to shimmer. "How much weight can the floors here bear?" she asked Helen.

It wasn't a rhetorical question.

"He's not angry with *me*," Helen replied.

This answer made no sense; Kaylin wondered what other question she'd missed.

"The amount of weight the floor will bear is irrelevant. Unless he is displeased, he will not strain the capacity of the floor. Even were these physical ruins, and structurally unsound, he would not strain them to breaking; the choice is his."

Squawk.

"He is not in a terribly *happy* state of mind, on the other hand." Helen also took a step back, toward the wall. "You may want to give him room," she added, as the gentle glow that now imbued his form began to brighten. "Also, Corporal Handred, it is best if you avoid touching the floor."

Since Helen meant this in all seriousness, Kaylin kept her mouth shut. This was harder than it should have been, because the floor wasn't the only thing being transformed.

The familiar was no longer a small dragon; the adjective *small* was fast becoming inaccurate, as well. As she watched, she realized that the floor wasn't actually glowing; it was reflecting the light at the center of the translucent familiar. Which was odd, because the floor's surface wasn't reflective.

"Is it not?" Helen asked.

"Not to the rest of us. I'm including Teela in that."

She had watched transformations before, and they always made her vaguely uneasy. This one didn't; the small dragon had become a thing of light; the light was bright enough that after a few seconds, it had no shape; she had to look away. She looked back as the radius of contained light grew, and grew again, becoming a perfectly balanced sphere on the tower floor.

Helen had been right: the sphere itself continued to gain both size and height; in the end, only a person's width of safe floor space remained between the walls and the light.

"Do you know what he's doing?" Severn asked her. He'd wound the weapon chain around his waist, and didn't bother to arm himself; he did, however, take up position closest to the door. Teela had done the same.

Kaylin nodded. "I don't know *how*, so don't ask."

It seemed particularly fitting that the sphere itself began to elongate; she recognized the shape it took. It was an egg. It was a *giant* egg.

"Do you think baby Dragons also come out of eggs this size?" she began.

"No. And before you ask, yes, I've seen one, and yes, it was during the war," Teela replied.

The egg cracked. Kaylin was grateful. She knew that Teela had centuries upon centuries more experience with war—but she was cowardly enough to want to think of her role in that war as brave and heroic. She did not want to think of it as slaughter or baby-killing.

But she knew that Bellusdeo had value to the Emperor—to

her *entire* race—because she was the last of the female Drag-ons. And she wasn't the last because the rest had up and com-mitted suicide.

Bellusdeo had flown *to* the High Halls. She was fighting to protect the Barrani there, regardless of what had occurred in the past. People *could* change. Kaylin had.

The crack in the egg travelled from its peak to the floor, joined by smaller cracks on its way down. Those cracks forked, and forked again, covering the surface until no more of the surface remained. At the center of what had once been egg, folded awkwardly into an egg shape, was the not-very-small dragon.

He stretched his wings out first, shaking their tips too damned close to Teela's face. Teela had one of the best poker faces in the Halls; she didn't even blink. She did curse him in loud, clear Leontine when he knocked her off her feet with a lazy swish of tail, though.

He brought his wings in, lifting and elongating his neck. End to end, there wasn't enough room in the tower to con-tain him—not fully stretched. He snorted in Kaylin's direc-tion, but didn't roar. She was grateful.

"We'll be back," Kaylin told Helen, as she climbed up the side of her familiar. "Ummm—it's okay with you if we do come back?"

"I think you had better, dear. I imagine someone will need to prevent me from strangling Mandoran." She headed to-ward the door.

"If I haven't strangled him yet," Teela replied, leaping with far more grace onto Dragon back, "I'll resent it if you do. It will mean all my prior effort at self-control was wasted."

"And that is *not* the lesson we wish to teach, clearly." There was no threat in Helen's voice. Before Kaylin could ask, she added, "Annarion is not nearly as…difficult. He has a much better sense of responsibility. Probably too much better." She left the tower by the door, which would have been totally normal—if she'd opened it first.

Severn didn't immediately join them; instead he cleared his throat. When the familiar swiveled to face him, Severn asked permission. A small hint of smoke cleared large dragon nostrils; Severn correctly interpreted this as a yes.

"Remember," Kaylin said, as the familiar's body tensed to leap, "that none of the rest of us can fly."

Kaylin loved to fly. Or rather, she loved to hitch rides with people who could. In this case, people was a bit of a stretch.

The familiar, however, was not a small aerial footprint. This wouldn't have been a problem on most days—not at this time of night. But she could see the telltale tunics of the Halls of Laws' Aerian division. The Aerians wore magical clothing when they went on sky patrols; the cloth glowed. The cloth didn't *have* to glow; activation depended on circumstances.

Kaylin wanted to tell them that these were the *wrong* circumstances for light; it made them trivial targets. She remembered that the Dragon Court was probably melting *streets* by now, and reconsidered.

"Teela—can you see Clint?"

"Yes."

"Can you tell him to pull our forces *back?*"

"You want him to know that we're here and we failed to respond to the emergency call-up?"

"No—but I'd rather get docked pay than lose them all!"

"And if *you* were their commanding officer, I'd be happy to comply. You're not. You don't get a say."

"Then find me the Hawklord!"

"Not worth the effort," Teela shouted back. She had to

shout. The Dragons were roaring. "We're obvious enough. He'll find *us*."

"I'd like him to find us before the mages decide we're an incoming threat!"

"Then you should have thought of that sooner."

"What? You didn't!"

"Yes, kitling, I did. I just don't *care* about anything but getting to the High Halls as fast as possible. I assumed you had the same thought."

"Incoming," Severn said, raising his voice. It was going to be an evening of raised voices.

The familiar, however, was watching rather than listening; he was on the move before the lightning that was traveling in the wrong direction—ground to sky—unfurled in full magical glory. The familiar immediately headed toward the High Halls. He roared, and Bellusdeo, grounded, looked up; she roared back.

"Drop me off there," Teela shouted. She indicated Bellusdeo, but the familiar didn't have eyes in the back of his head—and he wasn't all that keen on following anyone's orders anyway.

The Hawks were not yet thick in the air, but they were present.

Kaylin craned forward to see if she could catch a glimpse of the ground just beneath the massive body of the mostly translucent dragon. She saw people. Many of them were running *away* from the combat zone, which was more sense than a lot of the citizens of Elantra usually displayed.

Some people, on horseback, were riding toward it.

The familiar flew over them all, folding his wings as he approached the High Halls at speeds that should have made landing impossible. Teela's hold on Kaylin's waist tightened as Kaylin ducked. The familiar crashed *into* the High Halls.

But he didn't hit them.

And he didn't, apparently, absorb much in the way of shock—none of his three passengers were thrown clear. Only two of them were cursing. He wheeled, flapping to gain speed and momentum, and when he had enough of it, he headed right back to the High Halls.

Kaylin could see what he was doing: he was ramming the barrier. The barrier, like the dragon, was translucent—but it was thick. He had chosen to attack it from the heights.

"Couldn't you breathe on it?" Kaylin shouted.

The familiar roared.

"Fine. Shutting up now."

The third time the full force of his very large body struck the barrier, it cracked. Or it sounded like it cracked; nothing apparently changed. The familiar then paused, hovering, until the Barrani poured out of the High Halls, gleaming in the magical light.

Ynpharion—the barrier is down.

She felt his acknowledgment. He was too busy for actual words, since apparently condescension took effort. The familiar reached dirt, briefly; Teela slid off his back and ran toward the Halls. Kaylin, on the other hand, ran toward the golden Dragon with the obviously scorched wing. The wing was bleeding.

Maggaron was standing by her head, waving a monstrosity of a weapon—one which Kaylin didn't recall him having for any other part of the evening. She didn't ask. She was just grateful that he had it.

"What," Bellusdeo demanded, in her angry, rumbly tone, "are you *doing here?"*

"Being useful," she replied. She placed a palm against smooth, golden scales; they were almost uncomfortably hot to the touch.

"I am not dying," Bellusdeo snapped.

"I'm willing to take this crap from Teela," Kaylin shot back. "But I can see one gaping, bleeding *hole* in your right wing. If you die here, the Emperor is probably going to torch the entire city in a rage."

"Maggaron, get rid of her."

Maggaron effected not to have heard, and given his ears were closer to the speaking parts of the golden Dragon than Kaylin's, that took effort.

"Even your Ascendant thinks it's necessary."

Smoke came out of flared nostrils. "He is like a cat, except for the parts of him that remind me of puppies. *Fine*. I would *never* have allowed this in my own kingdom—there'd be far too much in the way of politics and security at stake. Here, I do nothing of worth or value, so it doesn't matter what you know."

A pillar of radiant, white fire shot up from ground to sky; it seemed to travel forever, and it burned whatever it touched. The air was filled with the sound of Dragon pain.

Bellusdeo surged to her feet, and Kaylin, without another word, clambered up her back. What Bellusdeo had said was true: she looked terrible. This would be because she felt terrible. Her arms were shaking, and her legs were unsteady. But she'd easily located the Dragon's injuries, and she'd set about healing them.

She was unprepared for the strangeness of the Dragon's actual body. She'd never been allowed to heal one before—and frankly, in Elantra, where there were Dragons, the need for healing usually went in the opposite direction. There were very few fights that involved Dragons to begin with, and when there were, she wouldn't bet against them no matter what the odds were.

Bellusdeo's body was not a single thing. It wasn't a harmonious whole; it was a duality. The human form—or what Kaylin thought of as the human form—wasn't actually human in any way; it was inextricably wed to the draconic mass. Both of these things were like—like skin or armor; the Dragon could choose which of the two it wished to face outward.

"Bellusdeo—don't even try to fly. Not yet—I'm afraid I might—"

"Afraid you might what?"

"—turn you back into your human shape. I don't—I've never—"

"Honestly, if you weren't on my back, I'd bite off one of your arms. Maggaron, get on."

Maggaron replied in *Norannir*. Kaylin knew only a little of the language, but she understood what he meant, even if the words were foreign: *no freaking way.* He was usually polite and painfully earnest and deferential; here, the earnest was on display. The rest? Not so much.

Bellusdeo roared.

He stood his ground.

Kaylin gritted her teeth and clung to golden back—it was warm, if nothing else—and tried to guide the Dragon's insane physical body back to something that resembled its normal, healthy state. She wondered if this would be any easier if she were a Dragon herself, but kind of doubted it. It might have helped if the Dragon weren't expending so much energy having a hissy fit.

But when the column of white turned bloodred, expanding to fill the street and to destroy the grounds of the buildings on either side, she understood exactly why Bellusdeo wanted to be up in the air.

Flying in, low to ground, and approaching that deadly magical pillar, was another Dragon. He was a shade lighter in color than Bellusdeo, but it didn't matter; there was only one Dragon missing.

The Arkon had arrived.

"All the rest of the Dragons are *in the air*," Kaylin shouted, kicking the patient because she happened to be on her back. "You're powerful, yes—but you're *one* Dragon. One *injured* Dragon."

"The rest are not *in the air*," Bellusdeo countered. "Diarmat and Emmerian have landed."

They hadn't landed anywhere near Kaylin.

"If you want to be helpful, find them and heal *them*." They wouldn't let Kaylin anywhere near their injuries—and Bellusdeo knew it.

"It's different."

"Because I'm the precious, singular *girl?*"

"Because I'm not *living with any of the others*." Kaylin was *so* tired. What she did not need now was to fight with her roommate. But this wasn't enough of an explanation, and she knew it. "And because none of them—except maybe Tiamaris—are actually my *friends*. You are. So you have to put up with it."

"Teela doesn't."

"Teela's never had most of her arm blown off. And *yes,* she *would* put up with it. She might not speak to me for a week, but she'd accept it." The wing was mostly closed. It was tender. Kaylin hadn't even tried to replace lost blood; from bitter experience, that type of healing flattened her completely.

At the moment, even healing the easy injuries was painful; Bellusdeo was almost in a frenzy of panic and fear—because the Arkon had arrived, and because the *idiot* had chosen to *land in the street*. Kaylin was—although she'd never admit it—fond of the Arkon; her own panic was hard enough to deal with.

Bellusdeo's was—like everything else about her—larger

and deeper and more visceral. Kaylin got all of it, because of the healing.

Kaylin understood that the Arkon, of all the Dragon Court, meant something to Bellusdeo—he was her only link to the past, to her childhood, and in the end, to the world that she'd unintentionally left. He was, inasmuch as a cranky old man could be, her friend. He was the only one of the Dragon Court with the seniority to criticize the Emperor.

And he was *right* to criticize the Emperor.

Kaylin slid off Bellusdeo's back. Bellusdeo was either going to fly or she wasn't—but Bellusdeo couldn't do what the familiar, still waiting on a lawn that would probably be blackened, scorched earth in a few minutes, could.

She ran to him; he was pawing the ground with very, very sharp claws. The claws, like his teeth, were the only solid parts of his body; everything else was translucent.

Are you finished? he asked. She nearly fell off her own feet. The surprise of his voice was a welcome gift; it gave her a little boost of adrenaline. It pushed the exhaustion back. She climbed up—with Severn's help. Tightening shaking legs, she said, "I'm on."

The familiar pushed himself away from the ground, and gravity let him go, as if he weighed nothing.

Bellusdeo was yards behind; Kaylin could hear her roaring—in her mother tongue—at her Ascendant. But she could flex—and flap—her wing, and Kaylin knew Maggaron would give in; if he didn't, she'd leave him behind. At any other time, Kaylin would have thought that for the best; what could Maggaron do in the air?

But as she was on her familiar's back with Severn—both wingless, and both unprepared to fight on the back of a creature whose wingspan was far greater than their reach—she let it go. Bellusdeo teased Maggaron mercilessly—but in the end, some of his words did reach her. And she wasn't exactly overflowing with good sense of her own at the moment.

"Kaylin!" a familiar voice shouted. Kaylin looked up. Tiamaris was flying toward her. "Get Bellusdeo out of here, now!"

"She's not exactly *listening* to me!" Kaylin shouted back. Her voice had nowhere near the power of the Dragons'—but they had better hearing. How, given their native speech, Kaylin honestly didn't know. "You want her out? You drag her out!"

Someone else roared. Kaylin didn't understand the language, and she didn't recognize the voice. Which meant it could only belong to one Dragon. She sincerely hoped the Emperor didn't attempt to give her the same orders Tiamaris had, because her answer would essentially be the same, and she didn't have the energy to funnel it through politeness and groveling.

It was Sanabalis who said, clearly, "Support the Arkon!"

She heard other roars, other commands; she thought she could discern the thinner, higher voice of the Hawklord in the mix. But she was on a Dragon's back, and she could see the only other golden Dragon in the Court. He had landed. His wings were high, and even at this distance, Kaylin thought his eyes were a deep, bloodred—it must have been her imagination; she was too far away to see them clearly.

The ancestor was not. He turned his attention from the sky; he gestured and the rain of Dragon fire that was even now melting stones around him in a wide circle parted harmlessly above his head. His eyes—his eyes were silver. She knew, because he turned as the familiar flew in a straight line toward his head.

His hair was black; it reflected nothing. His skin was alabaster, his lips both perfect and cold as they turned up in a smile of recognition.

She heard roaring, felt wind rush past her, and tightened her legs as the familiar banked sharply; white fire—fire, not lightning—raced from the ancestor's hands toward the spot the familiar had occupied scant seconds ago. He was, in spite of his bulk and his shape, *not* a dragon. He moved with the speed of a sparrow. Or at least the maneuverability.

Her arms suddenly began to burn.

Given the magic being thrown around, this wasn't surprising. But it was new. *The Arkon,* she thought. She said nothing.

He is important to you.

Yes. He is.

Then tell me what you wish me to do—and what you are willing to sacrifice for it.

Help him, Kaylin said, as white fire sizzled past her hair. *Buy him time.*

The familiar continued to dodge white fire—and if nothing else, the target he provided spared some of the Dragon Court. Kaylin knew that Diarmat and Emmerian had landed because they could no longer maneuver in the air. A dark shadow cut across her—from above; it was the Emperor. It couldn't be anyone else.

And the sacrifice?

Kaylin almost said: *anything.* But there was a gravity to the question, a weight, that gave her pause. The familiar was not an enemy. But he was not, perhaps, a friend, either.

No. I am yours, and I have chosen to serve you—but there are rules in all things, and those rules define both you and my place in your world. I can interfere, Kaylin. As I can, I do. But this intervention is not interference; it is an act, and it is not, cannot be, free. What will you surrender to me in return for the intervention you desire?

Can you stop the ancestor?

Yes.

How?

Silence.

What do you want?

I? I want nothing. This is not about what I want; it is defined, entirely, by what you want. Will you sacrifice the lives of one of the Dragons? Will you sacrifice Teela, or Severn, who are closer? Will you sacrifice some of the people in the city you are sworn to protect?

No! And no, and no, and no. She stared at the marks on her arms, willing them to *come to life* when she needed them. She would give him the words. She would give him *all* the words. But...without them, she wouldn't be able to heal.

Nothing comes without cost, Kaylin. Even were I to want what you want—and I do not disdain it—there are actions I cannot take if you are unwilling to make the sacrifice required. I am sorry. If you will save your Arkon, if you will save your city—

She almost plugged her ears, but it wouldn't have stopped the words.

The words are not yours to offer.

She had named the familiar. She had seen the shape of a name at his heart. Even thinking it, she knew that she couldn't contain the whole of it—not to use against him; not to demand obedience.

You are wrong, he told her. *Is that what you will sacrifice?*

She had made the attempt to force someone to do something against their will by use of their name only twice, and it had caused her intense, visceral pain. And she knew, as the familiar flew, that this is not what he meant. She could live with pain. She *hated* it, but she could live with it—as long as it was hers.

Pain wasn't the reason she hesitated. It had never been the reason she hesitated. To use the name—given or taken—was to use the person; it was to reduce the people described by the name at their core to the level of a weapon, a fancy dagger, no more. They became tools, without will or decisions of their own.

She was *willing* to do this when she believed she was working to save *them*. She was willing to do it when the alternative was death—hers or theirs. But even then, the memory was something she shied away from; it burned. It burned the way all her memories of life in the fief of Barren did, even at this remove.

It made her hate herself.

Yes, the familiar said. *But that, Kaylin, is a powerful sacrifice. What you might achieve, should you make it, would be of note to any of the sorcerers of your world. What you lack in self-respect as a consequence would be given you by every other person of power or note.*

Kaylin wasn't religious—but time in the midwives guildhall had exposed her to a variety of mortal religions. The familiar—dodging flame and *buzzing* the damned ancestor as he did—was giving her the same choice that devils and demons and gods offered some poor, hapless, desperate fool as a test.

To refuse was to pass the complicated test. It had always been clear to Kaylin, in the stories. To refuse was to *win*.

It was *not* clear now. She heard the Arkon roar. It was defiant, that roar, and laced with pain. She heard Bellusdeo roar in frenzy, and she knew, Maggaron or no, the golden Dragon would take to the skies. She would join the Arkon.

CHAPTER 24

Severn's arm tightened around her waist. *Kaylin.*

He was aware of what she felt. He might be aware of the entire conversation.

Yes. She felt his breath against her cheek; it was warm and silent. *The Arkon would not have landed without cause. The Emperor would not attack without intent; they are aware of the Arkon's presence. They must understand what he plans; Sanabalis asked that we support the Arkon.*

But—

The city has survived for centuries without you. It's possible it would have perished to the Devourer had you never been born—but even that, we can't know. The Dragons are not foundlings. They are not lost children. They are not—they have never been—as powerless as we were.

Severn—the Arkon—if he—

Dies?

Yes!

Do you think he's not aware that that's the risk he takes? I've told you before: you can't save everyone. You can't ever save everyone. Do what you can do. Push yourself to do more, and you will break.

Loss would break her. Loss would break her in a hundred different ways. She meant to tell him as much, although it wasn't necessary; he knew.

This is the only way out of the past, he continued, arm around her waist, chin in the crook of her neck. *You are measured by the choices you make when it's hard. It's never as hard as when you're afraid. It's never as hard as when you have something to lose. You've made choices you still hate yourself for—it's only in the past few months that you've been able to even think of them without self-loathing.*

Fire. White fire. And red. Kaylin's arms were in so much pain she thought the skin had been flayed off them—slowly. Her legs weren't much better. But the back of her neck, which mostly had Severn's face in it, was numb.

It's the choices you make when it's hard *that define you. And when it's hard, all choices seem bad. The familiar asked you—*

You heard that?

Yes. I think he meant for me to hear it. He asked you what you were willing to sacrifice.

Yes.

Sacrifice the things you can. Sacrifice only what you can look back on with pride—or at least acceptance. It's not easy—it's never been easy—but we're not children, anymore. We can live with the choices we've made because we can—barely—believe that we had no choice.

Kaylin said nothing.

You won't believe that, here. The Dragons and the Barrani have choices. They've made plans. This is their fight.

It's my city, too.

Yes. It's our fight, too. But we do what we can do.

I can do this—

He shook her. And then, he loosed his hold on her waist. *Can you?* he asked.

Can you? the familiar asked. His voice was deep; it was calm. She had no idea if he would fight her should she attempt to take control of him. And she knew that if she somehow managed what seemed monumental—holding enough of the name she had seen and only vaguely remembered in mind for long enough to *use* it—something would break.

She didn't really love the small dragon the way she loved Teela. She considered him mostly a pain, with built-in advantages that only barely outweighed the negatives.

Negatives?

Attacking a sleeping Hallionne? Destroying Severn's favorite knife while I had it?

He snorted. It was loud. *You wouldn't have made it to the West March without my intervention.*

I said there were built-in advantages.

He snorted again. *You wouldn't have survived to be* called *to the West March without my intervention.*

Fine. Sorry. They vastly *outweigh the negatives.*

Snorting, apparently, was the gesture of choice in large dragon form.

But the point is—things will change. Unless you want *me to do this.*

No one who has will and thought and desire wants to be enslaved. I told you: this is not, in the end, about me: the path that we follow will be carved or worn smooth by you and the choices you make. That is true no matter what you decide. Your decisions define what we are. They have since we were first joined.

You mean since you hatched.

Do I?

She had more to say, but spent most of her breath cursing

as she attempted to put out the fire that had caught strands of hair. Most of which was no longer pinned up.

I'd rather you bite off my arm.

Yes. Which is why it would be no sacrifice to you. Not in the moment in which you make the decision. If you want the power, there is only one way to obtain it.

But WHY?

Because that is the price you must pay for power.

Kaylin thought of Teela, of Bellusdeo, of the Emperor.

You misunderstand. The price they pay, they pay—but this is your *price. What you want of me is inconceivable levels of power and strength, instantly. It is not power you have gained through use and growth and experience; it is not of you. But it is within your reach— and it is only, in this place, within* your *reach. Decide.*

Severn's arm tightened again.

And she knew that she could not do it. She could not surrender her friends—any of them. She couldn't give over the responsibilities she had toward the citizens of Elantra—even the ones she despised.

They're going to die anyway, a treacherous part of her mind said. *Why not make those deaths* count *for something?*

Because, she answered, even if they were strangers—or worse—they meant as much to someone *else* as her own friends meant to her. She wasn't preventing pain—she was just passing it on as if she were playing a game of hot potato. And maybe that's all anyone really did in the end—avoid things, and pass them on. But Kaylin had struggled to reach a place in her life where she no longer believed that, and she wanted to *stay* there.

Even if people die?

Yes. It felt like no. *Yes, because I could never tell people how I'd saved them, or why. They'd resent me.* She inhaled. *I'd resent them if our positions were reversed. I'd resent them if they deliberately, knowingly, sacrificed others to save me.*

Barrani will die here, tonight. Barrani have died.

Yes. But they chose that death. Theirs isn't the same kind of sacrifice. It's not certain. There is always the chance of survival. Always. If I die here, I'm not going to be happy—but I chose to be here. I demanded it.

Yes. *Yes, Kaylin.* The familiar came to an unexpected stop a yard above the ground. It was sudden enough that both Severn and Kaylin lost their seating. They managed to slow their fall against the familiar's body, and spilled onto the ground. Even before they'd come to a stop, they were both rolling out of the way; Severn was up first.

He was spinning up his weapon chain at the edge of molten rock. What had once been solid dirt was now a pit in the ground, with glowing orange practically floating on top of it. It would kill either of them to touch it.

It was agony to walk; it was worse, to run. If Kaylin had had the time, she'd've ditched all her clothing, the friction was so bad. She heard Bellusdeo roar somewhere above her head, but didn't pause or look up; she made a beeline for Severn's back, because she knew what the spinning chain could do.

She just wasn't certain it would work against the ancestor.

The Arkon didn't even bark at her. He didn't have the voice for it. He was—to her ear—intoning words that sounded painfully familiar, even if she couldn't understand a single one of them. She kept her eyes on the ancestor, although she wanted to look back to see if what she suspected was true.

The Arkon was speaking true words.

"Go, Kaylin!" Severn shouted, without looking back to her. "Go to the Arkon!"

She hesitated; it was very brief. Fire once again shot up in a blinding, brilliant white column; she couldn't see what it hit, if anything. The Dragons could resist it, although they clearly weren't immune; she recognized Diarmat's commanding bellow. He spoke Elantran; some of the Palace Guard must have arrived.

Or the Swords and the Hawks.

The Emperor roared.

Kaylin didn't understand a word, but the voice that followed was Bellusdeo's. She could guess. She didn't stop to look; she ran in a straight line from Severn to where the Arkon stood. He was in Dragon form, although his voice was almost—almost—normal.

And he was reciting true words. His voice reminded her very much of Sanabalis's voice, on the day she had heard him tell the Leontines the story of their beginning.

The ancestor's fire flared from behind, catching more of her hair. She wheeled to see Severn. The fire parted at his chain, but joined again beyond him; it was much, much weaker. Her hair still burned. Her lip was bleeding—movement was painful. And she had to move, and quickly.

The Arkon's eyes were bloodred. They were also the size of Kaylin's head. He glared at her, his eyes rounding; she could see fire and its destruction reflected in them. That, and herself. Severn was invisible.

He didn't break the flow of his speech to shout at her, and he didn't sweep his extensive jaws to throw her out of the way; on a night like this, that had to be counted as a win. She continued toward him, ducking under his head until she stood directly between his gigantic claws. She didn't remember the Arkon being so *big* in his draconic form.

But at least this way, she couldn't see his eyes.

What she could see, as he continued to speak, were the words that formed in the wake of his voice. They were golden, and in size and shape very similar to the runes engraved in

Helen's heart—but they were floating in the air. She couldn't speak them. The Dragons—with knowledge and practice—could. The Arkon had that knowledge.

It was why he had chosen to land.

Bellusdeo was screaming in Dragon frenzy—but to Kaylin's ear, it sounded more like rage than pain. She let it go. There was nothing she could say to Bellusdeo now. Nothing she could say to the Arkon. He clearly had a plan—and he didn't have the time to tell her what it was.

Do you understand what he's trying to do? Kaylin asked the familiar.

Yes. I do not believe he will succeed.

Kaylin closed her eyes. It didn't shut out the noises of combat. It didn't shut out the very mortal voices that had joined the fray, coming from above and behind. It didn't shut out the crackle of fire and the harsh thunder of magical lightning.

But it did shut out every visible thing that wasn't a true word. True words, when spoken, had physical shape and form. Even the Arkon's.

She trusted Severn to be aware of where she was; she trusted the Arkon's magical protections. The latter were being tested—and the less she thought about that the better. She thought of the words. She looked *at* the words formed by his speech.

And she remembered, as she so often did, Tiamaris's words. True words had an innate shape; a sense of "right" or "wrong" that had almost nothing to do with comprehension. She took a deep breath, and headed out of the Arkon's shadow and into the glow of words. She could touch them; they were solid. She had to open her eyes because the ground beneath them wasn't always *as* solid.

And yes: people were dying.

Barrani were dying.

Aerians.

She had no doubt that mortals on the ground would join them. The Aerians seemed to be carrying something—fine netting, line, something—as they circled. When one fell, someone flew in to pick up what they'd been carrying. Whatever it was, it didn't catch fire the way—

The way wings did.

At this point, the discomfort magic caused her couldn't get worse; she wasn't numb, but she couldn't gauge power or direction. There was just too much of it. But the heart of whatever defense—or offense—the Emperor's forces intended was here, where the Arkon was. Where he was speaking.

Where he was telling some ancient, difficult story.

She reached out and touched the true words that had form. She adjusted the fall of lines and strokes, the subtle placement of dots, the fine, spidery wisp of light that looked almost accidental unless seen as part of the whole shape. She could do this without speaking.

No, Kaylin, the familiar said. *You can't. You are speaking.*

I'm not—

He's right, Severn said. *I can hear you. I'm not the only one.*

The ancestor's skybound attacks ceased, at least briefly. As Kaylin moved between one stable patch of ground to another, touching words, jostling them, discretely changing the way the elements of each aligned, a new voice joined the Arkon's.

She knew she had never heard the voice before.

She felt as if she had heard it every day of her life.

And she saw the words form, across from the Arkon's, their shapes and patterns far clearer and far more consistent, their form in harmony—that was the word Tiamaris had used—with the meaning that would forever escape her.

She almost stopped breathing, then. She understood that all the Imperial forces combined—many of whom were now also dying—would possibly, on a very very good day, be equal to this *one man* on a bad one. She understood why the Barrani feared them; she didn't understand how the Barrani had *survived*.

No, the familiar said. *But you are here. The Arkon is here. The Barrani you have chosen to support are here. All elements of your life are now in play. Remember what your Teela told you, Kaylin. It is important that you remember.*

Teela had told her *a lot.*

Mortal memory cannot *be this defective. What she said, she said in my hearing, although she spoke to you.*

This was not helpful. Kaylin continued to move between the Arkon's summoned words, but she knew that his summoning was too slow, too laborious, and her refinements too haphazard; the ancestor's words were pure.

They were pure and essential and whole, and he spoke them so bloody quickly.

Think, she told herself. *Panic is not helping anyone.*

She looked at the words assembled before her—the ancestor's, not the Arkon's. Why did the Barrani fear—and loathe—their ancestors?

And she understood.

His words were not simple words. They were true *names.* A visceral, terrible *anger* gripped her as the realization sunk roots. The ancestors had tried to destroy their lesser kin in order to possess their names, because their names *were* words of power. They were almost the ultimate words of power: they contained the essential essence of life.

And every word—every word he had chosen to speak, every word that was now on display to her eyes, if no one else's— had once *been* the heart of a living being. She had seen words like this in the Lake of Life. She'd touched any number of them in her search for the word that might, somehow, make the High Lord whole.

She had even taken one such word for herself, blindly and without intent. She had no idea how to return it; she'd never asked. The Consort had never demanded its return, although she knew.

And she was certain, if the Consort could see what she now saw, her rage and fury would know no bounds. Kaylin wasn't the Consort, but she had touched what the Consort guarded, and she felt an echo of the revulsion the Consort would have known.

These were lost words. Lost lives. They would not return to the Lake, although the Barrani who had been brought to life when they were bestowed were long dead. They did not belong here. They did not belong in the hands of a creature who destroyed life, rather than created it.

"Arkon," she said, knowing he couldn't answer. "If there's anything you can do to cover me, do it. I can see the source of his power, now—and I think I can break it."

Looking up to her familiar, she said, *Can you carry me again? I need to reach the words, and the ground will kill me.*

Yes.

And I don't have to kill people?

No, Kaylin. He moved as he spoke. He didn't land. Instead, he gripped her shoulders with his solid talons, and lifted her. *That is not the choice you have made. What is done—or not done— now, will be done by you. Or failed—by you. I give you what your Hawks would give, if they could hear you or see you; I give you what your Bellusdeo would, if she understood the whole of your intent.*

She wouldn't survive it. The Hawks wouldn't.

That is not guaranteed.

Her feet skirting molten rock, the air rippling with heat, her eyes watering at the ash and debris the wind threw at them, Kaylin approached the ancestor's words.

★ ★ ★

They were true names.

They were true names, and his story would either consume or destroy them—because she was certain he was telling a story, just as the Arkon was. Both stories were true. That was the nature of the words they used.

She had touched—had *taken*—true names from the Lake. She reached out for the closest of the words the ancestor had spoken, and grabbed it. It was smaller in shape—and weight—than the single, long stroke that had been a component of the High Lord's; it weighed less, and it didn't cut her palm.

Why could you destroy the barrier? she asked, as she gathered a second word. A barrier—faint, golden, sprang up around her; it wasn't evenly centered, and it followed her with a delay.

The barrier?

That surrounded the High Halls. She picked up a third word; she could not easily grab a fourth. Her hands were full. And there were more than four words.

There was also an angry demigod standing in the streets. He gestured and the ground *froze*. Stones cracked. Shards flew. He was coming, Kaylin thought.

I can intervene.

That's not a small intervention. I couldn't bring that barrier down.

No. But your Arkon could. Your Sanabalis, with time, could. Your Evarrim—

He is so not mine.

—could. They could not do what you asked of me; not in isolation. What you asked of me is possible. Even in your world. But to do it, the world itself must be altered, the shape broken, the word at its heart—vast and complicated—redrawn. No one who lives now in these lands you call home could do this.

She remembered Teela's stories of Sorcerers of old. Stories of the sundering of worlds. Stories of what was done to summon a familiar at all. She even thought she understood why someone might consider it worth trying.

What you are doing now, Kaylin, you can *do. I do not change you or alter you or alter the rules that govern this world; I do not change the name at its heart; I do not devour any part of its essence. Your Lady* could *do what you now do. She is the only other who might gather what was taken, because she has seen the Lake, and she serves what it represents. But so, too, have you.*

She couldn't pick up a fourth word. She tried.

What am I supposed to do *with them? How am I supposed to send them back to where—to where they should be?*

I cannot answer that, Kaylin; I do not know. But there is one who does.

The shell of shielding around her grew brighter as wind flew, pushing everything but Kaylin and the words toward the Arkon. The familiar hissed.

Ynpharion.

Lord Kaylin. There was no resistance at all in the communication; it was almost as if he was waiting—or hoping—that she might reach out for him. He failed to acknowledge this, if it was true.

Is the Consort still with you?

Yes. We are not alone.

I don't care. But damn it, the Consort *would. The fighting is going on outside—how many guards does she need?*

Silence.

Fine. I need you to ask her a question for me—and I need the answer right now.

Ynpharion turned to the Consort. There were a half dozen Barrani guards in this chamber; they wore white armor. They were hers. But among the Barrani, that meant almost nothing. Teela's guards had attempted to assassinate her.

You are right, Ynpharion said, and Kaylin realized that the attempted assassination was probably not common knowledge. Teela was going to kill her. *She will not, as you well know. But we do not trust where we have choice. Men and women of power do not. No one who is in possession of something highly coveted can afford to take that risk.*

I need the information. I think we can—we can take him down if we have it.

What information, Lord Kaylin?

I need to know how true names return to the Lake when the Barrani who possess them die.

She felt his shock and his fear. *You cannot ask that question.*

I have to ask that question! The ancestor is using true names for power. Barrani true names. I can gather them—but I can't gather all of them if I can't send some of them back!

He was frozen for one long moment; had she been standing beside him she would have shoved him out of the way. The screams and the sobs and the orders blended in her ears with the spoken ancient words; the air was thick with smoke and cold with ice and loud with magic.

Let me see.

Kaylin didn't even hesitate. The lack of hesitation disgusted him; he had firmly classified her in the "too stupid to live" category. But he clawed some of that disgust back, and she felt one small, hard, Barrani resentment unknot. *You cannot—you cannot speak of this to any of my kin.*

Except the Consort. I know.

You are speaking of it to me.

I don't have a choice, Ynpharion. How do I send these back?

And she felt the knots of other fears tighten, robbing him of breath; she felt his fear and his sense of humiliation war with his certainty—and hers—that if she was given this information, the fight might, somehow, be winnable. He cared about his people as a race; he cared less about the individuals—even those he knew were dying in the streets of this city.

The Consort was the heart of the Barrani. And the Consort had gone out of her way to preserve a lowly, irritating, stupid mortal for a *good* reason. Not for weakness. Not for indulgent sentiment. Lord Kaylin had *touched* the Lake of Life. Lord Kaylin had drawn words from its many waves. Lord Kaylin *was* the emergency measure.

And no one knew this. No one but the Consort and now, because Lord Kaylin was desperate, Lord Ynpharion.

But he could not ask this question of the Consort. Oh, he could ask—but she could not answer. Not where it could be heard. Not where it could be questioned. Not where *any* answer could be used as a weapon in some future war or some hostile coup.

There was only one way.

Kaylin understood what he intended to do; she caught it as he withdrew. She was motionless for one long breath. *Ynpharion—don't. You're right. She has* reason *to keep me alive. I have a use, if only in the absolute worst case.*

And I do not. He didn't argue. He didn't try.

And you don't. She didn't even *like* Ynpharion. He was a constant misery.

This amused him; the amusement steadied him, because otherwise, he stood on the edge of a personal abyss. There was only one way in which he could ask that question; only one way in which the Consort might ever answer it.

Ynpharion turned to the Consort, bowed low, and rose. He closed his eyes. He *had* to close his eyes. He could not bear to see pity—or worse—in the Lady's face.

Open them, Kaylin told him. It was an unexpected command. He almost fought her—but they didn't have the time, and he knew it. He opened his eyes.

He opened his eyes to see the sudden glow of gold in the Consort's eyes. He had surprised her, because, in silence, he now offered her the whole of his true name.

And she understood why. She lifted her head. "Lord Kaylin."

But it was Ynpharion who answered. "I must ask a question. It must be answered. There is only one way to ask, Lady, and only one way in which you would ever tender that answer to me. Please."

The glow of gold diminished; it shaded into a golden brown, which shocked Ynpharion, who had expected pity or disgust instead. He gave her his name; she accepted it. She *spoke* it. Her touch was *not* Lord Kaylin's touch; it was strong and certain and complete. But it had to be, because to answer this question, it was the only way to be certain of safety.

That, he thought, and his death.

Kaylin was witness; she was on the inside of Ynpharion. She heard him ask the question.

The Lady says it is not dissimilar to choosing a name.

This was not a helpful answer. And Kaylin wanted the answer to *be* helpful; to be *defining*. Because Ynpharion had given up everything, eternally, to receive it.

She chose our names, he said, voice soft. *She gave us life. I have to have faith that it is not in my destruction or enslavement that she will find her power. She is the mother of our race.*

Kaylin didn't point out that *this* Consort had almost certainly not chosen Ynpharion's name. She was struggling to remember what dipping her hand into what hadn't even *looked like* a lake had felt like.

She closed her eyes; the familiar carried her, and anyway, the ground was now solid. It wasn't *flat,* but it was solid. The Arkon was attempting to keep her from being turned to scorched ash. While speaking. She could, of course, see the words. She carried three. One, she set down; she couldn't say why. But the two, she lifted.

And as she did, they gained weight. Their size didn't change; their shape wasn't altered. But they grew *heavy*. As heavy, she thought, as the words she had first chosen in the High Halls, from the Lake. Their edges felt sharper, harder; she thought they would cut her palms.

And she didn't care. Because the High Lord's name had been heavy—and she had only carried one small part of it. The name she had taken, without thought, for herself, had been heavy. The words themselves hadn't been so damned heavy when she'd picked them up—and now was not the time to be struggling with their weight.

The Consort says: yes, it is. She says it is the only way. The Consorts carry the names any distance required—she says you will understand this: you are a birth-helper.

A midwife, Kaylin told him.

But not all births, she says, are simple; some are deadly. When a mortal birth goes wrong, you have the power to stave off death.

I'm not trying to deliver a baby.

No. I am sorry, but she seems to feel you will understand the weight of life.

These words aren't alive.

Not on their own, no. She says—

Time seemed to slow in the sphere in which Kaylin stood. The wind whipped debris toward her, and only in her direct radius did it suddenly crawl to a dead stop, suspended in mid-air. She turned; she saw that splinters just past her shoulder suddenly *flew* as they moved beyond her.

Lord Kaylin, I must see. *No—not the street and not the ancestor; I can see those. I must understand what you* do *when you aid birthing mortals.*

There was nothing—in any of those memories—that Kaylin

feared to share. She did as he asked. She felt his disgust, but it was tempered by genuine curiosity, and as he watched—and it was *fast*—that curiosity became something entirely other. Ynpharion was moved.

I did not know, he said.

His ignorance was a matter for *any other day.*

Apologies, Lord Kaylin. I have…transmitted…your memories to the Consort. She is frustrated. But she says that if the infants themselves are of insignificant weight to carry, they are not insignificant to you. It is that that you must…translate. You have carried words from the Lake. You understand what they can—and must—mean for our kin.

They are like your infants. You cannot know, when you deliver a living child to its parent what that child will become. You cannot know if you will be forced, in future, to hunt them or kill them. You cannot know if they will remain at the side of their parents or murder them and turn against them. You know nothing. *But it is the same nothing that the Lady knows. It is an act of hope and faith, not certainty. It is an act of the moment.*

The words were heavier, now. Kaylin regretted taking two. They were warm in her hands, but they had edges, and she knew her hands were bleeding. *No one's waiting for* these *words,* she told him. *It's not the same as babies. It's like delivering a child from—from a corpse.*

She thought you would say that. But she says: trust. You understand what they mean—to the future of our people. The ancestor did not. Release them, and they will return to the Lake, and to that future.

But—but—

How do they return on their own?

Yes! Kind of really, really, *need to know that, about now.*

She says—I'm sorry—that if you gather them as you gathered— shock. Absolute, utter shock.

Kaylin knew what the Consort had just told him. And she knew, as well, that had he not surrendered his name—and his freedom, his future choice—she would never have done so. *Ynpharion*.

...If you gather the name as you gathered the remaining part of the High Lord's name, if you feel and understand the weight and the measure—

I don't!

—of their value *and their necessity, it will be as if you were drawing them from the Lake itself. And when you release them, they will return. You can touch them and take them—I told her this—but if you cannot imbue them with your own sense of their potential, they will not...move.*

So she wants me to just—just—throw them away?

She knows that you will never do that. They are lives. They were not meant to be bound and used as they are being used now.

As, Kaylin realized, Ynpharion was being used now.

They were not taken from the Lake. They were forbidden their return. She does not understand how—but she says that what you feel now *is what she has always felt. In your hands, she says, if you gather them* the *same way, you are seeing to their rebirth.*

How can she know this?

She doesn't. She feels *this. This is why,* he added softly, *so few can become Consort, no matter how many might have that ambition. There is some part of the Consort who carried the weight of our names, no matter how briefly, in every one of us. She says you will know when it is time to release them.*

CHAPTER 25

Kaylin couldn't raise her arms, they were shaking so much. Two names, she thought. And there were more. She'd carried one part of one name through the High Halls. One. But she'd known when to release it because she was carrying it *to* someone. No midwife *ever* just dropped a newborn babe. They placed the babe in the arms of its mother, father, or nurse. They released the infant to safety.

You carry these, Ynpharion said, as if anticipating the question she couldn't even frame, *to their kin. To their home. The Lady says you will understand,* he repeated, as if by repetition he could drive away her panic. *It is not safe, but you will understand. She says she is sorry.*

Whatever it was she was supposed to know or see, it wasn't happening. Kaylin lowered herself to her knees; felt the ridges of frozen rock bite into her left kneecap. She let loose a few choice Leontine words—but she did it quietly. And in a much softer voice than Leontine generally demanded.

She could hold them—but honestly, not for much longer; she was afraid that she was going to lose her right hand. She didn't—and couldn't—understand the very essence of Barrani life. The words weren't infants. They weren't babies. They weren't wed to flesh, to vanish when flesh failed. She couldn't give them to their terrified, stressed out, underslept, elated parents when her job was done.

For some midwives, there was no parent to give the child to. And in that case, midwives didn't just throw the child away.

She inhaled slowly. Exhaled slowly. These were not newborns. They had lived. Their owners had died. She hoped they had died. She had a sudden, cold memory of Barrani undead, and wondered.

What part of life existed in eternity?

This. And this word, either of these two, could be the reason a Barrani infant opened its eyes. What he saw, what he liked, what he hated—were somehow influenced by the life force that these words represented. How many other Barrani had carried these words at their heart, until that heart ceased to beat at all?

How many more would?

None, she thought. None if the words remained where they were, riven from the living by an ancestor who saw the lives—of others, of course—as nothing but a source of power.

Even if the words couldn't cry—and of course, they couldn't—they were far, far more than that. They were precious. Precious and so very heavy. But she couldn't drop them. She couldn't leave them here.

In the outlands, at the edge of a constantly shifting landscape, she had—without thought—saved one word; she had added it to her forehead. That word—that word had no weight; it had shape and form, but far less substance.

She could not do that here. Because here, she knew, was where these words belonged. The Lake waited. The Lake that was not a Lake in any real sense of the word. The first time Kaylin had seen it, it had been the surface of a table. A large table.

She hadn't walked to the cave in which the Lake was physically housed; there'd been no one there to show her the way. But she *had* touched the Lake, regardless. She had run her hands through the flow of the current of words, fingers sinking through what appeared—to her eyes—to be wood grain.

She had been in the High Halls, then—in the oldest part of them. She was standing outside of that building now, in streets that were barely patrolled by Swords, and never by Hawks. There was no desk, no table; there was no cavern, containing endless, golden waves, composed of words such as these, moving as if alive—as if joyfully alive.

Inhale. Exhale.

No desk. No table. But the streets—broken, melted— beyond which the rich and the powerful sheltered—were the streets of her city. They were Elantran. The men who flew in the air above where she now knelt were Aerians; the men who ran *toward* death and danger, mortals, all. Almost all.

The whole city was her home. The High Halls were part of that city. The High Halls, and the Barrani, and the doorway that lead, at last, to the Lake itself. She had sworn the only oaths that really mattered—to her—so that she could join the Hawks.

She couldn't reach the Lake of Life from here. If *she* could, so could the ancestor—and that was never, *ever,* going to end well. It was what, she knew, he wanted. Why else come here?

To harvest, Ynpharion said.

Over my dead body. And that seemed increasingly likely as time wore on, even if it passed much, much more slowly in this small space. *Tell the Consort that nothing's happening. Nothing's changing!*

No, not nothing. The slow, slow bloom of white fire with

tips of blue grew in front of her eyes, spreading in slow motion. From its heart stepped the ancestor, and to her eyes, he moved far more quickly than the fire she *knew* sprang almost instantly from the ground.

He met her eyes, his slowly rounding; his lips parted.

He spoke.

He spoke, but it was not his voice she heard. She looked down at the words on her skin, at her full hands. The Hawks' weaponsmaster would have had her head for looking away from her opponent—but watching him told her nothing she needed to know to survive.

She heard the *words* speak. No—she heard the words as if they were part of a long recitation that someone else was speaking. Just as she heard the Arkon's distant words. Only these two—the ones she held—had voices, if they could be called voices. And yes, she thought, she understood. When she could hear their voices—and that was the wrong word, but she didn't have a better one—she set them down. In this space, they were as whole as they could be.

She heard the long, slow syllable of a cry of rage—the beginning of a word that could be heard by ears alone, elongated.

She could still see the words she had finally released; he couldn't. Not any more. And she could still hear them. She moved quickly—as quickly as pain and shaking legs allowed—to gather two more words, one in each hand. They grew heavy and cumbersome as she held them; she had already knelt, lifting her face as she did to watch the slow approach of the ancestor.

She knew he'd kill her when he reached her; it was only a matter of time. Time, she thought, knowing Severn would be here soon, his weapon's chain breaking magic or reflecting it. Severn wouldn't survive. Not unless she finished what she'd started.

And she couldn't rush it. She tried. But she'd never been able to rush a birth, either; swearing or praying didn't work. She held the words until she could hear them speak—and simultaneously be spoken—and only then did she let them go.

She wasn't prepared for the Barrani.

She wasn't prepared for Teela, who moved as quickly as the ancestor, slowing to his speed as she cleared whatever temporal barrier the Arkon had erected around Kaylin. She seemed to be flying—which was wrong; Teela did many things, but flying wasn't one of them.

She carried a sword. A greatsword.

Kaylin's hands were full; the weight dragged them to her lap. She tried to shout Teela's name; nothing left her lips. Nothing. She closed her eyes. She had to close her eyes.

The ancestor's power was rooted in these words, and if she couldn't break the connection and send them back to the Lake, they were *all* dead. And Teela knew it. Severn knew it. So did the Arkon. Kaylin needed to listen to something that wasn't her fear; to listen for the voices of the words in her hands, speaking in a language she didn't, and couldn't, understand.

Only when she heard them did she set them down and open her eyes again; she was still standing—or kneeling—in the streets, and moving without vision was just asking for trouble. It was just Teela. Tain was running toward the gap between the ancestor and Teela, and behind him, the Barrani Hawks. They carried swords—but their swords weren't the equal of Teela's, which seemed like forged lightning.

The Dragons were no longer unleashing fiery death on the streets. But the Aerians were flying low, now.

Focus, Kaylin. She shook her head to clear it, and inhaled slowly, which helped. She lifted the next two words, and closed her eyes.

The Consort is coming, Kaylin. She heard the fear in Ynpharion's voice and her eyes snapped open.

The Consort is not *coming! Has the High Lord lost his mind?*

She is coming, he replied, and it was clear that he agreed with everything Kaylin hadn't yet put into words. *She understands exactly what you are doing, Lord Kaylin—but she does not feel you will finish in time; our enemy will destroy the streets and half of the High Halls, or he will retreat, taking what he has gathered over centuries* with him.

She'll die. And then, upon the heels of that thought, *if he has her, he can reach the Lake—*

She says it is not that simple.

It is exactly that simple!

What you are doing she can do more quickly. She will not let him flee if there is any chance—at all—that she can save what he holds. She does not worry about the lives she spends here. She worries about what he can do with the names of the Barrani who have fallen tonight. The Dragons harry him. He cannot do what he must do to harvest the fallen—but he has altered the conditions of the terrain upon which they now lie. The words will not be his without work on his part— but without the Lady, they will not now return to the Lake itself.

I can do it—I'm here.

He didn't believe her.

And because he didn't, the Consort wouldn't. *You don't believe it, Lord Kaylin. You want it to be the truth—but you don't believe it. You are willing to risk your life—but you are, in the end, mortal; she is the Consort. She is the guardian of the Lake, the mother to us all. What you face and survive, she is certain to face and survive.*

He was disgusted to have to explain this. And frustrated.

And it didn't matter. *I'm not* the mother of an entire race—I *risk so much less—* She stopped. She had to stop. The buzzing of fear in her mind was the only thing she could hear—and it wasn't helping anyone. Not even Kaylin. As she inhaled—

slowly, as she'd been taught—the voices of the words in her hands became sharp and clear.

Almost as if they were people. She set them down—gently, although it probably didn't make a difference—and moved again. And again. She could beg the words to wake—if that's what they were doing. It didn't make a damned difference. Begging never had.

Teela landed, both feet planted and knees bent, five yards from where Kaylin now knelt, runes in hand. Her back was all Kaylin could see of her. Severn was where Kaylin had left him; it was Kaylin who had moved out from behind the magic-breaking barrier of his chain.

The ancestor spoke. In High Barrani.

The words—all the words that Kaylin had not yet wakened— shuddered with the impact of each syllable. Kaylin was already sitting; if she hadn't been, she might have frozen. Or fallen. There was a force in the ancestor's spoken words that only magic could give it.

Teela was not as fast as the ancestor, and the ancestor was very close to her. But she was hit—in a manner of speaking— by the sound of Dragon fury: a roar. The roar shook the earth beneath everyone's feet.

Kaylin recognized the voice. Bellusdeo. Bellusdeo had come. Maggaron came in from the ancestor's right, weapon raised. He wasn't as fast as Teela, but he had both stride and reach. Bellusdeo—in full Dragon armor—was steps behind.

And above her head, like the heart of a very bad storm, Kaylin heard the Emperor's roar. It was perhaps the first time she was honestly grateful that she couldn't understand native Dragon speech. Teela, having caught the ancestor's attention, moved toward Severn; Severn shifted position.

The words spoke, and Kaylin set them down, picking up the next two.

Teela shouted. Her voice wasn't as loud as Bellusdeo's—Bellusdeo who was carrying a sword, of all things—but Kaylin heard it clearly. She had only heard it a handful of times in her life; it was a Barrani battle cry. She was calling the Hawks. Tain, almost at Teela's side, skidded to a halt and turned, repeating Teela's shout almost, but not quite, exactly.

"Kaylin!" a familiar voice shouted. The syllables were elongated and stretched, but recognizable. "Get the hells *out of the way!*"

Teela replied in her stead. "She can't! Whatever aerial attack you employ is going to hit her!"

Cursing. Long, Leontine words. They were almost immediately swamped by angry Dragon. And by the sound of horns.

The ancestor dodged the downward arc of Maggaron's mace. The street didn't. Ice cracked. Stone. The ancestor lashed out at the *Norannir* with his weaponless hand—he carried no weapons that Kaylin could see—but the blow clanged off Bellusdeo's armor. It sent Bellusdeo staggering back, out of Kaylin's line of vision.

The pillar of white fire rose in a column. Kaylin was sitting within its radius. Everyone one else was standing.

A familiar golden bubble enveloped them all.

"Teela—call the Hawks *off*. The familiar can't protect all of them!"

"Not now!" Teela snarled as if she were Marcus.

Kaylin knew why; the words. She tightened her grip on them, because something had almost pulled them out of her hands. In panic, she looked at the rest of the words that the ancestor had summoned; they were moving. They were moving away. He was calling them back.

Panic didn't describe what she felt—the word wasn't strong enough. It didn't change anything, either. The words—the words would be lost. Only the ones she had managed to grab would return to the Barrani.

The Barrani Hawks had arrived. They were armed—with swords, not their usual sticks—but wearing the tabard of the Halls of Law: the Hawk. They didn't attempt to close with the ancestor. There was no room left; Severn, Teela, and Maggaron—especially the wall of Maggaron—were already too tightly packed for fast maneuvering.

Teela was attempting to move the fight. It was working. But the words would go with their enemy.

No, Kaylin, the familiar said. She had almost forgotten about him. *The Consort has arrived.*

She wore white armor, and her hair was a white spill; her brows, white, were furrowed, her lips thinned. She came in from the left, in an opening created entirely by Teela. The ancestor was parrying her blade—with his hand. He'd yet to lose his hand. Teela, on the other hand, hadn't lost the sword.

The Consort didn't speak. She glanced once at Kaylin, nodded, and sprinted toward the words that were farthest away from the private. She didn't lift them; she didn't touch them. But it was clear to Kaylin that she could. Instead, she spoke.

And her language, like the Arkon's, like the ancestor's, was opaque to Kaylin. It was not opaque to their enemy. He turned, leaping above the arc of blade and mace; he leveled one hand in the Consort's direction.

Ynpharion was there before the blow landed. He knocked the Consort to the side, rolling as lightning crackled an inch to his left. Kaylin had never watched him fight before. But Ynpharion was a Lord of the High Court; he could. Of course he could. He knew—as Kaylin did—that one hit was death.

The Consort stumbled and righted herself. She was still speaking. Not singing, not quite—but there was a musicality to her voice that the Arkon's lacked. The ancestor lacked it, as well.

The ancestor leaped toward the Consort as if gravity were meaningless. As he did, the Aerian Hawks finally dropped whatever it was they'd been carrying. It was a net. It was a net made of steel or iron or possibly glass; it reminded Kaylin of a spider's web. She set the words in her hands down and scrabbled toward the next two.

Bellusdeo returned to the fray. She was limping. Had Kaylin's hands not been full—but they were. She called the Dragon by name—but she wasn't the only one trying, and her voice didn't even register as sound in comparison.

Diarmat's did. Kaylin couldn't see him; the ground on which she knelt was the bottom of a basin, and the voice came from somewhere up top. Whatever he said, Bellusdeo ignored. Or mostly ignored. She didn't charge in to the fight; she came, instead, to where Kaylin knelt.

Kaylin looked up. *Not me,* she mouthed, over Diarmat's bellow. "Go to the Consort. Keep her alive."

Bellusdeo nodded, grim now. "You understand that I'm in the position I'm in because of the Barrani?" she asked, as she turned.

"Yes." Kaylin held her breath after the single word escaped her mouth.

"And that you'll owe me for this?"

She exhaled. "Yes." She wasn't certain that Bellusdeo could hear her answer, given every other noise—but Dragons had good hearing. The Consort didn't appear to notice Bellusdeo; she spoke, and spoke, and spoke. But Bellusdeo came to stand between the ancestor and the Consort's white back, lifting her hands as she did.

Kaylin couldn't tell if the Dragon was using magic; at this

point, her skin had passed beyond agony to blessed numbness. But she recognized the start of a sigil, and she saw the air around the two women thicken.

Maggaron shouted, *"Bellusdeo."* The Dragon nodded, no more. She'd chosen the ground she was going to stand on. Light—fire light, reflected light, magical detritus—bounced off golden armor. The armor was *dented*. The breastplate just below the ribs had buckled.

Bellusdeo's magic was no match for the ancestor's.

But the Consort had not arrived alone.

Ynpharion was not an Arcanist. Evarrim, however, was. It was Evarrim's magic that now filled the uneven, small basin. Kaylin recognized his signature. She couldn't see him, but she could *hear* him. She could hear the sound of combat. She realized, as she squinted, that he wasn't suddenly going to become visible. He was in the basin, but he wasn't in the basin that could be seen by almost anyone else in the street.

Evarrim was doing what Mandoran had done, somehow. What he himself had done in the outlands when he had crossed into the gray mists to deliver a message to Kaylin and Severn. She was never, ever going to *like* the Arcanist, but the contempt in which she held him lost what little traction was left.

Two more. Two more words to set loose.

Maggaron roared. He wasn't a Dragon; he had a giant's voice. Kaylin squeezed her eyes shut, bowing her head. She was doing everything she *could* do. Rescuing an eight-foot-tall, armed *Norannir* wasn't on the list. He was fighting alongside Teela and Tain; if they couldn't keep him alive Kaylin had no hope of doing so.

The netting dropped by the Hawks landed in the basin. Where it touched ground, fire instantly guttered. Kaylin had never seen anything like it. Then again, she'd never seen a full mobilization of the Swords and the Hawks before—certainly not as backup for Dragons.

The Arkon roared; the ground shook. Kaylin ducked instinctively, curling over the words in her hands although magical fire and Dragon breath wasn't going to harm *them*. The ancestor gestured; strands of net parted. The Arkon roared, and Diarmat shouted in response.

Kaylin wasn't privy to their plans. She set the words loose and looked up as the Consort's voice banked. The Consort herself had not moved or shifted position; nor had Ynpharion. But both wavered slightly in the air before Kaylin; the Consort looked vaguely transparent. So did Bellusdeo.

Hands empty, Kaylin rose. She covered the uneven ground in striding leaps, reaching for both Bellusdeo and the Consort. Ynpharion's eyes widened; the barrier surrounding them let Kaylin through. She caught both women by the arm, and as she did, the marks on her arms began to glow an even, bright blue.

What are you doing? Ynpharion demanded.

Keeping them both here!

The Consort continued to speak as if neither Kaylin nor Ynpharion were present; as if the ancestor was not struggling to either reach her or put her out of reach—possibly permanently—of the names that he used for power. Kaylin had weakened him. She would need another hour at a conservative guess to free the rest of the names.

The Consort wouldn't. She didn't appear to need to touch the individual words; she only had to speak. This left Kaylin's hands free; she tightened her grip on both Dragon and Barrani as the ancestor spoke again. The ground tilted.

Although Teela, Tain and Severn were moving in concert, none of their blows seemed to land. Some were deflected, but most were simply sidestepped. Maggaron's luck was no better, but he was slower than either of the Hawks, and the ancestor landed a kick that sent him flying. Bellusdeo cursed softly, but didn't move.

"I don't think he can crack your protections," Kaylin said, surprised.

"That is the hope."

"But I think he *can* move the ground they're centered on."

"I noticed a shift in the texture of the landscape—but he'll kill her if I move. I don't think whatever it is he's doing is guaranteed to end in our deaths."

"Have you ever been in the outlands?" Kaylin shouted.

"I wandered the heart of the shadows."

"I don't think it's the same."

"No." Bellusdeo sucked in air. Ynpharion had time to shout a warning before he was thrown clear with a metallic clang; no one could see what struck him. Bellusdeo tensed, clenching her jaw; she fell silent. The Consort raised her voice; the ancestor attempted to speak over her. Both spoke deliberately, slowly, evocatively—but the ancestor was doing it on the move. He was fighting on two fronts, one of which couldn't be seen.

Kaylin felt another surge of magic; she could *almost* hear Evarrim's voice. It was weak, attenuated—and she wasn't at all certain it was because he was out of phase. She looked up to see her familiar flying in a tight circle over the edge of the basin in which the fighting was taking place.

I cannot, he told her, before she could ask, *go to your Evarrim. Not without you. And you serve as anchor for your Consort. Evarrim will not be fighting alone for much longer.*

Kaylin frowned. She started to ask what he meant.

The shouted *WHAT HAVE YOU DONE WITH MY BROTHER?* told her all she needed to know. Annarion had arrived. She looked across the basin to Teela, but Teela was occupied; her cheek was bleeding, and she had drawn her left arm to her side. She could wield the sword one-handed, but was wielding it far more defensively than she had been. It was a greatsword. If she was aware of Annarion's presence, she said—and did—nothing that indicated it.

The ancestor stumbled; Severn's chain seemed to actually clip his arm; sparks flew.

"Teela! Is Annarion with Evarrim?"

"Yes!"

From the heights, another net fell. It had about the same effect as the first; strands were cut before they landed. This time, Kaylin watched where they fell. The netting wasn't rope; it was metallic. It didn't ensnare the ancestor; nor did it trap Teela or Severn. It hit the ground and lay there like a necklace snapped and lost in transit.

White fire leaped across the pit; red fire followed. The fire had come from Bellusdeo. She could, apparently, breathe and maintain a spell at the same time. Her eyes were—and had been since her arrival—crimson-red. They still weren't as disturbing as the Arkon's.

"How much longer?" Bellusdeo shouted at Kaylin.

Kaylin looked at the visible words. There were fewer than there had been when Kaylin had started to gather them; they were less substantial to the eye—or at least to hers. Kaylin was certain the Consort could see them. She thought that the Arkon might. "You can't see them?"

"No."

"Keep up the protections you're casting—whatever they are—and I think we'll be clear to move—" which meant pulling up stakes and fleeing as quickly as humanly possible, "in maybe five minutes. Whatever the ancestor is doing, he's not as strong as the Consort."

Bellusdeo snorted. Loudly. With smoke.

"It's not as strong as what *she's* doing *with the words*. Better?" She looked at the Dragon and added, "You fractured something."

"*I* didn't fracture it. Blame the ground or the ancestor. Don't even *think* it. I can stand. I can't run. I can't fight *well*. But I am not mortal. I am not frail."

"Your wing—"

"Yes. And it *cost you,* Kaylin. You would have made a terrible, terrible soldier. If we lose here, it's the battle—and quite possibly the war. I can't do what you're doing—whatever it is. Do not weaken yourself further until it's done."

"And if I—"

"I'll heal." The second syllable in the sentence expanded into a roar.

She would. She would, Kaylin thought. She looked up to see Teela and Severn. They had both taken injuries in Helen's dining room; Teela's left arm looked broken now. But they *moved* as if injuries were minor insults—there, but not life-defining. Not life-ending. Tain was not injured—not yet; he formed most of the offense. He was wearing the Hawk and it glittered in the light of multiple spells. His eyes, at this distance, were black, as if the pupil had expanded to take up all the space.

Above them, a third net fell—a third, final net. The Aerians were far fewer in number, and Kaylin felt her throat constrict. At this distance, she could see the Hawklord. She could see Clint. She could see—of all people—Moran.

If I don't make it, they will.

It brought her a peculiar peace, a little bit of calm. She was very, very tired.

"Kaylin—" Bellusdeo shifted in place; Kaylin felt an arm slide around—and under—her shoulders. She heard a soft Leontine curse—Leontine, from a Dragon. "You idiot."

She was. She knew it.

"Do you think you're invulnerable?"

Kaylin shook her head. Or Bellusdeo shook her; the motion was similar.

"Lady," Bellusdeo said, to the Consort. "Are you finished?"

She was. Kaylin could see proof of it in the ancestor, whose movements had slowed. He was still far faster than she was; he was still stronger than the Dragons in their human forms.

The Consort's voice receded. She turned for the first time since she'd arrived. "Yes, Lord Bellusdeo. I am in your debt."

"It is never wise to accrue the debt of the Barrani—or so it is said."

The Consort's smile was tired, but sharp. "You understand."

"Lannagaros!" Bellusdeo roared. She lifted Kaylin bodily and, to Kaylin's humiliation, hoisted her up onto her left shoulder.

The Arkon was silent.

"We need a lift!" Bellusdeo spoke in Elantran. She moved to the edge of the basin, grimacing at the climb; she walked slowly.

The Arkon appeared at the edge of the basin—in his human form. He was, to Kaylin's shock, bleeding; his forehead was scored, and his cheek; his armor—like Bellusdeo's—was dented. It was worse. But his eyes were only crimson, now. "I am not," he said, "capable of carrying you all at the moment; I do not think I could even lift Private Neya." He glanced beyond them, his smile sharpening.

"But I do not think we need fear the ancestor anymore." He gestured, his hands grasping air and twisting it sharply, as if the air were somehow solid.

Kaylin could only barely turn her head. "Bellusdeo, put me down."

"Don't," the Arkon said, before Bellusdeo could properly ignore her. "Lady. It is time to leave."

Ynpharion?

I am alive. I was thrown some distance, and I believe my leg is broken. I am, if the Dragon is concerned, out of the area of effect.

What area of— Oh. The nets.

CHAPTER 26

"Speed is to be desired," the Arkon added, in a pinched voice very much like his library voice.

Kaylin turned her head, which was difficult, given how she was being carried. "Teela and Severn are still fighting him!"

"Yes."

"If it's not safe for us we can't leave them—"

"Private."

"Bellusdeo—*put me down.*"

Bellusdeo did as Kaylin asked. But not until she had climbed up to stand by the Arkon's side. She kept one hand on Kaylin's arm as Kaylin turned toward the pit.

"Corporal!" someone shouted. The Hawklord. There were three corporals standing in the ice and stone of the ruined street, fighting. Only one of them looked up: Tain. "Now!"

Tain drove his *sword* into the ridged, malformed stone on which he'd been standing.

The strands of cut netting that lay across the ground like scattered decorations began to glow. To glow, Kaylin thought, and to *move*. They reminded her of smaller, finer versions of

Severn's weapon chain; they were delicate, and—as the ancestor had already demonstrated—easy to sever. She turned to
the Arkon; he appeared to be *sweating*. Kaylin couldn't recall
ever seeing a Dragon sweat before. His hands were out, palms
toward the ground, fingers bent—and moving.

He reminded her, in that moment, of a puppeteer.

And the chains responded as if he were; they rose like
slender, flashing snakes, twisting and spinning in place. Fire
bounced off them, as it did off Severn's chain. Severn had one.
The chains on the ground, finer and more fragile, were many.
Tain shouted Severn's name, and Severn shook his head; his
own chain was in motion. Kaylin understood that he meant
to retreat, and that he meant Tain to grab Teela and make a
run for it.

Since grabbing Teela without her express permission or desire was courting a different kind of death, and the Hawklord
was shouting orders, Tain settled for second best: he caught
her, shifted his grip and tossed her over the edge of the basin
that fire and magic had formed.

He then leaped up himself. This left Severn. Only Severn.

Kaylin held her breath.

She looked up to see her familiar, tracing the same circumference in the air that the basin occupied on the ground. A
giant, translucent dragon was impossible to miss—but none of
the Aerians in the air, none of the Hawks on the ground—and
the Hawks were here, if Tain's presence was any indication—
seemed to notice him.

No one but Kaylin noticed when he suddenly dived, folding
wings and plunging groundward. No one flew into him, and
he struck no one on his way down—but the Aerians avoided
the flying masses of the Emperor and Sanabalis; they didn't
alter their flight paths to avoid the equally spacious familiar.
The Hawks on the ground did feel the earth shudder as he

landed in the center of the basin, which seemed to Kaylin's eye to be a field of slender, spinning stalks. The ancestor's magic, severely interrupted, didn't burn Tain; it didn't—more importantly, and she felt guilty even thinking it—harm Severn.

Severn could see the familiar.

So could the ancestor. His back, black hair unimpeded by anything as everyday as knots, was turned toward her; she couldn't see his expression. She could hear the silence that fell across the basin as he lifted his head and faced the familiar.

The familiar roared.

The ancestor spoke in a language Kaylin didn't recognize. She wondered if it was a language that could be taught to the merely mortal, or if only Dragons—and possibly Barrani—could speak any part of it.

The familiar replied. This time, his voice was modulated; it sounded—to Kaylin's ear—like Elantran did when pushed through a throat the size of a cart horse. A Dragon's voice.

The ancestor spun, turning, his eyes bright and widening as he met Kaylin's steady gaze. He continued to speak, his voice high with disbelief. The Arkon grabbed Kaylin by the shoulders and spun as fire enveloped them.

"Put me down!" Kaylin shouted. The Arkon didn't seem to be impervious to this particular fire; his beard was singed. His hair. Barrani hair, she was certain, would have been untouched. Kaylin wondered at the differences between immortal hair—and at her own unbelievable stupidity in even thinking about it at a time like this.

Her arms were awash with blue light. She reached out and grabbed a handful of the Arkon's hair, and the small fires guttered against her palm, as if they were the weakest of candlelight.

"Yes," the Arkon said, releasing her—although he didn't look happy about it. "He is your familiar. But Kaylin—" He shut up before the rest of the warning could leave his mouth. "Go. Go while our protections still have effect."

She stumbled into the basin, legs shaking. She cursed. She drew the first dagger of the evening, although she was pretty certain it would be useless, here. She wasn't even sure why she had entered the basin until she heard Annarion's voice.

What have you done with my brother?

She heard, as well, the sound of distant blades: steel bouncing off steel. The ancestor leaped before the familiar could snap him in two. She couldn't see Annarion. She could see Severn as he backed toward the basin's edge, his chain spinning before him.

She couldn't hear Evarrim's voice.

At any other time, she might have tendered regrets for his death to the Barrani, but they would have been insincere. Good manners. She wouldn't weep at his death now, but she would regret it. That surprised her.

She took a step forward. Two. Neither were enough to carry her into the range of the ancestor; nor were they nearly enough to bring her to Severn's side; he was almost at the opposite end of the stretch of land that, empty of the rest of the combatants, now seemed so large.

The ancestor moved only once to follow Severn; the familiar cut him off. He moved like a graceful feline, not a lumbering giant, although he was that, now.

The third step brought her closer to the ancestor and the familiar.

The fourth step took her away from what remained of the city streets.

She recognized the gray, shapeless mass on which the familiar and the ancestor now stood. Annarion had materialized to the right of the ancestor; he wielded a sword that reminded her of *Meliannos,* although she knew it couldn't be.

Annarion made a *lot* more noise here than she'd heard when she'd been trying to avoid fire, magic and the dissipation of the words. His eyes were black.

They were *all* black. His features were accentuated, the lines that spoke of anger sharper and harsher. Annarion appeared to be fighting almost alone. The familiar now hovered above him—in almost the same position he had held in the normal city skies. Or rather, the city skies; nothing about this night and its attack were remotely normal.

She could see Evarrim. The Arcanist lay face down in the fog, his hair a black, perfect spill, his right arm stretched above his head, fingers pointing, as if he'd collapsed in midspellcast. It was to Evarrim she ran. Her dagger—which had made the transition with her—was about as useful here as it had been in the streets of Elantra during the fight. But it was her talisman. She didn't throw it, but she didn't sheathe it, either.

She did shift it into her left hand as she knelt by Evarrim's side. Her fingers fumbled for his pulse. If Barrani anatomy wasn't human anatomy, the crude similarities made it fairly easy to determine whether or not the Barrani in question was still alive.

He was.

She leaned in. His face was turned to the side, his eyes closed. His eyelids looked bruised, but the rest of his skin was normal, flawless Barrani skin. "Evarrim." He was breathing.

When his eyes shot open, she jumped, but managed not to fall on her butt. "What. Are. You. Doing. Here." His voice was a dry rasp, but his eyes—bloodshot—were dark blue.

"The Arkon and the Hawks set up some sort of trap while Teela, Tain and Severn distracted the ancestor in the real world; the Consort managed to sever him from the source of his power."

"Not an answer."

Kaylin exhaled. "I came looking for you. I think you're going to be stuck here if you don't move." She held out a hand; he looked at it as if a cockroach had hitched a lift in her palm. On the other hand, cockroaches were apparently less offensive than actual death; he took the hand and allowed her to pull him to his feet. His weight was close to dead weight, and Kaylin wasn't all that steady on her own feet.

The blood that wasn't on his back was a large, expansive splotch across his chest and his upper thighs. None of it clung to the mist he had fallen into. Kaylin suspected that was for the best. She hesitated until she looked at the ruby circlet he wore on his forehead. There was a black crater where the gem had been. Stepping closer, she tucked herself under his armpit, and put an arm around his back to brace him.

He looked even *less* pleased, but endured without comment. Or rather, endured without comment about her proximity. He was watching the ancestor and Annarion, his eyes narrowed to edges, his lips thinned in about the same way.

"Why," he demanded, "did you not command the familiar to destroy the ancestor earlier?"

"I haven't commanded him to destroy the ancestor at all," was Kaylin's tight reply. She was remembering, now, that there were still plenty of things to detest about the Arcanist. She was not about to answer his question. She knew damned well what his response would be to *that*. "I don't know if he's trying to destroy the ancestor; it doesn't seem like he is, to me."

No, Kaylin. I am waiting. If the ancestor is destroyed now, Evarrim will perish. Come to me, he added.

"He's waiting," Kaylin told Evarrim.

"For what?"

"For the two of you to leave." She glared at Annarion, who was far enough away he couldn't see the expression.

"Leave him," Evarrim told her, making the effort to modulate his tone so it at least sounded reasonable. "He will not, I think, be stranded here. He is not without power and presence on this plane."

Kaylin could see that. She thought he fought with more savagery and power than he had in Helen's dining room—although admittedly she hadn't actually seen him in combat there. But his eyes were not Barrani eyes. His facial structure was more accentuated, and his hair seemed to have a life of its own. Where his feet touched ground, fog warped and dispersed, leaving something solid in his wake. It was a solid Kaylin recognized.

Chaos.

Neither the familiar nor the ancestor had the same effect on the fog, although the familiar hadn't actually touched the ground *here,* such as it was. "I can't leave Annarion," she told the Arcanist. "I don't think he'll come back."

"We would be better quit of him—what he does now is not natural."

"You're here."

"Yes. And I know how I arrived. He could not have arrived the same way."

"Can you return now?"

Evarrim stiffened. "Yes. I can return now."

"Then go back. I won't be lost here—I have the familiar."

"You are, as expected, unreasonable." He looked as if he had more to say. What he did say however was, "You have my gratitude for your intervention."

She had not even tried to heal him. "Corporal Handred is using his weapon very near to where the familiar is hovering in our world. I think the Arkon is doing a variant of the same spell—but with much weaker chains."

One dark brow rose.

"Meaning, if you're going to arrive anywhere near where the ancestor is standing, don't."

"Noted." He grimaced as Kaylin withdrew her arm.

"You owe me nothing," she told him. "Everything you did, you did for the Lady's sake."

He chuckled, which surprised her. "You are becoming more familiar with the social mores of my kin."

"Yes. And so far I've even survived them."

She didn't watch Evarrim go, and made no attempt to follow. Instead, she approached the two men locked in combat, looking for an opening of some kind. There wasn't one. They both moved far too quickly. There would be a safe opening in the combat when one of them was dead.

Kaylin.

We can't leave Annarion here.

No. He should not have come. These lands are not safe for him; they are far too destabilizing.

At least we don't have Mandoran.

No. I believe Helen contained him when she realized Annarion had departed. Mandoran will not be best pleased.

At the moment, Mandoran was not her problem. Annarion was. He maintained the shape and form of a Barrani—but his grip was tenuous. Kaylin didn't think it would last. She thought his eyes had grown larger and darker as the fighting progressed.

He had not killed the ancestor. Watching him, Kaylin thought he might be capable of it. But only if he continued with the transformation that was slowly taking place. Of the two of Teela's cohort who'd come from the West March to

Elantra, Annarion had been the more reasonable. None of that reason was in evidence now.

"Where is my brother?"

Do you know where Nightshade is? she asked her familiar.

No.

Could you find him?

Under one of two circumstances, yes.

I'm going to assume that one of the two is the one I've already rejected.

Yes.

The other?

You travel with me.

This sounded a lot like "I can find him if you find him first" to Kaylin; she didn't argue. Instead, she said, *Can you help me pull Annarion out?*

His silence went on a beat too long. *Yes. But I do not think we will be able to fully contain or constrict the enemy if I do so. I believe Annarion may be able to kill him, in the end.* Even as he spoke he shifted, heading toward Kaylin, who stood a good five yards from the wide-ranging blades.

Kaylin, watching, wondered what would remain of Annarion in the end, in that case.

The familiar's feet did not solidify the ground as he landed. But his eyes were the size of her head, and they looked very, very much like the chaos that Annarion was leaving in his wake. She climbed up on his back; he was warm and solid, and even resting there soothed the trembling ache of her limbs. He pushed himself off the ground in one lazy, slow leap.

Gravity didn't seem to be an issue in the outlands. And these were the outlands, even if they weren't in the West March.

The familiar circled inches above the moving heads—and weapons, which were more important—of the two combatants in the gray zone.

The ancestor is a danger, the familiar said.

Yes. Kaylin exhaled. *But there's an entire Dragon Court and probably every Barrani Arcanist in the city who can deal with the ancestor, now. I wasn't willing to sacrifice total strangers to kill him. There is* no way *that Teela would be willing to let Annarion go.*

It is not Teela's decision.

No. It's mine. But I don't want to lose him, either.

Interesting. Why not?

Because he's important to Teela. And he's important to Nightshade. And because I *like him.* She wasn't as certain about Mandoran. On the other hand, if he didn't stop getting in Bellusdeo's face, her certainty would be the least of his problems.

She took one deep breath. *I'm not the Emperor. I'm not the Hawklord. I'm not even a* corporal *yet. I'm a private. Sometimes I get to make decisions based on what's right for* my own *life. The Barrani still exist as a race. They faced the ancestors before. They won.*

He said nothing.

Teela was unhappy about Annarion for a long time. She finally found him—found them—again. Maybe he'll commit suicide some other *way. He almost certainly will. But he can do it on someone else's watch.*

Everything has consequences, he said, in a rumbling internal voice that seemed, for a moment, larger than the inside of Kaylin's head.

Yes. Everything does. Breathing does. Not breathing. Stealing. Not stealing. Killing—and not killing. I've done all of it. Some of the consequences are good. Some are bad. I used to want to find something safe and good and preserve it forever. I used to think that was possible.

You still do.

Bastard. *I still* want *that, yes. Because everyone* does. *I don't believe I* can *have it because everything changes. But some of the changes are good. And some of the bad leads to good.*

Some of the good leads to bad, to use your terminology.

Yes. But not all of it—and if we don't try, we're just surrendering. We're giving up. We don't reach for anything. Speaking of which, she added, tightening her knees, *grab Annarion.*

That would not be wise.

Then swing in slowly enough that I can grab him without losing an arm or my head.

That would be even less wise.

Kaylin looked across to the fighting and said, "We're going to lose him. He's not going to come back."

Had you not interfered, Kaylin, he would never have come back to begin with. Perhaps that is his fate.

Fate. If Kaylin had been born to any other race, her eyes would be red, blue, or distinctly gray by now. *Fate,* she said, *is bullshit. Take me down if you're not willing to risk it yourself.*

She felt, of all things, his amusement; it was rich and thick and it pushed the anger aside, which left simple determination behind. She finally sheathed the dagger she'd been carrying.

The familiar swooped in low. His wings passed *through* the two combatants without touching either. They looked like ghost wings; she'd expected them to be as solid as the part of his body that was currently supporting her weight. She tightened her knees, folded forward and to the side, and reached out with her right hand.

She caught Annarion by the shoulder, and saw the arc of his blade as he *moved.*

The familiar's wing became solid in the blink of an eye. Both the ancestor and Annarion were almost flattened by it, which was enough—barely—to knock Annarion back. It probably saved Kaylin's life; it certainly saved her arm. She pulled him up—was surprised at how easy it was. He seemed to weigh almost nothing.

His eyes *were* black. They looked very similar to the familiar's eyes, but his expression lost some of its focused rage as he blinked. "Lord Kaylin?"

Ugh.

"We're leaving."

"We can't—my brother—"

"I give you my word—as a Hawk, as Chosen—that I will *find* your damn brother. But you won't be able to come back to us if you stay here. You've already been here too long." When he stiffened, she said, "Mandoran, Teela—tell him. Tell him he has to come back with me. Because I'm leaving, and he's going to have to kill me if he wants to stay and fight."

Fire—purple flame—engulfed them both.

It didn't burn. It didn't—to Kaylin—*feel* hot. She looked beyond Annarion to the ground, where the ancestor stood; mist surrounded his feet in swirls that reminded her more of sand than liquid. His hands were gloved in flame as the mist thickened. Purple flame. She couldn't see his eyes, although he was looking up, at Annarion.

Annarion, dangling over the familiar's side, cursed and attempted to turn; Kaylin tightened her grip. She was aware that the familiar was somehow helping, because her arms were not strong enough to hold Annarion above the ground for long. Or maybe it was just the outlands, and the laws of gravity didn't apply.

The familiar didn't insert his usual opinion. The mist continued to thicken around the ancestor's feet. It also rose. The fire that surrounded the ancestor's hands left them, flying upward, toward where Annarion dangled. It enveloped him again. It failed to burn. It failed to find any purchase at all, and if flames weren't normally purple or magical, these still appeared to need some kind of fuel.

Annarion wasn't a Hawk; he didn't curse. "What are you doing?" he demanded.

"Breaking my arms, by feel," she replied.

"The fire——"

"That's probably the familiar." Her arms were still glowing with harsh blue light; her clothing dampened the brilliance—but not by much. "You can thank him later." The mist continued to rise until it obscured the ancestor completely. "I don't think he can follow us."

"He's not going to try to *follow*," Annarion said. "He's going to retreat. He'll try to escape."

Kaylin, watching the mist thicken, agreed. "I think you damaged him, here. I'm not sure he can escape the force he's facing on the other side of the divide as easily." She hoped not. "Is he still on the other side?"

"Yes. The outlands are more…flexible." He grimaced as the pillar of mist collapsed, dispersing to ground fog. No sign of the ancestor remained. Annarion levered himself up and onto the back of the Dragon, sitting rather than dangling by her arms.

Ynpharion.

Lord Kaylin. She felt his tension—and also, fractured leg. He was exhausted, in pain, worried—but underlying all that was a subdued, strange sense of triumph. His usual suspicion and disgust at the hint of her presence was entirely absent. It felt…odd.

What is the ancestor doing where you are? Is he still there?

He is. There was a long pause. *The Dragons are landing.*

The Emperor?

Yes. The Emperor and the members of the court who remained in the air. Do you wish to see what unfolds?

She did. She knew it was hard on him, and wondered why she approached Ynpharion—the only person whose name she knew who despised her. Severn was there. But she had never been comfortable reaching out to Severn this way. No; she had never reached out to him like this. This was like…invasion.

Ynpharion's general sense of disgust returned. Kaylin was guarding her thoughts about as poorly as she always did when frazzled and stressed. *I do not understand mortals,* he finally said.

Would you take the name of someone you—you cared for?

In a tone that was very like Teela's on a bad day, he said, *Watch, Lord Kaylin.*

The indigo Dragon was the first to land.

He looked like a gleaming shard of night; his wings did not settle, but spread. To either side, Barrani fanned out; they faced the ancestor, but were extremely aware of the crimson-eyed Dragon in their midst. He lifted head, elongated neck and looked down to the center of the basin, where the ancestor stood his ground, alone in a field of glinting, twisting strands.

The Emperor roared. Kaylin didn't understand any of the actual words—but the sound crushed syllables, compressing them into an expression of rage so intense fire would have been superfluous. She knew why. Something had attacked his hoard.

Something would pay.

He leaped; Sanabalis and Tiamaris found room to land in the space he vacated. Neither of the two shifted into their human forms.

Above the basin, Aerians deserted the sky; one or two remained. They would carry the crystals that would add the evening's events to Records; even if they fell, the crystals would retain what they saw.

The Emperor landed as the ancestor leaped. The ancestor didn't sprout wings—but he didn't apparently need them. Depriving him of the power of true words had not deprived him of power. His fire, here, was white. White and blue.

The Emperor's was red.

White and red met in a horizontal pillar; the ground, frozen briefly by the ancestor's magic, once again began to melt. The heat, on the other hand, didn't bother the Dragon. It bothered Kaylin; she was so tightly enmeshed in Ynpharion's view, she could feel it. She would have taken an involuntary step back, but she wasn't in her own body, and Ynpharion's leg was in bad shape.

Tiamaris leaped into the air above the basin; his breath fanned the ground upon which their enemy had chosen to make his stand. The fire burned nothing that wasn't already molten.

The ancestor didn't turn; he shifted only his left arm. He didn't even look over his shoulder to see where he was aiming. But his fire—if it was fire—hit Tiamaris's left wing, just as it had hit Bellusdeo's. Tiamaris was silent as he crested awkwardly toward the ground. Sanabalis chose to leap, rather than fly; the reasons for that were obvious. He added breath in an orange-white cone, and this caused the ancestor to stagger for the first time.

Diarmat and Emmerian weren't immediately visible.

What is the Arkon doing? Kaylin demanded. She was, in the safety of the outlands insubstantiality, holding her breath, which was about as useful as it sounded.

Bleeding, was Ynpharion's calm and unconcerned reply.

What? Why? But she knew. The chains were still spinning. They inhibited the ancestor's power, somehow, and the cost of that inhibition was still being paid.

Arrows flew. Kaylin couldn't tell whether or not they'd been fired by Swords or Barrani. It didn't matter. They disintegrated feet away from their target; ash remained in a growing cloud. The advantage of having a Dragon for an opponent was its size. At a distance there was just that much more of a target.

The Arkon's counter enchantment will break, Ynpharion said. *The speed at which the ancestor casts will be matched, once again, by his power.*

Sanabalis moved closer, bridging the distance between landing and enemy; his fire continued to burn, and it struck the white fire shields of his enemy as if it were a battering ram. But the white fire wasn't a gate; it wasn't a door. It was a wall. Kaylin looked for cracks; she found none.

The street beyond the basin's lip exploded in small columns of flame to either side. They trailed down the street's center as far as the eye could see.

Kaylin lost sight of the combat in the center of the conflagration because Ynpharion threw himself out of their range. Ynpharion's hair wasn't as lucky; it burned; white flames seemed to cling to whatever they touched. Like anything that clung, it could be removed—but not without effort. Not without power.

She turned to see the high ridges of indigo wings. She saw similar ridges of gray—or silver; given white fire, they were one and the same. She saw the peak of tail slam ground, again and again, as if to break something. Whatever it was, she couldn't see it.

But she could see the minute gold joined the battle. She knew it wasn't the Arkon, either; it was—of *course* it was— Bellusdeo. She was of a size with the Emperor, but her eyes were the darker red. She didn't draw breath; she didn't roar. She didn't attempt to land in a triangular point to close off any obvious avenue of escape; instead, she rose.

Kaylin, who'd healed her damaged wings once this evening, would have cursed in perfect Leontine had she been the owner of Ynpharion's throat.

What is she doing? *Tell her to stop! Tell her to stop right now! If Tiamaris couldn't remain in the air, she won't—*

Do you honestly think I have any control over a Dragon Empress-in-waiting? Ynpharion's disbelief colored the force of his words.

Of course not. And if she did step fully into Ynpharion's body—if she did take the control he had offered—Bellusdeo was just as likely to breathe on her as she was to listen. The golden Dragon—the erstwhile roommate—rose to dizzying height—at least to Kaylin. The Dragons had remained high above the ground during the early leg of the fight, because at a distance the ancestor's magic was too attenuated to instantly kill.

But she knew Bellusdeo. That wasn't what was happening here.

Take us to Bellusdeo, she told the familiar. *Take us there* now. Silence.

You can stop him—

This time the silence was Kaylin's. She hated everything about the marks and the familiar and the outlands and the ancestors for one long, solid breath. It burned the back of her throat. She returned to Ynpharion.

Ynpharion might have been the bearer of a memory crystal. He had gained his footing—bracing his leg with magic and will. He stood to one side of the Barrani warband, which now separated like a curtain. Through the gap walked the Lord of the High Court. He wore armor that looked like it would have been at home on a Dragon in human form. Kaylin prayed desperately that that's not where it had come from.

Ynpharion's sudden silence was not the right answer to that prayer.

The High Lord carried no obvious weapon. No greatsword. No staff. He wore a circlet very like Evarrim's, but the gem in its center was not a ruby. Nor was it diamond or emerald or sapphire. At this distance, Kaylin couldn't identify it; she only knew that it was huge.

Where he walked, flames guttered. Where he looked, rock solidified. His eyes, from this distance, were almost...green. Kaylin was shocked at the color.

Do not be, Ynpharion said, grim now. *What he does, he cannot do in rage; it will consume him. There are very, very few of our kin who can wield the power he has chosen to wield—and of those who might, only one—in my opinion—who could do so safely. He must maintain perfect awareness—and perfect control.*

But green? Green is the happy color!

Do not be facile.

The High Lord walked; the ranks of the Barrani closed at his back. Kaylin couldn't see the Consort's distinctive white armor anywhere.

"Arkon," the High Lord said, the spoken words delivered as if they were incantation. "We are in your debt."

It was a signal. The fire that burned in patches between melted rock suddenly expanded. The fire didn't burn the Emperor or Sanabalis. But it didn't *touch* the High Lord as he made his way toward the ancestor.

The ancestor glanced—for the first time—away from the Emperor. What he saw in the High Lord caused his eyes to widen. To widen and then narrow into dark, lash-framed edges. A silence fell upon them all, broken only by the sound of fire. Elemental fire had a voice that Dragon fire didn't; Dragon fire sounded a lot like miles of breaking earth. It was hard to even see the ancestor, the heat caused so much distortion.

Is nothing *going to drop this guy?*

As if she could hear the thought, the hovering golden Dragon reversed the direction of her skyward climb, folded her wings, and dived.

CHAPTER 27

She dropped the way a bird might have; her body straight, her legs drawn in close. Weight increased the speed of her descent. She came in on a very steep angle, and once she'd set her course, she didn't deviate.

Even Ynpharion was impressed. *We once spent our lives at war with them. She is the essence of the historical flights.*

She seemed to fall forever; it was barely a few seconds. She disappeared beneath the eddies of ash and the height of flames.

The earth shuddered at the impact. For one long breath, silence reigned.

And then the flames went out.

It is over, Lord Kaylin, Ynpharion said.

Where is Bellusdeo?

She is alive. She is with the Emperor. Perhaps you can hear them. The last was said with just a touch of humor. *He does not appear to be pleased with her intervention.*

Thank you, she said. She let him go. Or let herself return.

She had been, in the past ten minutes, more aware of his body than her own.

Exhaling, she leaned back into Annarion. This was not, sadly, deliberate. He put his arms out to either side of her.

"I'm not going to fall," she told him, as the familiar continued his flight. Her voice came out in a whisper barely louder than the familiar's wings.

"No, you're not. Teela would kill me."

"It wouldn't be your fault."

"How long did you say you've known Teela?"

She laughed. It hurt. The laughter faded as she gazed into gray and seamless horizon. "Do you know why your brother was made outcaste?"

"No. Because you are not Barrani, I will take no offense at the question."

"Is it more offensive to ask you than to ask anyone else?"

"He is blood of my blood. Your question implies that my knowledge implicates me in his crime—whatever the alleged crime might be. In the hands of my people, the question would be highly political; it is the type of question that Evarrim might ask. He would, of course, drip with sympathy while speaking. Regardless, I do not know."

"The Consort doesn't know either. Or she lied to me." Kaylin was exhausted enough that the thought didn't offend her. "But the Consort seems to like your brother."

"Yes. The Consort's position, however, is unique. She can afford to like—and forgive—whomever she pleases. Social stigma cannot be wielded as a weapon against the Consort; she cannot be toppled. She can be killed, but that serves none of my kin."

"Did you know her?"

Annarion was silent for so long, Kaylin thought he'd chosen not to answer. "Once, yes. But she, like Teela, has lived in this world for centuries. I do not know if she has changed as much as Teela—and I am not at all certain I want to find out."

"If you still want to take the Test of Name, you will, though."

"I know. At the moment, I am more concerned with my brother's absence. You haven't spoken with him since the ancestor was brought down?"

"No. I tried." She hesitated. "He's not in the outlands. He's nowhere in our world. There are places where I can't hear his voice—"

"Oh?"

"If the Towers or the Keeper want to give me privacy—or give themselves privacy, more likely—they can stop his words from reaching me, somehow. I haven't asked how—and we can ask that. But not now."

"Now is?"

"Home. And no," she added, when he drew breath, "that doesn't mean Castle Nightshade."

Silence.

"I've promised that we'll find him. But now is not the time."

"We do not know if time is of the essence," he countered.

"No, we don't. But *I* know that we came *this* close to losing you. Not to death—but it would have had the same effect on everyone. Look—whatever you are now, it's not what Teela is. It's not what Evarrim is. We don't understand what you are—but I don't think any of *you* understand it either. And I'm sorry for that. I keep wondering if some of you wish you'd made Terrano's choice instead. This world—it's got rules. It's got physical laws. It's got boundaries. Most of us can't get around them.

"You did—for most of your existence. But you couldn't live *here* until now. So, please: live here. Relearn what it's like. Come back to the world. Or...don't. But don't walk out in a rage when you don't even intend to leave. If you decide that you can't live with Teela—if *any* of you decide that—do it properly.

"Because *I* have to live with Teela, and I can't just find an entirely different world to hide in when she's in a foul mood."

"She feels," Annarion replied, "that you already inhabit an entirely different world."

"Yeah. The mortal one." Kaylin frowned as distant thunder pierced the featureless sky through which the familiar was now flying.

The gray fog didn't magically clear at the intrusive roar of Dragons. The familiar hadn't returned them to the real world. Except for the sound of angry Dragons, the only voices here were hers and Annarion's. Even the familiar was silent.

"Ask Teela about the Hawks."

Silence.

"Teela doesn't know?"

"She doesn't know the whole of it. There were losses. She says to tell you that Clint isn't dead—yet."

Kaylin sucked in air. She was on the back of a translucent dragon in the middle of nowhere. She needed to get back. "Moran?"

"Is singed, but whole; she's taken Clint under wing. The Hawklord is likewise uninjured. Your Sergeant has lost half of his facial fur. Tanner broke his leg—upper left thigh. She asks if you would like her to continue." He added, in case this wasn't obvious, that Teela did not find list-making amusing.

"Tain?" Kaylin asked, pressing her luck.

"Tain is, according to Teela, a bloody idiot."

Which meant he was alive.

"Where are we going?" Annarion asked.

"I'm taking you back to Helen's."

"I—"

"If we get debriefed, I don't want you to be anywhere near the High Lord or the Emperor. I don't know what you did in Castle Nightshade. I'm certain it wasn't deliberate. But the ancestors were part of Nightshade's basement, and I got the impression they'd been there a long damn time.

"I don't think the High Lord or the Emperor are going to be thrilled if they find out you woke them. Given the damage done, and the lives lost, I don't think they'll *care* how it happened. You don't know what you did—and I'm fine with that.

"But I doubt they will be. They'll probably blame it on your brother—but he's already outcaste. There's nothing worse they can do to him."

"If you believe that, you do not understand the Barrani."

"No," Kaylin agreed. "But in this, at least, I understand Nightshade."

"We don't have to return to the High Halls. But the Castle—"

"You *called them* from the Castle and they came. You have no idea *how*. Gods only know what else might drag itself out of *Ravellon* to pay a visit. If you're in Nightshade, there's nothing that can take down another ancestor. And I'm not sure—but I think Castle Nightshade was waking. *If* the Castle is awake *and* the Castle accepts your presence without, oh, trying to kill you as a dangerous intruder, *then* it might be safe for you to stay there.

"But that's a lot of ifs. Given what happened tonight? Home—at least for the next little while—is going to be Helen's."

Severn?

Here, he replied. She felt a tinge of concern and relief in his voice. *Still here.*

You're injured, she said.

You're not. Relief. Again.

Annarion is with me. We're heading back to Helen's; given Annarion, I think that's smart.

It is. I have an indigo-eyed Teela and a slightly less irate Tain. If the Emperor and Bellusdeo don't stop their "discussion" soon, my ears—and the ears of every other person in the city—will be ringing for a day.

Glad it's you, not me.

So am I.

The familiar continued his desultory flight in the gray emptiness that passed for sky, until Kaylin saw the peak of a tower emerge from the fog. She recognized it: it was the tower they'd left. It was Helen's. The aperture was open; the room itself was empty.

The familiar landed, which took more time than departure had; the room really wasn't designed for Dragons. Aerians would have loved it, except for the lack of actual sky.

Annarion slid off the familiar's back; Kaylin waited. Having brought Annarion to the only place she was relatively certain was now safe—for the city, if not for Annarion himself—she intended to rejoin the Hawks. There were injuries, and she could heal them. But she couldn't heal them from across the city.

We cannot return that way, the familiar said. *And I am weary. It has been an interesting evening.*

But I have to go back. She thought of Teela's relayed message.

Annarion, apparently, was prepared for this. "Teela says Clint will wait. He's too terrified of Moran to actually expire."

"Teela doesn't want me there either."

"She feels that if you must meet the Emperor, doing it publicly isn't your best bet." He repeated the words in Elantran;

he did *not* speak them like a native. "The Emperor is already ill-pleased with you."

Great. "Why me, this time?"

"Bellusdeo was in danger."

"And that's my fault *how?* It's not like she actually listens to me!"

"Teela says: now that you understand the problem, stay home. She also says that she thinks Bellusdeo is heading here now."

"While the Emperor is *talking to her?*" Kaylin wilted.

"It's causing a bit of consternation in all quarters. Apparently the Emperor doesn't lose his temper often. Teela says the Arkon has joined the conversation."

"Tell her she wins. I'm staying put," Kaylin said, sliding off of her familiar's back.

"Teela also points out that your ability to heal is dependent on your own physical state, and she says—I'm sorry, I'm just the messenger—that you look like crap."

"That's not what she said."

"No. It was longer and more distasteful. Do you want it word-for-word?"

"I really, really don't." Her legs were shaking. She leaned back into the familiar's side—and fell over. Annarion caught her before her butt hit the stone floor. Or before her butt hit the familiar, who had shrunk into his small and squawky form.

Are you still there? she asked him.

Squawk.

"I don't understand why you can't speak when you're tiny."

Squawk squawk.

"Fine. I probably have enough people rattling around the inside of my head anyway." She knelt, picked him up, and plunked him across her shoulders; his entire body felt like limp lettuce.

Annarion stared at her.

"What?"

He shook his head. "I can see why Teela finds you interesting," he said. By way of compliments, it wasn't. She studied his face for one silent minute. His eyes were Barrani—and blue, but that was the Barrani resting state. His face had lost the edges that she found so disturbing in his fight with the ancestor.

"Helen?"

"Yes, Kaylin," Helen's voice replied. "I will close the aperture. You might want to send Annarion to speak with Mandoran. He's sulking."

"What have you done with the ancestor?"

"I did not think it safe to contain him here," she replied.

"Fine. Where did you contain him?"

"It is not someplace that you can easily reach."

"Are you being deliberately evasive?"

"Yes."

"...We need to find out what they did with Annarion's brother."

"I do not think it wise to ask him at this juncture. You are weak and exhausted. Annarion is too close to the edge."

"Not that I disagree, but edge of what?"

"Himself," Helen replied. "There are boundaries into which he—and Mandoran—have poured themselves, but those boundaries are not yet fully inhabited." There was an obvious hesitation before Helen continued. "It would be best for your city if they remained indoors for a while. While they are here, they will not be heard."

"Heard by what?"

"By beings who exist beyond the boundaries transcribed by the lives of the city's inhabitants. Mandoran and Annarion have willingly accepted those boundaries. I am sorry to say that they are not entirely aware of the ways they overstep them. Not yet. It is something they can learn. It would be best if they learned them in the West March, in the green—but I do not think they will agree to do so.' '

"I will not," Annarion said, with some heat. "Not while my brother is missing."

"And Mandoran will not leave you, as he has made clear."

Kaylin nodded and headed down the stairs.

"Bellusdeo has just arrived with her friend."

"And she's sulking?"

"No, dear. I think she's very, very upset."

"What color are her eyes?"

"Copper, I think."

Kaylin exhaled. "I'm heading down. Is she in a room?"

"Yes. She is in her room." Helen paused. "I am not sure she wishes to speak with anyone. Maggaron is standing outside her door, and she won't let him in."

Kaylin grimaced. She looked up at Annarion, who hadn't moved. "Did Teela understand *any* of what was said by the Emperor?"

"She says she did not." Annarion frowned. "I would consider that a lie. She is not adept at the language, but—no. She thinks it was probably personal."

Dragon voices did not lend themselves to the subtle and personal. "I serve the Emperor," she said, as she turned back down the stairs. "I've made my oath to the Halls of Law. I would die in his service. But sometimes I think he's the biggest idiot I've ever met."

Helen was not wrong. Bellusdeo would not leave her rooms. Nor would she open the door to allow anyone else to enter them. Maggaron, far from being happy that he could—

finally—occupy the same building as his Dragon Queen, stood
to one side of her door, looking morose.

"Did you understand a word the Emperor said?"

Maggaron shook his head. "He was afraid, for her. I have
learned, with time, that this is not the way to approach Bellusdeo. She does what she has to do. She did that, here. Without her..."

"She killed the ancestor?"

"Her blow was—the word, it means important?"

"Decisive?"

He nodded. "It was a risk—but the magical attacks hadn't
been working as well as hoped, and the Arkon's ability to
dampen the ancestor's magic was fading." Maggaron's shoulders slumped. "She is a warrior. She has always been that,
even when she—even as a *sword*. She's smarter than I am. She
sees the whole of the battle, she observes. She makes decisions based on those observations. Yes, she takes risks—but
Lord Kaylin—"

"Do not *ever* call me that again. Please."

He was clearly filing this under the peculiarities-of-Kaylin
category. "She was necessary. Her action was not a matter
of ego. It was a risk, yes. But it was a calculated risk. And it
worked. The Emperor should have been grateful. He should
have honored her choice and her attack.

"He did not."

"What did Bellusdeo say to the Emperor?"

Maggaron lowered his chin. Kaylin hadn't quite figured
out how someone so bloody *large* could look so vulnerable.
Clearly, it was a talent. When he lifted his chin again, she revised that opinion. "She said she would take the long sleep."

"I'm not going to ask you how you could understand what
she said when you couldn't understand the Emperor."

"I am her Ascendant. Even if she is no longer a weapon, I hear her."

"How likely is that? The sleep, I mean."

"I don't know. I do not understand the long sleep of the Dragons. I think—" He exhaled. "If you did not live in this city, she would leave it. I'm not certain she will not leave it regardless. If she does—if that is her choice—go with her." He looked pained as he added, "She won't take me."

Kaylin, who had knocked on the door until her knuckles hurt—to no visible or audible effect—said, "I'm not sure she'll take me, either. She understands what's at stake for the Dragons."

"Yes. I understand it, as well. But Kaylin—I won't see her sacrifice everything she is for the sake of the rest of the Dragons."

"No," was the fond reply. "You wouldn't. That's why *you're* here. You know that she's already sacrificed everything once— to fight the Shadows with you. To protect the world." Her world. And in the end, she had failed. "You know everything about the life she actually *lived* for centuries—and I think she needs someone who does. I don't. I understand it in theory— but I didn't live it with her. I can't be part of that history. Stay here. She'll ignore you, but she'll at least be aware that you *are* here, for her. I should go talk to Helen. I'm not sure if I'm supposed to sign something or not."

She was lying, of course. There were no signatures necessary to codify their agreement. Kaylin wanted a home—but the type of home she could make here couldn't be built on legalities. She found Mandoran and Annarion in the dining room, of all places. Mandoran had his feet on the table.

Helen was at its head; if Helen didn't tell him to remove his bloody feet, Kaylin didn't feel she could—although that took work. Both of the Barrani boys looked about as cheerful as Maggaron. It wasn't much of a housewarming.

Helen looked up as Kaylin entered the dining room. "We're having a bit of a discussion about the current difficulty," she said, smiling. She was the only person in the room who was.

Kaylin took a seat. She was tired. No—she was beyond tired. "Mandoran," she said, looking across the table at an obviously dejected Barrani, "no matter what else comes out of this, you saved us all."

The dark circles under Mandoran's eyes implied hangover from the hells. The bruises didn't help.

"We're going to find Nightshade," she told Annarion, when neither spoke. "But…before we even make the attempt, we need to understand what you can do. And you need to understand what you're doing. Tara said that the Shadows in the fief could hear you; we can't even approach the Castle if we can't figure it out and get it—get it under control." She exhaled. "Mandoran, how did you know how to reach Helen's heart?"

"How do you know how to reach the dining room door?" Kaylin frowned. "I can see it."

"Exactly."

"I can't see through walls and floors." She was too tired to be diplomatic. "Can you see it now?"

"…Yes." Staring at his reflection on the pristine table surface, he said, "You don't know what it was like. We were trapped in the Hallionne for a long time. We couldn't leave. The Hallionne rearranged itself to be a tasteful jail—but it was a jail. We could speak to each other, but we couldn't, for a long time, meet. We couldn't reach Teela, either. We tried." He exhaled and changed the subject. "Barrani don't sleep the way mortals sleep."

Kaylin nodded; she knew this.

"Hallionne do. We had traveled through the Hallionne

on the way to the *regalia*. We understood that they were not awake. But they were present. They were aware. They could influence their surroundings unintentionally. They could influence them according to the needs of their...guests.

"We were those guests, and we were bored. We experimented. Well, Terrano experimented. But what he saw, we saw; what he heard, we heard. We could not follow Terrano—not at the beginning. We couldn't see ourselves the way he was willing to see himself.

"But he showed us how to communicate with the Hallionne. To learn...was hard. We couldn't *hear* the Hallionne to begin with. He didn't speak to us. We had to listen. We had to turn our full attention to listening. Even for us, it was hard. I'm not sure Teela *could* learn. She doesn't understand half of what we say, and it frustrates her."

"And you?"

"It makes the rest of us feel guilty," he replied. "*Don't* tell her that."

"Do I look like an idiot?"

Mandoran was silent. Annarion was *loudly* silent.

"We never had to worry about secrecy. We listened, and when we could finally hear, we struggled to *speak*. To the Hallionne. We weren't Terrano; he learned more, and quickly. I think he was ready to abandon everything. He grew to love the cage so much it stopped *being* a cage, for him.

"But the rest of us were too anchored in our early lives and our regrets and our anger. They held us in place. What we did when we communicated with the Hallionne wasn't like speech. But it was a constant—and we think it still is. It's why Tara could hear us. And the Castle. And Helen."

"And the water."

Mandoran nodded. "We're not doing it deliberately. Stopping—it's like holding our breath. We *can*—but we have to breathe sometime. What I saw when I lead you to Helen's heart looked *almost* like the rest of the building to me. It's—" he frowned. "Subtext."

Kaylin stared at him.

Mandoran turned to Helen. "Is that the wrong word?"

"No, dear."

"Pretend I'm as stupid as you think I am," Kaylin said, trying not be resentful, "and explain it to *me*."

"If you tell stories about your life in the fiefs—and Teela says you do—you're talking about yourself. But someone listening could infer that you feel that anyone who has power is evil. The inference would be the subtext. It's not what you're *trying* to say—but anyone listening can hear it beneath the words. Buildings—buildings like Tara or Helen—are like those stories. They've got a lot of really loud subtext. We don't see it unless we look, but it's not hard to see.

"And once we see it, it becomes part of their story. We can move around in it the same way you move around the dining room. You can tell your stories in different order, right? You can mix it up, or forget something and come back to it? That's what we do."

"And the outlands?"

Mandoran looked at Annarion. "Your turn."

She almost expected Annarion to say *why me?*

"Because, idiot, you left Helen and went to fight the ancestor." Clearly, Annarion had performed to expectation, just not where Kaylin could hear it.

"I do not see things the way Mandoran does. He is probably closest to Terrano. When I look at the ancestor, I see what you see—but I see more. It is very much like the shadow you cast when you stand in light, at least to your eyes. I think. I have the same shadow, and it moves independent of me in the same way."

"So...nothing at all like the shadow I cast."

Annarion frowned, staring at Kaylin's shadow. He didn't disagree; he looked thoughtful. "I could follow the movement of his shadow. I could hear the voice with which his shadow spoke. I could become more like my own shadow to follow him."

"By switching places with it?"

Annarion looked as frustrated as Kaylin felt. "No. I don't know what you saw in the outlands. I don't know how you knew I was becoming absorbed in their narrative, their shape. I don't know what you saw when you found me in my brother's Castle. I know what Teela saw. It was...disturbing, to see it through her eyes. What I saw wasn't...what she saw. Helen is trying to teach us how to put the two together.

"But she says the listening we learned in the early years in the Hallionne isn't actually listening; we're shouting. We're demanding to be heard and seen. And we're not doing it the way you do. She thinks any Tower, any Hallionne, we entered would wake. They would see us as a possible threat because we're speaking to them in ways their intended inhabitants can't.

"A wakeful Hallionne or Tower can hear the rest of our thoughts; they can read our intent. Helen thinks of us as children." He said this last with a very pained expression. "But she says we have to learn to hear the subtext without making it part of the narrative—because we're changing the narrative and the nature of the story if we can't. And that...is hard."

"If you hadn't done what you'd done, we'd all be dead," Kaylin told him. "Both of you."

"If I had not lost my temper at my brother, we would never have been at risk," Annarion countered. "And I want to go back to the Castle now. Would it alarm you to know that I could see the path there while fighting the ancestor?"

Kaylin shook her head. She rose. "No. I just don't think you could have come back to here if you'd left to follow it."

"Lord Kaylin?"

She exhaled and sat down again.

"What Helen cannot explain—and what none of us understand—is how *you* could come to my aid. You are mortal. You are not of significant power."

"She is Chosen," Helen pointed out.

"So you've said. But that is not an explanation. How can you wander between the states without losing yourself in them?"

Kaylin reached up and wearily poked the small, limp dragon.

Squawk.

"I don't think he agrees," Mandoran said.

"Well, there's not a whole lot of other explanation. I'm not the one who can turn himself into a giant dragon and zip around the skies like a sparrow."

"No. But…if you can do this, you could possibly instruct *us*. You could teach us how to safely navigate between the states without being lost to any of them."

"I am not certain it will be as simple as that," Helen replied, before Kaylin could. "What Kaylin perceives is, I think, translated into what she is capable of perceiving in this world. Even if you look at the same thing, her view of it will be intrinsically different." She turned to Kaylin and added, "I really think you should send Maggaron to bed."

"I really think he won't go, and I'm lazy enough not to want to waste the colossal effort."

"You're probably right. I've never had a *Norannir* beneath my roof before. Are they all as he is?"

"If you mean as earnest, no. They're all about the same size when fully grown, though."

Helen frowned, eyes narrowing. "I would appreciate it," she told Mandoran, in as severe a tone of voice as she'd yet used, "if you stopped playing with the doors."

"I'm not doing anything to the doors," was his sullen reply.

"Anymore," Annarion added, which didn't make Mandoran any happier. "I think," he added softly, "you have guests."

"At this time of night?" Kaylin asked. She rose and headed out of the dining room. "I'll get it."

"I think it's for you anyway," Mandoran added.

"Teela?"

"Teela is going to be in debriefing until doomsday," Mandoran replied. This did, on the other hand, cheer him up. Kaylin was certain he'd pay for it later.

"Probably Severn, then."

"Severn and Tain are going to be keeping Teela company. So is your Sergeant. He looks ridiculous without facial hair."

"Avoid telling him that if you like your throat where it is. He's going to be in a foul mood for the next week. Or two."

"Until it grows back?"

"Some of the things we lost today won't. Grow back."

Mandoran's smile dimmed. "No. Apologies, Lord Kaylin."

CHAPTER 28

The small dragon lifted his head. Or tried. He made a meeping noise that sounded truly pathetic. Kaylin sighed and removed him from her shoulders, curling him carefully in cupped palms as she walked toward the door.

"Who do you think is visiting?" she asked. "Because if it's Barrani and ancient, I'm not going to be thrilled. I may scream in your ears."

Small and squawky covered his head with one wing.

Kaylin reached the door in the small foyer. She wondered, looking at it, if this had been the shape Helen had taken for Hasielle. It was far fancier than anything Kaylin had ever called home, because the Imperial Palace had never been home.

She opened the door.

Two men stood on the other side of it. One was older, and bent slightly with the weight of age; his hair was sparse, and his long beard white with a touch of gray. His eyes were orange. In spite of the bruising and the gash across his forehead, she recognized him instantly. "Arkon?"

He nodded.

"You look *awful*." She pushed the door out of the way and *almost* offered him an arm. Some sense of self-preservation prevented this. "Come in."

"I am, as you have so *kindly* pointed out, exhausted. I do not think I have been this tired in centuries. I am here as exalted page." The Arkon made no move to enter the building.

"Page?" She frowned. "Oh, wait—you mean the kids that run around the Palace opening doors and telling people how to get places?"

"Indeed."

She froze. His eyes lost some of the orange at her expression. No one—*no one*—asked the Arkon to serve as an errand runner. And if the owner of the Royal Library *was* running errands, as he'd just claimed, there was only one person the silent man standing to his left could be.

She looked up at him; she had to look up. He was not the tallest non-*Norannir* she had ever met, but he was easily the tallest Dragon. His hair was the black of Barrani hair, but the light from the foyer suggested blue highlights. It was currently pulled back; she thought it braided but didn't have the temerity to check. His skin, while pale, wasn't flawless; it sported a white and obvious scar that cut from the left of his nose, skirting lips and ending at the line of his jaw. His eyes were a pale orange.

"You understand," the Arkon said. "Or perhaps you do not. Let me introduce my friend. He does not spend much time in the streets of Elantra, and he is not, perhaps, as cognizant of its many customs as you yourself would be. He is a Dragon; I trust you will both recognize this, and attempt to treat him with at least as much respect as you treat...Lord Diarmat."

"Can we settle for Lord Sanabalis?"

"No. You treat him with appallingly little respect."

"I treat him with vastly more respect than he treats me— and vastly more respectfully than Bellusdeo."

"Indeed." He turned to the man by his side. "This is—"

The Dragon stepped forward. "I am Dariandaros."

Kaylin stepped back to let him enter the house. "I want to make one thing clear," she said, her voice more wobbly than she would have liked. She could hear the Arkon's sharp intake of breath in the background. The coward wasn't going to come in himself.

"And that?" The Imperial voice was very much like Diarmat's; it radiated death and a distinctly chilling lack of warmth.

"I'm Bellusdeo's friend. She's my roommate. This house is as much hers as mine. She's not a Hawk. She's not a Lord of the Imperial Court. She *is* a hero. And I won't have her attacked or cornered or intimidated while she's here." She exhaled.

The Dragon's brow had risen ever-so-slightly into his hairline. To her surprise, the color of his eyes hadn't shifted. She wondered if all the bad PR—about eating people or turning them into ash—was wrong.

"There is a reason," he said, although she hadn't spoken out loud, "that I am here as Dariandaros, and not as the Eternal Emperor. Understand, Private Neya, that as Emperor, I have responsibilities to the title itself. If I falter, if I am seen to lack confidence or direction, if I am seen as an object of scorn, and not a man worthy of both obedience and respect, the Empire stumbles." His smile was thin. It was not warm. "And I admit a personal predilection to be treated with the respect due an Emperor." He looked around the foyer. "This is to be Bellusdeo's new home?"

Kaylin looked out the door. The Arkon had vanished.

Squawk.

She froze and slid a hand up to cover the small dragon's mouth. "You didn't even bring any of your guards."

"I am aware that the Halls of Law and the Imperial Guard do not always see eye-to-eye; I am uncertain why, but I accept it as observable fact. I did not choose to bring Palace Guards. If I am to interact with you as a citizen, if I am to speak to you as if I were not Emperor, I cannot be seen *as* Emperor. So. I am here."

She led him to the right of the foyer, where she hoped to whatever god listened to the unrepentantly irreligious that she would find some kind of—of sitting room. The rooms she shared with Bellusdeo in the Palace had one.

And Helen apparently had one, as well.

"I don't—we don't have cooks," Kaylin said, feeling stupid. "And we haven't *really* moved in yet. We kind of just agreed in principle and then—and then the ancestors arrived. So— our, umm, hospitality—"

One brow rose. It was an expression she might have seen on the Arkon's face.

She entered the room; it was large, with slightly faded furniture—three chairs with high backs, one long couch with a slumped central pillow. There were blankets—Caitlin called them throws for some reason—draped across the top.

Kaylin chose one of the chairs. She didn't particularly want to risk sitting beside the Emperor.

The Emperor, without apparent similar concern, also chose one of the chairs. He sat straight-backed and stiff, as if it was extremely unusual for his knees to do something trivial, like, say, bend.

Kaylin felt awkward and ridiculous.

Severn, she whispered. *I don't want to panic you, but. Umm. Never mind.*

For some reason, this did not fill Severn with instant comfort. *What is it? What's happened?*

I'm at home. She tested the word in her thoughts, and some of the stiffness in her shoulders eased. Yes, she'd faced ancestors and true words and the magic that still made her arms and legs ache—but *this* was where she was going to live for the rest of her natural life. She had found a home. She had found a home in which Dragon paranoia wouldn't offend the landlord.

Or maybe it would, but at least the landlord wouldn't turn her out.

Kaylin—who's there? Severn's internal voice was much louder than it usually was. Possibly because he never used it.

The Emperor.

Silence.

He's here alone.

Why?

I'm not sure.

"You are wondering why I have chosen to visit."

She nodded.

"Am I so very terrifying, Lord Kaylin?"

"I've been repeatedly told that meeting you in person would be career-limiting, because I'd be dead."

His smile was slender and cold, but it was there. "And perhaps that is true. You seem…wed…to the informal. In some circumstances it would be highly offensive. But you are in your own home, and I have chosen to visit, not as Emperor, but merely as another Lord of the Court."

Kaylin wanted to laugh. If this was his idea of slumming, it was terrible. But probably to be expected from an Immortal. Mere Lord of the Court. The worst thing? He meant it.

"Why did you come? If it was to see Bellusdeo, she's not speaking to anyone."

"Not even you?"

"I'm part of anyone, so no."

The Emperor rose. "This was an exceptionally poor idea. I would not be here at all if the Arkon had not insisted."

"And why did he insist? What did he think you could do, here? You've pretty much insulted her. You've failed to acknowledge one of her few strengths. She helped *save* this city. She was critical at the end of the assault. She should be held in honor."

The difference in their heights seemed immense as he stood. His eyes were a solid orange.

But she thought she understood what the Arkon meant him to hear, and emboldened by a new home, she drew breath and chose her words as carefully as she could. Well, her remaining words. "What do you know of Bellusdeo's life before she returned to Elantra?"

He was silent.

"Do you know *anything* about her life?"

More silence. It was not, given the color of his eyes, a promising silence.

"Do you, in fact, know anything at all except the fact that she's female?"

"I know that she was swept away in the tides of the breaking of the portals," he replied. "She was young when the Arkon was, himself, much younger. She was one of nine, and they were connected. I do not understand how. I understand," he added, "what the Arkon understands."

Kaylin's jaw dropped at the last bit. "You *do not* understand what the Arkon understands. The Arkon sees Bellusdeo. Does he worry about her? Yes. Of course he does. But he doesn't worry about her because she's the last female Dragon—he worries about her because he *knew* her. And she hasn't changed as much as he has."

"Mortals breed. It is what they *do*. You do not understand her importance—"

"I understand her importance to *herself*. I understand what she means to the Dragons—the very few who remain—but you've done well enough without her before. You can't ask her to be something entirely different just *because* she's a girl!"

"She is hardly a girl," was his dry reply.

Kaylin was seated, but stood. "Let me take that back," she said.

Kaylin, Severn said, *be careful. He may have come in secret, but he is the Emperor.*

"It's entirely possible for you to ask her to be something she's not. I've seen it often. In the place I grew up—" *Kaylin, stop.* "—Which you're probably aware is the fief of Nightshade, what you're offering Bellusdeo so she'll pretend to be something she's not—would have been a daydream. What you're asking her to *do* for the life you're offering would have been a daydream, too. Most of the women who couldn't hide or make themselves incredibly unappealing ended up serving total strangers. They couldn't escape, except by dying. Which they did."

Kaylin.

She inhaled. Exhaled.

"People who have power often expect people who have none to make nice, just to survive. I made nice. I did worse."

She could feel Severn give up. He didn't stop worrying.

"What you're asking isn't nearly as bad. But the truth is: you've got power. She doesn't."

"I am not attempting—"

"You *are*. Do you think she doesn't understand what's required of her?"

She thought, for one long beat, he would breathe on her. The rising head of the familiar on her shoulder wasn't much of a comfort, in that regard. But she'd started. She'd probably never have another chance to say what she thought needed to be said.

"What, then, does she require to be...happy? What does she demand? I have made clear—inasmuch as I can—that I am willing to give her anything at all that she desires."

"She doesn't want your fear."

"And will you be naive enough to imagine that she wants my *love*? She is *not* mortal. She is *not* like *you*."

Kaylin flinched. Angry Dragons were never going to be something she could face without fear. "I don't know," she said, forcing herself to choose her words more carefully, "what love means to Dragons. I only barely understand what hoards mean—"

"Do not imagine that you understand what a hoard means."

"Fine. I don't understand Dragon love and I don't understand Dragon hoards. I don't understand all of Bellusdeo or what she wants, either—because I haven't known her for half my life. I'll accept that I'm *mortal* and *naive*. But I *won't* accept that the Arkon is. She will be—in future—the mother of her race. Until she has a daughter. Or several."

"She doesn't *have* to be Empress. She doesn't have to have children *with you*. If *you* care so much about the Dragon race and its continuation, you can offer to step aside." She folded her arms.

"Do you think I have not offered her the choice?"

Given that she had, Kaylin was at a momentary loss for words. Some of her ire left her, then. "Did you?"

"Yes. Reluctantly, but yes. I understand what is at stake for all of us, even if she does not."

"What makes you think she doesn't?"

"What she did *tonight*." His eyes deepened to an even, unfortunate red. His facial features rippled briefly. For one long, frozen moment she was afraid he was going to transform.

She held her ground. Mostly because she couldn't, for a moment, move. "What she did *tonight*," she said, through clenched teeth, "was *save* the city. Not more. Not less. She was Queen, once; she carried the weight of a country—and eventually what was left of a world—on her shoulders. She understands her own power, and she understands the responsibility that comes with it."

"She is not responsible for *my* Empire."

"If she's going to live here, it can't be just yours."

His eyes were bleeding red at this point. But Kaylin's would have been, too, had she been a Dragon.

"This city is my city," she continued. "The people in it are my responsibility. I don't *have* your physical power. On a purely personal level, you can do more good than I can. But that doesn't mean the good *I* can do is pointless. That's not the way the city works.

"You want Bellusdeo to be the mother of your race. I get that. But the Consort is the mother of *hers,* and she was in the street, fighting. The High Lord didn't order her to cower in the High Halls—and do you know why?"

Silence.

"Because there are things that the Consort can do that *he can't.*"

"You did not want the Consort in the streets, either," he said, voice cold. Cold, in Dragons, was better than heat. He was guessing.

Kaylin accepted the guess as the truth that it was. "No. I didn't."

"Why?"

"Because she's the Consort. She's the gateway to unimaginable power for the ancestors." That was the truth, but not all of it. "And because I *like* her. I don't have a lot of friends. I don't know that she wouldn't be insulted if I called her 'friend.'

I didn't want her to risk her life there. I thought I could do what needed to be done."

He looked down on her, as if she had just proved his point. "You understand."

Kaylin exhaled heavily. "I understand *why* you're protective."

"No, Lord Kaylin, you don't."

"Fine. I don't and can't. I'm not you. But here's the thing: I thought I could do what needed to be done so the Consort wouldn't have to risk her life—but *I was wrong.* Had it been up to me, she wouldn't have left the High Halls. And we would have failed.

"There isn't another Barrani Lord alive who means as much to the High Lord. Or to the Barrani race. But the High Lord accepted her assessment of the risk. He accepted the risk itself. I'm not saying it was easy for him—it was probably bloody hard. But he did it anyway. If you somehow think this means the Consort means less to him than Bellusdeo means to you, you are totally, dead wrong."

This time, his silence was less terrifying.

"I volunteer at the Foundling Hall between emergencies. I wouldn't let the foundlings out in the streets during an attack like this—unless it would save their lives. I would be terrified for them—and I'd be *right* to be terrified. They're children. The Consort is not a foundling," she continued, almost for her own sake at this point. "Yes, I was terrified. Yes, I wanted her somewhere safe. But—that's about *me.* It's not about what *she* needs. It's about what *I* want.

"I want all the things I love in life to be safe. Because if they're not, *I* lose them. It hurts *me.* I was angry at Bellusdeo for trying to fight while wounded because *I* don't want to lose her. Which is, again, about me. About what I need. I don't have the weight of a race behind my needs. I get that. But—this is still about *you*, not her.

"And some of it—some of it honestly has to be about *her*. Not about the fact that she can bear babies—or eggs, I'm not so clear on how that all works—but about what she can give, what she needs, and what she wants. Look—you're both Immortal. You have all the time in the world."

"We do not have that time if she dies. Twice now—that I know of—she has come close." He exhaled. There was no smoke in it. To Kaylin's shock, he began to pace. "You are right. I do not know very much about her life. She will not speak of it, with me. The only member of the Court she is willing to speak with at all is the Arkon."

"That's because the Arkon sees her. He's not interested in what she can—and must—give. He's worried about her," she added.

At that, the Emperor's brows folded. "He is."

"...He's worried about you."

"I advise, in future, that you think with your mouth closed." He paced the length of the room. Kaylin was surprised he didn't leave scorch marks in the carpets. "I was asked to come here," he admitted, his back turned to Kaylin, "because the Arkon felt that *you* might have insight that the Dragon Court currently lacks." He spun on his heel. "The rules that might once have governed courtship among our kind don't apply to Bellusdeo. She will not speak with me. I have tried—but all our discussions end in flame and fury. Diarmat resents the leeway she is already given, and he is my right hand at Court. How much must I compromise the stability of the hierarchy I have built to make her comfortable enough that she will not leave us?" He turned again. "I do not understand my own reactions, in this. I do not understand why she sees them as insults.

"You think I don't see her."

"You don't."

"Then help me *to see,* Chosen."

She could feel Severn's sudden amusement. *You asked for that.*

I am so not the person to be giving romantic advice. I haven't ever even managed to build one *successful relationship. He's insane.*

Severn laughed.

I mean, the most useful advice I can give anyone about relationships is: don't. And if you're going to try anyway, don't break someone's jaw when they kiss you. That's not useful.

Flame and fury, Severn replied. *It might be more useful to Dragons than you think.*

It's not funny.

Given what I feared when you started this interview, it is. I figured Helen would save you and you'd be under house arrest for the rest of your natural life.

"I can command you; I have that right. You are a Hawk. But I will not. I *ask* it. Help me to see."

"And if you don't, or can't? Or if you don't like what you do see?"

The Emperor turned. "I will let her go." His eyes were a shade of copper that Kaylin rarely saw.

"I'll try," she heard herself saying.

"I will leave her here. I believe that this home will not suffer the same fate as your last; I would find it almost amusing to see the Arcanists make the attempt."

"Because you don't think they'd survive it?"

"I am certain," he replied, "they would not."

Kaylin saw him out. It was weird to have to cross two rooms to reach the door. He didn't ask to speak with Bellusdeo, and Kaylin didn't offer. But as he turned to walk down the steps, she said, "Thank you."

He turned back, one brow lifted.

"For not killing me," she said, although he hadn't asked. "And for not being what I thought—what I was certain—you were, in regards to Bellusdeo."

He nodded. He offered no other reply.

"I think that he is not as terrible as you feared," Helen said, causing Kaylin to jump and spin. The Avatar was standing three feet away. "He is perhaps not as flexible as one could hope—but I think there's a chance, in future, that they may be able to speak to each other without melting the surrounding stone.

"Now, come to the kitchen. I don't normally cook, but dinner was very rudely interrupted, and you're hungry. We'll want to discuss your various roommates."

"What about them?"

"Who they are, and how many you think there will be."

"I don't—"

"Kaylin, if they mean you no harm and you wish to share your home with them, I will accept them. Your sense of home has been—by necessity—about the people in your life. I want to be your home. I want you to be at home here." She slid an arm around Kaylin's shoulders and drew her toward the kitchen.

Kaylin had never had a separate room for food. Or for eating. Or for sleeping. But she was tired, her body hurt, she was afraid of the news that waited her return to the office in the morning—and she let herself go, leaning into Helen and the sense, as they walked to the kitchen together, that this would be her home until she died.

★ ★ ★ ★ ★

But now Kaylin must find Nightshade and return him.
Don't miss CAST IN HONOR!

ACKNOWLEDGMENTS

I have been in a frenzied state of "catching up" in the past year. This has caused a little more household stress than ideal—but my children were born into a writer's house, and they more or less accept it. My husband, Thomas, is more actively helpful when I get snowed under (and I write this in December, 2013, when *snow* is the operative word).

My entire Harlequin team has seen me through the transition from Luna to Mira, starting with Mary-Theresa Hussey, but by no means ending there. I am, as of this writing, going to head out to watch my first ever cover model shoot, thanks to the energetic and lovely Kathleen Oudit, my art director, and I am really looking forward to it.

Terry Pearson not only read this book in its rough, chapter-by-chapter first-draft form, but provided his usual encouragement—and made sure that when I wrote "THE END", it *was* actually the end.

Before I forget: C. E. Murphy & Laura Anne Gilman listened to me while I pulled all my hair out trying to come up with the Emperor's *name*. (I had written background char-

acter sketches about the Emperor, since he's a fairly important part of the city—but everyone pretty much calls him the
Emperor. Or something far more obsequious.) In a round of
suggestions, Catie came up with several syllabic suggestions,
and Laura Anne pulled up one homage usage and the name
eventually came out of all those things.

I cannot write with placeholder names. If I need a name, I
invent one. If I get stuck on the name, I get stuck until I am
unstuck. I envy people who *can*. I know people who do. This
is not about artistic anything, but it *is* about process, and I've
been reminded, at some recent cost, that every process is individual.